Alive and Cutting

Alive and Cutting

A teenager's journey in therapy to understanding her self-harm

Richard Bryant-Jefferies

iUniverse, Inc.
New York   Bloomington

Alive and Cutting

Copyright © 2008 by Richard Bryant-Jefferies

This is a work of fiction. All of the characters, names, incidents, organizations, and dialogue in this novel are either the products of the author's imagination or are used fictitiously.

iUniverse books may be ordered through booksellers or by contacting:

iUniverse
1663 Liberty Drive
Bloomington, IN 47403
www.iuniverse.com
1-800-Authors (1-800-288-4677)

ISBN: 978-0-595-52963-6 (pbk)
ISBN: 978-0-595-63016-5 (ebk)

Printed in the United States of America

Other books by Richard Bryant-Jefferies

Counselling the Person Beyond the Alcohol Problem, Jessica Kingsley Publishers, London

The 'Living Therapy' series, published by Radcliffe Publishing, Abingdon, England:

> *Counselling for Problem Gambling*
> *Counselling for Eating Disorders in Women*
> *Counselling for Eating Disorders in Men*
> *Counselling Young people*
> *Relationship Counselling: Sons and their Mothers*
> *Responding to a Serious Mental Health problem*
> *Counselling for Progressive Disability*
> *Counselling a Recovering Drug user*
> *Problem Drinking*
> *Counselling a Survivor of Child Sexual Abuse*
> *Counselling Victims of Warfare*
> *Counselling for Obesity*
> *Counselling Young Binge Drinkers*
> *Counselling for Death and Dying*
> *Tim-limited Therapy in primary Care*
> *Person-centred Counselling Supervision*
> *Workplace Counselling in the NHS*

Also published by Radcliffe Publishing:

> *Models of Care for Drug Service Provision*

Book published by Pen Press Ltd, Brighton, England:

A Little Book of Therapy

Books published by iUniverse:

> *Binge! Would therapy resolve what his alcohol use never could?*
> *The Jigsaw of Life*

Disclaimer

This is a work of fiction. All of the characters, names, incidents, organisations, and dialogue in this novel are either the product of the author's imagination or are used fictitiously.

*

This book has been written to provide the reader with an appreciation of the emotional and psychological landscape that can be associated with self-harming behaviour. It does not intend to promote or glorify self-harming behaviour. Rather it aims to promote understanding and empathy towards those young people for whom self-injury or self-harm is their chosen resource and means of coping with their lives, with the emotional and psychological effects of their experiences, particularly those that are damaging and traumatic.

She slowly drew the blade down, feeling the sting, feeling a sense of freedom from everything that had been in her head. There was just that familiar yet quite singular sharp, sweet sting as the blade sliced through her skin. Not too deeply, but enough to give her that exquisite – for that was how she experienced it – sense of release from everything.

Chapter 1

The room was cold. A single naked bulb hung from the middle of the room emitting a dim glow. The little girl shivered and pulled the sleeves of her thin cotton top over her hands, and stretched the bottom over her knees which she had drawn up to her chest. It was an all too familiar experience for her. The heating was often switched off. She didn't understand why and whenever she complained of being cold she was told that they didn't have money for the bills, and to put on some more clothes. Being cold was how it was, she was used to it, but it still made her feel miserable.

She sniffed, she could feel the moisture running down her nose on to her upper lip. She was rarely free of a cold. She knew she was soon to start school and she sort of hoped that that would be better than being at home, but then that would mean not being at home. She sort of wanted that, but then she also thought about her mummy. She shivered again.

The little girl looked down at the doll that was on the floor just in front of her. It was old now, well, maybe not in years, but certainly in use. It was a well-loved doll. The little girl reached out to it and picked it up with her right hand, lifting it gently up to her face, pressing it against her cheek. 'You feel cold, Dolly' - that was the name she'd given to the doll because her mummy had always said 'dolly' and it had stuck. 'We'll be OK, we've got each other.' There were tears in the little girl's eyes. She blinked and sent a cascade of droplets down both her cheeks. She sniffed again.

Still holding Dolly to her cheek, the little girl rocked to and fro where she sat. 'I'll look after you, I'll always look after you. You're my friend.' Her eyes were still closed. She coughed.

The little girl had another friend, Mister P. He was a rather shabby looking teddy bear, desperately in need of a good wash. His fur was quite matted in places by the little girl's nasal mucous. The P was short for Paddington, but she hadn't been able to say that, and it had been her mummy that had been first to call him Mister P and that was how it had stayed. Mister P was sitting against the leg of a chair. She opened her eyes and looked at him. She wanted to be close to him as well. It wasn't something she was rationalising, she just knew that feeling him close to her felt good, somehow made her feel…, she didn't have the words for how it felt, she just knew she needed him.

Scrambling to her feet, she went over to him, picking him up with her left hand – she still held Dolly securely in her right hand – and held him by the top of the back. She lifted him up to her face and turned him to face her. 'We're going to play at Kings and Queens and you're going to be King and I'm going to be Queen and…', she turned to Dolly who she was also now lifting level with her face, '… and you're going to be the beautiful princess'. She sat down again, sitting Mister P next to her, resting against her right knee. She picked up a small blue plastic comb that was on the floor and began to comb Dolly's long, blonde hair. 'I've got to make you beautiful', she sniffed again, 'so that the handsome prince will take you away with him.' But there was no handsome prince, only Dolly and Mister P, yet she still hoped that one day he would come for her.

She always felt comforted when she was combing or stroking Dolly's hair. She didn't think about why, she just did it and could lose all sense of time as she sat and stroked or combed. She was always very careful. She could escape into herself as she did it, though she didn't think of what was happening for her in those terms. All she was thinking about was Dolly and making sure she was ready for the handsome prince to take her away. Her own hair was never as well combed as Dolly's.

There was a discomfort in the little girl's tummy. It was rumbling and growling a bit. She felt hungry. She hadn't eaten much, only a small bowl of cornflakes. It was now late afternoon. The hunger took her attention away from her fantasy world of Kings and Queens, beautiful princesses and handsome princes.

'Mummy', she called out, but it wasn't a very loud call. More of a whimper really. There was no reply, no-one heard her. She didn't expect a response. It was more instinctive rather than spoken with any expectation of a reply. Her tummy felt more uncomfortable, it was in fact cramping up, but she didn't know this was what it was, she just knew that it hurt and she didn't like it. 'Mummy', she called again, this time a little louder. She still hoped for a response, not because of expecting it, but because…, well, because she just hoped….

The little girl got up. It was still quiet. She picked up Mister P again with her left hand, she was still holding Dolly. 'Let's go and find mummy.' She walked to the door and pushed it open, turning right into the hallway. She could hear sounds coming from the bedroom. She went along to the bedroom door which was slightly open. She could hear strange noises coming from inside, not that they were new to her, but they were sort of strange nevertheless. She pushed the door open and went in. 'Mummy.' She stopped as she took in what she saw. A man, she didn't know who he was but she'd seen him before, was lying on top of her mummy. He was making sounds and moving. It was her mummy who responded to her call.

'Not now, go away.' The words were spoken with a hiss.

'But I'm hungry.'

The man had stopped his movements and had turned to look at her. She shuddered and stepped back. 'Fuck off, your mummy's busy. Can't you lock her into that room or something?' He paused, a sneer broke out across his face, 'or maybe she could stay, she might learn something'.

The woman hated him for saying that. She still loved her daughter, it was just that she loved the drugs more, and she needed to pay for them. But in that moment of hate she reacted. 'Fuck of, Mick, she's just a kid.'

Mick felt anger rising inside him. He rarely controlled it, never known how to. Probably because of the beatings he got as a kid from his drunk father. He'd only ever learned to act on feelings, not control them.

'Fuck you, bitch. You don't tell me to fuck off, got that?' He pushed down on the woman forcefully, suddenly pushing himself harder, and at the same time took her hair in his right hand and pulled her head down and back. She called out in pain. 'Or you'll get something else, something a little more permanent. Pretty face, yeah, you'd better look after it. I'll cut you up, slice you, yeah? You got a big mouth, might just make it fucking bigger.'

The woman felt real fear. She knew what Mick was capable of, she'd seen his handiwork on some of the other women.

'I do what I want, and you do what I want. You owe me, big time.' She could see the cold hatred in his eyes.

'OK. OK. I-I'm sorry. You've got me, yeah, come on, we're good, yeah? I make you feel good, you know I do.' She paused, aware that Mick wasn't safe. She spoke to her daughter. 'Go back to the other room and stay there. I'll come to you later.' She resolved then and there that she'd have to lock Katie in her room in the future when Mick was around.

The little girl turned. She heard her mummy groan as Mick pushed into her again. She walked back out into the hall but rather than go back to the lounge, she crossed over to her own bedroom, walked in and pushed the door closed behind her. She climbed into her own bed, getting deep under the covers and drawing her knees up once again. Still clutching Dolly and Mister P, she cried herself to sleep.

Chapter 2

The young woman sat in the waiting area, nervously picking at the side of her thumb. Her long, dark hair hung loosely over her shoulders. She was wearing a denim jacket over a thin black T-shirt and black jeans. Nineteen years old, yet she had experienced perhaps more in those nineteen years than many had experienced who were twice her age. Sitting in the corner looking down, her attention was seemingly focussed on the somewhat jerky movement of her hands. But her mind was somewhere else. When she picked like this she wasn't really that conscious of what she was doing. Her thoughts were elsewhere.

She didn't hear her name being called. Someone was standing close to her. He called her name again. 'Katie?'

This time she did hear her name. She looked up, momentarily stopping the movements of her fingers.

'That's me.'

Keith smiled gently. 'Hi, I'm Keith, you ready to come through?' The young woman that had responded seemed to Keith to look quite anxious. He watched her as she got up, noting that she seemed to move quite jerkily as if the energy in her movement was there and suddenly gone. She flicked her dark hair from her forehead as she walked towards where he was standing. Keith was aware of how thin she looked. Never mind counselling, somehow she looked more like she needed a hot meal. He put the thought aside as he turned and walked towards the counselling room.

Katie followed him out of the waiting area and along the corridor.

'It's not far, the counselling room is just here on the left.' Keith had turned as he had spoken. Katie did not respond. She was looking down. They reached the counselling room. Keith stood to one side and motioned for Katie to go in. 'Please go in, and sit on whichever seat you prefer.'

Katie hesitated, her chest was tight. She wasn't sure. She could feel her instincts screaming out to her to turn and leave. But she knew that wasn't the answer. She had to talk, had to face up to…. Her thoughts turned to images in her head, and sounds, horrible sounds of being shouted at, called names, and memories of being so painfully alone. She closed her eyes and swallowed.

Keith noticed her pause, he was standing behind her. To him it was as though Katie seemed to sway slightly. He was concerned.

'Are you OK?'

Katie nodded. 'Sorry. Where shall I sit?'

'Either seat, up to you.'

She chose the seat facing the door. She didn't like having her back to a door. Not since…. She took a deep breath.

'There's some water if you would like some.'

Katie nodded. She swallowed and realised just how dry her throat was. 'Thanks.'

Keith was very aware of the intensity he was experiencing. It was unusual. It could be tense sometimes, but this felt more so. He was aware that he had spoken to Katie the previous week, when she had phoned and they had fixed a time to meet up. She lived in bed and breakfast accommodation, organised by Social Services linked to her being a' looked after child' coming out of care, and now she had some contact with an independent agency although she didn't go to see them very often. He had explained to her then about counselling and what she might expect. Katie had said that she understood. She'd had counselling before, but it hadn't lasted long. 'Hadn't made a great deal of difference', was what she had said. 'Nothing had changed.' And she'd seen other people, usually social workers. But nothing really changed and she had told him that she was feeling worse and, well, it had been her doctor that had told her she needed to talk to someone and had recommended she talk to one of the youth counsellors that came to the surgery.

'I don't know where you want to begin, or what you want to say, but I hope that I can help.' Keith felt utterly genuine in what he said. He observed Katie as she sat, she seemed so very distant. Would he be able to help her? Others had clearly tried before. Yet he also knew that so often with therapy it was all about timing. The client had to be in a place in themselves where they could in some sense make use of the therapeutic process. He sat and waited for her to respond.

Katie was picking again at her thumbs. She felt ..., well, it was a familiar feeling. A sort of numb emptiness that was full of hurt. Those weren't her words, but they summed up what she felt. To Katie it was just awful, horrible, and she felt like she wished she didn't exist, sometimes anyway. That was on really bad days. But today, well, it wasn't as bad as that, but it wasn't good. Her thumbs were bleeding around the nails as they often did. The pain brought relief. Sometimes she cut herself as well, made her feel…. made her feel something other than the horribleness inside herself. Made her feel in control and more alive somehow. It felt like the answer to a lot of things, but it wasn't something she talked about. She took a slightly deeper breath and tightened her lips. She was shaking her head slightly from side to side though she was unaware of this movement.

'Just feel… dunno. Just know I need to talk but don't know what to say.'

'Mmm, that need to talk but…,' Keith paused. '… but what to say.' He spoke slowly, keeping his full attention on what was present for him as he sought to be open to the many impressions that were being made upon his senses. She sat, looking so thin, hunched up a little, somehow frail in one sense and yet that picking at her thumbs, it seemed so determined. It wasn't a distracted action. It seemed much more purposeful. So intense. What was behind it? He couldn't help but wonder what must be picking at her on the inside to be so intensely damaging herself. And she was damaging herself, he could see the scars on her thumbs and fingers, particularly around the nails. And he could see that she was drawing fresh blood. It didn't so much disturb him as sadden him, that she needed to do this to herself. But he also knew that it would be for a reason, and probably an extremely painful reason. He noted her long sleeves and wondered what other scars she might have. He brought his thoughts away from his speculations and let himself feel his own sense of the intensity of the moment as he sat in the silence that had developed, and waited to see if Katie wanted to say anything else. All this was speculation. He didn't know, but he just felt a strong sense of the presence of hurt and harm. He knew he could be wrong, and whilst it wasn't helpful to always jump to conclusions so soon, he also knew that sometimes first impressions could convey a great deal.

Katie didn't feel much from the picking. She could see the small droplet of blood oozing out. It was a familiar sight. But feelings of pain or discomfort? No. No, it wasn't enough to engage her, to really focus her on physical pain. The images remained in her head, as they usually did. They invaded her space, but from the inside. She wished she could pick them out, put an end to them, but she couldn't, at least, she'd never been able to. Pain could help to drive them away, those moments of sharp and exquisite pain. There was a sickly sweetness to that sensation. It didn't threaten, didn't overwhelm or suffocate her. It just took her attention and held it. But it didn't last, couldn't last. Bastards. Her jaw tightened. The picking became more intense. The blood more visible though it wasn't something she really paid that much attention to. Yes, there was something about the sight of blood, her blood, it seemed to have a particular meaning to her though she hadn't really worked out what it was. But it wasn't that so much as the sensation; she needed a sensation of physical pain sometimes to break herself free from how she felt.

Keith was aware that whilst he knew he could sit with people who chose to physically harm themselves – and he was wise enough to know that whilst the world would call it 'self-harm' that wasn't necessarily the experience of the person themselves – he also wasn't going to deny the discomfort that arose within him when exposed to descriptions of self-harming behaviour. Yes, he knew people self-harmed or 'self-injured' as it was also referred to for a reason, and usually a very painful reason, but it was as though he felt his own kind of physiological reaction. It wasn't so much emotional, though he felt for his clients, and for Katie as she sat there, the redness of the blood was clearly visible where she continued to pick at her thumbs. No, it felt more like his own physical self empathising with what Katie was doing to her hands, it was like a kind of physiological empathy to the physical damage she was doing. It wasn't enough to disturb him seriously, or cause him to lose his focus on Katie, but it was present, and he noted its presence.

Katie could feel the itching in her head, the scabs in her hair. She did pick at her head sometimes in desperation, and draw blood. But it wasn't enough to really hold her attention. She wanted something more to make her feel something other than the black cloud that could also be in her head, that seemed to fill her thoughts, and make her feel so utterly wretched, and so alone.

They both continued to sit in silence, though it wasn't a true silence, just that no words were being spoken. Thoughts and feelings were very present for them both, but not communicated verbally. Keith was struck by Katie's paleness. It wasn't that he hadn't noticed it before, but it seemed somehow more stark as he sat now, observing her hand movements. He didn't know why but the words 'tortured soul' came into his mind. They seemed to resonate in his heart more than in his head. They felt acutely present in his experience and wouldn't go away, as though they were urging themselves to be spoken. Should he? Were they rooted in his own assumptions? He knew better than to think too much. It was more than words just popping into his head. His sense was that they emerged into his thinking because of his striving to connect therapeutically with Katie, and they needed speaking at the time. They carried a certain power, a particular energy. He was nodding slightly to himself yet barely aware of his own head movement, it was so slight. Keith spoke. 'The words "tortured soul" are with me.' He felt a kind of relief – was that the right word – now that he had spoken? Was it relief? That didn't feel right. No, no, more a kind of ease borne out of a sense of the rightness of saying what he had said. He knew that words spoken in therapy by a therapist, particularly in highly emotional moments, or moments of deep connection, were important not just insofar as the words themselves, or how they were said, but the timing in voicing them.

Katie heard Keith's voice. It seemed distant and yet somehow close at the same time. She felt herself taking a slightly deeper breath, a moment in which something paused inside herself, a recognition at some level of a response to what Keith had said. But it was a brief moment, it didn't last, as though the part of her that recognised something in Keith's words was very much on the edge of her own awareness. Just for an instant there had been an inner stillness, like the pause between breathing in and breathing out. And then it was gone and Katie thought no more of it. She continued to sit, looking down at her hands, her elbows held in close to her ribs, continuing to pick small pieces of skin from around her thumb nails. She was only too well aware of the now swirling darkness in her head.

Keith had felt that he had said what he needed to say. He had expected, or was it hoped, for more of a response, more of a sense of connection. But the moment had now passed. Had Katie felt something? He did not know. And he wasn't going to say anything further. He needed to accept her need to be as she was, at this time, in the room, and being with whatever was present within her. He realised his lips had tightened, as if his body was telling him to remain quiet. He listened, waited, and sought to remain sensitive to his own experiencing. He knew he needed to be fully present, open and responsive to what was occurring. At some deeper, perhaps more profound level, he experienced a sense of trust in Katie. He was suddenly aware of a sense of knowing that she needed to be how she needed to be. It was something he already knew, but he now knew it differently, more certainty, it had a different kind of presence in his awareness. Maybe more acceptingly was a more accurate way of describing it. He was taking a slightly deeper breath, barely conscious of the change to his own breathing pattern.

Katie began to shake her head, ever so slightly. Her own breathing had become a little faster. She knew she had to talk to someone, try and get things sorted in her head, better still out of her head. Out of her head? Yeah, she needed that. That was the other part of her life that was so important. If she couldn't get the darkness out of her head, she had to get out of her head to get away from it. And she preferred drinking alcohol. It was numbing, but she also knew herself that wasn't the answer.

She needed to talk, she had to say something, but what could she say? The thoughts she had been having were fading. She continued to sit, not speaking. But her heart was pounding a little more. It wasn't that she was thinking about how she was feeling, that wasn't the experience that was with her. Rather there was now more of a blankness, but not an emptiness. Her head felt heavy, full, but she wasn't really thinking about it or about anything. It was like she just was, just sat, with a horrible darkness that seemed to fill her and overwhelm her. She could lose herself in it, that's how it was sometimes. No sense of time, just like living in a dark, blank stare, nothing going out, nothing coming in, and yet it wasn't empty. She closed her eyes, the picking stopped.

She felt her fingers tighten against her left thumb nail. She took a deep breath, trying to concentrate, trying to find herself somewhere inside what she was experiencing, struggling to find a sense of where she was. She bowed her head a little lower, she had released the grip on her thumb nail and was now clasping her hands together, her fingers interlocked. She tightened her grip, watching her figures growing a little redder with the tension. She took a deep breath and relaxed her grip. She struggled to concentrate, feeling a sensation somewhere in her head that seemed to be somewhere in the centre behind her eyes. It wasn't a sensation you could describe, more a kind of a focus.

Katie opened her eyes and looked down at her thumbs, speckled in the blood that she had drawn.

'It's no good, it's no good being like this. I can't carry on like this, I can't. I can't.' Katie stopped speaking as abruptly as she had started. She tightened her lips and her jaw, clenching her teeth together as she did so. 'I've got so much shit in my head, I can't sort it, can't…' Her words trailed off. She sat staring down. She knew Keith was there, she saw his feet and lower legs, and sensed his presence. It didn't feel uncomfortable, he didn't feel uncomfortable, it was all the stuff in her, in her head, that messed everything up.

'You really know that you've got to find a way of sorting that shit out.' Keith's response was instinctive, the words flowed from his lips, softly yet clearly. He felt for Katie. He was touched, affected by what she was saying and how she was saying it. He was particularly struck by the forcefulness and the certainty in Katie's words. She really did know that she had to sort out the shit in her head.

Katie swallowed. Yes, she thought to herself, got to sort it out. Keith's response seemed to affirm what she knew, it was good, sort of encouraging to hear him respond like that. His words were kind, understanding somehow. But how could he know what it was like? The thought became very present. And yet…. Something in her felt that maybe he did and that he'd really heard and understood how she needed to sort it.

'Have to.' She shook her head, taking a deep breath as she did. 'Have to, but don't know how.' She looked up as she spoke those last few words, saw compassion in Keith's eyes and looked back down again.

Keith felt himself nodding and taking a deep breath himself. There had been a kind of searching, an imploring in the way Katie had briefly looked at him. 'You know you have to, but it's about how you're going to do it? How….' The second how was not voiced as a question, more an affirmation, a statement. It wasn't an asking, but an acknowledgement. Keith knew that he did not know and wasn't going to try any clever responses that might, or might not, somehow force Katie into answering her question. He knew she was unique and that she would have her own way of doing what she needed to do, and in her own time. His job was to facilitate, or at least provide a *therapeutic* relational experience, which would help her to become more able to be both open to what she was experiencing and to express it. And in the expressing of it start to make sense of it, come to terms with it, whatever the words were that were right for her. But it wasn't for him to decide her process for her. He was there to offer support, human companionship on that most awesome and often most frightening of all human journeys, the journey into ourselves.

Katie appreciated that Keith wasn't pushing her in any way. She didn't want that. She wanted to be left alone, well, not really left alone, but left to just…, she wasn't sure how to describe it to herself. She was just glad that he listened. That felt good. She needed that. No-one really listened to her. Well, maybe some friends had, but they seemed to tire of her. And her parents? She was thinking of her foster parents, well, the last ones she'd had, though that was some time ago now. They hadn't really accepted how she was. They always wanted to try and encourage her, always being so bloody positive. They didn't get it, they really didn't. And then when she'd reacted against their son and, well, that was that. Showed how much they really cared about her. She felt herself taking another deep breath. The train of thought faded back into the darkness. She wanted some relief from the incessant feelings inside her, something, anything, that would take her away, if only for a short while. Cutting helped, it really did. Not too deep, but deep enough. She wished she was home, somewhere alone.

Katie knew that if someone asked her how she felt she couldn't really describe it, not really. It didn't feel like something you could describe, not clearly, not so that people would understand. Like a menacing fog, trapped in a heavy, black cloud. But those words didn't really capture it.

Would this counsellor understand? How could he? How could anyone? She felt so alone sometimes, like she was the only person in the world, and lost, utterly, utterly lost. And yet she felt curiously at home as well in her dark and lonely place. That was weird, but how it was sometimes. Yet now it was the sense of being lost that was very much present for her. And that didn't feel comfortable. It wasn't a new feeling, rather an all too familiar one.

*

Keith continued to maintain his focus on Katie as she sat, still looking down. He noticed the deeper breaths now and then, and what seemed to him like a heartfelt, silent sigh that would follow. He was struck by a sense of Katie's smallness, and it seemed as if she was in some way overwhelmed by the enormity of…, he didn't know what. Yet it was definitely the sense that he had. He was very aware of the silence, and of the distance that he felt between them. It seemed linked to how small she seemed. He felt as though he was straining in some way to be open to anything that might be being communicated to him. It was as though he was trying to boost his receptiveness. Although she wasn't speaking, her body language and the atmosphere in the room were conveying so much. He just wanted to be open and receptive.

The thought that came to mind was whether his sitting there was enough? How could he communicate to Katie that he genuinely wanted to be there, to hear whatever she wanted to say and help her make sense of things, or to simply sit with her so that she had a human companion in whatever was happening for her? He realised that his thoughts had drifted away from her and into himself, and his own self-questioning. He felt an urge to speak. Was it to meet his need to hear himself say something? Did he want to 'rescue her' from whatever was holding her attention? Was the silence uncomfortable and did he want to reduce his own, or her, discomfort? Was it his need, or was it something other? Was his urge to speak emerging from a sense of rightness and timeliness in reaching out to his client? He believed that clients could evoke or draw out of the therapist the response that they needed, as though some out-of-awareness communication took place that was more subtle than words or body language.

Keith believed that the therapeutic relationship was crucial, That meant conveying to his clients that he had some degree of empathic understanding for what they were saying or experiencing, that he felt a genuine warmth for them, and that he was openly and accurately able to be himself and not bring any falseness into the relationship. He believed these qualities needed to be communicated to, and received by, his clients, and that by so doing they were given a therapeutic relational experience through which constructive change or therapeutic movement could occur.[1] He felt he wasn't communicating to Katie that he accepted her need to be as she needed to be, and that he genuinely wanted to help her. He voiced what he was feeling, choosing not to think too much about the words, preferring to let the words emerge from his openness to what was present for him.

'I guess you have every good reason to sit and be as you are at the moment. I just want to say that I really do want to help and to understand you.' Yes, that was what he felt. He really did want to help and to understand Katie's world. 'And I accept your right to only tell me what you genuinely feel comfortable about me hearing.' He hadn't planned to say the last sentence but it emerged and again felt right. It was very much what he was experiencing and he felt good having made that visible to his client.

Yes, Katie thought, I have every reason. She knew she wanted to talk, to let someone into her world, but it felt so scary, more than scary, somehow terrifying. She hadn't talked to anyone before, not *really* talked. She was afraid of letting anyone in. Would they understand? Would they think she was crazy? But she didn't feel crazy though it sometimes felt it was making her crazy. None of this was comfortable for her. I don't know what comfortable means, she thought to herself, I just know what it is to feel awful. She knew it would be awful to talk. She didn't want to but she felt she had to. There was an air of gloom descending on her, and with it feeling of anxiety. The thought that was

1 These key relational qualities or attributes form a central feature in the person- or client-centred approach to therapy formulated by Carl Rogers, who formulated and wrote extensively about this approach. Keith's own approach to therapy is that of being person-centred.

with her found itself on to her lips. She heard herself speak, it wasn't that she was intending to say them, they just came out, and in a flat tone. 'Whether I talk or not, it'll be awful.'

Something in how Keith had responded had reached into Katie, had made a connection somehow, somewhere. It was tenuous, perhaps, but Keith responded. 'It'll be awful whatever you do, yeah?' He kept his response simple and short, making it a question in order to check out whether he was grasping correctly what Katie was saying. He knew that when people were struggling to describe something it could be so important that the therapist was able to convey to them that they understood, or what they understood. And, if they were not sure, that they wanted to check it out in order to be sure.

Katie nodded. 'Everything feels so heavy.' She spoke slowly, a reflective tone to her voice.

'Everything feels so heavy.' He conveyed his sense of what Katie was experiencing through his tone of voice. He spoke slowly, deliberately emphasising the words 'everything' and 'heavy', accentuating the first syllable in each word and dropping his tone as he said 'heavy'. It wasn't a carefully thought out response, it was actually quite spontaneous, an expression of the impact Katie's words had had on him. Keith deliberately responded using Katie's words. He recognised that when people were finding it difficult to put their experiences into words it was so important to really stay focussed on what they were choosing to say. Yet he also knew just repeating another's words could sound hollow and parrot-like. That was not the purpose at all. So many missed the point on this one. Yes, you reflect what a client says, but you do so out of a connection with the client's inner world. It is not a technique, more to do with the experience of connection. As a technique it would be little more than some kind of psychologically distant mirroring. Good therapy in his view was not about psychological distance.

Katie continued to speak. Yes, she had heard what Keith had said but wasn't really consciousness of how he had spoken. Yet the tone of his voice did resonate with her, though in that moment that resonance was outside of her awareness. Some part of herself felt heard. She spoke again. It wasn't so much a response as a continuation of what was present for her and which had urged her to speak previously.

'It's like I get so weighed down by things.' She didn't know how else to describe it. 'I just….' Katie shook her head and shrugged slightly, her head moving a little to the right as she did so. She took a short, deeper breath. 'I don't know.' Her head felt a bit weird, slightly dizzy.

Keith nodded and was aware he was frowning slightly, a symptom of his concentration. 'So weighted down, but… *so* hard to describe that weighted down feeling.'

She nodded, still looking down. It *was* hard to describe. She closed her eyes and immediately felt the dizziness more acutely. Her arms and her head felt heavy. She felt her shoulders droop and she wanted to lean back. She needed to rest her head against the back of the chair. There was a churning feeling in the pit of her stomach. It was an extremely anxious feeling of unease. 'I'm sorry, I guess people usually say more.' Katie was struck by the thought that she wasn't very good at this. She felt it was her fault, that she should be able to talk. But it all seemed so difficult. She took a deep breath. She was disappointed with herself. She'd felt so sure she was ready to talk.

'You feel a need to apologise, but not everyone finds it easy to speak about what is difficult, about what feels awful inside them. It's not easy. And we may simply not even want to, you know?'

Katie nodded slightly though she was looking down. 'I sort of knew that, but I also thought that I was ready, you know?'

Keith nodded, 'ready to talk?'

Katie nodded slightly again, still with her head down. She'd opened her eyes. 'Stuff in my head, you know?'

'I know what it can be like, but that's my stuff in my head. What I'm picking up on is how difficult it is for you, at this moment, to say much about your stuff.'

'Yeah.' Katie paused. Yes, she thought, it feels impossible, and it's been there for so long. 'And it's been there for a long time.'

'Feels like the stuff in your head has been there for a long, long time, yeah?' Keith could appreciate the difficulty. Sometimes people were ready to talk, as though they could no longer contain the feelings and thoughts that had been locked up inside them. But for others there was a knowing that something needed to change, yet putting the inner experience into words could seem so elusive. He knew people had to be given time, and in such an impatient society with everyone wanting instant solutions to everything, time was often a very precious commodity.

Katie closed her eyes and nodded slightly. Her stomach seemed to be churning more, the anxiety was more apparent. Her arms felt strangely numb in addition to the heaviness, and yet there was a tingling sensation as well. Her head still felt heavy and now her back felt stiff, she was suddenly very aware of it and moved a little to free it. Her shoulder blades and the middle of her back ached. She arched her back slightly, pulling her shoulders back to get a little relief. She felt tired too. Everything felt like such an effort. She took another deep breath and broke into a yawn. 'I sleep a lot. I'm not working or anything like that. Doctor said I needed to talk to someone, told me to come and see you.'

Keith nodded. 'Yes, she told me you seemed very low, tired, struggling all round.'

'Struggling with life.'

'That sounds big.'

Katie looked across at Keith, momentarily caught his eye and then looked down again. 'Yeah. I mean, why do I feel so messed up?'

'That how it feels, messed up and not knowing why?' Keith felt for her. She looked so withdrawn, so lost in herself. He sensed the struggle.

Katie went silent once more. She knew why, but why was it always all so horrible?

Keith felt an urge to ask Katie what happened. The silence following his response left him feeling that she did know. But he wasn't there to force it out of her. He knew that people had to feel ready to share thoughts, feelings, memories, that could provoke strong and difficult, frequently painful experiencing. 'Not easy to talk about.'

Although Katie felt an urge to talk, she could feel herself shrinking back at the same time. She wanted to let someone in, but she wanted to slam the door and double bolt it as well. She didn't want to be alone with it, and she wanted to as well because that was what she was used to, shutting herself away inside herself. She felt scared, and confused. The dizziness returned. She rested her head back on the chair.

'I do want to talk but it's not easy.'

'Can feel like the hardest thing in the world, to just...', Keith paused, '... let it out.' He spoke carefully and with warmth. It wasn't that he was trying to coax Katie to talk, that was not where he was coming from. He didn't want her to talk about her inner world, or past experiences that may have been difficult or painful, unless she was genuinely ready. No, he wasn't trying to encourage, rather to simply try to convey a warm and genuinely human presence so that, if she did wish to talk she would do so with a sense that whatever she sought to convey would be heard and accepted and that she would feel supported.

Katie was staring down at her thumbs, continuing to pick at them, She felt a little sting of pain, but it wasn't that much, not really. Not enough to make her feel different, better, in control. She hated how she felt. Why wouldn't it go away? Why? It was past, her past, she knew that, but the feelings, the fears, the terror – that's what it was – it stayed with her, and it was like it was getting worse. She hated it. It made her feel so alone, so very alone. It wasn't easy to try and put into words how she felt, what she was experiencing. She knew what it felt like but to find the words seemed impossible. Something just seemed to get in the way; like a part of her just slammed a door each time. The fact was that, put simply and crudely, she felt like shit. It was like she didn't matter, she meant nothing, just rubbish to be hated. It was as though.... Her thoughts stopped for a moment. The thought that had emerged was that it felt at times as thought she didn't exist; no, that wasn't quite how it was, more that she didn't really feel alive. Yes, that was closer to it. Other people, they were all out there, enjoying themselves, laughing, having fun, feeling great, having a good time. Her train of thought. What the hell did 'feeling great' mean? She genuinely did not know. But somehow she couldn't be like them. She didn't feel part of it and this left her feeling depressed. It made her feel sad just thinking about it. So much of the time she felt lonely. It wasn't just that which made her cut, though. Yes, sometimes it would, but it was generally a deeper feeling of having no control, of not really having anything of her own, anything that felt real.

Katie was still looking down. Well, her eyes were open but she wasn't really seeing; looking but not really being aware of what she was looking at. She was staring at her thumbs and fingers but she didn't really see them. She needed to feel and she needed the release. She needed to cut, something sharp and intense. She knew it gave her a different sense of herself, of her existence, something that cut through the numbness and the dark clouds that often took over.

Opposite her Keith was experiencing his own thoughts and feelings. He felt for Katie. Looking at her he was aware of how little he knew about her. He did not know her history, what had happened to her, but he did know that there would be a reason, and probably something that Katie didn't talk about, maybe never talked to anyone about. Or maybe she had and not been believed. But he couldn't start speculating or jumping to conclusions. He had to accept that he didn't know, and accept Katie as she was and how she needed to be. He could offer her the possibility of a therapeutic relational experience that would enable her to risk self-disclosure. He knew what a risk it could be to make something visible to someone else. And, of course, it could mean making something more visible to yourself as well. Sometimes things emerged that the person was not aware of. He knew how shocking such experiences could be to the person's sense or structure of self.

Keith didn't believe in forcing people to say anything. He knew how this could leave a person feeling very raw and exposed, and extremely vulnerable. Disclosing something painful that might have been kept locked away within oneself could, if suddenly forced into the open, leave the person with an open wound that their own inner psychological and emotional processes were not prepared for. It could be damaging and psychological traumatising. Human psychological process was not fully understood, but what Keith felt convinced about was that in the same way that the physical body has in-built mechanisms for self-healing where this is possible given the right care and supportive environment, then the same must be true for human psychological and emotional natures. It was just that we didn't understand them fully; what was needed to encourage self-healing or self-restoration, psychologically or emotionally speaking. However, he was convinced that the relational experience was a key element in this process and it was his job as a therapist to offer a set of relational and attitudinal qualities that would facilitate the inner healing process.

For Keith it was simple – theoretically though not always in practice – he had to allow Katie's own internal process to take her to the point where she was ready to disclose. A lot might need to take place within her, perhaps memories and experiences denied to awareness needed to become acknowledged and accepted. His role was to create the therapeutic environment and relational experience which would provide her with a sense of safety, or at least a sense that however unsafe she felt there was a kind of safety in allowing it to be expressed. He continued to sit, aware of his personal feelings of concern and compassion towards her.

Katie, meanwhile, had become aware of how on the one hand she felt uncomfortable being there, yet at the same time there was a certain OKness as well. It hadn't been as she imagined it would be. She'd expected lots of questions, someone probing, pushing, trying to get answers, and worse of all, trying to tell her how to live her life. She didn't need that, but she did know that she wanted to feel different. She felt herself taking a slightly deeper breath and let it out with a sigh. She heard Keith also taking a deep breath as well. He seemed to sigh with her.

Who was he? Could she trust him? He seemed to be trying to listen to her, but could he, could anyone, really understand? Would he listen, really listen? Or would he be like everyone else, telling her off, telling her to pull herself together, telling her to grow up. Would he tell her she was mental and send her to some shrink? Well she knew there was something wrong, but she wasn't crazy. Just sad, lonely, hurting like hell, scared to talk and wanting it all to end. And sometimes, worst of all, not having any feeling at all. Empty. Then she'd cut, and then she'd feel something ease inside herself, then she'd feel different. She didn't want to lose that. She needed that. She felt her anxiety rising at the very thought of losing it. Did she trust him? Did she? She didn't want to look up. She knew what he looked like. Say nothing, she didn't really know him. Better to say nothing, she'd be OK. She could cope. She always had. She was a survivor, she'd coped with so much. She found her own way through, she'd had to. So much…. Faces laughing at her, shouting at her, taunting her; feeling held down. Too many of them, always too many of them. Unable to fight back. Unable to breathe. She didn't feel angry, she'd lost touch with anger. She couldn't reach it and it couldn't reach her, though it was there, buried deep within. What she had was the feeling of sadness and loneliness, the emptiness and the anxiety and terror that had become unwelcome companions for so many years. She continued to look down and to pick at her thumbs and her fingers with her nails, seeing but not seeing the blood that she was drawing.

It seemed to Keith that for a moment at least, Katie had suddenly seemed even smaller, as if she had shrunk into the chair in some way. He had experienced this before with clients and invariably it was an indicator that a client was connecting with something deep within themselves, a deep feeling or memory, and often linked to something traumatic that had happened, something disturbing, something intense. He felt an urge to reach out to her in some way. Yet he was also aware of not wanting to take Katie away from whatever she was experiencing. At the same time, he wanted to ensure that there was some degree of relational contact and connection with her in the place that she had withdrawn into. He spoke gently, seeking to convey his presence yet he hoped without overly invading what was probably for her a very fragile place. 'Not a good place to be.'

Katie sighed as she heard Keith speak. She shook her head slightly from side to side. It wasn't a deliberate response, more instinctive. A human reaction to his human response. She took another deep breath. Something within her felt heard. Not completely, but something deep within her was recognising that her experience was being acknowledged; and in a non-condemning way. No judgement, just a kind of acknowledgement of how it was. Simple, and yes, he was right, it wasn't a good place to be, in fact it was a crap place to be. And yet somehow as well that acknowledgement felt good, not so good as to take away all the difficulty in what she was experiencing, but nevertheless there was something good about it, a kind of…, she didn't know quite what but it was a bit of a relief. It felt good that someone was hearing and responding; being there but not getting on her case, not having a go at her.

Keith had noticed Katie's head movement and heard her sigh. She wasn't totally absorbed into her own inner world. There was connection, communication, awareness of his presence, however minimal it might be. He knew he needed to try and keep that human connection. Yes, he thought, it's not just therapeutic connection; in essence it's about human connection, but one characterised by a therapists warm acceptance and compassion towards his or her client, and a striving to really hear what the client is communicating – verbally and/or non-verbally. Katie was responding to his presence; or maybe some part of Katie was. He knew how fragmented people could sometimes be.

He needed to maintain the relational contact whilst allowing her to be in the place where she had entered, to remain within that part of her inner world that she was currently moving around in. And he needed to be present and able to move with her in that world should she choose to begin to describe it more fully. He felt himself taking a deeper breath, in fact it brought to his awareness that for a short while he'd stopped breathing. His focus and concentration had been so intense, as if he was in a kind of suspended state, yet alert to what may be being communicated to him. Whatever was happening for Katie, whatever she was experiencing, he was struck with the thought that it was probably not new to her. He felt himself nodding slightly as the thought emerged into a fuller and more powerful presence in his awareness. 'All too familiar place?'

Katie nodded, this time more conscious of her response. It wasn't simply an involuntary, instinctive reaction this time, but a conscious agreeing with what she had heard Keith say. All too familiar. That summed it up. That was how it was, though she wished it wasn't. It was all far too familiar. She remained silent, the thoughts, feelings and memories still with her, filling her sense of self. This was her private world, a world that tormented her, a world she wanted to be free of and yet a world that could be strangely reassuring in its familiarity. And, more than that, a world that at times she would feel herself shut off from though it was always with a sense of doom. She didn't consciously shut it out, it just happened. That was somehow worse. The nothingness and the..., it was difficult to find words for it, she just knew it. But when the feelings were there, it wasn't really how she wanted to be either, but they filled her up, not allowing any psychological or emotional space for other experiences to impact on her awareness.

Although these were not the words she might have used to describe her experiences, for her it was more a matter of feeling at times overwhelmed by a horrible everything, and at other times an equally overwhelmingly awful nothingness. Anyone on the outside who looked into her inner world would probably have simply described it as a private hell. It had become very silent in the counselling room.

Keith intended to respond to the silence. He believed that silence itself was something to be acknowledged, indeed to be empathised with. His client was choosing to be outwardly silent. In one sense, respecting the silence was a way of conveying empathy. But there were times when he also felt he needed to acknowledge it verbally. Was this one of those times? He was aware that he was hesitating, and he often took that as an indicator that perhaps it wasn't the time. Something within him was causing that hesitation. He was aware that he was getting enmeshed in his own thoughts. That wasn't why he was there. He brought his focus back to Katie. She seemed so remote, and yet the intensity of her expression and her finger movements as she continued to pick at her thumbs made her more present. Verbally quiet but so much was probably going on for her. Such intensity. How alone with her thoughts and feelings must she feel? The thought passed through his mind, and it triggered a stronger sense of his caring and concern for her. What was the landscape of her inner world like? The words of the question formed powerfully in his mind.

He questioned himself. Was he simply curious, wanting to know to satisfy a need of his own, or was he experiencing something that genuinely had therapeutic relevance and value in voicing? If it was personal curiosity then he knew it was unlikely to be therapeutically helpful to voice it. But it had struck him so forcefully and had remained so present. Was it an impulse emerging from his connection with his client, being drawn out of him by her unvoiced need in some way? He had a choice, either try and push it to one side and focus back on the client, or say something to make it visible. Either way he was feeling it was a supervision issue, that he needed to explore his process with his supervisor to ensure that he was maintaining clarity or if some unmet need of his own was getting in the way or causing distraction. 'I'm aware of the silence, and whilst I want to respect that, I am also very aware of wanting to check if you want to tell me what you are experiencing. But *only* if you want or feel able to. I appreciate that you may need the silence.' He spoke softly, but clearly. He didn't want Katie to feel pushed or obliged in any way to respond. What he hadn't really appreciated was that his calm way of speaking also conveyed a certain reassuringly authoritative tone. And this conveyed a sense of safety.

Katie could feel the lump forming in her throat. She swallowed, but it would not go away. She felt strange. Yes, she knew she wanted to talk but she also knew she didn't as well. And that was the difficulty, the struggle. Hearing Keith speak somehow just made that inner struggle more present. He seemed calm. She felt anything but calm. He seemed somehow …, she didn't know, it wasn't something she was particularly dwelling on, he just seemed dependable. Maybe she could trust him, could talk, could tell him. She felt strange. Yes, the feeling of anxiety was very present for her. But she also felt something else. There was a kind of coldness that seemed to be spreading throughout her being. It wasn't just a physical coldness. She felt herself instinctively twitch, a sort of muscle spasm. She felt weak, as if she was going to faint. She could feel the energy draining, her head felt suddenly light. She swallowed and took a deep breath.

Keith noticed how even more pale Katie suddenly seemed. He felt a natural concern. 'Are you alright? You look suddenly very pale.'

'I'm feeling weird.'

'Can I pour you some water?' Keith glanced over to the jug on the table.

Katie nodded. Keith reached over and poured from the jug into one of the glasses, before handing the glass to Katie.

'Thanks.' Katie was grateful though she immediately noticed that her arm felt kind of strange as she reached over for the glass and brought it to her lips. But the cool sensation of the water in her mouth felt good; she was grateful for that. The strange feeling continued, almost like she was 'spaced out'. She sipped some more of the water before placing the glass back on the table. Did she feel a little easier? She wasn't sure. She knew she didn't feel right. Sort of weirdly light in the head but heavy in her body against the chair. And she could feel a strange churning sensation in the pit of her stomach. It was like an anxiety reaction, but somehow it felt deeper. She didn't know what to do or what to say. In fact, she felt as though she didn't really have the energy to say anything just at that moment.

Keith responded to what he saw, what, in effect, her body was communicating to him. 'You looked suddenly quite pale and withdrawn.' He didn't say anything further. He wanted to re-convey his attention and focus. He felt concerned and that was reflected in the way that he spoke. Clearly something was happening for Katie, he felt sure about that and he was not going to probe into what he suspected must be a very sensitive area. Again it was a case of his trusting her inner process. At some level he felt sure – and theoretically believed – that she knew what she needed, even though that knowing might reside outside of her awareness. It was for some a strange concept to grasp, but his belief was that the person was not merely the sum total of what was in their awareness. He knew that physiologically there were a lot of processes occurring for the person that they were not aware of. In fact, to be aware of everything that was happening throughout your body would simply pre-occupy you to the point that you couldn't do much else. The body had to function in some sense at a level beneath the radar of consciousness. So why shouldn't the same be true of psychological and emotional processes, and mental processes too? He knew he was working not only with the awareness that Katie brought into the room – in a sense 'the known' as far as she was concerned – but also with the material within her that existed outside of her awareness, or which might be known to her yet denied to her conscious awareness because if accepted it could threaten her self-concept or very structure of self. He also acknowledged that there could be conflicting needs or demands within her psyche, one area perhaps wanting her to disclose something, another wanting her to maintain silence. He also knew that where this was the case, the balance of power could change from moment to moment.

The anxious, churning sensation had moved within Katie, and now she felt her heart thumping in her chest as well. The urge to say something was getting stronger, in a sense it was trying to assert itself over those other elements of Katie that were trying to reign this urge back in. The result physiologically, and in her awareness, was the anxiety, the churning and now the thumping heart. A psychological struggle was in process causing uncomfortable physiological effects. She needed to say something. She needed to tell someone, but she was so afraid of what would happen. So much sadness, and terror, and anxiety. It all felt too much, all of it. She felt the constriction in her throat and tears were welling up in her eyes. She felt like she was fighting with herself. She closed her eyes and shook her head slightly from side to side, feeling a trickle of tears spilling down both of her cheeks as she did so. She swallowed again but it felt like she could not control it. It scared her. She couldn't bear to feel not in control.

Keith noted the tears and the shaking of her head. He also noticed how Katie's jaw had tightened and her lower lip had begun to quiver. He could sense the emotion in the room. He felt extremely focused as he maintained his openness and sensitivity to everything that was happening. He felt like he was tuning up his receptivity as he responded to what he was witnessing. 'You look so sad and upset, Katie.' He deliberately did not say 'it is making you sad and upset', which would direct the focus on to the 'it'. He was aware that what he wanted to empathise with was precisely what he sensed to be being conveyed to him – the presence of sadness and upset made visible by Katie's tears and her facial expression.

Katie bit her lip, trying to control her instinct to cry. Her breathing was in short bursts and she felt as though she would burst. Suddenly there was so much upset and sadness, so much to try and contain. She looked to one side, still struggling, wiping her cheeks with her hands and then her eyes. Keith indicated the tissues and Katie took one and instinctively buried her face in it. Control went, the emotional dam burst, she was utterly overwhelmed. And it was nothing like she had experienced before. The sobbing took over, each breath was wracked with pain. The cry of hurt and upset. It both brought a chill and a warmth to Keith. The chill was an instinctive reaction to the sound and the depth of distress he was witnessing from another human being. The warmth was the response of his heart to a person in pain.

Katie's eyes burned. Her throat felt so tight. Her breathing was difficult. She'd breathe out and the emotion would sweep through her making it momentarily difficult to breathe back in again. And when it did come, it was in short, sharp gasps. Not much air really getting into her lungs. For a moment she experienced wanting to regain control but then that was lost, she didn't have it in her to try any more. She succumbed to the emotions that were rapidly taking over. It felt as though the pain and the hurt was coming from so deep, so deep inside her. And the sadness. She realised she was aching with sadness. It was as if her insides were being pulled out of her. It was so utterly overwhelming that everything else in her experience vanished as the feelings continued to pour through her.

At the start Keith had felt quiet, inwardly and outwardly. There had been a certain stillness within himself. It wasn't that he had detached himself from what he was witnessing in order to avoid painful feelings himself, it was more a stillness emerging from his intensity of focus. As though all his senses had been not only put on high alert but had in some sense been gathered together into a single point within himself and then focused on Katie, like a sort of psychological laser beam. Yet that wasn't really a very accurate analogy. He felt enormous compassion for her, instinctively wanting to somehow make it all better for her and knowing, at the same time, that he couldn't, that only she could achieve that and, he believed, this would be facilitated by her experience of a genuinely warm, accepting, open and humanly caring therapeutic relationship. Now, as the intensity of Katie's upset grew, he felt his own heart beginning to thump. Yes, he felt enormous compassion for her as she sat, her face still buried in the tissue she was holding in both hands, her sobbing, her staccato breathing with her shoulders moving in what seemed such a jagged movement up and down as she gasped for breath. So much hurt; so much distress. How the human being has such capacity to hold it all in and then, when it breaks out, tears through us. He felt humbled as he sat. 'So much hurt.' He spoke softly, not wishing to disturb the process of emotional release that was occurring – was it to be thought of as release, or was it more a case of a person connecting with what they had been carrying within them and, for whatever reason, had been kept away from their awareness? He knew that wherever you placed the emphasis, it did help people, however awful it felt at the time. He knew that so often it was needed, a necessary part of the process of coming to terms with painful experience, and often the kinds of experience that had some degree of an emotionally traumatic impact on the person, either suddenly or sustained over time.

Keith could only imagine what must lay behind Katie's upset and distress, but he didn't want to let himself start to speculate in any way. Maybe he would know, one day, if Katie needed or wanted to tell. Katie needed his attention now, and it needed to be, and was, heartfelt. She needed his focus, his presence as a fellow human being. It wasn't that she would not survive if he wasn't there, if the release had come at some other time, for instance. He also recognised that this might not be the first time. Keith believed that the power of therapy was that another human being was there as a companion, a warm, caring and supportive companion, trying to understand and offer an utterly authentic and honest presence. For the counsellor there could be no masks to hide behind, no denial of experience, no unwillingness to reflect or express what was being experienced. His role was to be open and be in touch with his own experiencing as a human being. Yes, he thought to himself, most of all it is about offering the presence of another human being, and most importantly a human being with a heart.

Katie had heard Keith's words. They seemed distant and did not intrude. It reminded her that someone was there. But it didn't take her away from the feelings that were still so overwhelming. She felt like she would never stop crying and that it could go on forever. Her head ached, her heart ached, her whole body seemed to be in some kind of torment. There was tightness in her back and her chest. She moved slightly and winced at the physical pain. She was so stiff. She rubbed her face through the tissue. It was so wet it was breaking up. She screwed it together and reached for another to blow her nose, replacing that with another to hold against her face once more. Slowly the emotions began to ease a little. Her breathing had become less gasping. She was able to take deeper breaths and let the air back out through her mouth, each time with a faint sigh. So tired, so drained, she felt like a wet cloth that had been utterly wrung out. Gradually, a clearer awareness of being in the counselling room was returning. It brought with it a feeling of being suddenly vulnerable, of feeling like she would be judged. She heard herself saying, 'I'm sorry.' And then heard Keith's response, 'you feel sorry for expressing what you feel?'.

She nodded. Yes she did. Not that she'd had any choice. Keith's response had a very slight questioning tone. He hadn't wanted to reinforce any notion that it was right, or wrong. In fact, he'd intended for his words to be a more directly empathic response, but they were tinged with an underlying feeling within himself that she had no reason to feel sorry. He had just wanted to acknowledge what Katie had said.

Katie was drying her eyes. 'I must look a mess.' She had looked up and noticed Keith's expression. He seemed somehow so accepting of her in some way. She couldn't define what it was.

'Tears aren't the best thing for our appearance.'

'No, but I guess I'm not really sorry for..., you know.' Katie shrugged her shoulders as she finished the sentence.

Keith nodded.

'Just feels so much.' Katie shook her head. 'Just felt, you know..., I don't know.'

'Mhmm, too much to keep in, do you mean?'

Katie nodded, taking a deeper breath as she did so. She looked down again, feeling another surge of emotion. Not again, she thought. The inner ache was growing once more, the pain, the hurt. Her heart was thumping, her throat tightening. She felt so drained by everything and just wanted it all to go away. She wanted to feel different, normal – whatever that was. Anything but what she had been feeling and was still feeling. Yes, she had been upset in the past, and had cried herself to sleep so many times. But the intensity of what she had just gone through, and which was to some degree still with her, felt different. It was like everything had become one aching hurt, and it felt like it was throughout her body, her stomach, her chest, her heart, her head, throughout her very being. She began to sob again. She felt so tired, no energy to resist it, tired of it all, tired of everything. She wanted it all to go away. She reached for another tissue, holding it once more to her face. Keith noted her shoulders once again rising and falling as she sobbed and gasped for breath in the same way as she had done just a few minutes earlier. Her eyes and throat burned.

Keith was experiencing a powerful urge to reach out to Katie. She seemed to be so alone, locked into the painful world that was flooding out through her tears once more. Or was the sense of aloneness his own stuff, an effect of him separating himself from her world of pain and upset? Was he experiencing some kind of psychological or emotional reflex to protect himself? Why was he wanting to reach out? To meet her needs – as he saw them – or his own? He hesitated. He knew he wanted to convey some reassurance from his presence as a human being. He wanted to convey his warm acceptance of Katie and that it was OK for her to express her feelings, though he sensed that she probably had very little choice on the matter given the intensity of what he was witnessing. He tightened his lips and took a deep breath. Katie was continuing to sob. It was heart-wrenching.

He didn't want to invade her physical or psychological space. If he reached out to her physically he didn't want it misinterpreted. But his intentions were an open and honest expression of his concern and he knew the therapeutic power of physical contact and reassurance. Physical touch could convey more than words, a form of empathic responding not fully understood in many ways, and certainly a conveyer of compassion and caring. He spoke clearly, but gently. 'I see your upset, your distress and it leaves me wanting to reach out to you.'

Katie heard what Keith said and she appreciated his openness. It was somehow nice to hear. It made him feel more real, no, more present in some way, more of a human being. She had heard something of him. He was affected by what she was experiencing, it wasn't just her. She knew it wasn't but there was something about what Keith had said and the way he had said it. Yes, she wanted to be reached out to. For so long she had felt that need, to be cared for and comforted by someone who might really understand. His words stayed with her. They gave her a sort of refuge in some strange way. It wasn't that she wanted someone to feel sorry for her, she didn't so much want sympathy as wanting someone to acknowledge her, what it was like to be her, to live in her skin, as it were.

The emotions were subsiding again, her heart wasn't thumping to the same degree and her breathing had become a little easier. But she still felt tired. She took a deep breath which triggered a yawn. Her face felt so wet and puffy from the crying.

Keith hadn't moved closer or physically reached out to touch Katie after he had spoken. Katie hadn't seemed to indicate in any way that she wanted that, so he had continued to sit with the awareness of what he was feeling, maintaining his attention and focus on her. He watched the deeper intake of breath and the yawn that followed. She had taken the tissue away from her face and was drying her eyes and cheeks once more. He noticed that she was moving slightly in the chair. It made him suddenly aware that he hadn't moved for some while either. He felt the stiffness in the middle of his own back, and in the region of his right hip. He flexed his back slightly and took a deeper breath himself.

Katie was yawning again. The tiredness was sweeping over her yet with it there also came a certain calmness. She heard Keith speaking.

'That was a lot of emotion to release, a lot of feeling.'

Katie nodded. She swallowed, the lump had eased in her throat. She tightened her lips for a moment and blinked a few times, as if she was regaining her bearings. 'I-I just couldn't control it.'

'No, uncontrollable, just had to come out.'

'Is it always like this?' She hadn't planned to ask the question, it just formed in her mind and she voiced it. In a sense she was wondering whether what had happened was normal. She'd been to counselling before, but it hadn't been like this. Last time it had been questions and then being told what to do. That's what she thought it might be like again though the doctor had said that it wasn't about questions, it was about talking and being listened to. She'd had her own ideas and expectations, and had accepted that it might be upsetting, but not like she had just experienced. It had been the intensity and overwhelming nature of it that had taken her totally by surprise. She needed some reassurance now although to some degree she did accept that it was OK. Keith didn't seem phased by it. She wondered how she would have reacted if she had been with someone going through what she had. She didn't know. He hadn't seemed phased, but he'd been there. She knew he'd been there. It was something not just about the little he had said but the way he had spoken. There had been a warmth in his voice. It had been reassuring and yet, had it not been, she wondered whether she would have experienced anything differently. She didn't know. Her thoughts were disturbed by Keith responding.

'Sometimes. Depends on what someone needs. But yes, locked up feelings, hurt, can need to be released.' As he was speaking Keith was aware that Katie had not actually disclosed what the hurt was that she was experiencing, and what it was related to specifically. But he wasn't going to ask; much better to let her tell him in her own way if she wanted to.

Katie felt a little disconnected in herself. The tiredness and all that she had been through had left her feeling a little numb. 'Oh dear. I still feel very wobbly.'

'No rush. Take your time. We've still got ten minutes or so of the session left. You've been through a lot.'

'Yeah.' Katie nodded, more to herself as she spoke. She had looked up. Her heart had started to thump again but this time the intensity of emotion wasn't so present. She felt an urge, more than an urge, more of an inner command to speak. 'I need to explain.'

'Things that you need to explain to me.'

Katie nodded, biting her lower lip as she did so. 'I can't tell you everything.' She took a deep breath as she thought, "not in ten minutes".

Keith accepted that clients had the right and the autonomy to say what they needed to say. 'No, only what you want to tell me.'

Katie nodded again. 'It's just that....' She paused. It wasn't easy. 'It's just that, you know, it's things, well, I haven't told anyone about, you know?'

Keith nodded. Yes, he knew how, as a counsellor, he could find himself being the first person to be invited into a client's inner world, into their memories, their experiences. It was always a very significant and human moment. He did not undervalue it. To be the first person to be told something was, well, it was in one sense an honour and at the same time he found it extremely humbling as well. He needed to be sensitive, and he felt sensitive. A client tentatively offers you their experience and you need to receive it carefully, gently, honouring the moment and what it contains.

Katie knew that if she started telling her story it would mean the feelings would return again. She didn't want that. She couldn't face it, not now, not again, and then to be on her own once more. 'There are things I need to tell you, but…', she shook her head, 'but not today'. Katie could feel her anxiety rising again as she spoke. She looked at Keith, a questioning look, and then glanced away.

'You've gone through a lot today, and it doesn't feel like the right time to say what you need to say.' Keith kept his focus very much on what Katie had said.

'No, I am feeling a little calmer, and I think I need that, and I don't want to get back into, you know…'. Katie paused. 'Maybe next time, I don't know, maybe. I need to feel a little calmer, you know?' To Katie it felt something of a relief to have at least said what she had said. Keith seemed to be accepting, she didn't feel any pressure from him, though she did feel pressure. Maybe it wasn't so much him as the situation, she didn't know, but she was aware of feeling this strange sense of relief, although there was still anxiety mixed in with it.

'Sure, feel a little calmer, and maybe you'll feel able to say a little more next time, maybe not. It has to be at your own pace and in your own way.' He added the final two comments as he wanted to communicate some reassurance that he wasn't seeking in any way to pressure her, but rather he wished to convey his respect for her autonomy, her choices. Keith then refocused on what Katie had emphasised, 'but at the moment it's important to feel a little calmer'.

'At the moment.' Katie nodded slightly. Her thoughts were ranging across so many different experiences. She took an involuntary deeper breath, tightening her slips slightly as she did, and holding it momentarily. She swallowed. 'I've had some bad experiences, you know, and they're not easy to talk about.' She thought of the bullying, the feelings of abandonment, of being so alone in herself, and of a deep sense of disturbance which she had never understood but seemed to exist at the core of her being.

Keith nodded himself in response. It was only the first session. Katie had already expressed a great deal of emotion. That was more than for some clients. Katie had, in a sense, used the time during the counselling sessions to release, to express, make visible her emotion, her hurt, not just to him but in a very important sense to herself. She had not described events, circumstances, experiences, or indeed what she was actually experiencing in words. It had not been a verbal dialogue that had taken place so much as an emotional one. He didn't believe therapy was just about words anyway. Communication could take other forms, as could empathic responding. And he also recognised that for some people the non-verbal was their language of disclosure. In particularly this was the case for those whose hurt, pain, trauma, had been experienced and internalised in a non-verbal way, for instance at a time in that person's childhood before they had command of language. Severely traumatising experiences could be so intense, sharp and painful that the person might not experience it in a manner that involved language-based thinking. They were simply a raw and overwhelming experience impacting on the person's awareness and structure of self, embedding itself in a manner that by-passed language-based thought processes.

Keith was aware of not knowing what had been Katie's past experiences. Katie clearly had things she wanted to say and she was making it clear that today was not the time. He respected that, responding to her last words. 'No, not easy to talk about.' He was aware that his own lips had tightened as he had finished speaking. This was not a moment to smile, it would certainly not have been congruent to his own feeling of the seriousness of the exchange that was taking place between them. There was a very clear seriousness in Katie's tone of voice. She was living on an edge that marked the border between what was undisclosed and what was to be disclosed, between the known kept invisible and the known made visible. And, as he knew so well, there could also be the presence of the unknown that could emerge into awareness.

Katie nodded instinctively to Keith's response, and then lapsed back into silence. Yes, it was a relief to have acknowledged that she had more to say, and that it was acknowledged but not invaded.

Keith knew that it wasn't always disclosing in detail that was the key step. He knew that having someone else in effect bear witness to a secret, and who received it with the degree of respect and compassion deserved, was incredibly important within therapeutic process. But for many people simply disclosing that there was something further to disclose, without the detail, was a big enough and courageous enough step that, in itself, could threaten the person's structure of self. The fact that someone else knew something about you that you had kept hidden, yes, it could bring relief, but it changed things as well. And it could lead to disclosure to others, family, perhaps, or within support groups related specifically to the issue disclosed. It was always an extremely significant first step that deserved acknowledgement. Yes, the word courageous was very much in Keith's mind as he sat opposite Katie, and he wanted to acknowledge that in some way. But he also knew just because he felt she was being courageous didn't mean that she was experiencing that. In fact, he knew from past experience that often a client would say it wasn't courageous but a matter of necessity, or even simply desperation that impelled the disclosure.

'I don't know how it feels for you to have said that there were things that have happened, bad things, and that you want to talk about them another time, but for me that feels courageous to acknowledge that here, and I realise that may not be how you experience it.' Keith noted that Katie had looked up and they shared a moment of steady eye-contact. Katie smiled, it was only a slight smile, but it made an impression on Keith. She hadn't smiled much during the session and though Katie wasn't aware of that herself, Keith was. Katie wasn't sure that it was courage on her part to have said what she had said. It wasn't something she thought she had. She'd survived a lot of crap, yes, but did that make her courageous? She did what she had to do. Was that courage? She didn't know. But it somehow felt that Keith in some way understood. She couldn't describe it in words, but something occurred in that moment of eye-contact. A meeting at some level. She felt stronger for it. Was she being brave coming to counselling? Mad, maybe…, no, that wasn't fair. She knew she had to change, something had to change. She couldn't carry on the way she had been, she knew that. Maybe she was a little brave, perhaps. She looked away as she followed her train of thought.

'It's where I'm at, you know?' She shrugged and pursed her lips

'Mhmm, says something about where you are at right now.'

Katie nodded. 'I don't know if it's courage, though, well, maybe, I don't know. But it's not easy, nothing's easy, you know? Head full of shit so much of the time.' She paused. 'I just want to feel normal.' She looked back at Keith and again it felt as though there was a moment of significant contact.

Keith sensed a real yearning in Katie's voice, a kind of desperation. 'Desperate to get the shit out of your head and try to feel normal, yeah?' He spoke slowly.

Katie had looked away again. It left her feeling sad. She wasn't even too sure what normal was. She knew what her normal was like, and she didn't want that any more. She couldn't change her past, but she couldn't keep being affected by it.

'It's not easy, you know, but you get by, do what you have to do, yeah?'

'Yeah, what you have to do.' Keith was nodding slowly. He knew how it could be for people though exactly how it was for Katie he could only guess. But he had seen pain, sadness, a certain look of desperation in her expression. He'd felt a kind of desperate reaching out. It pulled on his sense of humanity. It touched his heart. He was glad to experience a genuinely human response and he hoped that it would be conveyed in his facial expression, his words and his tone of voice.

Katie pushed a memory aside. She didn't want to get into that just now. And then she thought about how she brought herself relief. Seemed crazy in a way, but it worked. Not too deep, just enough, yeah, enough to get by.

The session drew to a close. They agreed a date and time for the next session, in fact they agreed the next three sessions, once a week. Keith felt good that there was what he sensed to be a commitment from Katie, and he knew he felt committed to be there to try and help her.

Katie felt she needed to do this. However unsafe she could feel in herself it did sort of feel safe to be there. She needed to do it. She had to. It was how it was. She just hoped she didn't have to keep re-experiencing what she had been through today. Though she also knew she probably would. It never really went away, but it had been so much more intense today. Like she was sicking something dark up from within the very core of her being. Her short life – she was only nineteen – had been one of constant upheaval ever since she had been taken into 'care', as they called it, and even before in so many ways. She wanted to be different, feel different, but she didn't know what that meant. She wanted to leave it all behind. The thought that had struck her was that she wished she could feel she had something to smile about.

The session ended and Katie got up to leave, Keith opening the door for her and checking she knew which way to go. Katie thanked him and headed back along the corridor.

Keith watched her walk away. She seemed to be walking in a purposeful kind of way, and her words came to mind, 'do what you have to do'. Keith went back into the room and spent a while sitting and reflecting on the session, preparing his thoughts so that he could write his notes. Something struck him that he hadn't really noticed in the session. Katie had stopped picking at her fingers. It had stopped after her intense emotional release. He hadn't noticed it at the time, too engaged with what was happening and the emotional intensity of it all. Something had happened causing her to stop. Probably not a conscious or deliberate choice to stop, but whatever had been urging the need to do that had maybe eased.

He knew that some people's lives had been and still could be a kind of living hell. Was this how it was or had been for Katie? He realised that he was looking forward to their next session, to hearing more and to offering the kind of therapeutic relationship that he believed would help her to come to terms with whatever had so clearly affected her. And he also knew that deep within him was a concern, a sense of unease, a sense that he was going to go on a therapeutic journey with Katie that was going to be disturbing. He took a deep breath and hoped that he would be able to offer what she needed, what her own inner process of change and growth, needed from him. She was young. She'd mentioned the 'shit in her head'. She seemed too young to have her life and her sense of self messed up in a way that would affect her life chances. She still had so much of her life ahead of her. He realised he was shaking his head. He saw too many young people messed up by life, well, not so much by life, the truth was it was often by people, and often though not exclusively by adults who should have known better.

Chapter 3

A week had passed and Keith was sitting in the counselling room waiting for Katie to arrive. He had given a lot of thought to that previous session. His expectation was that Katie might now say more about her past, but he also knew that what she had said the previous week about there being more to say and that then wasn't the time to say it, didn't mean that today would necessarily be any different. He recognised all too well how a lot could happen in a week, and that internal emotional and psychological processes could leave people feeling very different, not just week to week, but even hour to hour, and in extreme cases minute to minute. He well appreciated how a person could have very different priorities from one week to the next.

Keith hoped that he would be able to listen to what she had to say and communicate that he heard and understood her accurately. He was nodding to himself as he thought about the difference between listening and hearing. In his view hearing went deeper than listening. Yes, he could sit and listen to a client's words, but he needed to really hear them, and hear what was behind them too. He put his musings to one side and drifted back into thinking about whether Katie would feel able to say what she might want to say. This question stayed with him as he sat and waited. Strangely, he had no sense of concern as to whether Katie would attend. He did not know why. Yes, he knew that people did not always keep appointments, but he did not have a sense that this would happen, not this week anyway. And yet, on the face of it, there was no reason to think that way. Katie may have been considering making some very painful disclosures, and she could have changed her mind. He wouldn't blame her for that. Too many people spoke of therapy as a soft option. They didn't understand.

He felt he related well to young people. He wasn't sure why, but maybe being a father with teenagers himself who were always bringing their friends round helped. He could engage them in conversation, taking an interest in what they were up to. So many young people seemed to value talking to someone who was older. He guessed he probably came across as a bit of a father figure to some of his clients. It wasn't a role he sought to take. He knew he was not there for that. But he also accepted that for many young people, particularly those from broken homes… now there was a nice British way of avoiding describing the reality, he thought to himself, broken hearts usually, broken relationships, broken lives, but we call it broken homes. He was shaking his head as he thought about how some, or was it many, young people may not have experienced a consistently present father figure, or having an adult taking a genuine interest in them, their world and their concerns. Yes, some had, maybe many had, but he tended to find himself working with those who hadn't, and who had learned over the years not to trust anyone but themselves.

He wondered about Katie. What had been her experience, what was her story? Did she trust easily? What had been her relational experiences? He didn't know. What he did know was that she was a young woman struggling with herself and living in a setting that indicated that something had probably gone wrong for her in her life. And the question for him now was whether he could be the person that could offer a therapeutic relational experience that would make a positive difference.

Keith had worked as a counsellor for over 20 years and during that time he had listened to the stories of many young people, and quite a few older people as well. So often there were parallels, he just saw people at different points in their journey through life. *Journey through life.* He shook his head. For some it seemed an easy journey, for others anything but. Yet he knew from experience how resilient young people could be. He thought as well about how often adults talked about younger people as if they were all the same, and in such a dismissive way. Yes, young people had problems, and maybe society's values and the whole way things were going were making it worse – break up of families, material values, rampant consumerism, violence on TV and in the games that kids seemed to get so addicted to. And all the chemicals in the food, not to mention the drugs on the streets or the alcohol fuelled violence which seemed just about everywhere, as if the whole country was drinking. And so available and accessible to young people. Everything so loud and intense. Something was going very wrong with society. He felt sure that you couldn't just blame the young people. Something was happening to them, something about the society and the values that governed it were not healthy. He knew that each young person was unique with their own individual story to tell. Yes, they could appear the same, following the latest fashion and social trends. But whose fault was that? Who created fashion? Who drove the advertising and the marketing? Who made the films and who designed the games? It depressed him sometimes when he thought about it, and yet he also knew that people could move on and make a difference in their lives. And that was his business, to do his bit; not to push, but to listen and to give that therapeutic space for young people to get themselves together. He wanted to offer an opportunity for them to free themselves from – what had Katie called it – the shit in their heads, and start to make their own choices and to get away from the intensity, the have now pay later, quick fix, fuck everyone else attitudes that seemed to him to be symptoms of a society where materialism was in control and addictions were becoming not the exception but the rule.

He glanced at the clock, still a few more minutes before Katie's appointment time. He wanted to clear his mind, be fresh, so he could listen to her without irrelevant thoughts and feelings of his own getting in the way. Closing his eyes he took a few deep breaths. Keith found it important to centre himself in this way. He began focussing on his breathing, feeling the shift in his head as he left the chatter of his mind behind. He felt a quality of stillness arising within himself. It felt good. He felt centred. A few more deep breaths and he opened his eyes once more to check the time. He got up and headed out to the waiting area to see if Katie had arrived.

The waiting room was busy and Katie had found a place in the corner. As soon as she had seated herself she had automatically looked down, not wanting to catch anyone's eye. She preferred it that way. She wasn't sure whether it had been a good idea to come. She'd had a crap week – what was new? No-one seemed to care that much. She'd got by though. At least she had a place to live, if you could call it living. What did she have? A room in bed and breakfast accommodation. At least she had a TV. Everyone else seemed to have so much more. It wasn't that she really craved lots of possessions, but a few things that she could feel were really her own would be good. Yeah, she had her music, she needed that. It was important to her. But what else did she have? She continued to sit, oblivious of the people around her. She was picking at her thumbs. She sighed but without really being aware that she had.

Keith called Katie's name but she did not respond. She looked distant. He went over to where she sat.

'Hi Katie, good to see you.'

Katie heard her name and looked up, noticing Keith smiling. It was a gentle kind of smile. Warm. She nodded and stood up, following him towards the counselling room. Keith opened the door and invited her in. She sat down in the chair she had sat in the previous week.

'Glad you made it.'

'Yeah.' Katie lifted her left hand and rubbed her left eye as she replied. Her eyes felt gritty and she was tired. She took a deep breath but said nothing more as she lapsed into silence.

Keith sought to maintain his own sensitivity and presence. He didn't want to in any way impose a focus on Katie, though he did want to communicate his emotional availability to her. 'So, anything you want to talk about? I'd be happy to listen.' He was genuine in what he was saying. It wasn't coming out of a text book on how to start a therapy session. He deliberately didn't make mention of what Katie had said the previous week, knowing that she might well have a different agenda now.

Katie was thinking back over her week since she'd last been there. It hadn't been a good week. The place she was living in at least gave her a bit of independence but it got her down. She got her money each week but it wasn't much, not nearly enough. Everyone else had nice things, why couldn't she? Life wasn't fair. Life was shit. She was looking down and realised she was looking at Keith's shoes. They looked expensive. Different world. Different fucking world. Did she want to tell him anything? Did she? So many people in her life always asking questions. But Keith was different. He didn't really do that, he just sat. Wasn't sure what she felt about that, but it was how it was. She'd get by, she always did. You just had to wise up, know what you could get away with.

She thought about her week. She'd been out a few times, got drunk – good feeling. She smiled as she thought about it. She'd had sex a couple of times, well, it was the deal, wasn't it. Let them buy you the drinks and, yeah, a trade. She didn't care, that's how it was. And then there were the bad times, the sad times. Feeling nothing. She'd feel herself sliding into it. Then she'd want to cut. And she was cutting deeper, and it sort of worried her, but not all the time. It made her feel …, better? Different? Alive? No, just made her feel something…, anything….

'I'm pissed off.'

The words took Keith a little by surprise, they were voiced with a sudden intensity and yet a certain flatness that he somehow wasn't expecting.'

'Pissed off?' He responded, aware of his surprise yet seeking to match the tone of how Katie had spoken.

'Yeah. I mean, you know, what is the point, yeah?'

'Point in…?'

'Anything.'

'Doesn't seem like any point in anything, yeah?'

Katie shrugged and lapsed back into silence, not sure quite what she meant or why she had said what she had said. She wasn't sure she was pissed off at anyone or about anything, just how she felt, how it was. She didn't feel like saying anything else, so she didn't.

Keith found himself taking a deep breath. He wondered whether to respond straight away or to give Katie time to be with what with whatever it was that was pissing her off. He wondered what the world looked like through her eyes; and he knew that he did not know, and he also knew he'd be a fool to make assumptions. He could only really see into Katie's world if she let him in, if she let him see through her eyes, through her thoughts, her feelings. At the moment all he knew was that she was feeling pissed off about something. He wondered if she was pissed off with him. Katie spoke and it took his attention away from his speculation.

'What's the point in talking? What difference will it make?'

'You don't see any point in talking, can't see how it can possibly make a difference.'

'It won't, will it? I'll still be me, stuck in the crap B&B, head full of shit. That's how it is. It won't change anything.'

'You can't see it changing?' The exchange was quite rapid.

'How's it gonna change? Someone going to give me somewhere nice to live and money to buy some decent stuff? See me settling down, nice house, kids?' She shook her head. 'Too many messed up kids.' She spoke the last words with what sounded to Keith like a kind of venom.

'Yeah, far too many.' Keith realised he was saying what he felt himself rather than empathising, and he hadn't really picked up on what Katie had said before, but the moment was lost, Katie was speaking again.

'I don't give a shit. I get by, that's all there is to it.' Katie felt a sadness well up inside her but she pushed it aside. She wasn't going to feel like that, not here, not now.

'Do what you have to do. You don't give a shit, just gotta do what you have to do to get by.' Keith deliberately spoke slowly, partly because he wanted Katie to hear that he had heard her, and partly to give her time to hear what he was saying, to hold her on the focus that had emerged.

'No-one gives a shit.'

'Mhmm, that's how it seems, no-one gives a shit.' Keith didn't add anything to suggest that Katie might be talking about how people related to her, though he suspected that this was at least part of what was being said. That might not be easy to acknowledge, it could be too close, too much to own. It wasn't what she was saying, she was being general and he respected that.

In many ways Katie hated her life and yet somehow it was what she was used to, what was normal, what felt right. And then it didn't as well, not when she was with other people. But then her mates were like her, so that was OK. Not that she had many mates. She spent a lot of time on her own, except when she was out drinking. That was how it was. She had begun to pick at her fingers and she deliberately dug her right thumb nail into the corner of her left thumb against the nail. She felt it. She liked it. She liked the pain. She hated herself.

Keith noticed the thumb movement and what seemed quite a violent jab. He felt his jaw tighten. He noticed a slight smile on

Katie's face. Was it a smile, a slight curl of the ends of her mouth? He responded to what had occurred.

'Good feeling?'

'It helps.'

Keith found himself nodding slightly. 'Pain helps?'

Katie shrugged, not sure that she wanted to say much more.

Keith sensed that Katie might not want to give much away. 'And it's not something you want to talk about.'

Pain did help, Katie knew that, knew that only too well. Pain, a familiar friend, or familiar enemy? Part of her life, a big part. She'd been hurt so many times, what did it matter? What did anything matter? 'You're not gonna be able to change anything.'

'You don't think I can change anything, but do you want anything changed?' Something felt suddenly very intense to Keith as he finished his response. He hadn't simply empathised with what Katie had said, he had gone further. It was a risk. How would Katie respond?

Inside Katie a voice screamed 'yes', but outwardly she just shrugged. She sat, staring ahead of her, thinking but not thinking. She felt the all too familiar darkness once more, and that sinking emptiness. She was alone, no-one understood, no-one could understand. What was the point? She closed her eyes. She didn't feel sad, or angry now. This was a place where quite simply she just did not feel. She sat. It was a state of heart and mind for which there weren't words. It was like she didn't exist. No thought, no feeling, no sensation. Nothing. If it wasn't for the emptiness it might have been described as a place of peace. But it wasn't. It was a place of retreat, of escape, a place where you couldn't be reached, but it wasn't a place of safety.

Keith felt a strange intensity. He felt as though his senses were on overload, the silence in the room seemed strangely audible as he sat, focussing on the young woman sitting opposite him. Once again she seemed strangely distant whilst profoundly present. Time passed, one minute, then another. Where had she gone? She was sitting there and yet somehow she seemed to have retreated from his psychological reach. He didn't want to disturb her but he wanted to keep in psychological contact, however minimal. He knew how important this could be. He sought to offer responses that some called 'pre-therapy'. He spoke softly, wanting to communicate but not disturb. 'Katie is sitting, saying nothing.' Katie heard the words, they were distant. She felt nothing. She continued to sit, staring down.

Keith remained silent again. He knew that he needed to offer a therapeutic relationship to his client. However distant she might be, however enmeshed within her own inner world, he knew the importance of human-to-human contact of a kind that expected nothing, accepted everything and could be trusted wholeheartedly. 'Katie is staring.'

Katie continued to sit, and stare, and say nothing, and feel nothing....

Minutes passed, the intensity continued for Keith as he held his focus on his client. He could feel his heart beating, it sounded loud. He felt as though he dared hardly move, the stillness in his own body seemed somehow important, as though the slightest movement would disturb something. The thought came to mind of standing in a field, a rabbit startled but now standing still, ears pricked, listening for the faintest sound that would cause her to scurry away into the bushes. He realised he was holding his breath. He let himself breath, slowly, gently, his attention remaining focussed on Katie as she continued to stare down. Where had she gone? Was this a familiar place for her? What experience in her past had created it for her to escape to, if that was what it was?

Katie was not thinking, it was as though she was in suspended animation, but she was experiencing. The darkness was about her and within her, making it difficult to have any sense of her own identity. She had first entered this place many years ago, as a very young child. The events that had caused it were not in her awareness, she had been very young, very, very young. She could not recall now the violence, the pain, the shouting. Yet it was close, just out of reach, leaving her constantly on edge, uneasy and prey to bouts of fear that she could not understand. It was then that she drank, or lost herself in her latest sexual adventure, but in truth it was no adventure, just a few minutes of sordid intensity that momentarily took her to another place and made her feel wanted. She knew how to bring herself out of the darkness. Pain - that sweet, sickly sharpness pricking her consciousness back into life.

'Katie is continuing to sit and say nothing.'

Katie heard Keith's voice. It drew her. 'Say nothing', the words stayed with her. 'Say nothing.' What else can you say when there is nothing to say? She felt herself breathing, she had not been aware of it for a while, partly because it had been so shallow and partly because of the place in herself that she had entered. She felt herself take another deeper breath. It gave her a contrast, something else, something that defined a sense of her existence. She breathed. She felt herself breathe. She felt herself. She felt. She ... existed. A deeper breath, and a blink, another sensation. She moved slightly in the chair.

Keith swallowed. 'Welcome back.' Was that the right thing to say? He felt as though that was what he wanted to convey though it might seem strange to anyone looking on.

Katie nodded, ever so slightly, taking another deeper breath as she did so.

'Go there a lot?' Keith wanted to keep his tone normal, be matter of fact about it.

She nodded again, a little more actively.

'Not a good place?'

Katie shrugged. It wasn't good or bad, it was just..., well, it just was. She didn't like it, and yet somehow its familiarity had a strange comfort to it.

Keith had experience of working with people who had their own deep recesses within themselves that they could seemingly lose themselves in. He knew that whilst there might be similarities, everyone's experience was uniquely their own. Trying to reach out to one person by using another's experience was not always helpful. But one thing he did know was that people could either describe it or they couldn't. His sense was that perhaps Katie was someone who maybe couldn't, hence the shrugs. And often that was an indicator that the place was first entered at a pre-verbal stage of life. It wasn't a certainty, nothing ever was, but he was certainly open to the possibility.

Katie felt suddenly alone. She was back to being her familiar self, but with an acute sense of vulnerability. She felt anxious, more than anxious. She tensed and looked up. Keith felt his jaw tighten. He saw something in Katie's eyes, a childlike innocence and yet there was fear in them as well, a look that struck him with a sense of someone seeing something that they couldn't make sense of but it frightened them, maybe more than frightened them, scared them, perhaps terrified them. He felt his heart go out to her, a tender, caring feeling, an urge to protect, to make better, to restore something that seemingly had been lost. So much emotional intensity. Nothing had been said, nothing had been verbally communicated to him about anything, yet he felt his eyes moisten as his own emotions rose to the surface.

Something in Katie felt strangely reassured by what she saw in Keith's eyes. Something touched her and yet it was unbearable too. She looked away, aware that her own emotions were suddenly very present. She didn't know what she was feeling, but she felt a sudden wave of discomfort. She didn't like or understand it. She felt strangely confused. It was as though for a fleeting moment Keith knew, or somehow understood, but he couldn't, not really. And he certainly couldn't care. No-one cared, no-one ever had. She felt herself hardening inside. No, no-one cared, and no-one could be trusted.

More time had passed during the silence than either Katie or Keith had realised. Katie moved in the chair, returning her gaze downwards once more. Keith had become aware of how stiff his back had become. He moved it uncomfortably, stretching his spine and pulling his shoulders back.

Katie lifted her hands up to the sides of her face, her little fingers over her eyes, which she had now closed. She opened them, her eyes dropping down a little further. She moved her hands up a little until her eyes were covered, and she closed them once again. She was holding her breath. Another uncomfortable surge of emotion had arisen from somewhere. It wasn't raw or sharp, more of a wave coming from deep inside herself. Sadness, loneliness, she felt weak, light-headed. She let her hands drop down her face as she lifted her head up a little. She suddenly felt a strange coldness, and her hands felt numb, her arms heavy. She sat back in the chair.

Keith noticed how pale Katie had suddenly become.

'You OK?' She clearly wasn't. He wondered why he had asked such a stupid question. 'Can I pour you some water.'

Katie nodded. She had here eyes closed and was breathing through her mouth.

Keith poured out a glass of water from the jug on the table. 'Here.'

Katie opened her eyes, took a deep breath and leaned forward to take the glass that Keith was handing to her. She held it in both hands and sipped slowly. It felt very cool, refreshingly so. 'I feel like I need some fresh air.'

'I'll open the window.' Keith got up and released the catch to push the window open. There was a cool breeze. It reached Katie's face. She took another deep breath and slowly blew it out. She closed her eyes again, she felt quite spaced out in her head. The light seemed very bright in the room. Katie looked down and sipped the water once more before reaching over and putting the glass on the table. She took a much deeper breath and blinked.

'Feeling a little better?'

Katie nodded. 'Yeah.'

'Happen a lot?'

She nodded. 'Don't feel faint though, but, yeah, it happens.'

'You seemed to me to sort of retreat into yourself for a while.'

'Yeah.'

Keith was aware that he was maybe asking too many questions. He was still physically quite tense. He deliberately dropped his shoulders and immediately realised how raised they had been with the tension. Accept. The word came strongly into his head. Don't try to make anything happen, don't try to 'do therapy', just be fully present, hold the connection, allow your client to be as she needs to be. Accept, unconditionally and warmly.

Katie was back with thoughts of trust. Could she trust Keith, really trust him? It wasn't just a matter of needing to be sure he was OK, that he would listen. She knew she needed more than that. It was more a matter of whether it felt safe. Safety was key. In truth, she'd never ever really felt safe. If anything, feeling unsafe was much more normal for her to the point that feeling unsafe had a certain safety to it, or at least a normality. It was familiar, a known experience. Though she didn't think of it that way, it had all become rather upside down for her. There was a safety in feeling unsafe because it was familiar, she knew how to cope with that; but feeling safe, no that was weird, unsettling and didn't feel safe at all.

Yes, Katie thought to herself, I can handle feeling unsafe. She'd coped with that for so many years, survived a lot of crap in her life, but to feel safe, what did that mean? What did that really mean? The truth was that for Katie there was no sense of what safe felt like, and that was a genuine human tragedy, and a product of the life she had led.

Katie was confused. Yes, she knew she needed to talk but what did she really want? She knew she wanted to feel different. She'd had enough of so many things in her life – at least that was how she felt some days. On others, she just did what she had to do to get by, and part of that was finding ways of avoiding thinking about herself, her life, how she felt about everything.

There were times when she felt she would explode with it all. At other times she felt nothing. Hers was a world of extremes, an all or nothing existence that strained her to the core of her being. A roller coaster ride? Some might think so, but that was not how Katie experienced it, not really. A roller coaster was too smooth. Yes, it threw you around and the ups and downs could be extreme, but there was a smoothness and a flow, a sense of journey to and through the ups and downs. Katie's inner and outer worlds were not like that. The transitions were too sharp, too sudden. Her inner world was volatile, not smooth. It bumped her around. It was what she was used to but she had grown to realise that it wasn't really normal, not what it seemed that other people experienced. But what did feeling normal really feel like? She saw people going about their lives in the streets, the shops, the cafes and the bars, but apart from in the bars normal seemed, well, boring.

Katie had regained more of her sense of self as she had continued to sit. She felt a little more solid in the room. She heard Keith's voice. 'I guess it must be so difficult to put into words. Sometimes we experience things but don't know how to describe them.'

And don't always want to, those were the words in Katie's head in response. And yet…. She felt pressure inside herself. She wanted to talk, she wanted to let it out, let something out. She wanted to release it. She knew how. She cut to release pressure, tension. And she cut to feel. It had become an important way for her to control and to engage with her feelings. It met so many needs and she always felt better for it. Yet she also knew that it wasn't the answer, not something she could keep doing even though it had been part of her life now for a few years. She knew that it wasn't good for her, but there was no denying the fact that it did make her feel better. And that was what encouraged her to continue. And anyway, so what if it wasn't good for her? Why did her well-being matter? Who cared? Who'd ever cared? Her thoughts took her back into past pain, abandonment and loneliness.

She did not know why she said it, but somehow something of what Keith had just said coupled with the feelings she was reliving as her thoughts ranged over her past pushed the words out of her mouth. She heard her thought coming from her own mouth. 'How do you describe what you *never* had?'

Keith felt himself take a short deep breath and momentarily held it. Katie's words felt so incredibly heartfelt. There was something utterly despairing in her tone of voice, a yearning and an emptiness all bound together.

'How do you begin to describe what you *never* had.' Keith responded without the questioning tone, his empathic response a statement. He kept the emphasis the same as Katie's, and waited. He could only imagine what Katie had never had, but it was for her to communicate it if she could. He held his attention on her and maintained his sensitivity towards what he was experiencing inside himself, which was caring, compassion yet most of all a sense of sadness. He voiced the last of these feelings, basically because it was the one that felt so dominant. 'Leaves me with a profound sense of sadness.'

Katie stayed silent. Yes, it was sad, really, really sad. And she felt it too. She sniffed, and swallowed. She went to speak but couldn't. What was there to say? She'd been here before, though generally on her own.

So much to say, and she didn't want to leave again without saying something. She sniffed again. She wanted to look up but she felt ashamed. She kept looking down. 'Life's been shit, you know?'

'A really shitty life, yeah?' Keith felt very still within himself, really wanting to reach out and connect to his client and to the inner world that she carried with her, that she was beginning to explore in his presence, but which he could not enter unless she invited him in. And even then, it would be a fragile world and he knew that he must tread carefully.

'You'd have to have been there to understand.'

'I guess so, been there…, or been you?'

'Yeah, both I guess.'

Keith nodded. 'Yeah.' He paused, 'I'd like to understand if you feel able to tell me a little more.' Keith's words came from the heart. They were a genuine expression of what he was feeling and wanting. It wasn't a therapeutic response coming from his head and learned in some textbook. It was real to him, alive, emerging from himself as he sat in therapeutic contact with his client.

Katie nodded in response. She heard the genuineness in Keith's voice. She looked up. 'You're not just saying that, are you?'

'No, I mean it.' Keith spoke slowly, maintaining the eye contact that had momentarily developed between them. Katie pursed her lips, and shook her head. 'Life's always been shit, as long ago as I can remember.' She sniffed again, and reached for a tissue and blew her nose. 'Always in trouble, always getting grief…' Her voice trailed off and she looked down again, lapsing back into silence.

'Always in trouble, always getting grief, shit as far back as you can remember, yeah?'

Katie nodded, taking a deep breath as she did so. Her heart was beginning to pound. She didn't know where to start and she suddenly felt very anxious about what would happen if she really tried to tell her story. She turned to look out of the window. 'Fucked up, big time.' She felt her eyes moisten.

'Mhmm. Fucked up by life, big time.'

'By life, by people, you know?'

'Mhmm, people can sure mess you up.'

'Now here I am with a shrink.' She turned back to face Keith, 'no offence'.

'None taken.' Not that Keith considered himself a shrink.

'Crap parents, crap childhood. I guess you've heard it many times.'

'I've not heard how it was for you.'

'No, I guess not. My parents were useless. Dad, well, don't remember much about him. Mainly mum, but she was all over the place. I didn't understand, but I know now it was drugs. I was taken into care, well, taken away, care home for kids. Don't really remember much but I know I…' she shivered, 'always seem to go cold when I think back to it all.'

'Something about them or being taken away that makes you grow cold?'

'Don't know.'

Trying to be too clever, Keith thought to himself. Must keep my responses simple, not try and tease out differences that just direct Katie into thinking about anything in particular. He couldn't afford to push her, try to get ahead of her. It didn't work, push and a client will resist, and rightly so, they are protecting fragile areas of themselves. He re-affirmed the focus on what Katie had already said. 'They were useless and you got taken away.'

'I really don't remember much about them, except mum always shouting at me, sometimes hitting me, and I just, I don't know, I sort of flip out.'

'Mhmm, flip out, like you kind of escape from what you're remembering?'

Katie nodded, 'something like that. I don't want to talk about it.'

'Sure. And there's no pressure here to talk about anything in particular. It's at your own pace and it's your agenda, your time.'

A momentary silence arose as Katie took a deep breath. She didn't want to feel pressured. 'I had foster parents, and times in kids homes. Never really felt settled anywhere except, well, with Mrs Albert.' Katie instinctively took another deep breath. Maybe that had been a happy time, but it had also been a time of being bullied and picked on at school as well. It took her away from the momentary good feelings about the Alberts. 'I never really felt settled, not really. Nothing felt right, I don't know. Never felt right. Always felt, I don't know…, don't know what I felt.'

'Mhmm, really hard to know what it was you were feeling.'

Katie's thoughts moved to later in her childhood. 'I'd get angry, you know? Didn't really do too well at school, didn't see the point. Teachers were crap. Always getting told off. Used to bunk off. That just got me more grief. Just passed around. Like a fucking parcel, passed round.' She shook her head.

'That's how it feels now, like you were just a parcel being passed around.'

'Didn't have many friends at school, got picked on a lot. Had one good mate, but she grassed me up. Bitch.'

'So she's not a friend any more.'

'Too right.' Katie could feel the anger, but she also felt herself going quiet as well. 'Never really sort of fitted in, never liked being told what to do. Always had to ask why? Always had to try and do things my own way. Spent a lot of time on my own.' Katie lapsed back into silence again. Her words brought back memories. Times at school in breaks when she tried to keep herself away from everyone else. She wanted friends, and she did have them for a while, earlier anyway. But they drifted away. She never really knew why. She'd feel so hurt by it. She'd get really sad and depressed. And always so alone. That was how it had been. She was still a bit like that.

'Something about being told what to do, wasn't what you wanted. Ended up on your own a lot.' Keith responded in a way that finished with the comment that Katie had made that had lead her into her silence.

'Does my head in all of this.' Katie shook her head in. 'What's the point…, to anything? I mean, you know, what's going to change, yeah? What's gonna be different? I've been fucked up and that's how it is, how I am. It's OK.'

'It's OK to feel that way, is that what you are saying?'

She shrugged. 'How it is.'

Katie paused. She didn't like feeling like she did, no it wasn't OK, yeah, it was how it was, but she wanted something else. 'No, no, it's not OK, but it's what is.' She shrugged. 'What's gonna change?'

'You wonder what can change, what can be different?'

'I've had to survive, had to find my own way. That's how it is, how I am. Yeah, it's tough, it's shit at times, but that's how it is. And I get on with it. I do what I have to do, yeah?'

'Yeah, and you sound strong and clear about that.' Keith wanted Katie to hear what he was hearing from the tone and the manner of what she was saying.

'And yeah, that's how it is, and yeah, there are times when….' Her voice trailed off.

'Times when…?' Keith spoke softly, gently inviting Katie to say more if she wished.

Katie shook her head. The thought was around whether it was all worthwhile, the struggle, but that was all she knew and she knew she'd struggle on. Yeah, she was a survivor. She'd been around. She'd learned how to cope with shit. 'I think I need to go, I'm feeling a bit weird again'. It was an excuse. She didn't feel weird but she wanted to go. 'Need a bit of fresh air, yeah.'

'Sure. It's been intense, you may need to take it easy. I respect your need to do what you need to do.' Keith was very aware of the abruptness, but recognised that perhaps something had maybe emerged within Katie that she did not want to address or acknowledge, and needed to deal with it in her own way which did not involve sitting in a room with a counsellor.

'Yeah.'

'So, you want to meet up again next week?'

'Yeah.' She didn't want to and yet something inside her was nagging at her that she ought to. But she didn't want to appear to not be making her own decisions. 'Yeah, I'll come.'

'OK.' They set the time and Katie left.

Keith sat back in his chair, still coming to terms with the suddenness of Katie' departure. Should he have tried to keep her longer, explored more why she wanted to go? Or would that have just played into something? Would he have been like a teacher to her, trying to tell her what she ought to do, what was best for her? Was counselling the best thing for her? He didn't know. He knew it helped people, but not everyone took to it. He felt that Katie saying she wanted to go and his not trying to persuade her otherwise was therapeutic. It showed acceptance and trust. Trust. Did he trust her? He trusted her to be as she needed to be and he could see that how she needed to be was the result of her life, leaving her feeling 'fucked-up', as she'd described it. He hoped she'd come back. He believed talking helped, and more importantly being heard, really heard at a very human level. So often what got messed up was the human bit and that bit then desperately needed another human response to begin to heal. But you couldn't heal a wound until the muck had been drained from inside it. He rather suspected Katie had some mucky emotional wounds, some open, some closed but containing emotional shit – how else could you describe it? He hoped he could help by offering a therapeutic relational experience that would begin to encourage the muck out, clean the wounds and provide opportunity for Katie to maybe find a direction in life that was right for her as a young woman freed from the conditioning effects of a shit life.

Katie got back to her room. She felt pressure. She felt tense. Talking and thinking had stirred things up. She needed release, and something to focus her. Then she'd go out, find someone who'd buy her a few drinks, get pissed, get shagged probably, feel good. Stop thinking for a bit. She opened the front door and headed up the stairs, her room was on the second floor. She knew what she needed to do. She opened the draw and took out the box of tissues, her flannel and the razor blade. It was all routine stuff for her. She felt an excitement, and an expectation, was that the right word? She had a sort of churning feeling in the pit of her stomach, an anticipation. She placed the blade on the flannel, with the tissues next to it on the bed. She took off her jacket, glancing down at her arm, halfway between her shoulder and her elbow. She'd not cut for a few days and the last cut had healed, a thin and slightly raised line where she had picked the scab. She now felt the anticipation more keenly.

There were times when she cut to feel, and times when she cut to release, and this was a time to release. She always felt more excitement when it was the latter, probably because she was more engaged with her feelings, more energised, and more aware of what she felt. She sat for a moment or two. She didn't like to hurry it. It was like once she knew what she was going to do and everything was ready, she could somehow stay with that anticipation. It was a kind of rush. Katie picked up the blade in her right hand, holding it firmly between her thumb and forefinger. Her attention returned to the top of her left arm, deciding where to draw that thin red line. She felt almost light headed as she held the edge of the blade against her skin on the outer edge of her arm. She pressed the point in, feeling herself tense with the familiar prick of stinging pain. Yes, it felt good. She slowly drew the blade down, feeling the sting, feeling a sense of freedom from everything that had been in her head. There was just that familiar yet quite singular sharp, sweet sting as the blade sliced through her skin. Not too deeply, but enough to give her that exquisite – for that was how she experienced it – sense of release from everything. It was as though her whole awareness became transfixed, held by the sensations that were coming from her upper arm and stimulating her brain and her senses. It felt good.

She looked as the blood seeped from the cut. Bright red. Her blood. It meant something. Her blood and she was in control. She chose to release it. Nothing else mattered. Nothing. The stinging pain absorbed her and released her. She took a deep breath and closed her eyes. She rarely cut again. It never felt the same, the sensation from a second cut was always disturbed by the sharpness of the first. She looked at the blade. Her blade, her blood. She placed it on the flannel, closing her eyes once more and appreciating the feelings she was experiencing. It was a kind of high. Yes, it hurt, or course it hurt, but that was the point. That was what gave her the focus that she needed to feel the release. And seeing her blood, blood that she had chosen to release, that was also important to her. Yes, she bled every month with her period, but that was different. She had no control over that. But this she did have control over. It was *her* body, they were *her* feelings, *her* sensations. She didn't like to think about it as her pain. It wasn't about pain, more about sharpness and intensity, focus, control and release. And yes, it felt good.

Katie reached over and picked up a tissue, folded it and placed it against the cut which was still oozing in a couple of places. She knew it would heal. So she'd carry the scar but she didn't think of them as scars. Each one was a mark, a kind of symbol of her freedom. It was her body. She'd do what she wanted. And whilst the initial rush had now begun to subside, the slightly buzzy sense of self that it left her with remained compelling. She sat back, supported by the pillow and head board, holding the tissue to her arm and drifted in and out of sleep. It didn't always affect her like that, but sometimes it did. Again, it depended on her mood and what she was cutting for. It was a different experience when she was flat and numb and cutting to feel something. There was an edge of despair then, but not today. Now she just felt good and she wished it would stay like that forever.

Chapter 4

The week passed in its usual way. Katie had been out drinking on a couple of evenings, had sex with different men on each occasion and cut herself a couple more times. She had also spent time in town with a girl she'd got to know as a result of attending a local educational support group that was helping young people either get back into work or education. She found it boring, it always seemed so pointless. How was *her* life ever going to be any different? But she'd sort of got on well with Bernie and they'd met up now a number of times. The previous night she'd drunk a lot, more than usual, and today she was feeling grim. She'd been sick in the night and still felt very wobbly. She was due to go to her counselling session but didn't feel like going. She didn't see any point. Too much effort, and for what? Her mood was low as well, partly tiredness, partly the alcohol still in her body. She'd been asleep most of the morning and now just felt too lethargic to bother. She lay there, staring at the peeling paint on the ceiling. She was also in some pain as well. It burned when she urinated, she'd had that before, quite often in fact. She'd go to the doctor when it got too bad and he usually gave her antibiotics; and usually a lecture about safe sex. She didn't care. She was on the pill, she was safe enough. Yeah, she'd got pregnant 3 years ago, but had miscarried. She had no idea who the father would have been. Didn't matter. It was over. Now she just wanted to sleep.

She thought back to the previous night. In the pub she'd got chatting to a guy who hadn't been in before. Bernie was with her, and she got off with his mate. They'd all had a few drinks, a few laughs, gone on to a club, more drinks. She'd had some pills to keep her going. They always helped. Then, yeah, back to her room and..., she couldn't remember much about it now. Dean was his name. He'd gone now, headed off sometime, he hadn't stayed that long. Typical, get what he wanted and gone. She hated that, but that was how it was. It often left her feeling depressed, used. But it also gave her what she wanted as well. Yeah, it was what she wanted, and it was OK at the time, but it didn't always leave her feeling good. Often she'd end up in an all too familiar numb and unfeeling place in herself.

The radio was on, an electric beat filled the air. She heard it but didn't hear it as well. Like it was there but she wasn't paying it much attention. She just drifted in her head, thinking and not thinking, feeling like she didn't want to do anything but just lie there. The peeling paint hadn't changed. The tiredness swept over her again and she drifted back off though not exactly to sleep, just lying seemingly hypnotised by the music and, yeah, just lying. No thoughts, her head felt full of nothing, just a kind of aching heaviness.

As she lay there she could feel that familiar darkness descending on her. It wasn't something she could have easily described, it was like a kind of thick, black fog that shut out everything. It wasn't new to her. She'd experienced this for as long as she could remember. Usually it just meant she'd do nothing. When she felt a little more energised she'd cut to give herself some relief, but she hadn't got the energy to do that now. Too tired, too hung-over to do anything except just lie there and let the black oblivion take over.

*

Keith was sitting in the counselling room, it was almost time for Katie to arrive. He'd been thinking a lot the last week about that last session, and how he needed to be in himself to be of help to her. He had been concerned at how she had left and wondered what effect that would have on her. Yes, she'd made her own choice, but what had she been feeling? What had been happening for her that had made her need to go? He knew how complex human beings were. The human personality was shaped by so many factors. He had only begun to experience something of Katie's personality. He didn't really know her, and yet he did feel that there had been moments of profound contact, connection even at a human and therapeutic level. And yet he knew that she was struggling with so much, things she was either not able or not wanting to talk about, at least not yet. He wondered if she would say more today. He didn't want to hurry her. It could take time and that her internal psychological processes could not be hurried. His role was to offer a therapeutic relationship, and that meant listening to her and letting her know that he was hearing her, being genuinely present and authentic, and to feel that unconditional sense of caring and warmth for her that was so important in therapeutic relationship. You couldn't make yourself feel that way, but when it was genuinely present it could make a big difference.

Of course, what form that difference would take you could never be sure of. But he knew within himself, and it was a kind of core belief for him, that it somehow all came down to love. People who didn't experience love in their lives, particularly their early lives, got messed up more than those who did, but that love had to be unconditional and that was rare. He was thinking of a quality of love that was to do with compassion and caring, feelings that emerged from the human sense of humanity. Most of the time people felt loved not simply because of who they were, but because they behaved in particular ways. That subtle conditioning, 'conditions of worth'[2] was the theoretical term, that influenced how we thought about ourselves and how we ought to be, what we ought to show of ourselves to the world in order to be and feel valued or at the very least accepted. Love could mean so many things to people, he thought to himself. And how many people couldn't see love as being anything beyond love of what they wanted, meeting their needs, their cravings. There was so much selfishness attached to love. No, he felt clear that for him love was about caring for the other person, his client, without any expectation of anything from them. He thought to himself how important caring was, caring about others, caring about ourselves. To have the capacity to care seemed to somehow make a person a finer human being, that was the notion that his train of thought led him to.

Keith glanced at the clock. It was time for Katie's appointment and he went out into the reception. No sign of Katie. He checked with the receptionist but there had been no calls. He decided to head

---

2 'Conditions of worth' is a phrase used by Carl Rogers to describe the conditioning that people can experience, particularly in childhood but also in adulthood, that makes them believe they are only to be valued, loved, cared for if they meet the particular requirements of significant others.

back to the counselling room and give her a few more minutes before checking again. He hoped she was OK. Keith knew how difficult it could be for people to come to counselling. The reasons could be many. Sometimes things arose as a result of the counselling that left the person wondering if it was worth it, leaving them feeling they were getting worse, not better. Of course, that wasn't everyone's experience, but it was common for people to feel more overwhelmed and wretched once they had begun to explore themselves and to get more in touch with the deeper, often more painful elements within their structure of self. Others found very early on the release from sharing what they needed to talk about, and to have it heard and witnessed by another – bearing witness was an important part of therapy in his opinion – could in some mysterious way leave the person feeling unburdened and much stronger in themselves.

For Keith there was a deep respect for people who entered into therapy. He knew that for some it wasn't that they had much choice, they were desperately in need of someone to talk to, to help them make sense of themselves. He knew it wasn't an 'easy option', not if the client was really working at becoming more in touch with themselves, and beginning to challenge the external conditioning that had shaped their sense of self. Starting them on a path to greater authenticity was the way he thought about it. It meant facing up to conditions of worth and, through the experience of a positive and supportive therapeutic relationship, beginning to redefine who one was. But first you had to know yourself. Wasn't it the Delphic Oracle that had said something along the lines of, 'man, know thyself'? He wasn't sure, maybe he'd got that wrong. Never mind, the words had meaning to him, whatever their origin. So often people thought they knew themselves, but you could so easily be blind to your own behaviours, and behind them were attitudes of heart and mind that could be rooted in areas of the self that were simply unknown or denied to awareness.

He thought of Katie as she had sat opposite him in that last session. She had seemed so thin, so pale. She hadn't looked healthy. He wondered how well she looked after herself. Did she eat well, or was she surviving on a meagre diet of junk food? He knew that some young people faced with what felt like insurmountable problems could become anorexic or bulimic, a way of gaining some kind of control in their lives. For others it was a case of alcohol becoming a major feature, reducing their interest and attraction towards food. There was no doubt Katie had a lot on her mind, a lot to say that was not being said. Had she decided to stop coming for counselling? He knew that clients could find themselves looking over that edge within themselves and shrinking back, preferring to find other ways to drown out the discomfort. But that rarely worked in a sustainable way. People needed more and more of whatever they were using to dampen down the discomfort, and that something could then become a problem itself, be it alcohol, comfort eating, excessive exercise, other substances, pretty much anything.

It seemed to Keith that society was becoming more and more addictive in so many ways. He put the thought aside, realising he was at risk of losing track of time and losing his focus on what he was there for. Five minutes had passed, he decided it was time to check at reception again.

He returned a couple of minutes later, still no sign of Katie. He would sit for another five minutes and if she still had not arrived he would go and get himself a mug of tea and think about what to put in a letter to her.

He drifted back to his previous train of thought. So many people seemed to choose behaviours that could become addictive. The list seemed endless as Keith pondered on the things that could become an addiction: eating, particularly foods that are fatty, sugary, and/or highly processed; not eating/dieting, exercising and working-out. His thoughts turned to the internet, whether it was for checking email, or going to chat rooms, shopping for clothes or the latest electronic gadget or just having the experience of buying or getting bargains. And there was, of course, High Street shopping too. Entertainment was another area, watching soap operas, computer games, following a football team, music with so many people seemingly addicted to sound who cannot abide silence. There were the things most often associated with addiction: drinking alcohol, smoking, taking drugs, betting and gambling and, or course, sex addiction. He thought of the violence on the streets and how people seemed to get addicted to watching or participating in violent behaviour, horror, risk and danger. So many things that could get out of control, even what might appear innocuous activities, like cleaning, could get out of hand and be considered an addiction.

Everyone, no maybe not everyone, but certainly most people seemed to be seeking some sense of satisfaction from their life experiences, which was fine, but it all seemed to be so much more intense these days – or was it a sign that he was growing older? Keith smiled to himself. Would he want to be a young person today? In many ways, yes, the opportunities for travel and experience, the money that could be earned as well if you were in the right line of business. Yet even with that came temptation to over-indulge or to engage in high risk behaviours. Then there were those who couldn't make it to that kind of experience, who maybe lived in the 'wrong side of town', brought up perhaps in poverty and not just economic poverty, there was a poverty of the soul in so many areas as well. What did he mean by that? For Keith it was about meaning and purpose, and of values. What were the value that governed people's lives these days? So much self-centred living, so much glamour that was actually quite hollow; the cult of celebrity being, in his view, one example of this. Discrimination remained a real problem, too. Racism hadn't gone away. Ingrained attitudes remained, deep distrust of people who were 'different', fuelled at times by certain areas of the media and stirred up by politicians in so many countries for their own ends. He didn't like thinking that way but he knew it was true.

He knew that it was often early life experiences that conditioned the choices that the person made later in life, the things that deep down they knew could give them a good feeling, or get them away from bad feelings. Then there was the issue of the emotionally damaged parents passing their damage on to their children. Contentious issue, he knew that, but how many times had he seen young people whose inability to express feelings or maintain some kind of steadiness in their lives seemed to link back to their own earlier experiences and the way they were related to by parents and significant others.

More than five minutes had passed; he went out into the corridor and along to reception. It could get quite busy, and quite hectic at times. But at the moment there seemed to be a lull. He looked over to the reception area and the receptionist behind the desk.

'Hi June, any sign of Katie?'

June shook her head. June, who was middle aged, had been working at the surgery for a number of years now and knew a lot of the patients quite well. She was pleased that there were youth counsellors now available. She had a bit of a soft spot for some of the young people. Yes, she knew some of them did seem to cause problems, but she always wanted to think the best of them if she could. She'd known Katie for a number of years, Katie had been something of a regular at the surgery, and she knew she'd had a tough time. She never said much but she'd seen comments in her notes when she had been filing letters.

'Oh well, there's still time of course. Maybe a bus was late or something.'

'You going to see her next week?'

'I'll write to her with an appointment.'

'I've known her for a number of years, she's not had it easy.'

Keith realised that June might be about to start to tell him information that he had not heard from Katie, and he didn't want that. 'Don't say any more. It's best for me not to know. I can be more genuine with her if I only know what she chooses to tell me. I prefer it that way.'

June didn't really understand. She thought the more someone knew the more they could help. She shrugged in response to what Keith had said and was about to say something when the phone rang and interrupted her. She picked up the receiver.

Keith asked if it was Katie, June shook her head. He asked her to call him if she arrived, and June nodded. Keith turned and walked back along the corridor to the kitchen and put the kettle on. He was going to have a little more thinking time. He was sorry she had not come, and felt some concern. Yet he also realised that she was making a choice and one that, for whatever reason, she needed to make. He'd write to her and then if there was no response he'd need to let her doctor know.

Ten minutes later and Keith was sitting down with his tea. Katie still had not arrived so he began to compose a letter to her. He wanted it to be more than just a sorry you didn't turn up, here's your next appointment letter, the kind often churned out without any personalisation and certainly no therapeutic tone. For Keith, letters to clients were an extension of the therapeutic process and relationship. They were an opportunity to convey his genuineness, his unconditional positive regard and his empathy for his client. He began to type.

Dear Katie

I'm sorry you have not been able to make it today. I do not know the reason, but I hope that you are not ill.

I am aware that it has not been easy for you during the first two sessions to express some of the things that you have or are experiencing, and maybe you are questioning whether you want to continue with the counseling process. This would not be unusual. I hope that you will feel able to continue should you decide that that is what you would like.

I can offer you an appointment for 11.00am next Thursday. Please would you call me at the Youth Counselling Service Number to confirm that you will be able to attend?

Hoping to hear from you and to see you then.

Kind regards

Keith Burton

Keith felt satisfied with the letter. He didn't want to make it too long and involved, better to keep it simple and to the point, with what he hoped would be a tone of warm acceptance and invitation to continue, but without in any way impacting on his client's autonomy. He decided not to print it off straight away, just in case Katie did arrive late or phoned.

He picked up a counselling journal and was flicking through the pages when an article caught his eye that asked the question whether we were becoming an addicted society[1]. It caught his interest.

> "We use all kinds of behaviour to gain a sense of satisfaction. We want to feel a particular way or have a set of inner experiences as a result of our actions. Each day we make choices, and our choices are driven by the experience of what brings us this sense of satisfaction. Often what defines it are the

conditioning experiences that we have had in early life, though such conditioning can also occur later."

Keith stopped reading and thought about what he had read. Yes, we are constantly making choices, even when we don't feel that we are, or are simply doing something out of habit. It may not feel like a choice but it is. He continued to read:

"Indeed, the major conditioning factor in our society could arguably be said to be 'consumerism', with advertising playing a significant role in shaping our desires and thus what we need to feel satisfied. Eat this, buy that, travel here, drink that, wear this, do that. In a consumer society, the more we have, the more satisfied we should feel — and yet it does not always work out this way."

And what psychological and emotional impact does this kind of society have on someone who, for whatever reason, is unable to 'have the goodies', as it were? Keith pondered on this thought, thinking about the young people he had worked with, many of whom were struggling to find a value system that they could live with, and which often was counter-consumerism. Yes, many were conditioned into it, but many also rejected it and were seeking alternative lifestyles. He found himself thinking that nowadays the shopping malls were in a sense becoming the new temples, where people worshipped at the feet of consumerism. Was that too extreme? He didn't think so. He thought of the Christian values that had shaped his own thinking and rather cynically found himself wondering if society had now introduced an eleventh commandment – "Thou shalt consume…", or should there be an addition to the Sermon on the Mount: "Blessed are the consumers for they shall find…." What do they find? He smiled, and shook his head. How many times had he heard people, particularly young people, talk about how life felt out of control. And he immediately thought of one ex-client who cut herself quite badly, in fact she had been hospitalised on more than one occasion. For her it had always been a case of 'I cut and I feel and therefore I know that I am'. Yet he knew as well that while the act might be the same, the motivation and the resulting effect would be unique for each person. He felt his lips tighten at the thought of the fact that people, and often though not exclusively young people, found themselves needing to self-harm.

He returned to the article.

> "What we do may feel very much a social experience, something we enjoy from time to time, or even every day, with a sense that it is a free choice and not something we are driven to do. But for some of us in relation to some activities there comes a point at which our choice is no longer free. We still think of it as free choice, but there is now something demanding. We have to have a drink or buy that latest fashion, we have to be seen at a particular venue, eat another bar of chocolate, or gamble on another scratch-card."

Hmm, thought Keith, and it can be more damaging, his thoughts still with that previous client. And so often low self-esteem seemed to be linked to self-harming behaviours, even though the person doesn't so much want to do themselves harm as simply feel different or, as he had heard it described on many occasions, to simply feel. He thought of himself. Yes, he could get drawn in. He thought of his early life, how he had frequented the amusement arcades and how that had got out of control: the sounds, the urge to win, or to win back what you had lost, or to simply beat the machine. He thought too of the way the machines tried to make you forget you were spending money. He shook his head. Crazy days but at least it hadn't got too out of control. It had for one of his friends who had developed a serious gambling problem. What a society we live in, with people trying to represent gambling as a harmless action that we should all be free to pursue. Yes, he knew it could be, but then his mind went back to an incident in his newsagents a couple of weeks ago, a woman buying scratchcards as though there was no tomorrow, and making some comment about how she might as well spend her money on them, at least she had a chance of winning something. He'd remembered wondering what that money might otherwise have been spent on. Healthier food on the table for her children? People did make choices, the article was right, but sometimes people didn't think about what they were not choosing because they were too busy choosing something else. And the reality was that people were just too damn good at making lousy choices. And poverty could make people desperate. Then there was internet gambling too. It seemed that these days he got more junk mail related to on-line gambling than anything else. He returned to the article once more.

> "We may still have some control, in that the urge to satisfy a compulsion may not interfere with our daily responsibilities. But while we may not experience them as a problem, if we continue with such habits then changes can occur. We begin to buy things on our credit card that we cannot afford. We drink more to feel a particular way, but it leaves us short of money to pay the rent. We return to the casino because we want the buzz that comes from being part of the scene, and we want to feel a winner. We need to look a certain way so we don't eat as much and we exercise more and more. Slowly, we find ourselves pursuing such behaviours to the point where they begin to dominate. Our variety of experience diminishes as we become increasingly centred on the behaviours that are now habitual features of our lives. Slowly and inexorably, we put ourselves at risk of addiction."

And so many people did, Keith thought to himself. And he seemed to be seeing more and more young people who were getting caught up in behaviours that they felt pressure to continue with, and for whom they were getting out of control. Alcohol featured highly, so did sex, drugs, and shopping. It used to be sex, drugs and rock and roll, and now it seemed more like sex, drugs and shopping! So much time spent shopping, and he was aware of the amount of shop-lifting as well that went on. Again, not everyone, but some did. Often to pay for some other habit that had got out of control. Or to have what society keeps telling them they must have. And the advertising, the pressure to buy and to have. And the sexualisation of young people, particularly girls. The sexualisation of girls was, in his view, one of the really damaging features of Western Society. Dressed up as freedom it was actually oppressive, feeding into the fashion industry and sexual consumerism. Young people robbed of the innocence of their childhood. He'd read recently about a seven-year old girl pulling a knife in the playground in an argument over a boy. Society needed a name for the sexual exploitation of girls for financial gratification. It wasn't paedophilia in the traditional sense, and yet… At times Keith felt quite depressed about the way his society was going. There were times when he could understand why Islam encouraged modesty in dress, for both girls and boys, with families in particular encouraging values and behaviours that protected them from what is such a damaging, exploitative and predatory society. He continued reading.

> "The individual's behaviour, their neurological functioning and the resulting internal personal experience are bound together. The habit takes over. Neural pathways fire up like default pathways as we continue with our addictive behaviour, increasing the level of obsession or compulsion. It could be argued that any behaviour that brings intense experiencing, and is continued over time and to excess, creates a kind of neurological, psychological and/or chemical dependency.

He thought about self-harm and the chemical release that must occur for the person. A rush of endorphines, perhaps? Was it only the pain and the impact that that had, or was there something more? And then there was the ritualistic element. That was quite common too. He gazed out of the window, watching a tree sway in the breeze, its leaves moving gently, almost hypnotically. There was something simple about nature, he thought to himself. Uncomplicated. He knew that was a simplification but it left him aware that for the tree life was somehow uncomplicated. It did what it did, grew from an acorn, spreading it's roots and branches as the seasons passed, dropped it's leaves in autumn but grew them back again next spring. The tree knew what it was about, well, maybe that was going too far. But the tree was designed, as it were, to be a tree, and that was its function through life. And as it dropped its leaves it provided sustenance as they rotted into the ground, it provided acorns for the squirrels and branches for the birds to make nests in or simply to sit and sing from.

What of human beings? Are they so clear about their roles in life? And are their lives satisfying enough? Or did they need something else? Always this urge to experience different things, at least for some people. Try this, do that, so much to do, to fit in. At least for some. And for others every day, every hour seemed an eternity, people messed up by bad experiences or caught in cycles of abuse. And how behaviours could get out of control. His thoughts turned to Katie. How was she experiencing life? And what was happening for her? He wondered whether there might be a connection between his thinking about the self-harming client and Katie. Did Katie self-harm? He knew it was more widespread than most people would want to accept, and was on the increase. He took his thoughts away from his speculation, he wanted to continue what he was reading. He had time.

> "An individual's behaviour, neurological functioning and resulting internal personal experience are bound together. A habit takes over as we continue with an addictive behaviour, increasing the level of obsession or compulsion. It could be argued that any behaviour that brings intense experiencing, and is continued over time and to excess creates a kind of neurological, psychological and/or chemical dependency. So how can we identify whether we have an addiction, or an obsession or compulsion that is tending towards addiction? Try and deny yourself that something that you do habitually, and see what happens. A word of caution: this can be dangerous if we are talking about substance use, particularly alcohol. In this case, suddenly stopping when there is physical (i.e. chemical) dependence can be life-threatening, and a gradual reduction is much safer. But otherwise, try to deny yourself a particular experience and observe what happens, what internal dialogue starts to take place: 'you don't have a problem', 'do it anyway', 'you're in control'. Deny yourself an episode of your favourite soap opera. There will be a sense of loss – yes — that is normal, but is it more than this? Is it genuinely depressing? Do we feel anxious, on edge, pre-occupied with thinking about what we are missing?"

Or do people simply find that they cannot stop. Keith thought about his own choices, habits and routines. What would he deny himself? What was his addiction, if he had one? He liked his sport. Was that an addiction? Would he be able to freely not watch football on TV, or not go to a match when City were playing at home? He rarely went to away matches these days. Was it a habit, a choice or an addiction? It felt like a choice, something he did, he enjoyed doing, it was social, a few laughs with friends. But how would he feel if he could go but made himself not go? He rarely missed a home match. Then there was his love of coffee. Hmm, yes, maybe that's more of an issue, he thought to himself. He liked his early morning double expresso, and at other times of the day as well. And he didn't like going without it, left him feeling very uncomfortable. Yes, he could see what the article was getting at more in relation to that than football.

> "We generally think of an addiction as a personal behaviour, but what of collective, societal addictions? As a society, do we generate collective addictions that people are conditioned into, simply in order to be part of 'normal society'? And from this perspective might individual addictions also be considered as symptoms of an unwell society, a society that preoccupies itself with experiences and behaviours that assume an importance incongruent to their true value? And what of the young people being conditioned into these social norms from an early age?"

Societal addictions? That was an interesting concept. Hmm, societal norms creating societal addictions. Keith's thoughts went back to gambling, and alcohol, and shopping; and reliance on all kinds of substances, not just illegal drugs. "Experiences and behaviours that assume an importance that is incongruent to their true value" was a rather telling phrase. He'd have to ponder on that some more.

Keith checked the clock, it was half an hour since Katie's appointment time and he felt sure she was not going to arrive now. June would have called him if she had arrived though he did go out and check with reception once again. No contact from her so he re-read the letter, printed it off, signed it and addressed the envelope, and went outside for a five minute walk to get some air.

---

1 Taken from *an addicted society?* by Richard Bryant-Jefferies' (March 2006), published in *Therapy Today*. British Association for Counselling and Psychotherapy. Full article at: http://www.therapytoday.net/archive/mar2006/cover_feature1.html

Chapter 5

It had been a fairly typical week again for Katie although she was feeling a strange kind of unease in herself from time to time. She'd thought about the counselling on and off. When she had received Keith's letter her initial reaction was one of feeling pleased that there was another appointment but then immediately feeling that unease again. She didn't know what to say. She didn't know if she really felt comfortable enough to talk about herself, *really* talk about herself. And yet she did know that he was somehow different, not like other people she'd seen in the past. So she had made up her mind to attend and see how it went.

She'd lost it a couple of times during the week. Too many drinks had left her feeling bad, but at the same time that felt OK as well. Katie's view was that you just got on with it, and did what you did to feel good, or forget feeling bad, when you had the chance. It was worth it. Few laughs, mess about, it was OK. She hadn't cut again during the week. That wasn't unusual. It wasn't like some daily thing for her. She was glad for that. That might be a problem, but she didn't have a problem. No, she had control and that was what she wanted.

It was time to leave her room and head off to the counselling session. She glanced around it, the clothes piled in the corner, the David Beckham and Robbie Williams posters on the wall. If only…. She picked up her bag, swung it over her should and opened the door, closing and locking it behind her. She had her earphones in and switched on her MP3 player. She walked down the stairs humming to the tune in her head. As she opened the front door the cold wind took her by surprise. She shivered. It wasn't too bad, just the first shock. Pulling her jacket a little tighter she headed out along the street towards the bus stop.

Keith was pleased that Katie had made it to the counselling session. She had come in and sat down with what seemed quite a determined air. Keith had decided to acknowledge that she had not made it the previous week and then leave her to take whatever direction she wanted.

'Sorry not to see you last week but I'm glad you made it today.' Keith was genuine in what he said. He wasn't just saying it.

'Yeah, wasn't too well last week.' Katie wasn't intending to go into much detail.

'You OK now?' The moment he stopped speaking Keith realised that he had unwittingly placed a focus away from Katie's not feeling OK the previous week. He knew he shouldn't have done that and rather should have the emphasis more open.

'Sure, yeah, I'm OK.' She knew she sort of was at one level, but not really. Though it was hard to really accept you were not OK. No-one wanted to know, not really. Someone says, "how are you?", but they don't really want to know. She'd decided a long time ago that people could be pretty false.

'Good. Well, how do you want to use the time?'

Katie had been thinking on her way over to the session. She was determined to try and say something more this week. But it was still difficult knowing what to say. She didn't want to talk about everything. 'I've gotta talk. I know I haven't said a lot and, well, last week I wasn't so sure that I wanted to come back, but that's not going to help, is it?'

'Not coming won't help?' Keith felt optimistic that Katie was going to disclose a little more.

Katie shook her head. 'No, I had some time to think about it. I mean, not last week. I mean, well, yeah, I read your letter….' Katie paused. 'Yeah, it's not easy and I'm kinda glad you said what you did. It's not easy.'

'No, no it's not easy.' Keith felt strongly that he needed to keep his responses focused very much on what Katie was saying. It sounded as though Katie was now more ready to talk and he had to be careful not to block that in any way by making assumptions, interpretations or just by getting ahead of her. She would need to go at her own place.

Katie took a deep breath. She was looking down, picking a little at her thumbs again, but not with the same intensity that she had in that first session. It was more of a reflective action rather than an intense act. Katie was thinking back. It really was not easy to what to say first. Should she start at the beginning, or what she was feeling now? She didn't know.

Keith noticed Katie shaking her head slightly. She looked quite absorbed with whatever was on her mind. He decided to respond. 'Lot to think about?'

'Just don't know where to start.'

'Too many starting places?'

Katie smiled slightly. That was an interesting way of putting it. 'Yeah.' She paused, thinking again about events from her past. It went back a long way, some things from before she could remember them. 'Just had so much shit in my life.'

Keith nodded, 'uh-hu, too much shit, yeah?'. He waited for Katie to continue.

Yeah, Katie thought to herself, far too much. 'Feels like I've been passed around, you know?' Whilst Katie's awareness was in the present, part of her was very much connected with the thoughts that were going through her head from the past.

'Passed around?' Keith was not sure what Katie was referring to. He was aware of frowning slightly as he responded

'Taken into, well, huh, they called it care, but….' Katie was shaking her head again.

'Didn't feel much like care to you.' Keith empathised with the feeling rather than the event.

Katie shook her head. 'No. Got taken away from my mum when I was four. Care, fostered, more care, and so it went on. Lot's of different people. It was OK to start with but…', Katie lapsed into silence. One set of foster parents had come into her mind, she'd been with them from about eight to thirteen. Longest time she'd been with anyone but it wasn't the happiest time of her life, far from it. They'd been OK to begin with but they had problems and started taking it out on her. They had a son, younger than her, and he became a real pain. They'd fight. He'd get her into trouble.

Keith could only begin to imagine how being taken away at aged four would feel. And how did a child deal with that? And what had caused it to have to happen? What was already happening to Katie before that had caused such a dramatic act to have to take place? He put his questions aside. 'Started OK but got worse, yeah?' He deliberately ensured he ended with the focus on what Katie had last said, to allow her to flow on from where she had reached herself.

'Got into trouble. This one place, they were OK, I guess, to start with anyway, but their boy was a little shit, you know? Always giving me grief. I just, well, we used to fight but there was this one time. He was pulling my hair and just wouldn't stop, little shit. I hit him, I hit him fucking hard.' She looked up. 'Broke his nose, blood everywhere. They took me away, but I guess I felt good about what I'd done.'

'Good to hit back?' Keith kept his response simple and short, allowing Katie to keep her focus.

'Brilliant.' Katie felt good as she spoke. It was good to talk about something that had made her feel, yeah, alive somehow. 'He asked for it. Been a pain for so long. I mean, he was sort of OK as well to start with but he just got more of a pain as he got older, as he sort of became more aware that I wasn't his real sister.' Katie paused as she thought back. She could still feel the sense of satisfaction. 'He had it coming, he really did.'

'Mhmm, you sound really clear and strong on that, he really had it coming.' Keith could certainly sense from Katie's tone of voice that she was connecting with some strong and satisfying feelings.

'I've had to put up with so much crap, all my life. Before I'd always sort of, well, you know, just put up with it. But I'd really had enough.' Katie could feel quite a triumphant surge of energy as she spoke. She knew that it had been a turning point in her life. Yeah, OK maybe she'd had a few more problems since but, so what. She needed to sort some things out, but she knew she was a survivor, and she'd get by.

Keith responded. 'Yeah, had enough. A real turning point, no longer putting up with any crap.' He paused. 'You really had had enough.' Keith really felt connected with Katie as she had been speaking. It wasn't just what she was saying or the way she was saying it. She had, in a sense, become more present, more alive to him. There was more feeling in the way she was speaking. Here was a young woman who was recalling a kind of defining moment in her life, a sort of turning point. He still did not know a great deal else but that did not matter. He valued and appreciated what Katie was telling him, and the fact that she was willing to disclose an action that she no doubt got into a lot of trouble over.

'It taught me to stand up for myself.' A pause. 'Yeah, OK, so I got taken away from that family, they didn't want me after that. Told me I was an ungrateful little bitch and said I didn't deserve having anyone care for me.' She snorted. 'Well they were shit at caring. I got taken to a kind of home for a while, which was also shit.' Katie paused again. 'Yeah, I did get a lot of grief over it but I knew I was never going to put up with anything after that. And I don't.' She looked at Keith, and it seemed to him there was in part a kind of challenge in her expression and yet there was something vulnerable as well.

'So a really important change, and it made you feel and behave differently. You stood up for yourself and that's how it's been ever since, yeah?'

Katie hadn't been looking down whilst she had been talking. It wasn't that she had thought about it, but it was the longest she'd been looking up, a significant shift from the first two sessions. She wasn't maintaining constant eye contact, not many people did, but she was holding her head up, looking away and then looking back now and then. She nodded in response to what Keith had said. 'And I'd do it again.'

'You'd do the same now.'

'Only to people who won't back off, you know?'

'Someone who gives you grief and doesn't back off…, doesn't know when to stop?'

'I don't just stand my ground, I'll fight back, teach them a lesson. I'm not going to let anyone mess about with me. I make my own choices, yeah?' Katie held the eye contact that had now developed. There was a definite kind of defiance in her eyes, as if she was ready to show just what she meant if Keith gave her grief. Keith noted it, and responded.

'You'd take anyone on if they gave you grief, that what you mean, including me?' He was warming to Katie and to the dialogue that had developed between them. It felt sharp and real, and very much in the present. OK, so Katie was talking about an incident in the past but the feelings were very much about now. For Keith that was very important. Yes, Katie certainly felt more alive to him and he felt more of a connection between them.

Katie held the eye contact a little longer, smiled slightly and looked away. She felt she'd made her point. She thought back again and acknowledged to herself that she had changed. That she had in a way become more angry since that explosion. Until then she'd been sad and withdrawn, a quiet little girl never really saying very much at all. And always getting picked on at school. She felt her jaw tighten as she thought about it. There were a few people she'd like to meet now, but she'd moved out of the area. Maybe she'd go back someday, maybe settle a few scores. She was glad things had changed. The little shit had done her a big favour. Made her feel strong. Yeah, she almost felt grateful to him.

Katie had returned to silence. As Keith looked on his sense was that this was an active silence. Katie was experiencing things, thinking maybe about what she had disclosed and how she felt about it. She looked quite intense. Not a stressed intensity, and he thought that maybe intense wasn't the right word. But she did look focused, concentrated, yes, that seemed to be more in keeping with what he was sensing. He briefly wondered how her train of thought had developed, but put that speculation aside. He wanted to keep himself responsive to whatever Katie was wanting to communicate to him and didn't want to drift of into his own private world. He brought his thoughts back to that sense of her being quite focused, with perhaps a lot happening for her internally. He believed in being transparent and open and he shared his experiencing.

'To me, you seem to have a lot of thoughts about it at the moment?'

Katie nodded. 'He did me a favour.' She wondered momentarily what Keith must think. 'He wasn't a small kid. OK, a couple of years younger than me, but he was taller than I was.'

'Younger, bigger and it feels like he did you a favour.'

'I'm glad I let him have it.' She looked a little more intently at Keith. 'You probably think it was wrong what I did. I wouldn't blame you, everyone else did.' She was curious what he would say. Would he say what he felt? Would he be able to be honest with her? She thought he might, but no-one had actually ever said she had done the right thing. Well, a few friends had when she'd told them. But none of the adults had ever given any indication whatsoever that what she had done had been in any way OK. Far from it. But *she* knew. She knew how it had affected her and what it had meant to her. It would just be nice to feel that people didn't keep judging her all the time and putting her down. The two always went together.

Keith was responding. He knew what he was experiencing and he responded openly and honestly. 'Katie, I'm not going to judge you and I don't feel like I am in a position to anyway. What happened was understandable. You had reasons to explode. It triggered something in you. It became a very significant moment for you, to the degree that you are even saying that he did you a favour in provoking your reaction. Sounds to me like you did what you needed to do.' He was tempted to add 'and you still do', but decided not to. Such a comment he felt would have taken Katie's focus from her past and into the present. He preferred to let make that choice. At the moment he wanted to simply empathise with what she had said and leave her with her own chosen focus.

Katie agreed with how Keith had summed everything up and it was not just what he said but the way that he said it. It was like, yes, that's how it was. And it was significant and, yes, she did change, and weirdly she was grateful. And she liked to hear that she did what she needed to do. That was how she was, and had been ever since. She felt herself smile, but it was interrupted as other memories started to make their presence felt to her. By then she had begun to speak. 'I really had put up with so much, I mean… yeah.' Katie noted a ripple of emotion but didn't want to show it. She decided not to say any more. She didn't want to get into anything heavy. She rather appreciated feeling good about herself, about something positive that had happened, even if no-one else saw it that way at the time, or since for that matter – except maybe Keith. No, she needed to be and to stay strong. She liked that, though she knew it wouldn't last, it never did. She'd have a bad day again and feel all stressed up. She sort of felt like maybe she needed to explode more. It did her good then. Now she didn't explode the same as that. No, now she got release from cutting. And as the thought came into her mind she felt strangely uneasy and suddenly quite sad. That wasn't what she wanted, it really wasn't. But it happened. How did she get to doing that? She didn't want that any more. Yes it had felt good remembering how she had felt when she had lashed out, but behind that there were years of sadness, and that sadness could still be with her, and very intensely. She swallowed. She could feel the emotion but she didn't want to show it. She tightened her jaw, she could feel her teeth biting together, and stared down at her hands, not knowing what to say. It felt like she had so much to say and at the same time it felt as though there was nothing to say. Her stomach was knotted. She took a deep breath and let it out in a rush.

Keith noted her expression and sensed that there was a lot going on for Katie. He wanted to communicate his awareness of, and sensitivity towards, what she was happening. 'A lot?'

Katie nodded, her eyes momentarily closing as she did so. Another deep breath.

'Past or present?'

Katie sat silently for a moment before responding. 'Both.'

Keith nodded in response.

'Painful stuff?'

Katie instinctively took another deep breath, and nodded again. Her eyes were open but she was looking down. She didn't want to sort of extend beyond herself, it sort of felt uncomfortable but sort of safe inside her own skin. Keeping her attention focused inside herself felt more OK.

'Hmm.' Keith didn't saying anything more. He was taking a deep breath himself.

Somehow it seemed that although she hadn't said anything about what she was feeling, that she or it was being respected. She couldn't analyse it, she wasn't trying to anyway, but it was like Keith wasn't probing her with questions, rather just allowing her to be. That felt respectful. Yeah, not invading her space, or telling her what she ought to think or feel. She'd had a life-time of people on her case and she was glad to have relief from it. Someone who just listened, who tried to understand, wanted to understand. That was unusual, weird almost, and not something she was used to. She wasn't too sure what to make of it. She was left feeling a little anxious and uncertain, and yet there was a hint of a sense of relief as well.

As Katie continued to sit she felt a kind of shift inside herself. It was as though she was looking at herself, being aware of the different parts of her nature. She felt strangely calm as her thoughts ranged over her sense of who she was. She could be so many things. She'd known sadness, loneliness, and she could still feel them both very acutely. And, yes, she could explode, she could be very angry. Her thoughts moved on to other areas. Yes, she could feel frightened, but she didn't like to dwell on that. She couldn't afford to let herself feel like that. It didn't help, it got in the way. She had to be strong. She had to look after herself as best she could. And yet she also felt at times as though her life was a mess and there was no hope, no future.

She was aware of Keith, she wanted to look up but somehow felt unable to. She could feel emotions rising within her and the thought of someone caring about her was too much. She couldn't cope with that. It would somehow be too painful. She swallowed and forced the feeling back. She needed to be strong, independent and in control, and she was going to be. She could cope, she had to.

Katie responded to what Keith had said. 'Yeah, a lot of painful stuff.'

Keith did not respond immediately. When he did he simply said, 'and stuff not easy to talk about.'

'I don't know if I want to talk about it.' Katie really didn't feel at all sure she wanted to get into her feelings, and she felt sure that talking about them would do just that. And she felt a sudden sharp anxiety that she'd lose it, lose control, and she couldn't let that happen.

'Sure, hard to talk about painful things, and not something you're sure you want to do anyway.'

Katie could feel herself breathing deeply and blowing the air back out of her nose. Her breathing continued like that. She didn't know what to say, the anxiety continued to grow, her breathing becoming more and more rapid.

Keith could hear her breathing and the pace at which her breaths were coming. Panic attack. It just struck him. He felt concern.

'You feeling very anxious?'

Katie nodded.

'Felt like this before.'

Katie nodded again.

'OK, you need to take a slow deep breath and let it out slowly.' Keith thought she was heading into a panic attack.

But Katie's breathing was deeper and becoming more rapid. She was breathing through her mouth now, trying to swallow every now and then to slow it down. Her chest felt tight, her arms heavy and strangely numb. Her head felt light.

'Can you slow down your breathing a little?'

She shook her head.

'OK, cup your hands over your nose and mouth like this.' Keith lifted his hands to his face. 'Now try and take shallower deep breaths.' It didn't work, if anything Katie's breathing became even deeper.

Keith leaned over and poured some water. 'Try taking a sip.'

Katie reached over for the glass and lifted it to her lips, her hand was shaking noticeably. She held it to her lips but found it difficult to sip it. Every time she tried she felt an instinctive urge to take another deep breath. She forced herself to take a very slight sip.

'Try and drop your shoulders, try and let them relax a little.'

Katie couldn't and she felt herself spill the water. She took it from her lips and put it back on the table. There was deep pain in her stomach and chest, an aching hurt and she felt her eye's watering. She hated it. She had to stay in control. She had to! But the hurt and the emotions that were now engulfing her were too much. She shook her head, screwing her eyes tight to try and stem the tears that she could feel building up and threatening to burst out and down her face. She rocked forward, her forearms resting on her thighs, her hands clasped tightly. Her breathing became deep sobs. 'Oh God. Oh shit. What's happening? I feel…, Ohhh.' Katie tilted back in the chair, her eyes still closed, but she could feel the tears on her cheeks.

'A lot of feeling, a lot of hurt, it's coming out. It's horrible stuff but you are safe.' Keith spoke slowly, and calmly. He sought to reassure her.

'I-I d-don't feel safe.'

'No, scary, very wobbly?'

Katie nodded. 'I've felt bad but never, I mean…'. She took in a very deep breath and blew out the air, 'nothing…', she swallowed, 'nothing like this'. She felt hot.

'Things have built up, time for them to be let out.' Keith's tone remained soft and calm. He could feel his own sense of focus sharpening up. You didn't listen to someone going through this degree of distress without being concerned. He felt alert, and utterly responsive to whatever was happening or going to happen. How he was would be defined by Katie for the next few minutes at least, and probably longer.

'I feel *so* much…, so much pain.' It felt to Katie like she ached with it, like it was everywhere. It wasn't something she could put into words.

'So much pain.' Keith realised that in his concentration he was frowning quite intensely. He relaxed his forehead slightly.

'And I feel so hot.'

'I'll open the window.' He stood up and opened it, allowing a cool breeze to come into the room and brush across her face. Keith sat back down more on the edge of the chair, leaning a little further forward than he had previously

'That feels good.'

'Take your time.'

'Where does that, I mean, what happens?'

'Emotions get locked up, so to speak, inside us, that's one way of looking at it.'

Katie could feel her breathing returning to a more normal pace and depth. She reached over to the glass of water and took a few sips, it was refreshing. She held the glass between her hands in her lap. She was stiff, and tried to free her shoulders. 'Like last time, but more….' Katie shook her head and frowned, unable to really make sense of what had happened. 'Is that normal?'

Keith nodded. 'Yeah, it happens.'

'Will it keep happening?'

'Probably not, but it seems that there are a lot of feelings inside you trying to get out.'

'Yeah, that's true enough. Shit.' Katie reached up with her left hand and pushed her fingers through her hair, bringing her hand down the side of her face. She felt its wetness. She rubbed her hand down her cheek and then sought to rub the tears from around her eyes.

'Have a tissue.' Keith pushed the box closer.

Katie put the glass down, took two tissues and proceeded to dab at her face.

'Does it help, I mean, you know, this kind of thing?'

'Do you mean counselling generally, or what you've just experienced?'

'Both, I guess.' Katie felt a bit more of her normal self, though she wasn't too sure what that meant. More her ordinary self would be more accurate. She reached over to the glass of water and brought it to her lips. She took a couple of sips. Her throat felt a little raw and swollen but the cool water felt good. 'Does it happen a lot?'

'It happens, everyone's different, different needs, different reactions.'

'But it's OK, I mean, you know…, it is OK?'

'Yeah, it's OK. It's a kind of natural process, not something to be forced.' Keith was aware of feeling a shift in himself. He was now talking about something rather than responding empathically to Katie. But then he also recognised that after an intense emotional release people would sometimes need that, part of their process of re-establishing their sense of self, of coming back together after what could feel like a very fragmenting process.

Katie was taking another sip of water as Keith spoke. She paused. 'I wouldn't want to be forced into feeling like that.'

Keith thought about what to say next. He could be empathic, maybe he should be empathic. Or should he say something about the process given that they were in a more reflective, more conversational mode. He chose both.

'No, you wouldn't want to be forced into those feelings and I'm not sure that that would be a good thing anyway.'

'Why?' Katie was curious. She had a sort of interest in what made people become who they were and though she hadn't really read anything about psychology or that kind of thing, she wanted to know a bit more about this weird thing called counselling that everyone seemed to think was the answer to everything.

'I think we have to trust our own inner processes and when the time and the circumstances are right, then things happen.'

'You mean like having someone listen to you?'

'Yes, coupled with what's happening for you on the inside, as it were.'

Katie said nothing but nodded slightly. That made sense. She thought back to a few minutes previously, she hadn't wanted to show her feelings, she hadn't wanted have someone convey caring for her. She remembered that. It somehow stood out more as she thought about it.

'I didn't want to show you my feelings.'

'No, you wanted to keep them hidden away from me.'

Katie was shaking her head as she thought about what she had experienced. 'It was like I didn't want anyone caring for me.'

'Mhmm, you sure didn't want anyone caring for you.'

Katie could feel herself going very quiet inside and yet there was a strange sensation developing on her face. She could feel a slight pressure on her chest as well, and a churning in the pit of her stomach. She swallowed. 'But I do.' The words came out very quietly. Keith only just heard them, and was glad that he did. He maintained the same softness in his response.

'Yeah, but you do.' He heard Katie taking a very deep breath.

To Katie it seemed as though Keith's response came from somewhere a long way away. She felt suddenly very small. It was weird, very small, and very sad, and very lonely.

Keith felt spatial distortion. It was as though his sense of the room shifted, the walls becoming no longer fixed. Katie seemed to retreat from him. She seemed suddenly more like a little girl. It wasn't that anything had changed, and he knew he was seeing Katie as she was, a nineteen year-old woman. But she seemed small in some strange way. He stayed with his experience, not wanting to think about what was happening. He knew from experience that thinking could disrupt this kind of experience and intrude on what was happening. He had to stay open and sensitive to whatever Katie communicated to him. He knew that these kinds of phenomena generally had deep significance and could indicate that the client was encountering something very deep, often from the distant past.

Katie felt very, very strange. She was herself but not the self that she was used to. She did feel small, and the chair felt strangely large, as did the room and Keith. She knew who he was and she knew she felt scared, but not of him.

'I'm scared.' Katie's voice sounded very child-like.

'Scared?'

'They say horrid things about me, and they hit me.' Her voice remained the same.

'Horrid things, and they hit you. That's not very nice.' Keith didn't know who Katie was referring to and he wasn't going to ask. His job was to listen and allow the part of Katie that was speaking to feel heard and warmly accepted. What he was clear about was that at this moment he was not talking to Katie the nineteen year-old, but a part of Katie from another time. He had to talk to her as a child, relate to her as a child, as he would if he had a child as a client.

'No, it isn't.' Katie's voice was very matter of fact.

'It must upset you?'

Katie nodded, her head movements slightly exaggerated as they might be if it was a child responding. And he noticed that her facial expression had a slight pout to it, again something that young children were very good at.

Keith knew that the connection with the part of Katie that had emerged was still quite tenuous. He needed to build a relationship with her, or at least offer the opportunity for this to happen. Yet he also knew that in these situations too much probing could cause the part of the person that had emerged to retreat and break contact. What had Katie been saying before? Wanting someone to care for her, about her, he couldn't remember the exact phrase.

'You must want someone to care for you, look after you, make it better?'

Katie nodded, a little more vigorously this time.

'How old are you, Katie?'

'Seven, and I'll soon be eight.'

'You looking forward to that?'

'Yes.' She paused, looking momentarily as if she was looking into the distance. 'But I wish they'd stop being nasty to me.'

'Who's being nasty to you, Katie?' He felt that they had a little more connection, and he spoke gently.

'The other children.'

'The other children are nasty to you?'

'They call me names and tell me I'm stupid and look funny. They laugh at me.'

Keith felt his heart go out to Katie, to the part of Katie that was very present in the room.

'That must be awful.'

The Katie that was present nodded and was thinking of the faces of the other children, of the nasty things they said. She hated it and wanted it to stop.

'Please stop them.'

Keith felt the goose-bumps rising up his left shoulder and across the back of his head.

'I'd really like to.' Keith was utterly genuine in his response, yet he also knew that he couldn't. He was talking in the present to someone who was in that moment locked into re-living their past, not just re-living it, more a matter *living and being it* in the present

'Tell them I don't like it.'

'I'd like to tell them to stop and tell them that Katie doesn't like it.'

Katie nodded. 'Will you be my friend?'

'I would be very pleased to be your friend.'

'I don't have friends.'

'That's very sad to not have friends.' Keith could feel himself becoming a little emotional. What a thing for a child to say. He was completely focused on the seven year-old Katie that was sitting opposite him. He felt incredibly concentrated, utterly absorbed by the conversation that he was having.

'They say I smell.'

'They tell you that you smell, that's not very nice.'

Katie shook her head. 'And I don't.'

'No, you don't.'

Katie went silent and Keith waited, maintaining his focus. He felt utterly locked into the moment.

'Can I see you again?'

'Yes, you can see me again.'

'I'd like that.'

'So would I.'

Keith could feel another strange sensation in his head, a little dizzy, slightly spaced out, perhaps the result of his concentration. Katie did not seem so small and she was staring at him with her eyes wide open, a look of shock on her face.

'Wh-what just happened?'

'Were you aware of what happened?'

'I-I think so. I could hear myself but I sounded weird.'

'Mhmm.'

'Like I could hear my voice but it was sort of coming from me but not from me.'

'Your voice but not your voice.'

'Was it me?'

'Did it feel like you?'

Katie was taking a deep breath. She nodded. 'It felt..., I felt..., what happened?'

'What did it feel like to you?'

'I felt like me as I was. I know the children, they used to taunt, call me names, crowd me, push me around.'

'At school?'

'Yes, but also in the home I was in as well. I could hear their voices in my head as well as what I was saying. It was so real, like I was there, I mean, really there.'

'Like you were really Katie as you were then, hearing the voices as they were, what they said?'

Katie nodded. She felt shocked, She felt..., she wasn't sure what she felt..., anxious, uneasy, unsettled? All of them, and it was hard to describe.

'It was a horrible time. They used to taunt me and hurt me. They'd lock me in cupboards, keep me awake. Horrible, like a nightmare.' The tears had returned. Katie couldn't stop them if she had wanted to.

'Sounds absolutely awful.'

'And I couldn't stop them. They all picked on me. They wouldn't stop. I couldn't ..., I was all alone.' The hurt, the fear, the anguish rose to the surface once again and Katie collapsed forward in the chair, her head in her hands, the sobbing and the distress was painful for Keith to witness. For Katie it felt almost unbearable. She hated that period in her life. She couldn't stop sobbing and the sounds she began to make were haunting, penetrating, an almost inhuman wail that was painfully all too human. Keith reached over, he could not bear to sit and watch someone in such distress. Yes, it was in a sense his need, and it was spontaneous. 'I'm going to reach out to support you, tell me if you'd rather I didn't.'

Katie wanted to be reached out to. She didn't want to face and feel all of this alone. She took her right hand away from her face and moved it in Keith's direction. Keith reached out and held it. Katie's grip was strong. He sought to ensure that his grip was also firm. This was support, nothing more, he was clear on that. This was a human being sitting in their internal pit of hell, and he was not going to let her sit there alone as she had in the past and, perhaps, for a number of years since as well. That he did not know. It did not matter. All that mattered was that he responded from the heart for that was what Katie had not received, and he was not sure how much she had ever experienced heartfelt caring and concern towards her. He never underestimated the power of the heart.

The voices that Katie could hear, or at least relive, they were different to how she had heard them when she had retreated back to being a little girl. Then they were more vividly present, now they were more of a memory. It had been weird, something she'd never experienced before. Yes, she had her memories and they kind of came and went but that vivid hearing of those voices and the feelings had felt so intense, so real. Now they were memories and she knew they were memories. She relaxed her grip on Keith's hand; she realised her arm was aching. She felt Keith loosen his grip as well. She didn't want him to let go, and she didn't want to let go either. It was strong, for her. She needed that. She sniffed, she needed to blow her nose. She had to let go of his hand, but she knew as well that she didn't want to feel that separation. It seemed to be somehow all important, though she also knew it wasn't, and yet it was. She sniffed again. She felt Keith loosen his grip more and she did the same, reluctantly, and reached over for the tissues. She blew her nose, took another tissue and started to dry her face.

Keith had felt Katie's grip loosen yet sensed that she was holding him more than he was holding her. He wondered whether he should have reached out, and then put the thought aside. It had been the right thing to do. To have not reached out to someone in that state, who had already disclosed not having felt cared for and wanting someone to care, it just wasn't a human response to sit back. No, he felt that the needs of the moment were clear. Yes, he could not be sure how Katie might interpret it or feel about it, but that would be dealt with. He was not going to let some fear of misinterpretation stop him from responding from the human heart.

'I'm having a bad time, aren't I?'

'You must be feeling wrung out by it.'

'Yeah, phew, I suddenly feel so tired.'

'You've burned up a lot of energy.'

'Is this going to keep happening. I mean, it just takes over.'

'Yeah, it can do, but it can ease in time as well.'

'It does feel like I'm getting something out, and that's good, isn't it?'

'Mhmm, does it feel good?'

Katie nodded. She was looking across towards Keith. He somehow seemed quite strong in some way. It wasn't that he had a huge physical presence, but he had been there for her when she needed it, and that meant a lot. She wondered what it would be like to be in his arms. But she didn't fancy him, not like that. Putting the thought to one side, she felt suddenly felt herself blushing and looked away.

Keith had noticed the expression on Katie's face and the flush on her cheeks before she turned her head. 'Intense, yeah?'

'Hmm? Oh, yes, er, yes, yes it was.' She felt flustered.

Keith could hear the hesitancy in her voice. He felt he needed to respond to this. 'It can be quite intense. And sometimes it is helpful in that context to feel contact, support. You looked like you needed some support in that moment.'

Katie realised that Keith was explaining himself, and putting the experience in its therapeutic place. She didn't feel she wanted to say anything more about it. She could see that he cared but it wasn't anything more. How could she have been so stupid to think, to wonder…. She put her thoughts aside. She wasn't stupid. The memory had just come back of how the other kids had told her she was stupid. She hated that. She felt angry. He'd made her feel stupid. Why had he reached out to her like that? And yet it was what she needed, she also knew that. She needed someone in her life. Yeah, she'd had boyfriends, and that was OK, though no-one for very long. One night stands, or maybe a little longer. But she never really wanted to get too close. Wanted to be in control of her own life.

'Yeah, and I think it's something I struggle with. I mean, I do, and I want someone to be there for me, to care for me, but that also seems weird, alien almost. Nobody ever has, or at least that's how it feels.'

'No-one was there for you.' Keith responded to the final comment, allowing the process of dialogue to flow.

'Not really, I never felt it. Maybe I couldn't or didn't want to, I don't know. Getting taken away, that affects you, you know? Messes your head up.'

Keith's response was utterly genuine, expressing exactly what he was experiencing in response to what Katie had said. 'I can only imagine how it affects you and learn about it from what you tell me.'

'It was a terrible time. And before, I mean, my mum was just…, I don't know, she didn't care. I mean she really didn't give a shit. Only interested in herself, so I understand now, from what I've been told. But I was four when I was taken into care. I just remember, I don't know, angry people. There was one nice woman, a social worker I guess, who I saw a lot of. She seemed nice. But she wasn't there for long, and you know, I was on my own. I don't think that's really understood, what it's like to really feel on your own.'

'What it's like to feel that alone at that age?'

'It's just so hard to understand. I don't know, it's sometimes hard to remember it, I mean, you don't, I was so young. But I do remember the shouting at home, and being cold and hungry, and there were always people in the house. I don't know who they were. But I was always alone, no-one cared, that was what hurt, no-one cared. But I didn't understand. I know I tried to get her attention, but she'd take me out, lock me in my room. She didn't want to know me, the truth is neither my mum nor my dad for that matter must have really wanted me, you know?' It was a sad thing for Katie to acknowledge. She bowed her head and felt her throat drying, her eyes had moistened.

'Not wanted by either of your parents.' Keith spoke slowly, aware of the emotional nature of what was being said.

'My dad wasn't around. He left anyway. Just sort of disappeared, I guess. Don't know what happened to him. My mum always had men around. When he was there they'd argue, then he just wasn't there any more. I know now there were drugs being used, I think that was what finally caused me to be taken away. But I don't know, it's a long time ago. The people that were involved aren't around. And anyway, I got moved out of the area. And that was that.' Katie paused. The feelings that had become present within her were becoming more intense. 'I get sad and I get angry when I think about it.'

'And you're feeling sad and angry now.'

'Angry at them for letting it happen. Why didn't they care about me? I was nothing to them.' She shook her head.

'Nothing to them, just nothing.' Keith kept his response simple and focused. It kept Katie in touch with that sense of nothingness.

'I feel like that sometimes.'

'Like… nothing?' Keith wasn't too sure what Katie meant so he responded with a questioning tone.

'Like I don't exist. Like no-one sees me, like I'm nothing.'

'Like you're invisible.'

Katie thought about it. That wasn't quite right. It didn't feel hard enough, somehow. No, she wasn't so much invisible although she felt like no-one saw her, no, it was something else. 'Not so much invisible, but not seen.'

Keith wanted to be sure that he got it right as it felt important in order to help Katie be clear what her experience was and to be in touch with the feelings and thoughts associated with that. 'So you knew you were visible, but no-one was seeing you?'

'I didn't exist to them.'

'Mmm, it felt as though to them you didn't exist.'

'And it…,' Katie hesitated. It was making her think of how she struggled during those times when she felt like she didn't exist, when she didn't feel anything, and how she coped, how she gave herself a sense of her own existence. She looked down. She didn't want to tell Keith what she did. It was her own private world, and she needed privacy, something to call her own, something that was hers and hers alone. She'd not had that in her life, not much anyway. She never really had anything she could call her own when she was in care, and the foster families she had been with, there had always been other children, and she knew she needed something that was hers, really hers, private and secret. Cutting was her own private world, she didn't want to let anyone else into it. She never did it when anyone else was around, and wouldn't.

Keith sat with the silence that had arisen. He could see that Katie was thinking deeply about something. He didn't want to intrude on that. She had been talking about something that was extremely important, the sense of your own existence. Being acknowledged by others was something most people took for granted. But when you have early life experiences of feeling you don't exist to other people, not wanted or cared for, it deeply affected you. And, yes, she most probably did get attention at times in her childhood, but somehow that could get lost beneath the hurt and pain, and the confusion of feeling you just weren't being seen.

Katie didn't want to dwell on it further, it didn't make her feel good. 'It wasn't all bad, you know? I mean it's not all like no-one cared, but….' Katie paused. No, it hadn't all been like no-one cared for her. Hmm. She felt her heart beginning to thump in her chest. An uncomfortable thought had come into her mind.

'Mhmm, not like no-one cared, but….'

Katie heard Keith's response, but she was engaged with her own thoughts. 'Some people cared, but by then it was kind of too late.'

'Too late?'

Katie tried to respond but didn't know what to say, how to put the thoughts that were coming to mind into words. It was more of a sense of something, but it was hard to get hold of. Something wasn't right, there was something else, but what was it? She knew that something didn't make sense, it didn't add up. There were people that cared, she did have good memories, but…, hmm, yes, she had the memories but there were no feelings with them. She could remember her first foster parents, Derek and Andrea Albert, yes, they did try, but what she remembered from that time was somehow…. She couldn't make sense of it.

Keith noticed that Katie's facial expression had changed. She was frowning.

'Something's making you frown.'

'Mmm. Something's not right, doesn't make sense.'

'Something about people caring or not caring, do you mean?' Keith linked back to what had been the focus prior to the silence and then the frown that had appeared on Katie's face.

Katie shook her head. 'The people I lived with. I was in a home for kids, you know, a Care Home for a while, and then they found me foster parents, Derek and Andrea Albert were there names. They were kind people. They really were, but I wasn't with them for long, well, I was, for nearly two years, but then I was taken back into care again and then, yeah, that was when things got really bad again. I mean it had been bad at school but then it was just bad all the time.'

Keith felt caught between wanting to be clear about the timing and the order of events in Katie's early life, but also wanting to maintain his focus on what Katie was saying and the thoughts and feelings that were present for her. 'So things got even worse after you were taken back into care? I'm just trying to get a sense of the order that things happened.'

'I was in the Care Home, then I went to the Alberts', then I was back into another one of those homes, then the Griffiths, the ones with the kid whose nose I broke, then back into another kids home again.'

'And that all started when you were four?'

Katie nodded. 'I was with the Alberts when I was five until I was seven, that sort of age, then back into care till I was nine, then the Griffiths, and then back into care at thirteen where I stayed.'

Keith nodded. 'OK, that's clear.' He paused, recollecting the focus that they had had prior to clarifying the timeline, as it were. 'But something about people caring and not caring doesn't make sense, which is what you were saying.'

'It's like, yeah, I mean, I guess, you know, some people cared but it's like, well, I mean, it doesn't feel like they did.' Katie knew what she was trying to say but it seemed hard to really convey how it was.

'So it's like you didn't feel anyone cared?'

'Yeah, well, they didn't, you know? Except some people did. Like I say, the Alberts were kind, they really tried but if I really think back it's like, I don't know, it doesn't *feel* like they cared.'

'Like you sort of know they did in your head, but not, what, in your heart? Something like that? Can't get hold of the feelings?' Keith had a sense that Katie was trying to tell him that she maybe knew one thing but felt something different, or simply didn't feel. But he wanted to clarify it.

Katie sat for a moment, thinking about what Keith had just said. It did sort of feel right. As he had spoke it had made sense, but what did that mean? How could that happen? What was wrong with her? That was the thought that emerged. Why didn't she feel what she thought? She felt herself going inwardly silent as another thought came to mind. It was a simpler one, more straight forward. It shocked her, not that it was a new idea, but somehow it was now taking on a deeper and more immediate and personal meaning in some way. Why didn't she feel? She took a deep breath and wondered what to say next. 'Is there something wrong with me?'

'Is that what you think?'

Katie nodded slowly. She was frowning as she did so, not an intense frown, more of a puzzled expression.

'You look a bit confused.'

'I am.' Katie paused. 'I mean, I do feel that no-one cared, I really do. I don't have a sense of anyone caring about me, not in a real kind of way. I mean, yes, there were people that cared, but it doesn't seem like they did. And I can't make sense of that.' It all felt quite disturbing to her. She didn't understand why, but it was unnerving and she felt a growing anxiety as she continued to sit trying to make sense of what she was now saying and experiencing.

'Hmm, hard to make sense of the two conflicting experiences.'

'It's like…, hmm.' Katie paused again. Another thought was with her that stopped her from speaking. What was in her mind was that she wanted to feel cared for, and she wanted to be able to feel that someone had cared for her and about her, and in a way she sort of knew that some people had, but at the same time she also didn't want to feel anyone cared for her either. And that was quite a sharp contrast. 'I want to be cared for, but somehow I don't want to either.'

'Mhmm, OK, so it's like part of you wants to be cared for and another part doesn't?' Keith was aware that he had introduced the idea of parts and wasn't sure now that he had said it that it was perhaps as helpful as it seemed as he was speaking. But it was said now and, in truth, that was how he experienced what Katie was saying, but he also recognised that it might not be her experience.

'I hadn't thought of that but yes, it is like that. I mean, most of the time I don't want anyone to care for me, I don't want someone to control me, you know?'

'Having someone caring for you would feel like someone else controlling you. That how it is?'

Katie nodded. 'Too right.'

'Mhmm, caring means control.' Keith made his comment in response to sharpen the focus that had developed, keeping his response minimal to allow Katie's own experiencing to find its own direction.

Katie's thoughts had gone back to her childhood, and in particular the phrase, "taken into care". 'They say they are going to take you into care. That's crap. They take you into control, they take control. That's what they really mean, but they don't have control. I had a shit time in care. Bullied, being picked on. No way was it care. And later, after the incident with Sam, the kid whose nose I broke, there was no-way that was care. It was control, that was all it was, "do this", "do it this way", "don't do that", "do what you're told".' Katie took a deep breath, her jaw tightened and she shook her head. She felt so angry. 'Fuck them! Fuck them all! They made my life a fucking misery.' Katie could feel the intensity building inside herself. She knew one thing, she felt angry, extremely angry, and she felt she had every reason to be.

'No care, all control, and you just want to say "fuck the lot of them".' Keith wanted his response to again be brief but he wanted to try and pick up on the themes that were emerging and leave Katie with a focus on her anger which was plain to see given the way she was speaking and the look on her face. He noticed, too, that she had tensed. She had gripped her hands into fists and looked as though the could explode at any moment. He waited to see how Katie would respond.

'Yeah, I do. I really, really do.' Her eyes were wide and blazing now. 'Fucking bastards, all of them.' She saw faces, the people in charge of the homes she'd been taken to, the other children, the Griffiths. She felt her lips curl up, she still felt that strong sense of satisfaction for hitting Sam, but she wanted to hit out at them all. Every single one of them. They'd all played their part in messing up her life.

'Every single one.' Yes, thought Katie, every single one. She had spoken slowly and deliberately, as if she was lining each one up in turn.

She paused in her thoughts, looking to the side and shaking her head slightly. A memory had come to mind of Mrs Albert. Yes, she had tried. More than anyone actually. Why had she been the one that had become ill? Maybe if she had stayed there, maybe things might have been different, but she had become ill. She found out later that she had died. Yeah, she remembered that. Then she remembered Mr Griffiths, bastard, he'd told her. 'You might have killed Mrs Albert but you're not killing us.' She felt the momentarily sadness towards Mrs Albert become anger once more. How dare he have said that! She wished she'd broken his nose as well. She hadn't killed her, she'd never have wanted that. She was the one who tried, really tried. They made cakes together. She could remember that, standing on a little stool at the table. She couldn't remember how she felt though, but she did remember it happening. And she took her out to the park and played with her on the swings. She could remember all of that. She felt her eyes itching and rubbed them. She'd felt sad. It was a happy time. But she couldn't remember feeling happy, and she immediately thought of the bullying and the name calling and being pushed around and punched.

Keith meanwhile sat in silence. He didn't feel a need or an urge to say anything. It seemed as though what had needed to have been said had been said and he had acknowledged Katie's focus and strength of feeling. He was sure that it would have triggered a train of thought which was probably now absorbing her. He would not disturb that process. She knew he was there. She knew he was hearing what she was saying. Now trust her own inner process to take her to where she needed to be within herself. But he kept his attention upon her, ready to respond to anything that Katie might say.

'I feel angry, I feel a bit sad. I don't know what to think about it all. I've got so much in my head, it feels like I want to explode.'

'Like your head's going to explode with it all.'

'It won't go away, just, well, yeah, does my head in.'

'Sure, so much of it just does your head in. Must be hard to cope with.' Keith was aware that he was introducing something that Katie had not said but it was a thought that came very strongly to mind in a way that it sort of demanded to be voiced. It wasn't easy to describe but it was something he experienced now and then and he recognised that often it was relevant. He had to be sure that it wasn't his own curiosity, or that he wasn't trying to avoid something by focusing the client on something else. He was aware of the risk of that and he wouldn't say something like he just had on a whim. It needed to have that depth within his own experiencing, and he needed to experience it at a time when he felt a certain depth – no, maybe depth that wasn't quite the right word - maybe more of a particular *quality* of connection with his client.

Katie's response within herself was immediate. She knew how she coped when she felt like that, what gave her release and relief, but she wasn't sure she wanted to say anything to Keith. 'I cope. You have to.'

'Sure.' Keith noted the slightly offhand manner of Katie's response which seemed quite incongruent to the expression that had been on her face, 'you cope, you have to.' And you're not going to tell me, thought Keith. And he respected that but he also hoped that maybe one day she would. But he wasn't going to push or probe, try and force something into the open before Katie felt ready to allow that to occur. He knew that if her own inner process wasn't ready for a difficult disclosure it could render her quite vulnerable. He wasn't going to risk that. He was also aware that the session would soon be drawing to a close.

Katie was thinking now about getting back to her room. She knew what she needed to do, and she knew it would make her feel better, take the pressure off. She didn't want people controlling her or telling her what to do. 'Is it time to go?'

'Almost.'

I need to go, got things to do.'

'Sure. It's been an intense session. You OK?' Keith was genuinely concerned, not that he didn't trust Katie, but he didn't want her to…, hmm, it wasn't for him to want her to do anything other than to become more congruent and more able to offer herself unconditional positive self-regard, as the theory described it.

'Yeah.'

Keith nodded. 'Next week, same time?'

Katie nodded in response. 'Yeah.' She didn't way anything else. Too many thoughts in her head. It made it difficult to really engage with what was going on outside of her skin.

'You take care of yourself.' Keith meant his words quite genuinely, but they were not helpful. Katie heard the words of someone telling her what to do, not the words of someone who cared about her well-being. As someone who had not really known much caring, at a deeper level his words stirred strong feelings about herself. I'll do what I fucking want, was what Katie thought as she got up to leave. What do you know, telling me to take care of myself. She wanted to say 'fuck off', but she didn't. She left in a very determined manner. Keith was left watching her leave thinking to himself that it had not been a very helpful ending to the session, and wondered what had happened. He was glad that he would be seeing his supervisor the next day for their monthly contact. He had to talk about his work with Katie. His last supervision session had been just before he had seen her for the first time.

*

Katie headed home. She felt angry, let down, confused. Too many thoughts in her head. She needed to stop it, get away from it all. She knew what she needed and she stopped off at the supermarket. She had some money, not much, but enough to get a couple of alcopops. That would see her through and she'd go down the pub later. She bought her drinks, they were on offer, she got four for the price of three. OK, so she'd spent nearly all her money, but she'd get by. It wasn't anything new. When she got back to her room she set about drinking them all, and it wasn't long before she was feeling the effects. She was still angry, pissed off with Keith and everyone else, in fact she felt that way towards the whole world. No-one gave a shit, that's what it felt like, no-one cared whether she lived or died. No-one. Mrs Albert's face came into her head. 'You'd miss me, I know you would. You're the only one.' She took another mouthful from the bottle. It tasted very sweet but she was used to that. She'd spent her whole life eating and drinking sweet things. 'Like I missed you.' She felt her eyes brimming with tears. 'Why'd you have to go and get ill? I'd have been OK if you hadn't. You

103

were good to me, you were, I know you were.' But she couldn't feel it, she just knew it. She wanted to feel it, but she couldn't. It wasn't a time of her life when Katie felt a great deal. She was still in a kind of shock from the effects of her parents on her, being taken into care, being bullied. No, it hadn't been a time when she had felt much caring even though she had been cared for. She took another mouthful. She felt sick, she hadn't eaten much that day, just some cereals for breakfast. She got up, feeling very unsteady as she walked towards the sink in her room. She knew she wouldn't make the toilet which was along the corridor. She didn't see the corner of the rug had been turned up. She tripped and fell, catching her head on the sink as she went down. It was only a glancing blow but it was enough to knock her out. She landed with a thud, her head fortunately missing the low cupboard a little to the side of the sink, which had a sharp corner and could so easily have caused much more serious damage.

Chapter 6

It was the following day and Keith was sitting opposite his counselling supervisor, Lorraine. He had been seeing her for supervision each month for about four years and they had formed a good working relationship. He felt at ease with her. She didn't sit in judgment of his practice, it was much more collaborative, and she respected both his professionalism and his humanity. Like him, Lorraine had a particular interest in young people and often their supervision sessions included discussion about young people in general and about the many difficulties they could face as they sought to make their way in the world.

Keith had not discussed Katie with Lorraine before. There had been a slightly longer gap than usual between supervision sessions due to Lorraine being on holiday. Now, Keith felt glad to be there, particularly after the ending of the previous session with Katie. And he also wanted to take some time to check out his own reactions to, and perceptions of, Katie. She was clearly experiencing a great deal, and he wanted to be sure in himself that he could be genuinely and openly available to her within the therapy sessions.

'So, what do you want to focus on today?' Lorraine sensed that there was a little bit of something in the air that she couldn't quite define. Anxiety, concern, unease? Keith didn't look his usual relaxed self. She waited for his response.

'A new client. I need some time to talk through what's happening. The last session has left me feeling as though, I don't know..., it's complex, I think I need some time to just range over what has been happening to make some sense of it and to get your feedback.' Keith was still very much with the end of the last session, but he was also aware of that phase in the session when Katie had connected with something deep from her past. And the issue of being cared for/not feeling cared for.

'OK, where do you want to start?'

'Katie's nineteen, she referred herself direct to the Service. The doctor had encouraged her. All she said at the time was that she felt she needed someone to talk to, that life was difficult and she had stuff to sort out.'

'Mhmm. OK. And your response to that?'

'It seemed normal. Nothing untoward about that. When she'd phoned – I didn't take the referral – we took the usual details. You know the system, the client phones the Youth Counselling Service and I called her back to make the appointment. Her doctor had encouraged her to refer. What was clear was that she was someone who had been in care and was now pretty much on her own. She said she'd had contact with Social Services in the past but she'd missed appointments and now didn't have any contact with them. Said she just wanted to talk.'

'And when she arrived?'

'Quiet, withdrawn. Picks at her fingers and thumbs a lot. Did that a lot in the first session. They really were a bit of a mess. She's clearly got what we therapists like to term 'issues', which I hate as a word. We all have issues, but some of us have a lot of crap to sort out, you know?'

'That how it is for Katie?'

'Yeah. She hasn't said a great deal about her past, or her present. Some references, you know? There have been a lot of silences though, and also some intense emotional expression as well.' Keith paused, the depth of feeling that had been expressed in those emotional periods within the sessions was still quite vivid.

'So, silences broken by intense emotion?'

'Mmm, there have been periods when it has become a little more conversational as well. She felt faint one session, and she had a panic attack in another.'

'That sounds intense stuff. How were you in coping with that?' Lorraine was concerned, not because she doubted Keith's ability, but that these could be events that could make a powerful impact on a counsellor, and part of her role was to offer support and to ensure that her supervisee's were not so affected by what they experienced in their work that it then had an adverse affect on their ability to offer the therapeutic relational qualities that were so important.

'It was OK. When she felt faint, which was in the first session, I think I opened the window for some air, I know she had some water. I was concerned. She went so pale. But she came through it OK.'

'Was it in response to anything being said?'

Keith shook his head. 'There was a lot of silence in that session. I think, well, I don't know. She may not have been well. She's very thin and I do wonder how well she is eating, you know? It may have all been too much, perhaps. She was certainly not saying much so if it wasn't a reaction to anything said, I don't think, more about what was happening within her. She does seem to be someone with a lot on her mind.' Keith paused. He recollected the silences. They had felt intense.

'A lot on her mind. And the silences, how were they?'

'Well', Keith found himself taking a deep breath and holding it for a moment, before breathing back out slowly. He spoke slowly and deliberately. 'A lot going on, and I didn't want to disturb what was happening. I responded on a few occasions, acknowledging her, acknowledging the silence. It's always difficult to know what's best. Trying to be sensitive to someone's needs, to their emotional landscape, is a challenge when you haven't really got to know them, but it's what we do, isn't it?' He tightened his lips, he was maintaining his eye-contact with Lorraine. 'I just..., I don't know, I think she's got a lot to say, but she is really finding it difficult to know what or how to say it. I seem to remember her saying something like that in the session, or it may have been in response to my commenting on how difficult it can be to talk about things or to know where to start.'

'Mmm, it's a challenge, isn't it?' Lorraine was struck by the fact that Keith seemed to be speaking in a manner that wasn't so easy as she was used to. He seemed to be struggling to find the words, and there was a hesitancy. It was the challenge to him that her response was directed at.

'I didn't want to invade her inner world. I don't know how robust that is, or how fragile. But she's a survivor, no doubt about that, but probably at quite an emotional cost.'

'What's your sense?'

'I think she's built a kind of emotional shell around herself and it's enabled her to survive, enabled her to not be overwhelmed by things that have happened and impacted on her. I'm speculating a bit, but I know she was bullied and picked on at school. I know she had difficult times with being in care – where she was also bullied – and all was not good with some of her foster parents.' Keith paused, and shook his head. 'And I haven't mentioned her parents that she was taken away from, well, from her mother anyway. Father seemed to have already vanished. There was, it seems, negligence, maybe violence, I'm not sure. There were drugs and her mother seemed to have maybe brought her up a lot on her own, although how much bringing up went on seems questionable. A lot of men in the home, maybe, I don't know, I'd be guessing, but perhaps there was some degree of selling herself for drugs.'

'And Katie.'

Keith took a deep breath. 'Hmm, I know what you mean. And I don't know. Nothing has been said yet to indicate sexual abuse. And obviously I'm not going to enquire but wait to see what Katie feels ready and able to tell me. I don't want to plant an idea in her head, but given the little we know, it can't be ruled out.'

'Often it's a matter of sexual boundaries being in shreds.' Lorraine had heard clients herself from disrupted and disruptive families Where chaotic drug use was a feature, and children could certainly be sexually at risk. Not always, of course, but it did happen. She didn't want to jump to conclusions, it wasn't always the case, but there was a raised probability. 'Do you have any sense of that?'

'Don't know.' Keith was shaking his head. 'She hasn't said much about it at the moment, and has made no reference to anything sexual.'

'And with you? How do you feel being there with her? Anything overtly sexual making an impression on you.' Lorraine was aware that there could be powerful sexual dynamics present, particularly though not exclusively where a client's sexual boundaries may have been badly affected by earlier life-experiences.

Keith paused. He wanted to think about that for a moment. No, he shook his head, it didn't seem to be something that was affecting him. He was much more aware of her being withdrawn, thin, and so much pain and hurt coming through. She seemed to be touching him more in the heart, and not in any kind of sexual way. It was compassion that he was feeling, and a caring. He felt sad for her. It didn't feel sexual for him. Of course he didn't know what was being experienced by his client.

'I don't think so. I just feel, yeah, sad and more caring towards her. I feel it more here.' He tapped himself on the heart area of his chest with his right hand, 'you know? She feels, I don't know, a real mixture. There's something vulnerable and there's something that makes you think she's finding her own way through everything and as I said she's a survivor in many ways.' He paused, he could see Katie's response to his having held her hand in that last session. 'Just a minute, I've just remembered something. She really did have a tough time in the last session, and on one occasion I held her hand. I said that was what I was going to offer if she wanted that. I felt I needed to offer some support, something tangible, I guess. She was sitting there, so cut off, so much pain and anguish, it was, I don't know, it just felt to me like a human response, but nothing else. Maybe, yeah, I guess there was a risk there, and I'm sure some would say maybe it wasn't appropriate. I don't know. But in the moment it felt right.'

'It felt right. And you checked it out with her before?' Lorraine wasn't going to be judgmental. She knew that there was a lot of debate around physical contact, and an older man with a teenage girl, could definitely have particular dynamics and issues, but she also wanted to acknowledge that for a male counsellor to reach out to a female client could take a lot of courage, knowing the risk of misinterpretation and, in a world of increasing resort to litigation, there could be other risks too.

'I said something, I'm trying to think what.'

'You said something before you reached out to her.' Lorraine nodded, feeling a little uneasy.

Keith was aware that he could feel his heart thumping. There was anxiety in his system. 'I'm feeling some anxiety here, I need to stay with this.'

'OK, so something about all of this is leaving you feeling anxious.'

Keith was frowning. 'I acknowledged her upset, how distressed she seemed…' He paused. 'Hold on, no, no, I'm getting confused here. The first or was it the second session, I said something about…, yes, that's right, yes, I acknowledged her upset and said that it left me wanting to reach out to her. Yes, that's right. But I didn't.'

'So, OK, you felt her distress, you felt the urge to reach out, but you didn't in that session.'

'But in the last session I did.'

'In the last session you did reach out.'

Keith nodded. 'Yes. What I said was along the lines of "I'm going to reach out to support you, but tell me if you'd rather that I didn't". Something like that.' Keith was trying to be sure he was being correct with what he was recounting from the sessions. He felt a little easier in himself as he was speaking.

'So, a different response but this time you did reach out.'

'She took her hand away from her face and reached it out. I held it.'

'Mhmm.' Lorraine was wondering about the anxiety Keith had referred to a short while ago and whether it was still present for him. 'And how does it feel now talking about it?'

'Calmer. I don't know, it just felt right. It felt like the human thing to do in so many ways, and now, as I process it, it does feel more I suppose fatherly.' He stopped speaking, his lips tightened.

'More fatherly.' Lorraine was pleased that Keith was able to clarify this. It was healthier for him and for the therapeutic relationship with his client if he was able to be fully aware of what was happening and what he was experiencing. What he was saying seemed thoroughly genuine to her.

'Yes. It's like I just feel that she needs someone there for her, someone steady, someone who is a therapeutic companion. And that sounds so…, I don't know.' Keith paused, collecting his thoughts. 'She needs a friend, someone to sit there with her as she faces up to and experiences the emotional turmoil that I've already witnessed. And, yeah, she needs some guidance and direction. And, I don't know, hearing myself say that makes me think that I don't trust her. Like I don't believe that her own inner tendency towards growth that we believe in as therapists can be trusted. But I do trust it, it's just that when young people have such a tough time they can end up taking really damaging risks and if they can be avoided, then that has to be a good thing. And I know people have the right to have their own experiences. But so many problems for young people today seem to be linked to either how society doesn't give them a healthy direction, or actually encourages really unhealthy attitudes and values. It's sad to see.'

'You sound passionate about it.'

'I am. Maybe too passionate.'

'You think you can be too passionate about caring about young people and how they are affected by society's values?'

'Well, when you put it like that, maybe not. But I guess it is about what I do with it.'

'How you express that passion.'

'And working with young people is part of that.'

'Mhmm, working with them is important as a way of expressing your passion.'

Keith nodded. Yes, he cared about young people and how they were affected by, well, life. He wanted to help them get on in life, find their own way and if possible unburden themselves of some of the difficulties that they experienced, particularly young people like Katie who clearly had so much disruption in her past. 'I want to help them find ways that enable them to cope better, you know?'

Lorraine was struck by the difficulty of knowing what was therapeutically best to enable a person to cope. She thought of the physical contact that had occurred between Keith and Katie. Katie had been in deep distress, but she was coping. Was she coping? She needed to check that out.

'I don't want to direct us away from your passion, but I am also aware of wondering how Katie was coping with her distress? What was happening? Did she really need you to reach out to her?'

'I don't know, I sort of assume so. She responded by reaching out to me.'

'After you had verbally reached out to her.'

Yeah, point taken. She has survived, she has coped. But how? I mean, it seems to me that sitting with another human being who really listens to you, hears what you are going through, seeks to support you, has to be a positive kind of way of coping with stuff. And I felt for her, I was human. I think we need to give and receive human responses, within boundaries, obviously.'

'Mhmm. And you felt and feel boundaried?'

'I do. But it is difficult as a male therapist. I do feel an oppression to hold back sometimes. I'm sure if I was a female therapist in that situation I might have moved closer, maybe even have held her, maybe. I don't know. But it does make you wonder if it wouldn't be simpler if you counselled people of your own gender. I don't know.'

'Mhmm.' Lorraine wasn't sure now was the time to explore that one. She was aware that the exploration had moved away from Katie specifically. 'Maybe we need to get back to Katie?'

'Sure, that's OK. It's good for me to acknowledge what I feel.' Keith paused, collecting his thoughts. 'I do need to be clear about not over-reaching myself in the sense of imposing my agenda on Katie, or any of my clients for that matter. I need to keep my focus on creating the therapeutic space, but I also think that the fact that I genuinely experience compassion is important.'

Lorraine thought for a moment and knew she had something she needed to clarify. 'I'm struck by the fact that we were a little while back talking about *passion*, and you have just said *compassion*. I'm momentarily caught on the contrast.'

'I think that, yes, I am passionate about what I do, but for me the compassion lies with the sense of connection, the sense of sitting beside or with someone who is going through pain and despair, it can feel like they're lost in their own personal hell sometimes, or trying to make sense of themselves or their lives. I feel for them, but I want to also say that somehow it's more than that, it's something about feeling *with them* as well.' Yes, Keith thought, that seemed to clarify it for himself and he wondered what Lorraine's response was going to be. 'Does that make sense to you?'

'It's subtle but there's a crucial difference in there somewhere. Feeling *with* in contrast to feeling *for*. Feeling *for* could so easily slide into sympathy or pity, it's sort of got that tone to it to me. And yet even as I say that I know that feeling for someone doesn't always have to be quite like that.'

Keith was back thinking about Katie. 'She'd been talking about the kids in care picking on her.' He paused, remembering the intensity of it, and the interaction that had occurred a few minutes previously. He needed to say something about that as well. 'It got to me and, yeah, it wasn't just that. Something else had happened a few minutes before then in the session. I just felt…, hmm, I do want to say felt for her. It's like, yes, there is a different tone. Feeling with is more subtle. Maybe it's rarer too. And I'm just wondering how this fits with empathy and sympathy and having unconditional positive regard for clients.' Keith was thinking about the therapeutic relational attitudes that were at the heart of the person-centred theory that was at the core of his practice. 'I think *feeling for* is more on the sympathy line, *feeling with* is more about empathy. *Feeling for* has more of my own emotional tone present, *feeling with* is more collaborative – that doesn't seem the right word, maybe mutual is better. Something shared rather than just my reaction. But it was very intense being with, and listening to, Katie.' Keith wanted to bring the focus back more specifically to Katie.

'Very intense to be with Katie, feeling for her, feeling with her and hearing what she was saying.' Lorraine said nothing further. She sensed that Keith was bringing the focus on to his work with Katie and away from his reflection on compassion. It was time to let that go and move on with Keith. She waited for him to describe what he was referring to. She was aware her focus was sharp, there was a need within her to be extremely attentive to what Keith was saying, and how he was saying it.

Keith nodded but knew he needed to now talk about what had happened in the session. 'She went back, deep into herself. I don't know the best way to describe the process, but a part of her emerged, it was quite distinctive. I know people can experience themselves in parts, and sometimes those parts can be extremely, how can I best describe it, like they have a kind of will of their own, sort of independent in some way, you know?'

Lorraine nodded, she did appreciate what Keith was describing. Keith continued. 'And in extreme cases this can be linked to dissociative states – part of her nature being cut off or cutting itself off from the rest of her structure or sense of self. And given what her past was like, and how much worse it may well be over and above what she has told me so far, traumatic experiences that could trigger dissociation may well be possible. But I don't want to get into that discussion at the moment. What happened was that Katie went back into herself and what emerged was a seven year old Katie, talking like a seven year, talking as if that time period was in the present, and looking small in the chair. There was spatial distortion of my perception. She just spoke as a seven year old about being picked on, being called names, how she wanted it to stop.' Keith felt goose-bumps as he spoke, and his own emotions rising. 'It was intense.'

'For you as well.' Lorraine could feel her own intensity building.

Keith nodded. 'Very much so.' He paused and swallowed, feeling the presence of his own emotion. His eyes felt watery. 'Yeah. I literally…, hmm, I was going say it felt as though I really had a seven year old girl in the room with me. I mean I know she wasn't, Katie's nineteen and she was the one sitting there, but in that moment, during the few minutes when I was responding to this seven year old part of her, I don't know how best to describe it, but she was there, and I was reacting and relating to a seven year old without any doubt at all. That's how it was.'

Lorraine took a deep breath. 'I can see and hear from what you are saying just how profound it was to have that experience. It does happen.'

'I know, and you know I've been there with other clients. And it gets to you.'

'And I want to also say that you must have been offering something to Katie to allow that part of her to emerge. She must have felt safe to do so.' As she stopped speaking Lorraine wondered whether she had cut across Keith and should have simply held his focus on it 'getting to him'. Keith was responding, she made a note to herself that this was something she may want to come back to, but recognised the need to go with her supervisee's focus.

'Katie said afterwards that she had never experienced anything like that before. So, yes, unless this was a part of her that previously emerged outside of her normal awareness, then this was the first time.'

Lorraine was taking a deep breath. 'Hmm, and you don't have that kind of experience without something happening to cause it.'

'No.'

They both lapsed into a silence, each having thoughts and feelings about how people can have so much to struggle with. Within her silence Lorraine acknowledged to herself that there was something incredibly human about all of this. What Keith was describing was on the real human edge of relational experiencing. And it was an area that mainstream psychology and psychiatry, in her view at least, didn't engage with very well. How often were people who 'heard voices' actually hearing traumatised parts of themselves clamouring for attention, or seeking to express themselves in ways that the person had been unable to when the trauma was occurring. Whilst she knew that wasn't the case for everyone, she also knew that so many people diagnosed with so-called borderline personality disorder, or those given the diagnosis of personality disorder, were actually people badly affected by experiences in life who needed time and space to try and re-integrate the extreme fragmentation that had occurred. She also knew that there were other factors as well, but so often people who struggled to function within the so-called 'norms' of Western society – and it had to be acknowledged that personality disorder and borderline personality disorder as concepts and diagnoses were essentially Western psychiatric inventions – were people who had learned to be different, and often had to be different in order to survive the chaotic experiencing of their early lives. If someone's early life experience is, in effect, psychologically and emotionally upside down and back to front, as it could be for some unfortunate people who suffered abuse, neglect and absence of love, then it was not too surprising that they struggled to adjust and fit into societal norms. Add to that the fact that often people who are struggling with this may turn to substances to alleviate their symptoms of inner distress, confusion, hurt and despair, and you had some very difficult people to work with, but a set of people who needed more than most the opportunity to experience normal, caring, authentic, consistent, reliable, honest human interaction and relationship. Lorraine believed that therapeutic relationship could offer that – genuineness and authenticity, unconditional positive regard and warm acceptance, and a willingness and ability to listen, hear and empathise.

'And she's only nineteen?'

Keith nodded.

'Getting support?'

'I don't know. She's in some kind of bed and breakfast accommodation. She had some contact with Social Services but that's not continued. She's in touch with an independent agency as well but it's not regular, on-going support.'

'Except you.'

'Except me.'

'What do *you* need?'

'Time to come to terms with what you've just said. Talking now is bringing it all together, making me aware in a more direct way what we are dealing with. And that sounds like an awful way of saying it. I don't mean it like that.' Keith in his earlier silence had become acutely aware of the human challenge of working with Katie, and of the sense of the unknown, and the not knowing how the therapeutic process would unfold. He was aware of having a sense of the awesome nature of his role as a therapist.

Lorraine could appreciate what Keith was saying. 'How would you like to put it?'

Keith thought for a moment, looking down at the floor as he did so. 'I know what it is.' He looked up again. 'It's that sense that you get, and I hear it far too often, "oh, just another typical teenager". OK, Katie's only just still a teenager, but there are just so many put downs in our society about young people. And some of them, and probably many more than society likes or wants to admit to, are, as Katie puts it, simply "fucked up". That's how she's describes herself.'

'Sounds pretty clear.'

Keith nodded.

Lorraine paused before responding. But before she could say anything, Keith started to talk once more.

'What's good is having the time here to reflect on all of this. It's so hectic out there, so intense, so do, do, do. It's good we have time out like this. So many other professions don't have this kind of reflective space. You need it. I need it. I need to have time to quietly take on board the immensity of what is happening. It's just so easy to make glib comment about people as if we can sum them up in a sentence. And we can't. And we are stupid, more than stupid, utterly ignorant when we try to do this. Each young person, everyone, is unique, with their own stories. And what each person needs is unique as well, unique to their situation, their experiences and how they have been affected.'

Lorraine could hear the passion in Keith's voice, and a note of what sounded like angry frustration. She responded to what she was hearing.

'Makes you angry.'

'Makes me bloody angry. How many youth counsellors are there? How many opportunities do young people get to talk, really talk, about the things that matter to them? We've got kids out there not just carrying knives, but carrying guns, partly to feel safe, partly to boost their sense of identity within the gang culture. What the hell is that about? How did we get to this place? Because something caused it. And I'm bloody sure that a big part of it is the breakdown of family structures and the rampant consumerism. Buying things for the experience of buying. The pressure to have this, do that, be seen wearing whatever the latest fashion is. People getting bullied or worse if they don't, and it happens. Kids have to wear certain clothes or else they're in trouble, serious trouble, on the streets. It's a real mess, Lorraine, I see it every day. You know, I really wonder what on earth we are doing because there is no doubt that the Western value system as it is currently being expressed is crap. We are telling young people and everyone else what they must have to be happy, and it involves buying things. And the people that can't afford it, well, they borrow on credit, they steal, or they get depressed, maybe drink, take other drugs, develop eating disorders to feel in control of something in their lives, whatever. We are a sick society, Lorraine, and we need to start asking some very serious questions about how we got here and what we're going to do about it, because there's no sound-bite quick fix that is going to resolve this.' Keith took a deep breath and blew it out. 'That's me. I've said my bit.' He still felt angry but he felt good having said what he had said.

'It's huge, you're right, and I guess we've all contributed to the problem by buying into the values of our society, and now, well, now maybe we have to change, and it's difficult.'

'It is, but if we don't? I don't know, I often think back to the…, and I know we've got away from Katie and I don't want to lose sight of her in all of this, and I'll come back to her in a moment, but what I often think of…, is it in *The Quest of the Holy Grail*, I don't know, it's in the myth anyway. You know where Gawain is shown the Holy Grail at the start but doesn't ask the question of the Fisher King, and has to go off and experience all kinds of different challenges, lessons whatever you like to call them, before returning to the Grail Castle and seeing the Grail again, and the Fisher King with the wound from the lance, and his realm a wasteland. And this time he asks the questions, "What ails thee?". Time and time again I find myself wondering when on earth our society, and maybe the whole world, but lets stick to our society, when are we going to ask of ourselves, "what ails us?". Because we are wounded and we are at risk of turning our society into a wasteland. And that might seem extreme. But is it, really? Maybe we're already in the wasteland. Anyway. I'm stopping. I need to get the focus back to Katie.'

'Man on a mission, a good mission, but you can't save society through Katie.' Lorraine hadn't really thought through her response, it was utterly spontaneous. Was it fair on Keith to have said it? She awaited his response.

'I know. I know. And I have to keep the balance right and a sense of proportion. But I see so many young people who are the victims of others whose values are upside down. And I know that there are good things happening and good people trying to make a difference. And then you have government making cannabis seem less harmless, extending access to alcohol, increasing opportunity for gambling which will make the businesses richer and the punters poorer, now wanting to force young people into continued education under threat of getting a criminal record – and lets face it those who don't engage with education often don't give a shit about having a criminal record. I know that's not every one, but a good few that's true for. And all the time the bosses in the banks and other industries make obscene profits, celebrities strut their stuff and shove their wealth in the faces of the poor, and we have violence and sex constantly on our TV screens, in games, on the internet, in films, and we wonder why we have so many problems....' Keith shook his head.

'You're full of it, aren't you?'

'I'm frustrated. I want to do more, but I don't know where to start.' And he thought of Katie leaving the last session. 'And I think I made a right mess of the last session. Katie got angry over something and left. It was the end of the session, but I did something that didn't help, something I must have said. And maybe I shouldn't have reached out. She seemed a bit flustered by it afterwards. I think I pissed her off. And that's not what I want for her or for any of the young people I work with.'

'No, I do appreciate that.' Lorraine was about to respond to what Keith had said but Keith continued before she had a chance.

'OK, I've blown. Let's get back to Katie. She's got difficult stuff to deal with. She's messed up about wanting to be cared for, feeling no-one did care for her in the past, but in her head knowing some people tried and wondering whether she's lost the ability to feel care from anyone.'

'That's a tough place for her to be in.'

'Upside down world. She wants to feel cared for, but, having someone care for her feels like someone having control over her, and she won't have that.'

'There's a great deal going on for her, that's an understatement perhaps, but I want to consider what you need to be available for her. And that physical contact....'

'Yeah, well, maybe that was…, hmm, looking back now, maybe that was in part in response to that period when she was the seven year old. I don't, and I mean, I genuinely don't think I was in that moment totally reaching out to nineteen year old Katie. I think I still had the seven year old with me as well. And I think it may well have confused her. I did pick up on that and say it could be very intense in therapy and that in that context sometimes support was helpful. I need to be aware of all of this. I think I was caught up in the intensity, the hurt, and the sense of the seven year old Katie even though I didn't think that at the time. But now, looking back, it makes sense and feels like that was what was happening. But I need to keep an eye on it.' He paused, thinking back to what Lorraine has asked him.

Lorraine didn't respond, sensing that Keith had more to say.

'What do I need? I don't know. Time to reflect. I need to stay with Katie's own pace of disclosure. I need her to find her own way forward. She doesn't want to be controlled, that is very clear. She doesn't want to be told what to do. She's not able to hear that positively. I maybe need to think about her wider support system, and check out who else she is getting support from and maybe encourage her to think about what else is available. But it has to be support, not control. And somehow, if she has shut down her feelings in terms of being able to feel someone's caring, then that's going to be a difficult area for her. It makes me think of something that I know I've mentioned before, that the relational quality that you didn't have is the one you most need, in therapy or anywhere else. If Katie didn't feel cared for, and let's be straight on this, didn't feel loved, then she may well have shut down not only her capacity to feel others' love for her, if she ever developed it, but also to feel love herself for anyone. So she may well find the unconditional positive regard that I seek to offer her as a therapist confusing, threatening, it is certainly likely to be challenging. I just have a sense of this little girl sitting there desperate to be loved, to feel love. And I can't say that without my eyes watering and feeling a lump in my throat. And I have to remember that Katie is a nineteen year old woman as well. And I am a man, and I do not want any sexual misunderstandings to arise. I don't feel that way towards her, I am clear on that.'

'Being sensitive, being open, being willing to self-question, taking time to really reflect on the process and how it is impacting on you and your responses. Tread carefully, yes?'

'Very, and at the same time be genuine. There's something about the need to be present and to respond to her, and to all my clients, in a genuinely heartfelt way.' This felt very important to Keith.

'Yes. And if you need to get in touch to check anything out between sessions, please do. OK?'

'Sure. Thanks. I'll keep that in mind as well.'

'So, we have explored a lot around your feelings and reactions to Katie, and what she is presenting. Do you feel you need more time to explore anything further?'

Keith shook his head. 'I feel as though I have clarified a number of things and actually I'm feeling quite drained and yet curiously energised as well. Strange, but that's how it is. I just need to keep my focus, not let my desire to make a difference get in the way, and convey the therapeutic attitudinal qualities: warmth and acceptance, empathy and try to be open and authentic myself. But I must watch my reactions. Tread carefully, yes, and I know this, but maybe when it gets intense and I get intense, that gets lost sight of somehow.'

'Like sensitivity to the subtleness can be lost sight of?' Lorraine knew she was using her own words but they were the ones that had come into her mind as Keith had been speaking.

'It is subtle, and whilst a client's reactions can be strong and the pain can be overwhelming, somewhere there is a fragile and sensitive part of them that wants a gentle response, which they so often don't get because they are reacting strongly to whatever is going on around them, and the people trying to help them. I mustn't get caught up in that. I need to hear the pain, the struggle, the whatever Katie brings, and be mindful of that something else that can so easily get missed or not heard.' Keith paused, the goose-bumps were on his back. 'The seven year old Katie. And maybe there are other parts or aspects of Katie still to emerge from an even younger age.' The goose-bumps grew, spreading across his back and up his neck. 'I think it is time to move on as I have a couple of other clients I want to touch base with you about. Is that OK?'

Lorraine nodded. 'I think you have become more accurately and authentically open to what you are experiencing and I believe that will help you to be more fully, and I would say helpfully, present with Katie.' She smiled. 'That feels like a good piece of work.'

The supervision process moved on to another of Keith's clients, but Keith did not forget the discussion and exploration in relation to Katie. It felt good to have processed it all to some degree, and yes it had touched off some of his own deeply felt beliefs and concerns. It was good to air them once in a while. He hadn't been like that in a supervision session for quite some time. He guessed it had built up and maybe something about Katie had just added a little more. There was something about Katie that had got to him. And he was glad. He needed to stay in touch with his own feelings and motivations, but they mustn't distort his experiencing of Katie and what she was communicating to him. He found himself at the end of the supervision session hoping she was OK, and hoping that he would be able to help her become who she needed to be and to be in some way a little freer of the psychologically and emotionally damaging effects of her past.

As Keith drove away from Lorraine's house he was thinking about how people thought therapy was a soft option. If only they knew....

Chapter 7

Keith arrived at the surgery at his usual time. He had five young people to see. It was good that he could see them there. Whilst he knew that it wasn't perhaps the most young person-friendly environment, he did pick up referrals direct from the doctors. They'd got to know him and that seemed to make it easier for them to encourage young people to see him. It was easier for them to recommend that they contact the counselling service, as had been the case with Katie. He felt well integrated into the surgery and had good professional relationships with all the doctors. There were times when he worked particularly closely with the doctor concerned, whilst ensuring that confidentiality was maintained except where his client had agreed to pass information on. He wasn't thinking of anything in particular today as he walked down the corridor to the counselling room.

'Ah, Keith, I need a quick word.'

Keith turned. Dr Armstrong was standing outside her door. She was one of the younger GPs, and quite pro-counselling.

'Sure. New referral?'

'No. I've had a letter from the hospital about one of your clients. She was taken to A&E last week and kept in for observation. You are still seeing Katie, aren't you?'

'Yes, I am, but I do need to keep what she has been telling me in confidence.'

'Yes, I know that, but, well, the liaison psychiatry saw her and they have recognised signs of self-harm, and they want me to keep in touch with her. I've seen her since she was in hospital, she fell over, drinking, banged her head.'

'And the self-harm; cutting?'

Dr Armstrong nodded. 'Not deep, but definite signs on her upper arms.'

'OK, well, look, I'm seeing her today. Don't tell me any more. I'll see if she wants to say anything about it to me. She hasn't mentioned this before but I am not surprised. I think she will need long-term counselling and so I expect it to be a slow process, so don't expect miracles. From what I have gleaned so far she has had a very difficult past.'

'I know a fair bit of the history, and I won't say any more because I know you don't want to get ahead of your clients.'

'No, as you know from my perspective it's best if they tell me what they want me to know as and when they feel ready to do so. But obviously there are some real concerns here. I'll need to tell her what I know, and then invite her to say more if she wishes. Maybe she will, but I don't think it's easy for her. She's not someone who is going to find it easy to trust people. That's why I'll be open, she doesn't need me keeping secrets from her about what I know.'

'Well, I've encouraged her to talk to you about it so whether she will, I don't know. I'm seeing her again later this week. She took quite a bang on the head. Anyway, just wanted to pass this on.'

'Sure, OK, thanks.'

Keith turned and continued on to the counselling room. He had misgivings. It was always difficult to know something about a client when they hadn't told you, and you were seeking to be transparent and open with them. He didn't want to force things out of his clients, but then, if she was cutting, it was now known to others. He was seeing her later and by then he would have decided how best to play it, but he felt sure that the appropriate, professional and ethical way would be to be open from the start and not play games. He knew something. She knew that the A&E people knew and that her doctor knew. It would be ridiculous to try to pretend that things she might now say were somehow new to him.

*

As Keith walked into the waiting room three hours later the first thing he noticed as he looked over to Katie was the rather ugly looking bruise on the left side of her forehead. It looked very painful.

'Katie, come on through when you're ready.'

Katie got up. Her head still did not feel too good, still very tender, but it was better than it had been. She was avoiding sudden movements, though, as they were still uncomfortable. And her neck was stiff and painful as well as her shoulder due to the fall. She followed Keith to the counselling room.

She walked to the chair as Keith closed the door. By the time he turned she was sitting.

'I expect you're wondering?'

'Yes and no. I do know that you fell and have been to the hospital. Dr Armstrong told me.'

'She said she would.' Katie felt and looked pretty fed up about it.

'You rather she hadn't?'

Katie shrugged. 'Doesn't matter, it's what happened. I've fallen over before, I'll probably fall over again.'

'She said you'd been drinking as well. That what caused it?'

'Maybe, I don't know, just got up and tripped and next thing I knew I was on my way to the hospital in an ambulance.'

'And they kept you in?'

'Yeah, and made me see a shrink whilst I was there. Gave me a lecture on drinking. I didn't need that. Said he was going to ask the GP to refer me to somewhere about it, but I told the doc I didn't want that. It's not a problem. She was OK, talked about how it affects you, how it can get out of control. But everyone does it and it makes me feel good. That's how it is.'

'So, the alcohol helps, makes you feel good.'

'Yeah.'

'And just one too many on that occasion, yeah?'

Katie was going to nod but realised immediately that was a mistake. Her head wasn't up to it. 'Yeah.'

'I just want to say that you have to treat alcohol with respect. I know it's everywhere and the pressure is on to drink to be sociable and everything, but it does a lot of damage. If you do want to talk it through a bit more some time, that's OK with me.'

Katie said nothing. She didn't want to talk about it. She'd had a crap week. She hated feeling like she did. She hadn't felt like going out, but it was boring being in. She'd listened to music a lot, and watched some TV. But it had been hard to concentrate to begin with, her head was so sore. And she found it hard to lay comfortably. She'd been given some pain killers and that helped a little. Sitting wasn't too comfortable either. She'd got some big bruises on her shoulder and she found it painful to lift her arm very high. Her neck muscles had been strained in some way as well and that tightness seemed to spread up over her head. The doctor had referred her to a physiotherapist. She was OK with that if it helped. But it was the other matter that concerned her. She'd promised to talk to Keith about it when the doctor had raised it. It wasn't what she wanted to do.

Keith knew what he needed to say. 'There was one other matter that Dr Armstrong mentioned.'

Here we go, thought Katie.

'And I know it's something you haven't told me about, and I respect that. But I need you to know that I know that the hospital reported signs of self-harm, of cutting.'

Katie looked miserable. She was going to get told off, she knew it, told to stop, told it was wrong. She really didn't need that. Why didn't anyone understand that it helped her to feel better.

'I know people cut for all kinds of reasons and that's your business. If you want to talk about it, then that's fine by me and I'll listen and maybe we can find some other ways of you achieving what it gives you. It's up to you, yeah?' Keith sought to convey his genuine acceptance of Katie's choice to cut, although he was aware as well that his equally genuine hope that she would find other ways of coping that could be less harmful was probably affecting his tone of voice and facial expression. Keith knew that for many young people cutting was a kind of resource used to simply survive. Without it, he was sure the suicide and attempted suicide rate would be a lot higher. He'd read somewhere that over 4,000 children under 14 were admitted to hospitals in England over the 12 month period to March 2007 after attempting to kill themselves.

Katie tightened her lips. She didn't want to say anything and she didn't want to nod her head either.

'And I know it's something you had been choosing not to tell me, and it's a secret that's been forced into the open. And I know secrets can be important, we can like to have secrets, particularly if we've gone through life with little space of our own. When people find something out before you are ready to tell, them well, that can be extremely upsetting, disturbing, it affects people in different ways. Anyway, these are things I wanted to say to keep things open.' Keith felt that he had said what he had wanted to say. He'd thought about it before the session but hadn't tried to formulate the exact words. He wanted to be open to the moment and to express himself in response to how he was experiencing being with Katie. He wasn't going to say any more on the matter, Katie had enough to make sense of and come to terms with in her life and he wasn't going to take over the counselling session with somebody else's agenda. Yes, cutting was a risk, but so was drinking which above certain limits could also be called 'self-harm'. Life was full of risks, walking out alone at night was a risk. He didn't encourage cutting, but he could appreciate why for some people it could have a positive effect on how they felt. But he also acknowledged to himself that he would always want to help someone find another way if he could and if it was what they wanted.

Katie had listened to what Keith had been saying. He did seem genuine and he wasn't having a go at her about it. But it didn't feel like something she wanted to talk about, or think about.

'You told me to take care of myself last week. Didn't do a good job, did I.'

'Well, things happen.'

'Shit happens.'

'That how it feels?'

'Yeah. Shit life, you know?'

'Only what you've told me.'

'Yeah, what happened last week. I felt pissed off with you. Wanted to get out of my head.'

'I know you were pissed off with me.'

'Telling me to take care.'

'It's what I said. I meant it. You'd had a tough session.'

'Felt like you were telling me what to do.'

'Didn't intend that.'

'Wouldn't have got pissed and fallen over.'

'My fault?'

'Yeah, sort of, not really. Just, you know, that's how it was.'

Keith nodded slightly. 'Yeah, how it was.' He paused. He was about to ask how Katie wanted to use the session but she had begun speaking.

'Had a lot of time to think this week. Couldn't do much else, haven't felt up to it.'

'Mhmm. Anything in particular been with you?'

If her shoulder hadn't been so sore Katie would have shrugged. But she couldn't so she pulled a face. 'Last week, what the hell was that about?'

'What in particular?'

'I really hurt, and I don't want to go there this week. I don't want anything too heavy.'

'Sure, I can appreciate that. You're feeling rough enough as it is.' Keith hadn't got a problem with what Katie was saying. She must feel awful, he thought to himself, the very fact that she had made it said something, unless she was under pressure from Dr Armstrong to attend. 'Therapy can unleash powerful and disturbing emotions, memories, all kinds of things. We take it slowly. No rush, no pushing, at your pace, yeah, you choose where you go, what you talk about.' Keith was aware of thinking back to the previous session and the way Katie had been with the emerging part of herself from her early life. Yes, he knew that could be disturbing to the person experiencing it in the present.

Well that felt good to hear, Katie thought to herself as she listed to what Keith said. 'Yeah.'

'So, you want to talk about last week? Or is there anything else more pressing?'

'I want to make sense of last week. Hearing myself speak like that. That was, shit, that was really, I don't know. Was that really me?'

'Did it feel like you?' Keith seemed to feel that they were saying something similar to what they had said the previous week, a kind of déjà vu.

'Yeah, it did. But I was sort of listening, and I was talking as well, except it wasn't me, but it was me. I can't make sense of it, I don't know, I just…, I don't know. Feels kind of weird, I mean really weird. That stuff happen a lot?'

'I don't know about a lot, but it happens.' Keith was aware not everyone had the degree of traumatic experiencing in their past that created that kind of fragmentation within the self. But he also suspected that it was more common than was generally thought.

Katie thought for a moment. Her head was beginning to ease a little, and her shoulder too. She'd taken a couple of the pain killers before she'd left and they were kicking in.

'And it was me, I mean, is that how it was? We've all got, I don't know, voices inside us?' Katie found it hard to really make sense of it because it had felt so real and yet like nothing she had ever experienced before. It was also quite disturbing, leaving her feeling unsure of herself, of who she was. She didn't like that feeling, but it was there.

'It's a way of looking at it.' Keith sensed that the tone of the session might be more around talking about what had happened rather than re-connecting with those areas of Katie's structure or sense of self.

'But who am I?'

'Big question, who am I?' Keith's response was quite matter of fact. It was a serious question and he wanted to convey his hearing of that seriousness in his tone of voice.

'Am I me now, or me then?'

'Maybe both, maybe the you now also contains the you then, part of what makes you who you are. It's just you hadn't really heard that part until now.'

'Like I didn't really know who I am. Like a bit of me that exists but I hadn't realised how much.' Katie paused and frowned, but only slightly as it was painful to tighten her forehead. 'So it's like that bit of me got sort of locked up inside?'

'Something like that.'

'I mean, I had a shit time but I didn't realise, you know. I mean, I felt so much. I sort of know about what happened but since last week I've felt it more.'

'Feelings that have been locked up, or that you've not allowed yourself to experience, that kind of thing?'

'Shit.' Katie eased herself back in the chair. It eased a little of the stiffness and wasn't too painful. A thought was with her, and it was something she'd thought about on-and-off during the week, but she hadn't really come up with an answer to it. 'So, I mean, OK, so part of me…,' she felt confused, not sure how to put her thoughts into words.

Keith saw the confused look and responded. 'It's confusing, not easy to get hold of. Part of you…?'

'Part of me that I don't know about sort of, I don't know, is there, suddenly, like it was. Like it's been sort of hidden away somehow, somewhere. That right?'

'Something like that.'

'So, I mean, if, yeah, if one part of me can be sort of hidden like that, I mean, you know, shit, what else?' Katie stumbled through the words to the question that was really nagging at her. What else wasn't she aware of?

'Yeah, what else, what else don't we know about ourselves.' Keith was aware that he had generalised rather than focused specifically on Katie. Why had he done that? Was he trying to make it easier on her rather than really directly empathising. He should have empathised. Katie was owning her wondering about what else might exist in her, and she was focusing on herself. He needed to trust her to be able to handle the awesome nature of what she was speculating upon. He added another sentence, 'and for you its what you might not be aware of about you'. What he didn't want to do was in any way to encourage any kind of emphasis that might mean he put ideas in her head. He didn't want to create the possibility of false memories but at the same time he also knew that false memories were unlikely where genuinely traumatic experiencing had occurred. As he had said in supervision, he needed to tread carefully, and sensitively.

'But I know me, and then suddenly I sort of don't know any more that I do know me.'

Keith nodded. It was a difficult thing to make sense of, even to do so intellectually, let alone when it was your own sense of self that was in question. 'Yes, you thought you knew yourself and then suddenly something new is there.'

'I feel…, I don't know how to describe it…, confused, sort of, but more. I don't know, sort of lost. And yet.., yeah, lost.'

'Mhmm, somehow lost in who you are, you mean?'

Katie went silent. She wasn't sure how much of what she was feeling was as a result of what had happened the previous week in counselling, or the bang on her head. She knew she just felt pretty grim, a bit like after a really heavy drinking session, only worse. 'I just feel really shit at the moment.'

Keith wondered what Katie meant. It was a word that could mean so many different things to different people.

'Mhmm, and I guess I'm wondering what shit means for you at the moment.'

'Weird, like I'm really hungover but worse. Like everything's sort of spinning around and, yeah....'

'And that puts you, your head, everything, in a spin.'

'I don't need any more of that.'

'No.' Keith wondered for a moment at how Katie's accident had coincided with what she was now having to think about. Yeah, her head really had been put in a spin, physically and psychologically. But to Katie it felt more than just her head. She felt in a spin; and she felt sad. That had also been something she'd felt more of this past week.

'I felt sad.'

'Sad?'

'Last week. I mean, yeah, I was upset, but I felt sad, you know, listening to myself. I mean....' Katie couldn't help frowning and that was uncomfortable. She took a deep breath, moving her head slightly and slowly from one side of the other. 'Yeah, really sad.'

'So did I.' Keith's response was delivered slowly and very much from the heart. Yes, and he knew that from his supervision session it had affected him more than he had realised at the time.

'You felt sad?'

'I felt my sadness, but your sadness was special, it was deep, and very personal.' Keith knew he had to bring the focus back on to Katie sadness.

'I did want them to stop but they never would.'

'No, they just kept going at you.'

'No escape.'

'No, no escape.'

Katie took a deep breath. She felt strange, a kind of buzzing in her head, like she was a little bit high, and that on top of everything else she was experiencing. She felt sort of suspended, like she was watching herself but from the inside, and in slow motion. At least, that's how it felt and yet things weren't going slow. She heard the voice again. 'Help me escape.' She didn't feel alarmed. It wasn't such a shock this time. But she felt the feelings, the sense of being trapped, of not being liked, of being taunted and pushed around. Yeah, she could feel all those things. She didn't know if she had heard the words or spoken them or both. But she couldn't sort of find out, somehow. She was looking at Keith but somehow not really taking in what was happening. She heard his voice.

'Someone to help you escape?' Keith had heard the change in Katie's tone of voice. He made sure his response was spoken softly, and clearly.

Katie felt a huge yearning for someone to help her escape. She wanted to say "yes". She then heard the voice saying 'yes', that oh so childlike voice. 'I don't like it here. Take me away.'

'You would like to be taken away.'

'Yes I would.' Katie felt herself swallow. She wanted to take herself away. She wanted to take that part of herself that was speaking away. But she couldn't, she didn't know how. What was she thinking? It was like it was part of herself but she couldn't reach out to that part. There was a kind of invisible barrier between them. And yet she felt what was there, the pain, the isolation, the despair. They were her experiences as well. 'I want to go somewhere nice.'

'Somewhere nice. What would that be like?' Keith was speaking softly, slowly, he felt as though he was putting his heart and soul into what he was saying.

'Safe, warm, nice people.' The voice sounded so small, so helpless.

'Safe and warm with nice people.'

Katie was nodding. She realised she wasn't aware of any physical pain and suddenly felt a tremendous rush of feeling. It was a new feeling, she didn't know what it was, and she wanted to speak. She felt the urge and the rush of feeling sort of carried the words out of her mouth. She heard them but wasn't sure if she had spoken them. 'I'll take you away, I'll look after you.'

Keith heard Katie's adult voice speaking, and he could feel the goose-bumps breaking out. His own eyes were full of tears. There was silence in the room, a very silent silence.

The voice had gone, and the strange sense of being somehow watching herself had also faded away. Katie sat blinking. She knew that it had happened again but this time it had been different. She felt like she had been sort of communicating with herself in some way. Last time she'd been too shocked. She didn't say anything. She didn't feel any urge to say anything. She just felt like she just needed to sit and not even to think. No, she didn't want to think. She didn't want to do anything. Just sit, just be still, be very, very still.

Keith respected the silence and the stillness that had emerged. It was as though there was nothing to say. What had happened had happened. It needed to be allowed to just be. The voice had sounded the same as the previous week, though a little more pleading and desperate. He didn't know what had happened. It felt sudden. Hearing Katie's adult voice seemed to stop everything, somehow. He didn't know what he meant by that. And he didn't want to keep thinking about it either. It didn't feel right. Somehow, and he couldn't explain why, the moment commanded silence. He set his thoughts aside.

Katie had never experienced anything like what was happening for her. The simple fact was that nothing was happening, and yet in a strange way everything was happening as well. She had never felt this calm, this still. She didn't want to move. She wasn't thinking about moving, she wasn't thinking, yet she was being. She still felt somewhat spaced out and she could hear the silence, it was intense. Yes, she knew her hands were in her lap, she could see them, and yes, they did feel…, no, they didn't feel like her hands because she sort of didn't feel them. They were there, they were hers, that was all that mattered.

She was aware that around the edges of her vision it was slightly blurred, but she wasn't looking, or thinking about it, just aware of it. She could feel her breathing, the air coming into the airway at the back of her nose. It wasn't warm or cold, it was just there, a sensation. She couldn't feel it going into her lungs, but she could feel her chest expanding and contracting. It felt very steady and rhythmic. She could just stay with that rhythm it seemed like forever. That's all there was, her awareness of herself, the sense of the air in back of her throat and the movement of her chest.

She felt the depth of her breathing beginning to increase. It was as though more air was rushing in and out. It felt good. She still felt that stillness, that calmness. There was a sensation in her feet. She'd sort of forgotten about them. And she was aware of blinking. She deliberately blinked more tightly and took a deeper breath. She was more aware of her body now, of the stiffness in her shoulder and neck, and the slight ache in her head. The tablets were still taking the edge off it. But it also seemed different as well. She seemed different. She looked at Keith. He responded to her look.

'How are you feeling?'

'OK.'

'Mhmm.'

There wasn't much more to say about it. She felt OK. Still a little spaced out, but that was OK. She felt strange but OK. 'It was different this time.'

'You experienced a difference.'

'I felt sad again, but I felt something else and I don't know what it was but I wanted to reach out, I so wanted to reach out.'

'To?'

'Me, the voice, that part of me that was there.'

'It sounded to me like you did reach out to her.'

'I lost track of what was being said. I don't know if the words were thoughts or actually words.'

'I heard you respond, and it felt deeply heartfelt, and it was deeply moving to hear you.'

'I'll take you away. I'll take care of you?'

Keith nodded, feeling his own goose-bumps once again.

'I know I felt myself wanting to say the words, and I know I heard them I just wasn't sure that I had said them.'

'You did, and,' Keith continued as another wave of goose-bumps went up over his head, down his back and into his arms, 'I think Katie heard you'.

'I wanted…', Katie went silent. It sounded crazy but it wasn't and somehow she knew it wasn't. She swallowed, her throat was dry. She reached over to the glass of water and raised it to her lips, sipping slowly. She put it back, and cleared her throat. 'I wanted her to hear me?' The slight questioning tone was there because Katie really wasn't sure what to make of what she was saying, or how Keith was going to respond.

'Mhmm, you wanted her to hear you.'

'And it wasn't just that. I really wanted to take her and look after her… me.' The silence returned. Katie was taking a deep breath. 'I was reaching out to me. I felt….' She didn't know what it was. 'It was like…', Katie frowned, 'it was like a …, a wave. Like it just…', she paused again, 'like it just seemed to pour through me. And I stopped feeling sad'.

Keith swallowed, more goose-bumps. 'Mhmm, that wave stopped the sadness.'

'I felt, I don't know, sort of whole somehow. I really don't know how to describe it.'

'That sense of somehow feeling more whole.' Keith maintained his empathic responding, enabling Katie to explore her experience a little more.

'There was a kind of, "yeah, it's OK", you know?'

'Something felt really OK.'

'I don't know how else to describe it.'

'OK, but hard to describe, and is it still with you?'

Katie nodded. 'Yes, yes it is. Maybe not as much, but yeah. And calm too.'

'So there's a calmness as well as a wholeness and an OKness.'

'And afterwards, when I was sitting there. I wasn't really thinking. I wasn't really anything, and yet I felt incredibly, I don't know, alive I suppose. Like I was really there even though I wasn't sort of doing anything.' Katie hoped she was making sense. She felt as though she was describing what she experienced but it was so new that she wasn't sure whether Keith would understand. It seemed somehow important that he did understand. Her thoughts went back to what had happened, to hearing herself speaking, that wanting to reach out. She felt emotional now, thinking about it. It wasn't a distress, an anguish or a pain behind the tears that began to seep out over her eyelids. It was something else, something different, something that she could not describe. But it was very present. It seemed to be centred in her heart, a kind of tickly pressure, but it was wider than that as well.

'Like you were really there, really alive.'

Katie heard Keith's response. The calmness that had been part of her experience remained and yet she also felt suddenly uncertain.

'What's happening to me?' She blinked as she spoke, sending teardrops down her cheeks. She looked at Keith who seemed to somehow convey a kind of understanding, even though he wasn't saying a great deal.

Keith knew instinctively what he needed to say. And it wasn't a case of deciding whether it was the right thing to say or not, it commanded him to voice it. 'I think you've just experienced caring, real caring, compassion maybe, towards yourself.'

'I've never felt like this. I feel very different.'

'Mhmm, a very different experience, but very real.'

'Oh yes, very real. More real than…' Katie paused. Hmm, she thought to herself, more real than everything. And that seemed in one sense too much but at the same time seemed absolutely right.

'More real than?'

'Everything.'

'That good, huh?'

'Yeah.'

Keith smiled. Yes, he thought, something had broken through into Katie's awareness and experience, something that was a marked contrast to what she usually experienced. He knew that people had all kinds of names for these kinds of experiences, and some people hung a 'spiritual' label on them as well. Maybe it was, he didn't know. It wasn't a word that Katie had used and he wasn't going to introduce it. For her it was about calm, wholeness, and feeling very real. Maybe something had shifted. And it was somehow related to that spontaneous response she had made towards that hurt and damaged part of herself. He thought of the theory that he applied in his therapeutic work and the concept of 'unconditional positive self-regard', self love but not the selfish kind. Maybe, perhaps, Katie had experienced something of that, and perhaps for the first time in her life. If so, he did not underestimate the likely impact, and what might happen once it began to fade. Her concept of self which might be of being someone who was unloved and unlovable may have left her feeling incapable of experiencing love. Perhaps now this was being challenged. Something in Katie had caused this to be the time for this to happen and he knew he trusted the inherent wisdom and timeliness of that process. His job was to co-operate with that and to not say or do anything to obstruct the inner psychological and emotional processes occurring within his her.

Katie stayed quiet. The truth was she did not want to lose what she was feeling. It was good. She didn't want to think about it much, just be in it, as it were. She hoped it would last forever, it was like being high but softer somehow. Yes, intense, but soft at the same time. Weird but not unsettlingly so. Quite peaceful in many ways. Peace. Was that what she had found? Was it that easy? She wasn't convinced. But for now it was a good place to be. She smiled.

Keith was struck by the thought that although he had noticed Katie smile before, it hadn't been quite like it was now. The thinness and paleness in her face was less obvious. She seemed to have a slight glow. He felt good himself. Yes, he thought, therapy isn't all about pain and upset, though he knew often it was. He recognised that there were times when metaphorically the sun came out from behind the clouds, long enough to bathe you in its warm rays and bright light. But then how quickly the clouds could return and feel thicker than before. That could be a desperate time. Was that ahead of Katie? He noted the thought and put it aside.

'You look quite peaceful with that smile on your face.'

'That's how I feel, but it's losing its intensity now. I guess it would be too much to hope to stay like that.'

'We'd spend all day sitting and smiling, and that's OK when it happens.'

'But I've got to cope with everything as well, haven't I?'

'Life, the universe and stuff out there, you mean?'

'Out there. In here.' Katie tapped the side of her head with her right forefinger. 'Yeah. I wish my life was different. I'm not feeling it like I do sometimes, but I sort of do know I'm, you know, messed up with it all, in spite of this.'

'And that's a tough thing to think about.'

'I don't want to be like that. I want to feel good, to feel normal. To just, I don't know…, I guess that's the problem.'

'That you don't know?'

Katie tightened her lips and nodded slightly. She was becoming more aware of the stiffness in her neck and the discomfort in her shoulder. She'd been sitting still for a while and had become quite stiff. She moved her back and winced as a sharp pain ran down her arm from her shoulder. 'Oooh.'

'Painful?'

'Yeah.' Katie found herself thinking back to the previous week. She felt so different now. She wouldn't have believed it. So much had happened, she thought to herself, or at least, another thought was with her, that not much had really happened, it had been a typical week only more painful, and in fact she'd done less than usual. But now she felt like so much *had* happened. A thought came to her mind. She felt her expression change and Keith noticed it too.

'You don't suppose this is all the result of me banging my head?' She was wondering if it was some strange brain thing that was happening to her.

'Does it feel like that to you?'

'No.' Katie felt sure about it once she heard Keith ask the question. Strange, one minute you think something and then the next moment you think something else. No, it seemed more than the effect of just a bang on the head. It all felt too real. Hearing herself speaking as a child, and hearing herself respond, and the wave of feeling and then that calmness. No, that all felt very real and not something she was going to easily forget.

There was some 20 minutes or so of the session left but Katie felt like she wanted to make her way home. Although the feelings were not as intense they were still present and she sort of wanted to take them home with her. Crazy idea, she thought to herself, but it was what she felt she wanted to do. She also felt tired. It was the first time she'd been out for any time since the fall, apart from seeing the doctor, and she felt like she just wanted to go back and lay down for a while.

'I feel like I want to head off and lay down for a bit, is that OK?'

'Sure. You've had quite a week, and quite a session today as well. So take it carefully.' Keith knew what he had said though he had said it slightly differently to the previous week.

Katie was in a very different place in herself and did not hear it as being someone telling her what to do or how to be. She wanted to take it carefully.

Keith continued to speak. 'You've become in a way perhaps more sensitive so out there may feel a little harsh. You might want to be aware of that.' Keith wanted to convey his concern that the contrast between the kind of intense quiet and calm that had developed within

Katie would be very much in contrast to what might be her experience once she left the counselling room.

'Yes, I will, thanks.'

They agreed to meet again the following week at the same time and Katie left. She confirmed that she was seeing the doctor again in a couple of days and Keith was glad to know that. He felt that it would be good for Katie to have someone to see during the week, someone to check she was OK and, yeah, the thought came to him as well, someone to convey some care for her.

On leaving, Katie did notice the difference. The world seemed noisier and yet she also felt a little distant from it, in a little bit of a protective bubble. She hoped it would last.

Keith sat back in his chair and stretched himself out. That had been another intense session yet with a completely different tone to it. He reflected back on his experience. His sense of self had somehow expanded and yet become more focused during that period when that younger part of Katie – was that the right way to describe it – had become present. Yes, it wasn't just the client that was affected. He smiled. It felt good to be touched by another human being in that way. The connection, the psychological interaction, being together on a client's experiential edge took him to his own edge as well. It changed him, enhanced his own sensitivities and appreciation of the marvel of the human person.

His thoughts turned to Katie. Something had touched her, and touched her deeply. Something had come into her awareness that was new to her and he felt pleased about that. A new experience for her to grow with, or into, he wasn't sure how best to express it. He thought about the concept of people having a tendency to become more fully their potential, the term to describe it from a person-centred perspective was 'an actualising tendency' – a kind of inner drive that is intrinsically present within the person to achieve the best they can, to fulfill their potential, but it could become blocked or distorted by negative experiences or other peoples' perspectives or expectations that could then undermine the person's sense of self, and lead to the person gaining a sense of fulfillment from quite damaging actions and behaviours.

He thought of the notion of everyone being in a *process*, as if you were not so much fixed and solid but fluid and moving. He knew that could seem like a rather strange concept, but it reminded him of something he had read many years ago, written by David Bohm, the theoretical physicist, something about how we are a very noun-based world, and that maybe we should think more in terms of verbs. It was the concept of thinking about trees not as fixed objects, but as being 'a process of treeing' that had made the impression on him. Flowers were 'flowering', the sun was 'sunning' and people, well, rather than a fixed human being we are each a process of 'human being'. He liked that. And it always made him smile when he thought about it. It somehow made the world more fluid and therefore less fixed, and for Keith fluidity meant opportunity for growth, change, and to become more than what we are. Yes, he thought, we are actually 'peopling' or 'personning'; our fixity is an illusion that we get caught up in.

And Katie? She was being Katie, being who and how she needed to be based on how she saw and experienced herself and those around her – in the past and in the present. Maybe she was becoming a little more fluid herself. Maybe she was experiencing caring, or compassion as he had mentioned to her in the session. Or maybe it was love; love for herself, or at least part of herself, a part that had been bereft of love, of being cared for. Was this the first step in her healing process? The thought gave him goose-bumps again. He realised he was quite prone to them, particularly when he was thinking about experiences that seemed to have deep meaning or significance in some way. He was glad that he had that kind of sensitivity.

He guessed that at some point during the week and maybe quite soon, the experience Katie was having would fade. Would it leave her feeling good? He hoped so, but he also knew that the structure of self wasn't to be changed that easily. Too many patterns of thought, feeling and reaction had been established over the years. Some might prefer to think of it in terms of neural pathways having been laid down. Yes, he knew people could have intense experiences that could seemingly bring about instant change, but he was sure they were rare. Often the intensity faded and the person returned to how they were, though now at least a little more aware of what was possible, and what they might now work towards. But he also knew that some would crash. The contrast would be too much, the loss too intense. The clouds would return and settle and the presence of the sun would be doubted. A dark and all enveloping depression could arise. He hoped that would not be the case for Katie, but he could appreciate that it might be the case.

Chapter 8

The week had begun well enough for Katie. The good feelings from the previous therapy session had stayed with her up to the weekend. She had seen Dr Armstrong who had been pleased that she was talking positively about the therapy and how it was affecting her. It had been over the weekend that Katie's mood had begun to slide. A heavy drinking session on the Friday night had not helped matters and by Saturday her mood was on the way down. The 'high' she had been experiencing, that sense of wholeness and calm, had now faded, and a more familiar gloom had started to descend upon her. She had been drinking more during Saturday, spending time in a bar where she had met a guy who she had then spent the night with. It had met a need to have someone close to her, to feel some intimacy, but there was no love in what happened between them. It was a case of two people meeting each other's sexual needs, an intense high except that for Katie it was meeting another need as well, the need for a sense of having someone close, holding her, making her feel wanted, however temporary the feeling. That was how it had been for Katie for some while. That deep need to have someone care about her and give her some attention would take over, particularly when she was alcohol-affected, as though the alcohol opened her to that needy part of herself. Sex was the only way she had learned to meet that need, except that whilst it did to a point at the time, it rarely lasted for long.

It was Sunday now and Katie had returned to her room. It was a wet day, the kind of Sunday that does very little for a person's mood even at the best of times, and these weren't the best of times for Katie. Her mood was in a bad place. She wasn't experiencing the feelings she had when she felt as though her head would explode, when she needed to feel some kind of release to reduce the tension within her. No, this was different. In fact, what she was experiencing was in many ways quite the opposite. She was actually feeling less and less, in fact the phrase 'dark and empty numbness' would have described what she was feeling. Not that she thought like that when she was in this state of mind. The truth was, she didn't really think much at all when she was like this. It was more a matter of being in suspended animation, as if her consciousness was put on hold, but it was a depressed hold. She felt no sense of wanting to do anything, but she did have enough self-awareness to know that she hated how she felt and that she wanted to escape from it, find some other experience to enable her to break free. It was also a state in which she felt she had very little energy. That didn't help. She knew that there were times when she could be like this for days. When it was like that she didn't care. Nothing mattered, and she certainly did not feel as if *she* mattered.

Katie couldn't recall the feelings she'd had from the last therapy session. They were a distant and very hazy memory now, far out of her reach as she lay on the bed. She had her music on, but it wasn't that she was really listening to it. That too was distant even though it was loud in her ears. She stared at the ceiling, looking at the cracks in the paint. She wasn't thinking about what she was seeing, it was just that they were there and she could see them and somewhere there existence registered in her awareness.

The rain continued against the window. It was getting quite dark. She felt heavy, tired, hungry and quite empty inside. Emptiness. She wasn't thinking about it, it was simply present as she lay there. It was as though it pervaded all that she was experiencing. She had no sense of time passing. An uncontrollable urge to roll on her side and lift her knees up caused her to move. There was no real thought about her movement. She held her knees to herself. It was a position she often adopted when she felt this way.

Her thoughts were back in her past. The times she had spent alone and cold, uncertain as to what was going to happen next. Always alone, no-one caring for her, at least that was how it had been for her first few years. Cold, hungry, empty inside. She would either lie in her bed clutching hold of her dolly and teddy bear, or sit in the lounge, propped up against the wall in the corner. In both positions she had her knees up. She needed contact with her body, something to make her feel a little less separate from everything, something to try and relieve the sense of being so very alone.

She didn't know how long she had laid there, Katie had no sense of time passing when she was in this state of mind. Was it simply a state of mind? There were her feelings to consider as well, though in so many ways they had shut down. The darkness spread both in her room and within her sense of self. She had mixed feelings about being in a dark room. Sometimes it was OK. At other times she hated it and had to have a light on. She couldn't explain why. Now she felt she needed to be in the dark, to let it take her wherever it wanted. This was generally the case when she was experiencing the darkness within her as well. She didn't care. She wanted to sleep. She wanted to get away from what she was experiencing and yet, at the same time, there was such a familiarity with what was happening for her that she also didn't want to lose it. There was a strange comfort in that familiarity even though she hated how she felt; the dark heaviness within and around her, seemingly pinning her into a state of physical and psychological immobility.

It was about an hour later when she awoke. She had drifted off to sleep, but had no idea for how long. She still felt the oppressive darkness but now she felt distinctly uneasy as well. She needed the light on. The darkness around her seemed suddenly threatening, as if it was going to swallow her up in some menacing way. Katie closed her eyes. The darkness from having her eyes closed always felt different to the darkness of a room when they were open. There were times when she would welcome this but not at this moment. She rolled over and reached out for the pull cord. She found it and heard the reassuring click and felt the light glowing through her still closed eyes. She lay for a moment, glad to have that sense of light. She tightened her lips, still feeling uneasy and wanting relief from the claustrophobic darkness that was still enveloping her. She knew that it didn't matter how bright the light in the room might be, in truth it never permeated inside her. Yes, it brought light into her eyes and it touched her skin, but it never cleared the inner darkness. She needed a sharper focus to engage with to do that.

She pushed herself up, lowering her feet over the side of the bed. She felt a bit dizzy. As she slowly got to her feet she realised just how unsteady she was feeling. She walked over to the chest of draws and opened the top draw. The razor blade sat where she had left it on top of the flannel. She picked them both up, and kicked the box of tissues that was on the floor closer to the side of the bed. Her movements would have seemed to an outsider to have been almost zombie-like, as if she was mesmerised in some way. She sat back down on the side of the bed. She knew that she needed to feel something sharp, something that would, quite literally, cut through the heavy darkness. She pulled the sleeve of her tee shirt up a little higher. The scars from the previous cuts were now visible on her upper arm. She paused for a moment, looking back down at the blade. It looked very cold and hard, and strangely distant, almost unreal, and yet it was her friend as well, a very close friend. It wasn't that she thought like this all of the time, but when she cut she could feel this way. It was borne out of a familiar knowing that the blade would give her a good feeling. Yes, it was her friend. She picked it up carefully and with a certain deliberateness, holding it between the thumb and forefinger of her right hand. She gritted her teeth and closed her eyes.

As she opened her eyes she lifted her hand, pressing the blade against the skin on her upper arm, carefully selecting an old scar, healed now, and pressed the corner of the blade until it broke the skin. She took a short, sharp intake of breath. Yes it hurt, of course it hurt, but it felt good as well. She drew the blade across her arm, slicing the skin as she did so. She saw the droplets of blood bubbling up. She withdrew the blade and looked at the cut. It stung and gave her an experience that took her away from her inner, oppressive state. Yes, she needed that sharpness. She needed to not only feel the sharp stinging but also see the blood, her blood. It looked so red, almost shining somehow. She put the blade down on the flannel and reached down for a tissue. She felt light headed as she reached over, but it passed as quickly as it had come upon her. She took a tissue and dabbed it against the scar, pausing only to take it away and look at the blood that was soaking into it. She looked back at the red line on her arm. She took a deep breath and smiled to herself. Yes, she needed this. She was also feeling familiar sensations in her stomach, not butterflies exactly, but a kind of tickly sensation. The stinging in her arm continued, she held both sensations in her awareness, closed her eyes once again and took a deep breath.

Katie must have sat there for ten minutes or so. She did feel some relief but she was also aware that the heaviness remained close, too close. When she was like this it never seemed that far away. But the cutting did make a difference to it, even if it seemed to be slight once the initial cut had been made. The sensation in her stomach had persisted.

She rarely cut more than once, it wasn't her style, her habit. But it was necessary sometimes and this was one of those times. She just knew she needed more. It was the intensity, the sharp intensity in contrast to the heavy and swirling blackness that had closed in on her. But she wanted the sensation to be distinctive, not lost in the sting from her already damaged left arm. She didn't often cut on her right arm, but today she knew that she was going to. She just needed more sensation. There was a kind of boost she felt from it and she rolled her tee shirt sleeve higher up on her right arm and picked up the blade in her left hand. Again, she selected the spot carefully, and again it was on the scar of a previous cut. For some reason this time it was more painful, she had less control with her left hand and had cut deeper and with more hesitation. It wasn't what she had hoped for but nevertheless it was what she felt she needed. There was no doubt that it did cause the heaviness to lift a little. This time the sensations in her stomach were more pronounced and her heart was thumping more. She put the blade down and picked up another tissue, pausing only to again look at the blood seeping from the cut. There was a sense of feeling more alive. She couldn't rationalise it, and in truth she wasn't trying to. She just knew that this felt better than how it had been in the swirling darkness that had been enveloping her. Yes, she had a stinging pain in both her upper arms now, but she could feel her heart beating too, and she could feel a particular thrill in her body, giving her a different, and somewhat compelling, experience of herself. She couldn't have explained it, she just knew that she felt more alive, more alert. Katie knew she wasn't going to sleep again, not now. She wanted to hold on to what she was feeling.

*

At the surgery the following week, Keith had already been called out by the receptionist. Katie got up as he walked into the waiting area and she followed him to the counselling room.

'How do you want to use our time today, Katie?', he asked as they sat down opposite each other in the counselling room. He thought about asking about her head, but had decided not to direct her there, rather to keep the start of the session very much open so that Katie could focus on whatever she wanted to address. He had thought about the previous session and was aware that they hadn't talked about her cutting, but he also recognised that other important experiences had occurred in that previous session and Katie had clearly still been affected by her fall. It was in his mind to say something at some point in the session, if only in order to convey his concern and positive regard for her, though he did not want to in any way undermine Katie's autonomy in choosing what she wanted to talk about and what she needed to do in order to cope, if that was her reason.

Katie had spent time herself thinking about the session as well, though mainly prior to the weekend. She was afraid that if she spoke about her cutting Keith might try to make her stop. And she knew she didn't want that, at least she didn't want to have to be without it because it was so important to her. It helped her get through, let go, feel different, free herself up a little. And yet she also knew, though it wasn't something she thought about when she cut, that she had to find another way. She couldn't keep doing what she did, it wasn't an answer, not a permanent one. She knew that, but she hadn't talked about it before. The nurse at the hospital and her doctor, yes, they'd both asked her about it but she hadn't said much. She'd said that it wasn't a problem, wasn't like she wanted to really damage herself, anything like that. Both had warned her, told her of the dangers, infection, cutting a large vein or worse. But she'd thought, 'fuck them'. She was a survivor. She'd had to put up with so much throughout her life and she'd survived; she was going to do it her way. That was how it was. And yet…, there was that small but insistent voice within her that said that she had to change, had to find other ways.

'Dunno', was her response to Keith. It was an honest response, she didn't know. What Katie did know was that she didn't want to end up feeling worse, that was for sure.

146

'Don't know what to do with the time we have?' Keith's empathy held Katie on her not knowing and the slight questioning tone to his response invited her to say more, if she wanted to.

Katie felt anxious. She was clasping her hands together in front of her, but they weren't still. Keith noticed the movement and wondered if Katie was going to start to pick at her thumbs again as she had done in the earlier sessions. She looked tense. He offered what he was experiencing. 'You seem tense to me, though I could be wrong.'

Katie took a deep breath. It was quite involuntary, a reaction from somewhere within her to Keith acknowledging her tension.

'Guess so.'

'More so than usual, maybe.' Keith just sensed that there was something different but he wasn't sure what.

Katie shrugged. She had been looking down at the floor since she had sat down. She continued in that manner.

Keith sensed a need to be very alert. It wasn't that he made himself become that way, it was a kind of natural and spontaneous reaction. Something about how Katie was being was having an impact on him. He noted it and stayed with it. 'Feels quite intense.'

Katie's heart was pounding. She didn't like it. It felt very uncomfortable. She swallowed, her mouth and throat had gone very dry, almost as though her body was making it difficult for her to talk, even if she had wanted to. She sniffed, and swallowed again.

'Shit week.'

'Yeah?'

Katie nodded.

'Want to talk about it?' Keith offered the invitation warmly though in a fairly matter of fact way. This wasn't by design, it was just the way that he responded. He was convinced that the best therapists were often those that sounded least like a therapist. He was honest enough with himself to know that he didn't always achieve this.

'Not much to say, really.'

Keith forced himself not to smile. How many times had he heard that. 'Not much to say about it, huh?'

'The usual.'

'Mhmm, just another usual shit week.'

Katie took another deep breath. Yeah, she thought, yeah. Something strange hearing someone else summing up your week for you. She wanted to say something more. She didn't want it to sound like it was all that bad, she didn't want to think that herself, not really. She wanted something to feel good about. 'Had a few drinks, few laughs, though'. It wasn't really what she was thinking or feeling, but she said it anyway, as much to experience saying something rather than more silence.

'Mhmm, few drinks, few laughs, so maybe not all shit then?'

Katie looked up. Keith somehow seemed to come across to her as wanting to hear. It didn't make sense. Why should she talk to him. She didn't know anything about him. Why should she say anything? She just knew she needed to. She could feel her emotions rising. Her heart was still pounding and the dryness in her mouth and throat hadn't gone away.

'Kind of got depressed, you know. Life's like that, yeah? Gets you down.'

'Life got you down this week.' Keith kept his response simple, not wanting to in any way take Katie away from what she was experience by causing her to have to listen to him.

'Happens most weeks.'

'Life gets you down most of the time, yeah?'

Katie nodded. She was looking down again. She tightened her lips. Another deep breath. She felt upset but didn't want to show it. She'd been there, done that, didn't want it again. 'I just want to feel normal, not feel so, I don't know…, I get so fed up.'

Keith nodded, 'that sounds like a real despair, wanting to feel normal but feeling so fed up all the time.'

'I can't get stuff out of my head, you know?'

'The stuff from the past?'

She nodded. 'I get really depressed, I mean, yeah, like a zombie, you know, but worse. Like a heavy…, I don't know, it's hard to describe.'

'It's heavy but hard to really describe how it is. You haven't got words for it.'

'I just curl up in bed, under the covers, shut out the world, but I can't, it's inside me.' Katie wasn't so much thinking what she was saying, rather she was just responding almost in a kind of automatic sort of way. She wasn't stopping herself, the words were just coming out, describing what was in her head, in her thoughts.

'Can't shut out what's inside you.'

'Just feel like I sink into, I don't know, it's like nothing but it isn't as well.'

'What you feel is like nothing, but you also say it's heavy, depressing, like a zombie, it's inside you and you can't shut it out.'

Katie wanted to nod, felt like nodding but her head didn't move. She could get stuck just thinking about it.

Keith wondered about asking how she coped, but held back, wanting to allow her more time being with what she was experiencing. He hoped she would offer an answer without his having to ask. He put his curiosity aside.

'I want to be free.' She looked up. 'I want to, I don't know, I just want to feel different, yeah?' There was anger in her tone now, an anger driven to the surface by frustration.

'You've had enough of feeling the way you do, you want different.'

There wasn't just the anger and frustration that was present within Katie as she heard Keith's response. There was also an aching hurt. It grew within her as she sat there, and she could feel her emotions rising. The urge to tell Keith how she was feeling became irresistible. 'I just feel like I've been hurt all over.'

Keith could hear the emotion in Katie's slightly quavering voice. He responded, 'so much hurt, it's everywhere.'

Katie swallowed, she didn't want to let her feeling get the better of her again. But they were so powerful. 'I-I just…, I don't know, I can't tell you what it's like.' She looked down again, finding her eyes following the pattern in the carpet.

'And you don't have to try to. There are just no words for how awful if feels.'

The tears in her eyes caused the carpet to become blurred to Katie's sight. The truth was that Katie just wanted to scream. There was a little girl somewhere deep inside herself screaming for attention, and she was that little girl and she needed attention, love, someone to really care for her, someone to tell her it was alright. But all Katie could feel at the moment was the aching hurt and a feeling of being very alone in the world, and very alone in herself.

'I-I don't want to be like this.'

'No, no you don't want to be like how you are.' Keith had been struck by an urge to say something more. The words simply felt right and he judged them to be forming in direct response to his being in emotional contact with his client. 'And maybe you want someone to hear and understand and respond to just how awful you feel.'

Katie nodded as she sat in the room, but in truth she was somewhere else in herself. There was a place within her where she knew she would never be heard, where she knew her pain and hurt would always be ignored. It went back a long way, a long, long way, to a time before she had any command of language to attach words to her feelings. This was one of the reasons why it was so difficult for her to verbalise feelings. They were very present and very overwhelming, but rooted in those early months and years of her life when she had no words to attach to what she experienced. All Katie knew was that the hurt was growing and deepening inside her. It felt as though from her tummy to her heart there was turmoil, churning, aching, and her head was spinning, She felt dizzy with it. The scream when it came was penetrating and to Keith in some sense primeval. It was a sound that seemed to come from some very deep place and it sounded to his ears like a vocal embodiment of utter anguish and despair. It was raw, it was cutting, at the same time both human and yet almost inhuman. He wasn't sure if the scream was coming from Katie the young woman, or Katie the child. He sensed that it was the latter. He responded as if he was listening to a child scream.

'So much to feel hurt about, I can hear you.' He spoke softly, keeping his words simple because of his belief that he was probably talking to a very young Katie. He wanted to connect with her and to enable her to feel a human response, a heartfelt human response. He knew it was an extremely sensitive time and that he had to get it right. His senses were, to say the least, on high therapeutic alert.

'No-one ever comes. They send me away. I get so cold, so lonely. Just me, Dolly and Mister P.'

Keith kept his focus on his empathy. He did not need to know who Dolly and Mr P were though he had a fair idea what they might refer to.

'Just the three of you.'

Katie nodded, she felt weak and her cheeks were wet. 'They were my friends.'

Keith noted the past tense. Where was Katie in herself now? He wasn't so sure, but he chose to continue to respond as if she was very much the child. 'They were really important friends.'

'My only friends.'

'Dolly and Mister P were all that you had, your only friends.'

She looked up. 'Mister P was taken away from me. When they took me away they let me keep Dolly but not Mister P. Don't know why, they just did. Never saw him again.'

'So they took him away from you when you were taken away.' Keith thought of saying something about how she had been allowed to keep Dolly but chose not to. What she had lost seemed the more important focus as that was the general theme Katie was following.

'I screamed, I know I did. They didn't care, they didn't want to care. They told me it was OK and they gave me another teddy bear, but I didn't like him. He wasn't Mister P.'

'You only wanted Mister P.'

There was a slight pause and Katie spoke again. It was still a very childlike voice. 'Why did they do that?'

'I don't know, but it seems a horrible thing to have done to a little girl, to take away someone who was so special.' Keith was very aware of how he was talking and expressing the idea of Mister P as a real person. He suspected that to Katie, at that time, that was exactly what he was, and probably even more so. He *would* have always been there for her, unlike people. He could have been relied on, unlike people. He could only imagine what he must have meant to Katie.

Katie was shaking her head. For her the loss of Mister P was somehow more devastating than the loss of her mother. In truth, being taken from her mother was at least as much a loss, but at the moment she was focusing on her loss of Mister P. 'I hated being in that "home", I hadn't really spent much time with other kids, you know? I didn't know how to cope. I had Dolly but they used to tease me and try and take her away from me. I can remember that.' She felt anger and sadness welling up. 'Bastards.'

Keith guessed by her use of language that Katie was very much her more adult self now reflecting on the past. 'Bastards to try and take her away.'

Katie was thinking about those times when she had been in care. She'd hated it. She never settled. And later she had always been getting into trouble, often being the one that did the more outrageous things. She'd been like that a lot later in her childhood. She didn't know why, just knew she liked people around her and reacting to her. 'I don't think they really understood what it was like, I mean, oh I don't know. I can't change anything. Shit happened, still happens, can't seem to get away from it.' Katie spoke with a degree of forcefulness. She was fed up and frustrated, and angry about how she had been treated. She looked at Keith, 'so, what can you do about it?'

'You mean, how can I help?'

'Guess so.'

'You want to be different? Make changes?'

Katie nodded. 'I mean, yeah, I can't be like this, not forever. I want…, I don't know.' She paused. 'That's the problem, I don't know what I want and it all seems hopeless anyway.'

'Seems hopeless the idea of somehow knowing what you want or getting what you want?' Keith wasn't sure which direction Katie was wanting to focus on, so he offered both.

'Both. I mean, look at me, living in a shit-hole, nothing much to do. Yeah, OK, so maybe I could get a job or something, but I don't know, it's…, I don't know…'. She really didn't and it did all seem so utterly hopeless.

'There's a lot of "I don't know" for you at the moment.' Keith spoke with what he believed to be a warm and accepting tone. He really felt he had heard Katie, she had spoken with a lot of feeling.

Katie appreciated the way Keith had responded. It made it feel like although it was her problem at least someone was listening, even if they couldn't really change anything. Who could? No-one could go back and change what she had experienced. 'I guess I want to change the things that can't be changed.'

'Such as?' Keith responded with genuine curiosity.

'Well, I can't change what happened to me. I can't change that my mum was crap, never there for me, only interested in getting off her head. That's where it started for me. She'd be with men, no time for me. I remember some of it, and some of it's gone now, but that's how it was. I just wasn't wanted, and that's a shit thing to feel. I've come to realise that.'

'Your mum didn't want you?'

'She didn't seem to care much about me.'

'Because she didn't respond to you when you needed her?'

Katie went quiet. Yes, she knew her mum hadn't been there for here, but she didn't really know why. She knew she wasn't going to be able to do much about that now. Her mum was dead. Overdose. Wasn't long after she'd been taken into care. She wondered sometimes if her mum would have survived if she hadn't been taken away; whether her being there had maybe stopped things getting worse, or had it just been too much for her? Sometimes she just felt vindictive towards her mum for giving her such a crap start in life. At other times there was a sadness. It was the sadness that now suddenly broke upon her. 'Maybe if it had hurt her so much to have me taken away, maybe that meant something.' She looked up, felt a lump in her throat and looked back down again.

Keith nodded, 'maybe'. He wasn't sure what to say. He was suddenly feeling caught in his own thoughts and feelings and was aware that in doing so he had distanced himself from Katie. He had been caught up in wondering about Katie's mum and what it must have been like to have her daughter taken away into care. He brought himself back to Katie and decided to be open about what he had experienced. 'I was momentarily thinking more about your mum and how it must have been for her, than about you and how it was for you. Tough experience for everyone.'

'Horrible.' Katie could still remember the day she was taken away. 'They just came, forced open the door. There was a lot of shouting and screaming. Mum was crying, but they refused to give way. Things must have been said. I'd seen one of the women before. They'd visited on other occasions. Mum had sort of made a fuss of me when they did, always seemed different. But I don't really know everything.' Katie felt herself going cold as she thought back to that time. It was as though her whole life had turned on that moment. 'If it hadn't happened, maybe things would have been different.' But even as she spoke the words she knew she wasn't convinced.

'For you, for your mum?'

'Both of us, but then, would she have changed? She might still have done what she did, maybe things mightn't have gone so bad so soon, I don't know.' Katie paused. 'I used to think there was something bad about me.'

'That you were bad in some way?'

'That it was my fault. Maybe it was me she couldn't cope with, I don't know. But things always go bad with me, always. Nothing ever works out. People get upset. People say they're there for you and then, yeah, then they're not. No-one really cares, not really, you know? You just have to do what you have to do to get by, that's how it is, always has been, always will be. Can't rely on other people. They shit on you.'

'Look after yourself, no one cares, do what you have to do. Other people shit on you.' Keith felt a real pang of his own sadness for what Katie was saying. Her world-view, her view of herself as someone bad, and of others as not caring, not being there for her was painful to hear. It was Katie's experience. He couldn't question her reality. That was how it was, and how it remained. He hoped it would change.

Katie was still focussing on how other people hadn't been there for her. And even though some people over the years had tried to help, and even now her doctor was trying to help, as was Keith, that didn't remove her fundamental belief that you couldn't rely on other people. She knew it, *really* knew it. It was as though it had been burned into her at some fundamental level. In one sense it made things simpler, she knew where she was, but at the same time there was also a deeper yearning for recognition and connection, a hunger for relationship. But she couldn't trust it. She didn't want to have to be reliant on anyone else.

'I need to be me. But I don't like how I am becoming.' Katie hadn't planned to say the second bit but the words just got spoken. Keith noted them and responded. Katie was able to acknowledge something important, and make it visible to him. It felt like a very important acknowledgement and he wanted to be utterly sure that Katie appreciated that he had heard what she had said, and that it had touched him deeply.

'That really touches me, that you really don't like how you are becoming. Something about how you are is just not how you want to be.' He was particularly aware of Katie's body language. She was looking down and seemed withdrawn. The way she sat made her look as though she was bent under the weight of something.

'I do things that I know aren't good, not really, but it's what I do. I probably get pissed too often, yeah, and, well, yeah.' Katie didn't feel able to add that she wasn't too caring about who she had sex with, particularly when she'd been drinking which was generally how it was.

'Mhmm, get pissed too often and that leads to…?' Keith had heard the way Katie had hesitated as she had spoken and he sensed there were things not being said. He didn't want to push Katie into disclosure, but he did want to show his readiness to hear what was not being said. His response had just a slight questioning tone, inviting her to say a little more if she felt able and wanted to.

'I've never had a relationship with anyone that's really, you know, lasted. It's always, yeah, I never sort of want to commit myself, you know?'

'Relationships are short, and you feel that it's something about you not wanting to have a commitment. Is that how it is?' Keith wanted to ensure he was clear. It felt important and he wanted to be sure that he was understanding Katie and that she could feel she was being understood. Both were important therapeutically.

Feelings were becoming present for Katie, feelings of profound discomfort. She felt a churning in her stomach and a cold numbness in her arms and shoulders. She felt light headed. 'I don't…', Katie paused. This wasn't easy to talk about, perhaps because Keith was a man. She wasn't sure how he was going to react, although he did seem to be someone who cared, but was he just like everyone who she knew that couldn't be relied on? Yet she also knew she had to say more, to let someone in, someone into her innermost thoughts and feelings. Or did she? The struggle within her was deep. Yes, she did want to talk, she knew she needed to, and yet…. It was making her extremely anxious now, and more and more uncomfortable. She shifted in the seat and looked up at Keith. Could she trust him, really trust him? Did she want him to know about her, about who she was, really was? Yes, at times she didn't like herself and how she had become, so what would he think? Did she care? She did. She was surprised by that realisation.

Keith was very aware that Katie had gone silent but it certainly didn't feel to him like a passive, empty silence. When she looked up he felt sure that he sensed a kind of searching look in her eyes. Words formed and they demanded to be spoken. He voiced them. 'Can you trust me.' He didn't make it a question, more of a statement that he sensed was an expression of what was present within Katie's inner world. As a person-centred therapist he knew his role was to be able to move sensitively within his client's inner world, trying not to disturb what was present. He sought to be a kind of mirror to reflect what clients were experiencing, but without leading or getting ahead of them. He realised, though, that in what he had just said he had probably got ahead of Katie.

Katie did not look away, but kept eye contact with Keith and nodded slowly.

The moment was profound. Keith instinctively knew it was crucial how he responded. But he also knew that the only helpful response was an authentic one. 'Whatever you choose to say or not say, I will listen, I will not judge, I want to understand, and I want to help.' His words were genuine. He did want to listen and understand and he was totally accepting of Katie being free to choose what she said or kept from him. And he did want to help.

For Katie this was a new experience. She was aware herself that it was her call. She had come to where she was now, and she had a choice. Her heart was thumping. What if she bottled it now? What if she said nothing? She knew she wouldn't come back. She knew there would be no point. It all felt so difficult, like she was taking a huge risk. But was she? What was the biggest risk, saying more? Or saying nothing?

'I want to talk, I need to talk, but...', Katie took a deep breath and shook her head. She felt anxious and remained silent.

Keith appreciated the depth of the struggle that Katie was having with herself. He could hear through her tone of voice a kind of yearning to talk and yet, quite clearly, she was also needing to stop herself, or part of her was stopping herself.

'You want to talk and need to talk, I hear that, and there's something else that is stopping you.'

Yes, thought Katie, yes that's how it is. She felt a sickly feeling in her stomach, her throat was dry, 'It's just that…', another pause, 'what I do, I *have* to do.'

'Mhmm, you really *have* to.' Keith waited for Katie to continue and at her own pace.

Katie knew all too well what her fear was, that she'd be made to stop, and she couldn't face that. She had to be able to release the pressure sometimes and to feel able to find a way out of the darkness when that descended on her. 'I get really stressed up, and I have to relieve it.' She paused. This was not easy and she knew that what she was going to say next was the big step. 'And cutting myself a little helps, I mean really helps.' Katie wasn't sure what she now felt from having said what she had said, but her heart was definitely thumping in her chest. She felt anxious, unsure how Keith was going to respond.

Keith nodded, appreciating that Katie had been able to say what she just had. 'That wasn't easy to tell me, was it?'

Katie shook her head. 'No, it wasn't.'

'And cutting yourself really helps to relieve that stress when it builds up.'

Katie nodded. 'I know it's not a good thing to do, I know that, but it really helps and, you know, lots of people do it.'

Keith wasn't going to disagree with her on that point. He'd long suspected that a lot more people than was generally recognised cut themselves, or sought harm in other ways, But what mattered now was Katie, what she was doing and why, and what the experience was giving her.

'And that's what matters, that it helps, yeah?'

Katic nodded again. She was looking quite intently towards Keith. It seemed to him that she was seeking a response, a kind of acceptance of what she was doing.

'We all do things to make ourselves feel better. Some are risky, others not, but it's all part of being human and finding ways to cope. For your own reasons you have discovered that for you cutting yourself gives you an experience that relieves stress. Is that right?' Keith wanted to be clear for himself and to be sure that Katie felt accurately heard and understood.

'It really does help, and I know, yeah, maybe it's not a good thing to do, but I haven't done myself any harm, not really. I'm careful.'

'You take care with what you do, is that what you mean, and that's less harmful?'

Katie nodded.' I don't cut deep, just enough…,' Katie paused, thinking about how it felt when she cut herself, 'enough to, yeah, get some relief.'

'Mhmm. So let me be sure I am getting this right, you cut when you are feeling stressed up and it gives you release from that. And you are careful.'

'Yeah.' Katie's thoughts had also moved on to the other time she cut, when she was low and depressed. 'I'm not always sort of stressed though, sometimes, well, I get really down and then it help me sort of get out of it.'

'OK, so cutting yourself, giving yourself the experience that it brings, helps you when you are stressed, to relieve the tension, and also when you are low, down, it kind of gets you out of that state as well?' Keith's response had that slight questioning tone as he checked out that he was understanding what Katie was telling him and wanting him to hear. He was aware, particularly in relation to difficult and sensitive issues, that what a client told you, and what they actually wanted you to hear, might not always be the same.

'It helps. It really does.' Katie paused. 'You're not going to tell me to stop, are you?'

Keith smiled but in a gentle manner. This was a crucial question and he knew his response needed to be honest. 'No, I'm not going to tell you to stop. I am glad you have been able to tell me and I do appreciate that it is important to you, really important. It helps you to cope. I'm not going to try and take that away from you, but I am going to be concerned that you do yourself damage. I'm going to hope that you keep safe. And I hope that by talking things through with me and exploring what causes you to cut, you may find other ways of coping, of getting what you need. But, no, I'm not going to stop you, but I'd like to understand what it means for you.'

'Makes me feel better.'

'Mhmm, better, but I wonder what *better* means for you?' Keith was aware that the word could mean so many different things and if he was to be able to communicate genuine empathy and warm, unconditional acceptance towards Katie he needed to have a clearer sense of her inner world, if she wished to let him into it.

'Relief. Release. Something to focus on.'

' OK, that's clear. The experience that comes out of cutting is a sense of relief and release, and it gives you a different kind of focus?' Keith was a little unsure with his last comment.

'Sort of different, but more just something to focus on. It's like, when I'm down I just, well, it's like nothing but, I don't know, it's hard to describe.' Katie paused.

'You say, "it's like nothing, but…".'

'Yes, but it isn't nothing. It's like being in a really thick, heavy black fog. It's like it's inside you, inside me.'

Keith responded in kind though he knew to empathise with her words would place the focus on her internal experience. 'It really gets inside you.'

'It is inside me. But, yeah, I don't know, it sort of feels everywhere as well.'

'Like it descends on you as well?'

Katie thought for a moment. 'It's like it's everywhere and I just don't want to know anyone or do anything. I get so depressed, you know, about everything.' Katie paused. She didn't like talking or thinking about it. It brought it too close.

'Sounds utterly overwhelming', was Keith's response, which was exactly how it felt from the way Katie was speaking and the look on her face.

'It's awful and yet, when you're in the middle of it, yeah, it's awful but somehow you don't care any more.'

'Like you're in a place where you're, what, too depressed to feel the awfulness of it?'

Katie had to think for a moment. Yes, that did make sense, somehow. 'I guess so. I just feel stuck and can, well, I go to bed and just lie there. I sometimes sleep a bit or I just do nothing.' She paused. 'And then I cut.'

'So you're in this place in yourself where you're feeling depressed…', Keith stopped, thinking about what he had said, 'does it make sense when I say it like that, or is that not how it is?'

159

'I suppose so, I guess it's in me but it just feels like it becomes all of me.'

'That's the overwhelming side of it?'

Katie thought about it more. 'I don't know that I can say it's in me, like a place in me, it's just there, everywhere.' That seemed to her to describe it more accurately.

'OK, it's suddenly there or creeps up on you?'

'Creeps up, I guess, but it's like, yeah, like I sort of feel it building up and then suddenly…. It's like a light that gets dimmer and then suddenly goes off. Something like that. I mean, it's not pitch black, but there isn't any light and it's sort of heavy as well, a kind of…', another pause as Katie tried to get the words to describe the heaviness. 'It sort of pins you down, physically, emotionally, everything.'

'Pinned down, like you can't move. Nothing in you feels able to move.'

'Yeah, and it's like I don't care, *about anything*. It's like nothing matters, what's the point?'

'Mhmm.' Keith nodded. He kept his response simple and focused. His intuition told him that these were key words that could be like a gateway into the experience that was behind their existence. 'Nothing matters, what is the point.' He spoke slowly and flatly, not as a question, more a simple statement of fact. He waited for Katie's response.

Katie was feeling strange, a buzzy feeling and her head felt strange, like it had expanded and yet she felt small as well. 'No-one cares.' The voice was childlike. 'I'm nothing.'

Keith responded softly and with care to keep to the words Katie was using. 'No-one cares, you feel like nothing.'

'Don't…', Katie's voice trailed off. 'On my own.' Katie felt very sad and alone as she heard the words she was saying emerge from within her.

'You're feeling all alone, don't…' Keith empathised and offered an opportunity for Katie to finish what she had started to say. He knew how the structure of self could be made up of parts, sometimes these could be normal and healthy, sometimes the result of traumatic experiences that led to each part becoming quite distinctive, to the point of their being outside of the person's normal awareness. And sometimes parts could act to stop each other breaking into awareness because the experiences they carried could threaten the structure of self that the person conceived themselves as being. Their self-concept was, in a sense, distorted by the fact that elements of their structure of self were being denied to awareness. Was part of Katie blocking her from connecting with something?

'Don't care.'

'Who doesn't care?'

'I don't.'

'Katie doesn't care.' Keith switched to using Katie's name. It felt right, it felt as though it was clearer, more relational given the way Katie was speaking. She sounded young, very young.

Katie shook her head and tightened her lips. She looked at Keith as though she was going to burst into tears. But she didn't, she just sat staring ahead of her. Then she looked down and started to pick at her fingers. It was a behaviour Keith had witnessed when Katie had first started to come to counselling. He decided to maintain contact with a pre-therapy response, used by some therapists to keep in contact with clients where there is uncertainty over whether there is any psychological contact being made or maintained. 'Katie needs to pick at her fingers.'

The finger movements grew more intense. She was really digging her thumb nail into her fingers and picking at the skin around her nails. The thought struck Keith with utter clarity that she was inflicting pain on herself, but it was an action from a time way back in her early childhood. Or was it? Do children do that to themselves, or was it more of a teenage or adult behaviour? He didn't know. Certainly Katie had learned to use pain to feel something, maybe something different, maybe just something. He didn't know. But this wasn't the time for speculation. He needed to get his focus back on Katie and on what was happening in the present.

Katie continued to pick and dig her nails into her fingers and thumbs. She had drawn blood. Keith felt an urge to respond to what he was seeing. It wasn't rational but he felt an urge to say something. He trusted it. 'Katie feels pain and hurt.'

It wasn't that Katie didn't hear what Keith as saying, she did, but his voice seemed somehow detached from her reality. It was as though it was coming from a great distance and wasn't really getting through to her, to the place that she had entered within herself. It was as though her world was empty, nothing was making any kind of impression upon her awareness. Yes, she knew she was sitting down but she wasn't holding in her awareness any sense of being in a counselling room or of being with Keith. In fact, her main focus of awareness was simply a sense of numb emptiness, a condition in which whilst she knew she existed there was a parallel sense of non-existence. It wasn't that she didn't believe she existed but rather she wasn't experiencing much sense of self that could give her a sense of self. It was as though her awareness had been put on hold. She sat, not thinking, her blank expression reflecting the blankness that had become her inner world.

Keith continued to sit feeling unsure just how present Katie was in her awareness, and therefore how aware she was of him and what he was saying. She seemed to be quite detached. Her expression was fixed. He could only guess what was happening for her. The truth was that he didn't know. The hand movements suddenly stopped. They had been the only movement. Now there was a strange stillness that added to the silence between them. He held the silence, maintaining feelings of warm acceptance towards Katie and aware that he was also feeling a very human reaction to the sense of disconnection that seemed to be present. He could not sense anything from Katie that was indicative that she was aware of his presence. And yet even though in some sense there seemed psychological disconnection, there was also an intensity present for him. He felt very concentrated. The stillness left him feeling he shouldn't move either, as though he should hold his breath and mirror the stillness that he was seeing in Katie.

For Katie it seemed as though she was floating in an emptiness, and that she had in fact become that very emptiness herself. This wasn't what she was thinking, it was just the state she was in. No thought, no feeling, nothing stirred from within her. She had no sense of time passing so when she suddenly became aware of taking a sharp deep breath she felt a kind of shock and her heart seemed to suddenly be pounding in a way that she felt sure would have made a noise. She was back in her normal awareness. Her body had jumped as well, some kind of reflex. She felt tired, her eyes felt gritty. She closed them, hoping to clear some of the grittiness. It only helped a little, so she blinked a few times, and that definitely made them feel less dry.

'What happened?', she asked.

'I'm not sure but you seemed to go very quiet and still and felt out of contact.'

'I don't remember anything. I heard your voice, I don't know what you said and then…, I don't know, I just don't know.' Whilst her eyes were moister, the tiredness had not gone away.

'Don't remember anything?'

'No, just, I don't know, blanked out I suppose somehow.' She frowned. 'I can remember feeling very alone, I remember that.'

'Mhmm, so that feeling of being very alone, that was with you.'

'And then, I sort of know but it's like, yeah, I sort of, I don't know, it sounds crazy but I feel like I sort of stopped.'

'Like you *stopped*?' Keith placed the emphasis that he did because it seemed to be what Katie was saying. She had emphasised the word a little in her own response.

Katie remembered a little more. 'Something about no-one caring.'

'Mhmm, no-one cared.'

'No, and that takes me back, and yet it's still with me. It still feels like no-one cares, not really, you know?'

'Mhmm, yeah, no-one really cares.' Keith responded quite naturally. He wasn't trying to say the therapeutic thing or the right thing, he was simply responding and being with Katie as she explored what she had experienced as best she could.

'Cares or cared.' The words just came out.

'Cares or cared. That says so much.'

'I know why things happened, I mean, you know, like I've said, I know my mum wasn't well, I mean, she had problems, yeah?'

Keith nodded.

'But it's still hard to make sense of how she was towards me. I still feel as though it's me, that it was me that made things difficult. And I know that isn't true as well. She should have been there for me, but she wasn't. She was only interested in doing drugs and stuff. But I do blame myself, I can feel it, it's deep. I should have, I don't know, done something.'

Keith felt himself feel quite heavy listening to Katie. He could really feel this awful, heavy sense of her blaming herself. She must have been very young, perhaps crying for attention and getting nothing. Being

163

ignored. Being starved of caring. How she must hunger for that now, he thought to himself.

'You feel as though you could or should have done something, or been different, but you were a small child, and adults should not expect young children to have to go through what you did. I hear you saying that you blame yourself, but what could you have done?'

Katie didn't know. She knew Keith was right, but there was this nagging sense deep inside herself that she was bad, she'd caused her mother to have problems which had led to her dying. It may not seem logical to anyone on the outside, but to part of herself it seemed the most logical thing in the world. And, at the same time, another part of herself knew that it was ridiculous, but that part had not found its voice. It remained quiet. Only the guilty and self-blaming part was present in her awareness to any significant degree.

'I could have done something. I know what you are saying, but inside me I know that it was me. There is something about me, I know it. Look at my life. It's been shit. Yeah, there have been some stupid people in my life too, but it's me that has never really…', Katie paused, 'oh I don't know. I just know that I'm different'.

'Different?' Keith was inviting Katie to say more so that he could understand, and convey that understanding back to her.

'I've always had problems, always. I've never really settled anywhere much, except for the Alberts, they really were the only ones that really cared.' She felt her eyes moisten once more as she thought back to Mrs Albert in particular. 'And, as you know, she died.' She paused, shaking her head and looking down. 'It's me, I'm bad news. I hate myself, I really hate myself.' The tears began to flow as Katie felt her sadness rising up. 'It makes me really sad,'

'Sad to feel the way you do, sad to feel you hate yourself so much.'

Katie didn't want to feel sad, she didn't like feeling like this but it was so familiar. Sometimes more intense than at other times. At the moment it felt intense.

Keith added a further response to what Katie had been saying. 'Leaves you with a profound sense of being "bad news"'. He sensed that this was the perception behind the feelings of self-hate and sadness. She had said it and he wanted her to know that he had heard what she had said. It just felt very important.

For Katie there were two reactions. Yes, she hated herself, and yet she also identified with the notion of being "bad news". It was a part of who she was, quite a large part in many ways. Uncared for, unwanted and everybody else's problem. That was how it felt. That was who she was. 'That's me.' She spoke with an air of resigned acceptance, or at least that was how Keith heard it.

'That's you, and you sound resigned to it.'

'What choice do I have?' She paused and repeated herself, a little more reflectively the second time. 'What choice do I have?'

'Mhmm, what choice do I have?' Keith responded in the first person, holding the question as Katie had voiced it.

'I am who I am. I don't like it, I wish I was different. I wish things were better. Every day seems a struggle. I don't know, I just don't know where I'm going.' Another shake of the head. 'I sure know where I've been, got a head full of that, but where I'm going, I don't know.'

'It's like you don't know where you are going but you'd like to know?'

'If it's good, yeah, but I can't see it. I mean, you know, people have shit lives, yeah? I see it, I do it too. Just existing day to day, getting drunk, messing around. Yeah, OK, have a few laughs, but it's madness as well. I don't know. I wish I could get some peace.' As she spoke those last seven words Katie breathed out a deep breath and felt her shoulders drop. Yes, that was what she wanted, more than anything else, some peace.

'If only I could have some peace.' Keith again responded in the first person. He had sensed the importance of what Katie was saying, the deep yearning that he could hear in her voice.

Katie took a deep breath. Those words seemed to fill her in some strange way. She closed her eyes. She knew that was what she wanted but she didn't know what it was like, not really, other than what she had felt in that previous counselling session and what she sometimes felt when she cut, particularly when she was stressed and needed to release. She knew it was be possible to have it without having to cut herself. 'Cutting brings me peace.'

'Mhmm, something about the experience of cutting puts you at peace.'

'When I cut to release tension, when I feel overwhelmed by everything, when it all builds up, it lets the pressure out, and that, yeah, makes me feel sort of more relaxed.'

'Being at peace is like being relaxed, and that's what cutting gives you when you're stressed out?' Keith sought to sum up what Katie had told him, to enable her to feel that what she had said was heard and that he understood how it all fitted together.

Katie nodded. 'Don't get me wrong, I like excitement as well, I like messing around and, yeah, you know', she was thinking about being with men, 'but I can't be like that all the time. I know I can't be like that, not keep being like that. I need to find some way to…'. Katie paused, she knew she wanted some peace in her life, peace in herself. She wasn't sure exactly what this meant, in many ways it was the idea of being in a place where she didn't have a head full of shit, the crap memories, the hurt, the everything that seemed to go around in her head, and which cutting, drinking, shagging seemed the only easy way of getting away from.

'Some way to…?' Keith hoped to help Katie say a little more, if she wanted or felt able to.

Katie was taking another deep breath and on breathing out she responded. 'I want to let go of it all.'

'Let go of, what, the past?' Keith ought to clarify what "it all" meant.

'And the present, everything. I just want it all to go away. I want to escape, be different, be someone else, not feel like shit, I don't want to feel alone like I don't exist. I want to feel cared for, I want to be noticed.' The words came out fast and with intensity.

Keith nodded. He was certainly struck by the tone of how Katie was speaking. She sounded very clear. He wondered whether he should try and show empathy for all that Katie was saying, or take her comments as a progression and simply respond to the last comment. He decided on repeating the last two statements of what she wanted.

'I want to feel cared for. I want to be noticed.' He spoke slightly slower than Katie had, simply offering an opportunity for the focus to be held and perhaps allow Katie to connect more deeply with what each of those two statements represented for her.

It was the wanting to feel cared for that made most impact on Katie. Yes, she did want to be noticed, that was important, but she wanted to feel someone caring for *her*, giving *her* attention, meeting *her* needs. Someone who, yeah, who really cared for and about her. Someone who wouldn't let her down or drop her. She shook her head. 'I want to feel important.'

'Important?'

'To someone. I'm not important to anyone. I'm everyone's problem, get passed around, that's how it was.' She paused. 'Too many people just take on kids for the money, not because they care, really care. Mrs Albert cared. The Griffiths didn't, just saw me as a way of earning money. Put up with me until I did something that was a real problem to them, something they really didn't like, and that was it. Not many people stick with me, you know?' She wondered about Keith. Was he going to be like everyone else? Could she really trust him, could she? She still didn't know, but she knew she'd talked to him about more than she had with anyone else. That sort of felt good. She did think she trusted him. It felt safe, and that was something. She didn't always feel that way. And as she thought this there was another part of her that was telling her that she didn't deserve anyone being there for her anyway, that she was bad news, a problem that people wanted to just go away. She pushed the thought aside. She knew it but she didn't want to think about it, not just now anyway.

Keith responded to what Katie had said. His response was influenced by his own reaction which was to wonder how she viewed him. 'I guess it leaves you not believing anyone would want to stick with you.'

'I'm as good as anyone else. Yeah, OK, so life's been shit, I know that, but at least I can look after myself.' Katie felt strong in affirming this and it was a good feeling.

'You feel you can look after yourself in spite of it all.' Keith reflected the affirming tone of Katie's voice.

'Yeah.'

'Mhmm.' Keith didn't add anything further. He accepted what Katie was saying. That was how she wanted to see herself and what she wanted to communicate to him. He wasn't going to challenge this. She had survived. She had come through some problematic experiences and a start in life that some simply didn't survive or ended up with very severe disturbance as a result, whether you called it mental or emotional or whatever. But Katie had survived and she was still able to draw on a particularly feisty attitude to life.

She didn't know why she said it or where it came from, the words were suddenly coming out of her mouth and it took her totally by surprise, as did the surge of emotion that followed. 'I wish my mum was here.'

Keith felt his senses go on high alert. This was a yearning from a deep place that had suddenly emerged, seemingly quite out of the blue. He wanted to somehow capture this in his response. 'If only my mum was here.' He tried to speak in a manner that captured the yearning he could hear in Katie's voice and to speak in the first person which could be such a powerful way of empathising. He wondered what was going to happen next. What struck him in particular was that the voice that spoke was very much Katie the adult. It wasn't coming from a child-like part of her nature; it was now, it was Katie as she was in the present saying it. Given the things she had said before he was struck by how present her statement felt, as though it had been etched into the atmosphere in some way. Before he could respond Katie had burst into tears. He saw her reach over and take a tissue, holding it to her face. The force of emotion was strong. The sobbing was intense. He could hear her struggling to breathe in as the emotions and the sobbing pushed the air out of her lungs.

'Deep down you really miss her.'

Katie nodded, but the crying and the release of emotion continued. She didn't understand. She didn't think about missing her mum that much, and yet here she was crying her eyes out, feeling so much, wanting her so much. It didn't make sense. She didn't understand.

'I-I don't understand. I didn't think I missed her.'

'Maybe old feelings have been locked up for a long while.'

'But she was never there for me. But I want her to be here.'

'Like you wanted her to be there for you so many years ago?'

Katie nodded, swallowing painfully and taking another tissue to dab at her wet eyes. 'Is that it? I'm still wanting her even now?'

'Maybe.' Keith thought for a moment, should he make something of the fact that she had spoken as an adult not as a child? He knew he couldn't dwell on trying to decide too long, clients didn't want to sit there watching their therapist trying to think of what to say next. It wasn't good therapy. He spoke what he had thought and trusted it was right and helpful because it had emerged into his awareness at a time when he was feeling strongly connected with his client. 'And I was struck that when you spoke it wasn't as a child, but as Katie now, Katie the adult. So it might have been a yearning from the past but it also felt very much in your present.'

Katie nodded again. 'I don't understand. But I want *her*, I want to be able to talk to her. I want her to listen. I want her in my life, and I can't. I can't.' Another surge of emotion spilt more tears and Katie buried her face in a tissue one more.

'And that hurts so much, wanting her and knowing you can't have her in your life.' Keith watched as Katie continued to cry, but the intensity was reducing. She picked up another tissue and blew her nose.

'Oh dear. I must look a mess.'

'Hasn't helped your mascara, but these are tears that I think you really need.'

Katie felt a little calmer. 'If she was alive I know I'd want to find her, you know?'

'Mhmm, I'm sure you would.'

'I know I'd be angry, and I'd have questions, but somehow as well, I don't know, I feel something else. It's sort of new. I don't know, I can't explain. It's like she's still important somehow but all I have are painful memories and knowing that she didn't …, I don't know, maybe she did care, but she just had too many problems.'

'It's like she cared but had too many problems to show you that care, yeah?'

Katie nodded. 'Maybe. I don't know. I get confused by it all.' She felt as though there were times when she just went around and around in her head. But she had to admit that the yearning to see and talk to her mum now were very present, and it was something new to her. She'd only felt the hate before, but that was no longer the only emotion present.

'So much to have to think about, it all gets so confusing.'

'It's like I fill up with it all. It stresses me out and, well, yeah, that's when I cut as well, to get some release, take out the pressure. It feels like I have to or I'd explode.'

'Builds up that pressure, so much going on inside you and cutting can release to stop you exploding.'

'Releases the tension. Kind of helps me relax.' Katie paused, tightening her lips as she did so and frowning slightly. 'And that's when I sort of find some peace, but it isn't really peace, just a sort of escape, I guess.'

'A temporary escape from the stress of thinking about it all.'

Katie nodded.

A silence settled down between them. It was as though some kind of agreement had been reached, as though both of them knew how it was and that for the moment at least there was nothing more to say. It was an easy silence. Keith sat and waited to see if Katie wanted to make any further response. He didn't feel any urge to say anything further, to try and push the conversation along. It had come to this place and he accepted that, as he accepted Katie's need to be as she needed to be.

For Katie the silence felt good. In a strange way it did have a certain kind of peacefulness about it and she appreciated that. Yes, somehow this was how she wanted to be. It did feel strange although the sense of strangeness wasn't strong enough to disturb what she was experiencing. She realised that she had begun to smile. That felt good as well.

Keith noticed the smile and responded in a similar manner. 'Something feels good?'

Katie nodded. She didn't want to speak, but she appreciated the acknowledgement. Yes, something did feel good. She had absolutely no idea why. But that didn't matter. Maybe she could be different. Maybe….

Time passed and Keith glanced at the clock. He had lost track of time. There were only a few minutes of the session left. 'We only have a few minutes but I don't want that to disturb what you are experiencing.'

The silence continued a little longer before Katie responded. 'Time to go then. I don't know why, but I do feel different, calmer somehow. It feels good.'

'I'm glad to hear that you are having that experience.' Keith was quite genuine in what he was saying. Yes, he knew that sometimes these kinds of experiences would happen but not necessarily remain with clients, that they could be a kind of glimpse of what was possible. He knew that there were times when something else fought back against it. Holding on to a sense of genuine calmness and relative ease was not easy, not when you had a structure of self that had been formed on the basis of hurt, rejection, loss and confusion. He knew that what was happening wasn't the end of therapy, but perhaps a beginning, a sensing of something different, of another possibility that could be reached, and not just by cutting. Katie had experienced different feelings towards her mum and was now experiencing, perhaps, different feelings towards herself. Only time would tell what the effect would be. He just knew he was glad that things were happening for Katie, yet he knew as well that there was still a long way to go.

As Katie got up to leave, Keith felt a need to say something more. 'You are experiencing something new, something perhaps quite subtle in many ways, so be aware that it's a noisy world out there and it may feel quite sharp for a while. Take it easy.'

'Thanks, I will.' Katie headed out of the door and Keith watched her walking down the corridor. He could only imagine the adjustments that were taking place within her structure of self, and to what effect. He said quietly to himself, 'hang in there, the change is starting'. He felt emotional himself, and he felt great respect for Katie. He just hoped all would be well for her and turned back into the counselling room to write his notes. He thought back over the session. So much had happened, a real rollercoaster of a journey with surprises along the way. Moments when something shifted, referred to as 'moments of movement' within the person-centred theory of therapy. It had been an intense session. He still felt very alert, his senses remaining very much alive, and yet he could also feel a tiredness beginning to creep up on him. It had been a demanding session as well. He knew that once he had jotted down his notes he would go out for a few minutes of fresh air and have a drink of water before his next client arrived.

Chapter 9

The calmness had not been maintained. Yes, it had stayed with Katie for a short while, most of the rest of the day, but it had faded. She had felt herself losing it and it left her anxious. As a result she had gone on a drinking binge. For some reason that she could not make sense of – not that she had tried to – it had seemed the right thing to do. She wanted to lose herself. She didn't want to feel the confusion, the tension, the darkness, the sense of being alone and anxious that were her normal states of mind. She wanted that calmness, but it had faded. And so she drank.

It had not brought relief but had rather opened her to a more intense set of negative feelings towards herself. It was as though the part of her that wanted her to hate herself, that carried those feeling that had been internalised so many years ago, was fighting back against her attempts to be different, to feel different, to make sense of her past and how it had affected her. It was a part of herself that wanted to keep the self-blame alive, and intensely so.

The blade cut deep, it needed to do. The darkness had closed in and she wanted to cut her way out. It was the only way she knew. She could have let go of the blade and it might have stayed in her arm, it was that deep. And it hurt. She was gritting her teeth, a sickly sensation in her stomach, but she knew it was the only way she could cope. It took her to another place, another depth within herself that she had not encountered in this way before, a place of darkness, yes, but a place of hate as well.

It wasn't the familiar darkness she was used to. It was different, it had a tone of self-hate within it, a desire to cut out of herself the feelings of self-blame and self-loathing that had gained control of her thoughts and feelings, but they were mixed with a sense of wanting to hurt and damage herself. That was not her usual experience.

One cut was not enough. Katie knew she had no choice. She had to cut, it was a kind of inner command. It was scaring her, but that didn't stop her. She needed another cut and another. The scene changed in her mind, she was looking at the wallpaper in her bedroom, so many years ago now. The weight and oh the pain, splitting her. She felt crushed. She saw this snarling face, she felt the man's breath. It stank. She recognised him. It was a new memory. It took her to another depth of hatred. She hadn't known his name, but she knew who it was. She gritted her teeth and dug the blade in deeper. Now she felt the hate, yes, that was the feeling she was desperately seeking out. She wanted to dig it out of herself and yet she didn't, it was her place of refuge. Yes, she hated herself but beneath that was another hate, of him, of what he was doing. She hadn't realised, but now she knew. Tears were pouring from her eyes. She was dirty and she wanted to see her blood, It was the only thing about herself that she felt was pure. The bright redness of it, she needed to see it, dribbling down her arm. She wanted to stab out at everything, everyone, and herself, who she was, what she was, how she had been and what she had become.

Katie drew the blade further, extending the latest cut. Her heart was thumping, she felt light headed, almost a kind of buzz. Yes, that's what she needed now. The cuts were all bloody and it was dripping down her arm. She felt herself smiling as she looked at it. But she wasn't smiling inside. She was terrified. She'd been raped as a child. She hadn't realised. She hadn't known. How could she not have know? How could she have forgotten? She was going mad. She had to be going mad. The alcohol was still in her body, affecting her thinking. She was dizzy, she'd cut far deeper than she would normally have done. She'd hit a vein and the blood was flowing. She'd withdrawn the blade and laid back, the buzziness had returned once again. She let herself be taken by it…

*

Katie felt awful. She knew she was lying down and there were sounds around her, strange sounds. There were voices, two people talking, she didn't know who they were. She was too weak to open her

173

eyes. Everything felt heavy and she could feel the stinging pain in her arm. She was dizzy, she didn't want to move even if she had felt that she could. The voices were clearer.

'Alcohol. Why do they do it? We have enough to do without people deliberately cutting themselves up. We've got people here who are really ill, who need help. People like her should sort themselves out. Why do they have to get drunk all the time.'

'I don't think that's fair, I mean, we don't know why. We don't know what happened. She may have reasons.'

'Kids give themselves too many reasons to get drunk, and not just kids, not that she's a kid. Old enough to know better.'

'But there may be reasons.'

The two people who were talking were staff at the Accident and Emergency Department. Katie's arm had been sown up and she was now on a trolley waiting to be taken to a bed on one of the wards. One was an administrator, the other a nurse.

'I don't know, drinking, self-harm, it's all the same thing if you ask me. People just do crazy things. It's a world gone mad.'

'We still have to try and do the best we can to patch people up and try and help people to be different.'

'She won't change. She's a cutter. They don't change.'

'People can always change if you give them the right environment, listen and try and understand them, help them sort out their problems, give them some hope for a better future.'

'Didn't have things like this when I was younger.'

'People drank.'

'Not like now, and so young, and just to get off their heads, and the drugs. Nothing like today. Madness. And there are people with real illnesses needing help.'

Katie heard what they were saying. She felt like shouting at the woman who was making such negative comments. More than that, she wanted to hit her, hard. But she didn't have the energy. She just wished she'd shut up talking about things she knew fuck all about.

'Always getting drunk can be an illness as well.'

'I don't think so. And cutting yourself. Never heard of it in my day.'

'They didn't talk about child sexual abuse in your day but it happened nonetheless. At least a few more things are out in the open today. And if it's not visible you can't respond to it.'

Katie heard the words and she was immediately transported back to the images and the feelings that had been with her when she had been cutting. That was her. Oh God, it had happened to her. She felt suddenly nauseous, partly because of what she was feeling and remembering, but also because of the alcohol she had consumed that had upset her stomach. 'I'm going to be sick.' She tried to get up but she couldn't push with her cut arm. The nurse who had been sympathetic to her had heard her and was lifting her head and back and calling for someone to get a bowl or something. There must have been one nearby because she felt something hard being pushed against her chest and up under here chin. 'It's OK, we've got you, there's a bowl under you. Let it go.'

Katie didn't need any encouragement. She felt her stomach heaving and the horrid sickly taste in her mouth. Again, and again. Her stomach was still cramping but there was soon nothing more to come out. She felt cold and sweaty. 'Sorry.'

'It's OK. Think you've finished?' It was the nurse that was still speaking to her.

'I-I think so. I feel awful.' Katie had opened her eyes. She couldn't see who was holding her from behind, but there was an older woman in front of her holding on to the bowl. She didn't look very sympathetic. She guessed which one she was. The woman took the bowl away, whilst the nurse eased Katie back down. 'You're doing fine. We've patched you up, but they want to keep you in. You lost a lot of blood but not enough for us to give you a transfusion.'

'I-I don't remember.'

'No, well, that's OK. You were lucky.'

'I don't feel very lucky.'

'Well, you were. It was a good job someone found you. It could have been a lot worse. You'd cut yourself real deep.'

'I had to. I had to.'

'I guess you had your reasons.'

'I remembered things.'

'Bad things?'

Katie instinctively felt her jaw tightening. She nodded, aware that her emotions were building up. She felt tearful and hurt, the kind of hurt that just felt like it was everywhere. She closed her eyes and felt tears trickling out and down the sides of her face.

'Want to talk about it? My name's Veronica by the way.' She came around the side of the trolley and smiled at Katie, who opened her eyes. She had a friendly looking round face, very dark skin and large brown eyes. Veronica had short, dark hair.

'I'm Katie.' She paused. 'Friends call me Kat.'

'Hi Kat. Pleased to meet you.' Veronica reached over and held her right hand, giving it a firm but friendly squeeze. 'You're gonna be OK. You'll feel bad for a while but you'll heal OK.'

'It's not the cuts that worry me, not now.'

'The things you remembered, huh?'

Katie nodded. Somehow she felt she wanted to talk. She didn't know why. 'I just feel so awful inside. I-I think I was sexually abused and I've only just realised.'

Veronica felt a surge of pain within herself as she heard what Katie was saying. Oh God, she thought, what a terrible thing to realise. She took a deep breath quite instinctively. 'That's an awful thing.'

Katie knew how awful it was. Memories that she simply had not had before were crowding in on her. 'I don't know how I'm going to cope. I can see him. He was someone who was around when I was a child. I got taken into care. Mum had a drug problem. It wasn't good. But I can see his face. I can feel him touching me, he raped me. It's awful. I feel like, I don't know, I just…' She shivered. 'How could it have happened? How did she let it happen?'

'I don't know, why do these things happen? They do. Some men are just animals, bastards. I don't know why they do it.'

Katie felt nauseous again, it was the effect of the memories. The whole thing revolted her, she wanted to throw her insides up, get everything out somehow, make herself feel clean. 'I'm gong to be sick again.'

Veronica called out for someone to get a bowl again. The same person who had taken it away returned with it and Veronica helped support Katie again. It wasn't that there was much to sick up, just a little, but it was more a physiological reaction to the psychological revulsion at what she now knew. The nausea passed and Katie laid back again. 'Am I going to be here long?'

'Until we get you a bed for the night at least. The doctors want to keep you under observation, and make sure you're safe and well enough to go home. We're giving you some medication to help you.'

Katie thought of her room. Wasn't really something she wanted to call home, but it was what she had. In fact, she wasn't at all sure she had ever really been anywhere that felt 'home', except for the Alberts. It always came back to them as being the one ray of light in her life. If only she'd been able to be with them. If only…. She felt sad; things could have been so different. Her eyes were moistening and Katie could feel her emotions rising. She felt tired and wanted to sleep. She closed her eyes and drifted. The urge to talk had passed. The sounds around her continued but they seemed a little distant now. She finally fell asleep.

*

It was a couple of days later when Katie was finally discharged. She had seen a number of people whilst she had been in hospital, including a psychiatric liaison nurse who had assessed her. She wanted Katie to see a psychiatrist but Katie didn't want that. She didn't want to be thought of as mental. She'd just had a shit life and needed to find a way of coping with it. The nurse had said that she was still going to refer her and that she'd get an appointment. Katie accepted it, but without much enthusiasm. She'd told the nurse that she was seeing a counsellor and that it had been helpful, hard going but it had been helping her make sense of things, it was just that she was finding out more and it was difficult. She didn't like the assessment. Too many questions. Keith hadn't been like that. She wanted to talk in her own way at her own pace, not be bombarded with someone else's agenda.

The day after her discharge she went to see her GP, Dr Armstrong. She was very concerned about what had happened and wanted to know what Katie felt she needed. She encouraged her to accept the referral to the psychiatrist but Katie still wasn't happy about it. 'I'm not mental', she told the doctor, 'I just need time to sort my head out. I can do that with the counsellor. He, I don't know, sort of lets me just talk. He doesn't ask questions. It's helped me make sense of things. It's just that

I'm remembering things.' She'd told her about the remembering of the sexual abuse. Dr Armstrong asked if she wanted to see a sexual abuse counsellor, that there was a local service. Katie said she'd think about it.

The hospital had prescribed medication to help Katie relax. Dr Armstrong told Katie that she was only going to prescribe small amounts and that she needed to come back in a couple of days for more. She was concerned that Katie might be at risk of overdosing, although she also knew that anyone who really wanted to do so could easily get over the counter medication for this if they really wanted to. But she wanted to manage the risk where she had some degree of control. She also checked out with Katie whether she was feeling suicidal, or had any thoughts about it. Katie confirmed that she wasn't feeling like that. Yes, there was a lot she didn't like about herself and her life, but she wasn't a quitter. She was a survivor and that was what she intended to continue to be. She'd been through too much shit and survived to give up now, though she knew as well that she now had more to cope with and life did get her down and at times she had wondered whether it was all worth it.

Doctor Armstrong also talked to her about the cutting. Katie told her that she knew it wasn't the answer to anything, but it helped. She said she couldn't promise she wouldn't do it again, but she really didn't usually cut as deep as she had. She didn't want that to happen again, she was absolutely sure of that. It really had scared her to know that she had lost control like that. She'd always had so much control with her cutting. She didn't want to lose that.

*

The next few days passed without further incident. Katie saw her GP as arranged. She kept taking the medication as prescribed and it did help. Katie found that she felt calmer, it took the edge off things. She was now sitting in the waiting room at the surgery and waiting to see Keith. It was still a few minutes before her appointment time. She was fed up with her room. The doctor had been clear that she should not drink with the medication she was taking. Katie hadn't liked that but had managed so far. She was a little wary as she sat there, wondering just how much she wanted to talk and how it would leave her feeling. She didn't want to stir things up any more than they already were. It was strange. The tablets made her feel detached from reality, and yet anxiety could still get hold of her though not as much. But she did feel different, her mood felt sort of flatter, somehow, it wasn't easy to put into words and in fact it wasn't something she really felt any great urge to do anyway.

She was looking through a magazine, not really paying that much attention to it. The images of the women on the pages made a subtle impression on her as to how a woman should look in today's society. But she wasn't really thinking about it. The medication made it hard for her to concentrate, and she felt tired a lot of the time. She was sleeping a lot and she was grateful for that. But she would wake up feeling very anxious. So many memories would crowd in on her though the anxiety faded a little while after she took her first table

She had been shocked by what had happened. She had never thought of herself as someone who would cut herself to do herself real harm. Yes, she knew it wasn't good but she did it to feel better not to make herself worse. Realising that she had the capacity to cut deep and without seemingly any regard for her own safety was unsettling to say the least; she knew she did risky things but that had been different. Knowing that she was now capable of really damaging and harming herself was disturbing and that was something she wanted to talk about. Being in control was important to her, and she knew that she hadn't been.

Keith had heard that Katie had been in hospital; Dr Armstrong had left him a brief note. She hadn't given him all the details, just that she had cut herself much deeper than usual and was back home now, that she was being prescribed medication and she was seeing her every couple of days. As he walked along the corridor towards the waiting area he was thinking back to the previous session with Katie. It had been a difficult one and yet there had also seemed to have been some kind of breakthrough. Yet he also knew that things were rarely that simple. Had some part of Katie surfaced and driven her to seriously harm herself? Or had something else happened? He didn't know, and there was little point in him speculating. It was Katie's perception, meaning and experience that mattered. What was *her* view and what had *she* been seeking to achieve? He needed to accept that Katie was getting regular support from her doctor and that he needed to offer her the therapeutic space where she could bring what was on her mind. He wondered what she was going to be like as he looked into the waiting area. Katie had her head down and was looking at a magazine. She didn't look any different except maybe a little paler. He called her name. Katie looked up, smiled and closed the magazine, putting it back on the table with the others.

She walked towards Keith. 'Hi.'

'Hi.' He turned and walked towards the counselling room, Katie a couple of steps behind him. As they entered the room Keith beckoned to Katie to sit, which she did.

'So, I know you've had a difficult week, Doctor Armstrong said you'd been in hospital.'

'Cut myself.' Katie looked down as she spoke. Her voice was somewhat flat in tone, but beneath the apparent lack of emotion was a genuine fear about what had happened.

It felt to Keith like something of an understatement. But it was good that she was upfront and talking about it, no sense of avoidance or awkwardness in that moment. 'Must have been serious.'

Katie nodded. 'Went too deep, lost a lot of blood, they had to stitch me up. I don't know, so much has happened since last week. My head's spinning with it all, trying to make sense of it.'

'Yes, you felt calmer as I recall, but things must have happened afterwards.'

'I felt bad again, about myself, like there was something bad about me. I don't know, it just came at me again and I cut, but it was different. I really did cut to hurt myself, I don't know, I just wanted to punish, hurt myself, like I was trying to cut something out. I remember thinking that I really needed to see my own blood, *really* needed to see it. It was awful. But I had to see it. I had to hurt myself. I *had* to. That scares me.' She could feel her anxiety rising as she spoke. The medication wasn't containing it.

'Having to do it, having to seriously hurt yourself, cut deep, see your own blood in the way that you did…?'

Katie nodded.

Keith continued, '… and the sense of *having* to do it.'

Katie held eye contact with Keith as she spoke. 'It was like I knew what I was doing and, yeah, I really had to. I couldn't stop myself. I just remember knowing that I had to cut deep, *had* to cut, and deep.'

The fact that Katie had repeated this showed how important this experience had been. Keith wondered if maybe she didn't feel that he had really appreciated what she was saying. He wanted to be sure that the sense of compulsion that was present for Katie was reflected in his empathy. 'It really is that *having* to do it.'

Katie's thoughts had moved on to the images that had come to her. She looked away. 'There was something else as well.' She swallowed. She felt the anxiety rising further, her stomach was beginning to churn. 'Things I, well, things I remembered.' There was a seriousness in Katie's tone of voice and expression, a seriousness Keith had not heard before. It wasn't that she hadn't been serious before, she had, but this was different. Her voice absolutely commanded Keith's attention.

'You remembered things when you were cutting?'

Katie nodded again. 'A man's face, and feeling hurt by him. He sexually abused me. I know it.' Katie continued to look down, she couldn't quite bring herself to look back up again. She'd got more of a sense of what had happened than she had had when she had first remembered. 'More than once.'

'You've got memories of being sexually abused.' Keith felt his own pain. Although he wasn't somehow surprised at what Katie had disclosed, he was nevertheless strongly affected. He wanted to close his own eyes. He knew part of his reaction was towards Katie and what she must be going through, the other part was for himself and his own feelings towards men that sexually abused children. 'I'm sorry that it happened to you and I'm sorry you are now having to cope with knowing it.' Keith realised his words would have very likely taken the focus on to his reaction and he wasn't too sure how helpful that was.

Katie looked up. She appreciated what Keith had said. 'Thanks.' She shook her head and tightened her lips. 'I hadn't realised. I don't know why. You hear about it but you don't think it happened to you. You think you'd know. But then, well, given the things that did happen to me I shouldn't be surprised. And yet I am.'

Keith nodded. 'Yeah, something that you wouldn't want to think happened to you, and then….'

Katie interrupted him. 'And then you know.' She closed her eyes as a surge of emotion arose within her, a mixture of sadness, hatred, and disgust. So many feelings. And her mum, what about her, where had she been? She knew it had happened at home. Where had she been? Her sympathy towards her mother that she had found the previous week was lost. She felt hot tears in her eyes and on her cheeks.

Keith responded, softly and clearly, 'and then you know'. He felt the silence grow in the room. For the moment there was nothing more to say. His role was to be present, authentically and humanly present, a companion to his client as she confronted her shattered emotional landscape.

What Keith had said summed up what was in Katie's thoughts. 'I sort of wish I didn't.' She closed her eyes, trying to control the tears and the hurt that were taking over.

'Like it would be better if you didn't know?'

'Maybe.' Katie was now supporting her head with her right hand, sobbing to herself. She felt utterly wretched. Since the memories had emerged she had spent a lot of time feeling this way. She'd talked to her doctor, and to her friend Bernie who had been around to see her. It was like everything had changed for her in a way that she couldn't really explain to herself. But she knew she was different now. She experienced herself differently. She didn't understand it and couldn't make sense of it, she just knew that somehow everything had changed.

'I….' Katie didn't finish. She wanted to say something but she didn't know what. She wanted to make sense of it but she didn't want to think about it. It was another part of a shit life. Was she surprised? In one sense she wasn't, but she was as well. It was the shock, the shock of knowing that it had happened to her. So what if it was a long time ago, yet it didn't seem a long time ago. The memory was knew, it was fresh, it didn't seem distant even though it had been when she was still at home so she couldn't have been older than four. She didn't know how old. It didn't matter, and yet it did. She did want to know. And yet she also felt the revulsion making herself recoil from it all. She didn't know the man's name, but she recognised him. The look in his eyes, it was so penetrating, so vivid. She wanted it to go away, it all to go away. She was taking a deep breath as she heard Keith speaking.

'I guess it's hard to find the words.'

Her thoughts were now back with her mum. Why hadn't she done something? Surely she would have done something if she had been there, she wouldn't have…. The thought left her feeling cold. She shivered.

'I don't understand, I mean, what goes around and around in my head is where was my mum? She wasn't a good mum, I know, and she wasn't there for me in so many ways, but what happened?' She shook her head which was still resting on her hand. 'She's not there. I don't have any recollection of her, just him, his face, so clear. It's horrible. It's just too horrible.'

Sitting opposite her Keith was very aware that he could only imagine what Katie was feeling. Yes, he had heard the words she had used, and he could see from the expression on Katie's face the utter horror of what she was remembering, but exactly what her inner world was like at this moment was beyond his knowing. He accepted that it was entirely up to her what she would feel she could trust him with. He needed to remain in touch with her, gently being present and letting her know that she was being heard and that he cared about her as another human being. He couldn't take the memories away, he couldn't change the past. Things had happened and things were today as they were. He knew Katie must feel very alone within herself and he just hoped he could help her to come to terms with what had happened. And he wondered as those words "come to terms" were in his mind, exactly what on earth they actually meant. He wasn't sure they were very helpful.

'The horribleness of him.' Keith deliberately placed the focus on the horribleness and wondered then whether he should also have acknowledged what Katie had said about her mum. But he wasn't going to add anything. He'd responded and if Katie needed to make visible to him again her thoughts about her mum he was sure that she would.

'I'd like to cut him out of my head, out of my body, out of me, I really, really wish I could.' Katie's hand was taking the weight of her head which felt heavy and full, like it was going to explode. She felt tired and she didn't want to be feeling any of this.

'Cut him out, make it all go away.'

'And I can't. He's fucked…', She paused, the word brought a pain in her heart and chest area. She couldn't finish her sentence.

Keith didn't respond straight away. He sensed the anguish linked to what Katie had said. If she had wanted or been able to say more she would have done. He wasn't going to push her. He needed to be beside her in this.

'Lots more painful thoughts and feelings, yeah?'

Katie was taking a deep breath, her breathing wasn't smooth but interrupted by the motions that felt so utterly overwhelming. She nodded in response to Keith. 'Why? Why me? Why am I always the one that gets the shit in life? Why?' Katie felt a surge of anger. 'Why do I have a shit mother, a shit life, bullied, and now this? I thought I was starting to, you know, make sense of a few things. Why this?'

'Yeah, feels like you got all the shit and you just want to know "why?".' Keith didn't respond with a questioning tone, he didn't want to respond in a way that might leave Katie thinking he wanted an answer. Rather he spoke in a more matter of fact way.

Katie moved in the chair, her arm was aching. She sat back, realising as she did so that her back was very stiff as well. 'I didn't deserve any of this.'

'No, you didn't deserve it.' Keith was quick to affirm what Katie had said. He knew that there could be a tendency for people to blame themselves, often because as a child that was what they had done and the belief lived on in some way. But he knew that the reality was that the child was never to blame. The adult was responsible. It was the adult that should have known better, the adult that should have had control. Yes, he knew men could have childhoods where they were abused, or be brought up in family systems where it was acceptable for there to be sexual contact with children. He knew it happened. But it wasn't an excuse, not really. A man should know that it is wrong to have sex with a child.

'I know I have thought, you know, there was something wrong with me, and, well, yeah, you know, being bad news. But….'

'But?' Keith invited Katie to continue.

'Not that.'

'No, not that.'

Katie went silent, aware of conflicting reactions within her. She wanted to shrink away, go very small in the chair, and she wanted to react angrily as well. She felt herself shrinking back. 'I didn't want….' Her voice had changed. It was a child once more.

'No, you didn't want.' Keith softened his voice. He empathised directly and again did not respond in a questioning manner, not this time. He wanted to be sure that the part of Katie that was speaking knew that the fact that she didn't want something was being heard.

'He hurt me and I screamed but he didn't stop.'

'You are a little girl, he was too big. You screamed, he didn't stop.'

Katie could feel herself being four years old. Yet she was herself now as well except that somehow that was secondary. The new feelings were so sharp, so present. 'He made me hurt so much.'

'Yes, he hurt you so much.'

Katie wanted to close her eyes and make what was happening stop, but she couldn't, it was as though she was just an observer, like someone or something had taken her over. It had, the traumatised little girl who had, perhaps, never spoken of what had happened.

'I want my mummy.'

Keith could feel goose-bumps breaking out at the back of his neck, down his back and into his legs. 'Yes, Katie wants her mummy.'

There were two Katie's in the room in that moment, both wanting their mummy. Keith was aware that he had never encountered anything quite like this. He knew he had to be absolutely in tune with what was needed, and the truth was that in his head he hadn't a clue what the "right" responses were. He had a young woman and a little girl in the room and whilst he knew he was currently relating to the little girl, he also was aware that the young woman was also there, experiencing whatever she was experiencing in this process.

Katie wanted to somehow reach out to the part of her that was speaking, to the feelings that were there inside her. But she felt unable to move, psychologically, or in any other way. She was transfixed by what was unfolding within her. She felt a surge of terror inside her. It wasn't her, the adult, but her, the child. 'Are you going to hurt me?'

More goose-bumps and a cold sensation in his neck and upper back. 'No', Keith responded, 'no, I am not going to hurt you.' He paused before adding, 'I want to help you'. He wasn't sure if that was the helpful thing to say but it felt, well, not so much right as words that just needed to be said.

The terror subsided a little. 'I'd like that.'

'You'd like me to help you.' Keith could feel his heart thumping. He wanted to hold his breath, it was instinctive.

'Will you be my friend?'

It wasn't what he expected. Again the little girl was speaking directly to him. Should he empathise or give a straight answer? He didn't know. He knew he couldn't spend time hesitating and thinking about it. He had to respond.

'You'd like me to be your friend?'

'Yes.'

'Then I will be.' He smiled.

Keith saw a smile breaking out on Katie's face. He heard adult Katie's voice. 'So will I.' She blinked rapidly for a moment, he had not noticed that before. There was a difference.

'Are you OK?' Keith knew instinctively that adult Katie was back in contact with him, it wasn't just the voice.

'I-I think so. That was…, ooh, I don't know. Was that me, well, I know it was. It was like before and yet this time it was very, I mean, I *felt* so much more.'

'Like you had feelings from the past that felt very real in the present?'

Katie nodded. She felt extremely tired all of a sudden and yawned. 'Oh dear.' It set Keith off who yawned too. 'It's catching', he commented. But he also felt incredibly moved by what he had heard and witnessed.

'I feel tired, incredibly tired but you know it felt good. I mean it didn't as well, I really felt terror at one point, I mean really. It was…, I can't describe it, just everywhere.'

'Mhmm, like the terror just overwhelmed all of you.'

'But it was her, me, I don't know what to say. It was, is, me.'

'It's you but a part of you that's been kind of locked away.'

'Not any more.'

'No, not any more.'

'Something happened at the end.'

'Mhmm.' Keith's response had a slight questioning tone, inviting Katie to say more. Yes, he thought, something certainly did, but he

186

wanted to allow Katie to explore it as she experienced it rather than start giving her his experience.

'I felt a change when you said about being her friend. It was like, I don't know, relief. It was like something suddenly seemed sort of OK. I don't know. Like, yeah, OK.'

'Being told I would be her friend, something shifted, something like a sense of relief kind of emerged within you?' Keith wanted to get clarity on this. It felt incredibly important not just for him to understand but that through understanding he might also help Katie clarify for herself what she had experienced. He knew that she needed to integrate. She was fragmented, parts of herself to some degree dissociated as a legacy of the traumatic experiencing at an age when the structure of self hadn't formed in a strong and resilient manner. He knew that whilst some people spent their lives managing fragmentation of this kind, not everyone could. And he hadn't worked with someone where it seemed so clear. He knew that all parts of Katie needed to be heard, understood and valued.

'It was like she, I, heard what I, she – how do I say it? – it was what she needed.' Katie couldn't work out what words to describe herself.

'She needed.'

'And I needed.

'You mean like you both needed to hear that?'

'Hmm. Sort of.' Katie paused. 'Maybe she did need a friend. I needed a friend. I know I spent so much time on my own. So, yes, I did need a friend, and I maybe still do in many ways.' She felt her eyes moistening as part of the conversation came back to her. 'We both wanted our mummy.' She felt a lump forming in her throat as she finished speaking. Her eyes were now quite watery and as she closed them she felt the tears spill over her eyelids and on to her cheeks.

'Yes. You both wanted your mummy.' Keith kept his response simple and responsive to the last thing that Katie had said. She had clearly processed her way through to this recognition and it wasn't for him to take her back to the start of what she had just said. His own emotions were very present too.

'And I still do, even though I know I don't understand her, I blame her, and know she was a crap mother, I know all that, but there is still that....' Katie shook her head. It didn't make sense in one way and yet somehow it did, in spite of the contradiction. It was how it was and she had to come to terms with it.

'Still something important, something between you.' Keith was also aware that Katie had also responded to the part of her that had spoken. It didn't feel right in that moment to introduce this.

Katie nodded. She knew it didn't make much sense. She felt a creeping emptiness inside herself. It was intense. She closed her eyes and wished it wasn't there. 'I just feel like there's something missing inside me.' Katie paused. Yes, she thought to herself, something's missing, a gap, it was hard to really describe, but she felt it, she knew it was there. And it seemed linked to the experience she had just had.

'Empty, something missing.'

'It's like I'm not…, I don't know, I want to say "all of me", but I am who I am, and yet this feeling of something missing is still there.'

'The something missing feeling.' Keith's response was slightly questioning but more of a reflection of what Katie was alluding to.

She thought back to her experience of hearing that younger part of herself speaking. In a strange kind of way it had felt like she had connected with something, rather than it being about something missing, but it was linked, she was sure about that. She felt a powerful thought come into her mind. 'It's what I said, we both miss her, we both want her, we both didn't have something we both need. But I don't know if it's me, her, it's confusing, and yet somehow hearing myself speak like that it also seemed really clear as well. I can't…', she shook her head, 'I don't know.'

Keith could see the confusion in her facial expression. 'So it's clear and yet confusing as well.' He could appreciate what Katie was saying. She'd had all kinds of disrupting experiences in her life, and been neglected as well, and all of this had contributed to her being how she was now. In addition she was now realising things about herself that just added even more to the awfulness of what she had been through. He wanted to say something to capture this but he didn't want to direct her away from her focus.

Katie nodded, not sure what else to say. Keith felt his urge to speak growing. He felt he wanted to communicate to Katie his sense of what she had been through, the enormity of it all. Was that fair? Was that helpful? She knew what she had been through. Did she need him telling

188

her what he was experiencing? Did she? Would it be therapeutically helpful, or was it simply his need to say something, his need for her to hear what he was experiencing? And yet he wanted to trust the urge to speak. It felt right. He knew that wasn't necessarily a good enough reason, but he also knew that when you were experiencing a therapeutic connection with a client it could move you to speak in ways or to say things that you might not normally have said, and yet often they proved to be helpful. He let himself be open to what he was experiencing. It felt right. It felt it was something emerging from the connection rather than simply his personal reaction coming out of a disconnected place. He needed to say something, he could feel a strange urgency about it.

'Katie, I am sitting here so aware of the enormity of everything that you have experienced and that you are describing. So much has happened and is happening. Things you are experiencing, realising, having to make sense of. I'm sure you don't need me to go into details, and I see you finding your own way to hang in there with it all, as you have always hung in there.' He didn't feel a relief in saying what he had said. Rather he felt a kind of steadiness, a sort of inner composure. He waited for Katie to respond.

It felt good to hear Keith say what he had said. Yes, it was enormous, it was huge, immense, everything. And she was hanging in there. Yes, she had survived so much, but at what cost? A heavy emotional cost. She'd been hurt and she was still hurting. She'd been abused, she knew that now, not just sexually, that was new to her and was still a shock. She hadn't come to terms with that yet. She wasn't sure she ever would. And yet, at the same time, even that in some strange way wasn't a surprise. Another thing to add to the roll-call of shit she'd gone through. But she was a survivor. She had coped. She wasn't going to let other people put her down. She did fight back. It didn't always help but it was her way of saying, "hey, don't mess with me". And she also knew she needed to feel wanted, to have contact with men in particular. She needed that, and she sort of felt like she didn't want that either. It wasn't straightforward, it wasn't clear, nothing ever was. She'd been having sex for so many years now, since early teens. That's how it was, how she was. Yeah, it was exciting, but it was something else as well. And yet she could also feel quite detached too. She did just feel like an object sometimes, just being shagged by someone, whoever it might be. To begin with it had been important who it was, but not any more. She was sad about that. She wanted that to change.

'I want to be in control.' It wasn't something Katie had thought about saying, but the words just came out. And having spoken them the experience of that wanting seemed more present to her. She wanted be in control of her life, yes, she wanted to be in control of herself, who she was, what she did, why she did it. Why she did it…, that was a big one. It was an area that she was growing more uneasy about. She heard Keith speaking though his voice was a little remote, her own thoughts being so very present in her awareness.

'Yeah, be in control.' Keith wasn't sure his response was as it might have been, he had perhaps not conveyed the wanting as strongly as he had heard it in Katie's voice. 'Something you really want.'

Katie tightened her lips and nodded slightly. Her thoughts had gone back over the past week, to seeing the man's face and knowing what he had done to her, and the cutting herself so deeply and being in hospital. Not being in control. She hadn't been, not then, she'd lost it. She'd lost so much. So much loss. She'd lost control, another loss, so many losses in her life. And having someone there for her, to care for her, to turn to, that was hugely present in her thoughts and feelings. And yet she knew she had to look after herself. She took a very deep breath and silently sighed to herself. So much loss….

Keith saw the deep breath and sensed that there was lot happening for Katie that she wasn't talking about. And that was OK. Therapy wasn't just about talking, it was about connecting with yourself, and that could be so difficult. Katie would have so many experiences, so many reactions to the events on her life. 'A lot to think about.' Keith spoke softly, wanting to communicate his empathy for what he sensed was happening for Katie, but not wanting to disturb the internal process that was taking place.

Again, Keith's voice seemed distant, but nevertheless for Katie it was somehow reassuring to hear. It summed it up, a kind of confirmation of how things were. She was still feeling that loss. It was a strange sensation. It felt as though it was all around her, as if she was inside the loss rather than the loss was inside her. She didn't like it. The loss had turned into lost. She was feeling lost, unsure of herself, who she was, who she really was. Yes, she was Katie, but what did that mean?

What did that *really* mean? It all seemed such a strange thing to think about, and to not have an answer to. Who was Katie? Was? No, who *is* Katie?

'I don't know who I am anymore.' Katie's voice was quiet and reflective. It seemed to Keith as he heard her words that she was speaking from a long way away. Physically, she was present, but clearly her psychological focus was in a sense somewhere else, maybe deep inside herself.

'You don't know who you are.' He paused. 'Who is Katie?'

Katie sat, she felt almost as though she couldn't move, even her breathing was shallow and it was as if she dare not take a deeper breath in case.... In case of what? She did not know. She just knew that something was requiring her to be very still. Keith's words were very present for her. He had said exactly what she had been thinking, though she had not actually said it herself. Who is Katie? The questions reverberated in her head. She felt as though everything had stopped. His words had affirmed something, and it went deep. She wasn't thinking of depth or anything like that, for Katie it was simply a matter of feeling very still and knowing, in an immediate and personal way, that she did not know the answer to the question. And it was as though she knew if she moved she would become again the person she was. Part of her did not want that. The stillness continued.

Keith felt the silence acutely. But he was not going to say anything further. What he had said had felt right and it seemed to him that there was a lot happening within the silence even though outwardly there was no evidence of this. He kept his focus on Katie, aware that he was hoping that whatever was happening for or within her was going to be helpful. No, it wasn't hoping, it was more than that. He knew that so long as she was experiencing unconditional positive regard from him, that his empathic responses were accurate, and that she experienced authenticity from him, then whatever was happening for her could be trusted to be part of a process of personality change that was inherently constructive. He continued to sit, respecting the silence. He did not let his mind wander.

Within her own silence Katie was aware of a stream of thought taking her back into her own past. So many things had happened in her life, so much that had caused her sadness and hurt. But it wasn't this that held her attention. She knew all that, she didn't need to remind herself of those things. In fact, all of her life seemed somehow distant, a bit like a film on a screen. Something to watch, to observe and you see yourself there, being part of it, and yet you are also just watching everything unfold. It felt as though someone was rewinding a tape in her head. She was recalling images from the different homes she had been in, the schools she had gone to. Each time there was a kind of urge to go back, to make another step into her past. It wasn't that she was in any way making it happen, it was just happening. She could only watch as scene after scene in a sense unfolded itself within her mind.

Time was passing, three, four minutes, the silence continued. To Keith it seemed that Katie had become transfixed, her eyes were open and she seemed to be looking and yet she didn't look focussed, not on anything that she might have had within her line of vision. He hadn't experienced this before. It felt not so much intense, just…, he wasn't sure. It was as it was. His last words had, perhaps, resonated with something for Katie. He had no idea what. He had simply been seeking to stay in touch with Katie and to convey what he felt she was telling him. He was aware that his concentration was making him feel a little spaced out. He briefly closed his eyes, hoping it would clear, and it did. He was also feeling as though he couldn't, or was it shouldn't, move. It was like the world was holding its breath in some strange way. He thought that seemed somewhat over the top, but actually it did feel like that. He continued to sit and wait. A zen-like koan came into his mind, the statements that are used to stop the rational mind so that something more immediate and whole can break into awareness. 'What happens in the moment when nothing happens'. He felt goose-bumps on the sides of his neck and down his spine as the answer flew straight into his head with an absolute assurance. Everything. Was everything happening for Katie?

Katie was back at home as a child, watching the scenes unfold. It was as if she was seeing the scenes through her own eyes as she was when they were occurring, and yet there was this sense of onlooker or observer as well. But it didn't disturb her. In fact, it seemed quite OK, and certainly nothing to feel any discomfort or anxiety about. She was seeing her mother. How she had been. She could see her shouting at her, hitting her. She saw Dolly and Mister P in front of her on the floor.

She saw the man's face who had sexually abused her. She felt strangely detached, and yet she wasn't because she could also feel a cauldron of feelings within her, yet they were contained in some strange way. At least for the moment. Slowly the images began to fade. She was aware once more of the room in which she sat, with Keith opposite her. A surge of emotion burst upon her, the cauldron had bubbled over, no longer contained it burned now in her awareness, as if it was consuming her whole being. Hurt, pain, sadness, terror, being utterly alone, and small and confused. The tears flowed and the heart-rending sounds that were her only way of giving voice to her feelings burst out of her, interspersed with an occasional desperate 'Oh God'. The release lasted some minutes. There was nothing Katie could do, it was more than she could contain, and she wasn't trying, she wasn't in a place to try to contain it anymore.

Keith sat with his heart-thumping and his own emotions churning as he witnessed the release of pain and emotion before him. He spoke softly, 'It's OK, let it go, let it out.' He didn't want his voice to get in the way of what was happening for Katie, but he also wanted to offer his presence and reassurance to her. He could see that what was happening was profound. He didn't know exactly what had happened for Katie, but he also knew that what was occurring was needed, not because it was something everyone had to experience, but rather it was necessary because it was happening, and happening now. 'So much pain and hurt, so much to let out.' He felt such a warm compassion for Katie as she sat in the midst of what he could only imagine to be a kind of human hell. A phrase from an affirmation came to mind, 'Let the fire's rage, the flames devour, let all the dross be burnt'. Something in Katie was burning up, it was excruciating to watch, and yet he knew that so often, where the pain and hurt were deep, this was the only way of resolving it.

Katie began to feel the emotions start to subside. She felt wretched, her face was wet, she needed to blow her nose, her body felt heavy, weak, her throat burned, her head felt like it wanted to burst and her heart…, her heart just simply ached, a fiery aching that still burned. It was there, in her heart, that the pain of her past resided. She swallowed and reached for a tissue, starting to dry her face. It was soon breaking up with the dampness. She reached for another and blew her nose. She swallowed again, the burning lump in her throat made it difficult. She looked up at Keith. 'I couldn't....' Her voice trailed off.

'No, too overwhelming.' Keith nodded slightly, he tightened his lips but smiled gently. His task now was to reassure and be a steady presence.

Katie took a deep breath and blew the air out. 'I saw it all.'

'All?' Keith sought to understand what Katie meant.

'My life. I mean, not everything, but it was like watching a film, I mean, it really was like watching a film.'

'A film of your life.'

Katie nodded. 'Going right back. One event after another. Just watching. I wasn't really feeling, just watching.'

'Like you were a kind of observer?'

'But seeing through my own eyes.' Katie paused as she was forced into silence by the overwhelming sense of what had happened.

'Seeing the events unfold through your own eyes.'

Katie nodded again. 'And I knew I was feeling things, but I wasn't, it was like they were there but I wasn't experiencing them.' She frowned.

'Mhmm, I have a sense of like watching a film without the sound, but this was without the feelings.'

Yes, thought Katie, yes, that was it. And actually, now Keith had said it, there hadn't been sounds, not really, or they had seemed somehow muffled. It was what she saw that was important. 'There wasn't much sound either.' She continued to frown, puzzled by it all.

'No feelings, not much sound, just images.'

'Painful ones.'

'Painful memories.'

'But not just that. There were some good images as well. But not many, it was mainly being bullied, being picked on, shouted at, hit, being on my own…'. And being raped. She didn't say this, she somehow didn't want to. She knew that was what had happened to her as a child, and in some respects had happened later as a teenager. She'd been what they called 'promiscuous' since she had been 13 or so, messing about, and a few times it had got out of hand, but she'd never tried to stop anything. She felt suddenly very dirty as she thought about it, and sad.

'So many horrible things happening to you.'

Katie knew she needed to say more. 'And, you know, being sexually abused as a child and, well, yeah, that affected me, I mean, yeah.'

'Yeah, it would.' Keith sought to affirm what Katie was acknowledging than empathise. It felt the right response.

'Probably been raped since, I mean, you know?'

'There have been other times?'

Katie nodded. She wanted to feel OK about it, but the truth was that deep down she didn't. 'A few times when, yeah, it wasn't really what I wanted but, well, hmm, a few drinks and well….' Her voice trailed off.

'Things get out of control, you mean, and a few drinks adds to the problem?'

Katie took a deep breath. She'd also had a number of infections as well over the years, numerous courses of antibiotics. 'I guess it all connects, I mean, what happened to me in the past, what I've been through all my life.'

'You've had a tough time, no doubt about that. And, yes, it's affected you in a range of ways.'

'Too much everything, too much booze, cutting myself, bullied, family using drugs. At least that's something I don't do, well, dabbled a bit but no, that's something I don't do, and don't want to. I suppose that's something.'

'It's a positive in amongst a lot of negative experiences.' Keith was strongly aware of his sense of the enormity of what Katie had been through, and yet she had survived, she was a survivor in so many senses of the word.

'It's strange, I'm feeling calmer again. It's like it kind of blows up and then, yeah, settles down again.' She paused. 'Or maybe I'm just tired.'

'Or both.' Keith glanced over at the clock, the session was due to end. Katie noticed his glance. 'That time?'

He nodded.

'I need to keep it together, don't I?'

'Have you got support, apart from your GP?'

'I'm still seeing her, next time is tomorrow. She wanted to avoid seeing me the same day I see you. I stopped going to the support group, but maybe I should start again. Bernie suggested that when I saw her, she's still going.'

'There are other agencies out there to support young people, you know?'

'Yeah, I know, but, well, I kind of need to find my own way, you know, that's me, independent, looking out for myself. 'She paused in silent reflection. 'Just not much good at it at the moment.'

Keith nodded but didn't respond directly. The session was up and he wasn't going to re-engage Katie in an exploration. 'You've always found your own way to survive, I guess that's how it is for now.'

'Hmm. Maybe I…, I don't know.'

'Maybe I…?' Keith responded as it felt important to help Katie to say or acknowledge what was on her mind.

'Maybe I do need to, you know, get more help, maybe.'

'I've got a new list of groups for different kinds of support, just been updated. Do you want a copy?' Keith wondered if he was pushing. Should he just have empathised with what Katie had said? He waited for her response.

'I'll think about it.' Katie got up. 'Time to go.'

'Sure. I hope your week goes well.' Keith felt sure he'd said the unhelpful thing.

'Can't be worse than last week.' Katie felt determined not to go back there again. 'See you next week.'

'Sure.' As Katie left the room Keith was aware of his own depleted energy levels. That had been an intense session. In truth they all were with Katie. In one sense he was glad all of his clients weren't like Katie, he knew he'd be feeling overwhelmed, but the reality was that some did have intense sessions, others not.

He knew he had a supervision session later in the week and he was glad of that. So much seemed to be happening for Katie, and so much was coming to the surface about her past. What a life, he thought, and is she the exception? Is she? The tragedy was that he knew she wasn't, that so many young people had their own versions of what Katie had been subjected to and had had to cope with, both physically and psychologically. But he did feel positive. Yes, things had gone bad for her with the cutting and everything, but she was also engaging in the therapeutic process and, as far as he was concerned, what was particularly important was that she was engaging with herself, she really was making connections. Yes, it was difficult, confusing, harrowing as well – he thought of how she had been during the last session. And yet, somehow he felt sure that things were moving in a productive direction. He was glad for that and for being a part of that process. Katie was clearly hanging on to her independence. Maybe that was a good thing. He wasn't going to undermine that. He turned and wrote his notes for the session and jotted down a few areas he wanted to cover in his supervision.

Chapter 10

'Katie.' Keith began. 'A lot has been happening for her both within and outside of the sessions.' She was the first client Keith was talking about in his supervision session with Lorraine. 'She's cutting, and deep, ended up in hospital. That shocked her. She's realised she was sexually abused as a child. She's had flashbacks and there's some dissociated experiences coming through as well, younger, child-like parts of herself have emerged into the therapy room and into the dialogue. It's been intense, very intense. And some really distressing releases of emotion. She's been through a lot, she really has.'

Lorraine as usual had one supervisory antenna focussed on Keith's clients and the other on Keith. 'So, difficult for her and difficult for you to witness and be a part of?'

Keith took a deep breath. 'Particularly so. I think we talked about it last time as well, but the sessions are intense, they really are. I've not had many clients with this kind of intensity at such a sustained level. Things really do move, and fast. There have been long, intense silences, but the most powerful have been related to hearing herself speak as a child. I want to process that because even as I mention it now I can feel the goose-bumps on my neck and a slight watering of my eyes. The way that she, as an adult and as a child, are both facing the same loss....' He shook his head as he thought back to how they had both wanted their mummy.

'Like it's there both in the past and the present.'

'On occasions it really feels like there are three of us in the room. I mean, it's like that anyway when a dissociated part emerges, but it seemed to become even more so.' Keith paused, aware that as he was speaking he was feeling a little spaced out himself. He commented on this, 'just talking about it and I can feel my head beginning to spin'.

'It's powerful, intense, it really gets to you.'

'It does. There has been so much happening, Lorraine, so much, and it is hard to know where to begin other than just going through it and see what emerges from it.' Keith felt sure that was the best way to approach it. He'd jotted down notes so that he could get things in order as he knew it would be easy for him to lose the sequence of events.

'OK.' Lorraine agreed that it was best to recount what had happened, to try and convey something of the flow of events and experiencing. Sometimes it was more helpful to move back and forward, picking up connections, and maybe that would happen now, but as she looked over at Keith and given his tone of voice, she had genuinely been struck by a sense of his being 'full'. Clearly, it was impacting on him in a physically experiential way given his reference to feeling his head spin. As a supervisor she knew that one of her roles was to allow her supervisees to process what they had been experiencing and restore, within themselves, an ability to be congruently and empathically present for their clients. She knew that when a counsellor was overwhelmed this can be difficult, the emotional and mental build-up can impact on how open and sensitive they can be. It is hard to be responsive to what someone is saying to you when you have a head full of the effects of the intense interactions you've had with other clients. Yes, it felt right for Keith to tell the story. It helped clients to do this, and it also helped supervisees.

'I've seen Katie three times since our last session. The first of those three sessions she came in having got drunk, fallen and ended up in Accident and Emergency at the hospital. I'd said something at the end of the previous session, and I can't remember exactly what but it was something like saying to her to look after herself, or take care of herself, I'm not sure.' As he spoke he was struck by the significance of the two words he had used given the content of recent sessions. 'May have been more along the lines of "you take care of yourself".

'So you suggested to her to "take care of herself" and that was connected to what happened?'

'She wanted to blame that. I mean, you know, people blame all kinds of things for drinking, but she did blame what I had said. She was angry with me, that's what she said the following week and it had left her wanting to get drunk.' Keith knew it wasn't his fault, and yet he also knew that maybe he could have been more sensitive although what he had said had been genuine.

'She became angry and drank on that anger, and it was towards you.' Lorraine doubted that it was probably that simple. She didn't make her response questioning, just left it as a statement and waited for how Keith responded.

'Well, yes, but I don't think it was just that. I mean, yes it was, but there is so much happening for Katie, so much depth to her pain and I think that it was just me using the words "take care", I think that it really did touch something in her. She hasn't been cared for very much in her life. At least, that's not how she has experienced it. One good set of foster parents, but the foster mother became ill and died. Otherwise, bullied, neglected and now she realises she was sexually abused as well.' Keith tightened his lips and shook his head slightly. 'She really has been through it, I just hope she can come to terms with it all.' He stopped and felt a smile break out. 'And I think she will. I don't know exactly why, but I think she will. There is so much happening and it feels like her…, I don't know the best way of putting this, but there is a lot of fluidity. I don't think she's sort of fixed or rigid in herself. I mean, yes, she will have rigidity about some things, we all do, but there is something very dynamic about her structure of self. Things are happening, interactions are taking place and, yes, she has got into some risky and dangerous habits and ways of coping, but I just think, well, she is a survivor. I hope I can help her now to survive the inner turmoil she is facing as she comes to terms with her past, with emerging memories and finding hopefully less damaging ways of coping with it all.'

'So, as you say, a lot going on for her, but that sense of fluidity seems important.' Lorraine responded to that because it had just struck her as being particularly important as Keith had said it. She knew that in terms of person-centred theory that movement from fixity to fluidity was a sign or stage in the process of constructive personality change, but that there could be a period within that emerging fluidity where it just felt like chaos; the fixity that had previously been a support system, something to rely on, was now no longer there in the same way.

'I think it's about not knowing what she has to hang on to. There was something about not knowing who she was in one of the sessions, and I don't think she knows.'

Lorraine nodded, 'and how does that affect you? Sometimes a client not knowing who they are means boundaries are blurred and that can impact on the counsellor'.

'I feel clear. I'm her counsellor. I'm there to listen and support her psychologically and emotionally as she finds a way through all of this. I'm like a point of reference, something hopefully steady and consistent in contrast to her inner world which must just seem as though it is swirling around in, at times, a quite uncontrollable manner.'

'I wonder how she sees you.' Lorraine's response was a result of hearing clearly what Keith thought he was, but it was all very much his perception.

'Hmm.' Keith nodded in response. 'Yes, good point. And I really don't know. I know she's been angry with me, but I also think she respects me, I mean, she is still attending in spite of what has been happening. So there's something there that keeps her coming back.'

'So, you sense a kind of respect?'

'She's not said it, but I think so. She knows that she's likely to get upset, and for some people that can put them off, but she is coming each week. I'm sure her doctor will be encouraging her to keep attending.'

'So there may be some external push as well.'

'Yes. But I'll take your point away and bear it in mind.' Keith paused. 'Anyway, Katie had got angry and got drunk and fell over and had to go into hospital. And, well, her doctor then saw me at the surgery and told me there were cuts on her upper arms, the hospital had noticed them during an examination. I had decided to make what I knew visible to Katie. But I did it in a way so as to acknowledge what I knew but hopefully without pressuring her in any way to talk about it. And I think I achieved that.'

'That sounds helpful. Always difficult when we are told things before the client tells us.' Lorraine knew from her own experience that it could throw up difficult situations. Her policy had always been to make what she knew visible, but to pick her moment so as not to cut across something the client was saying or to strongly divert the client's attention to a particular issue. It was about acknowledging so that in terms of knowledge about the client there was transparency from the counsellor. Knowing something about a client that the client doesn't know that you know can simply create a focus of attention within the counsellor that undermined their authenticity.

'She didn't look too happy about it, but I acknowledged what Dr Armstrong had told me and that people cut for their own reasons, and that if she wanted to talk about it I'd be happy to listen. I sought to make it clear that it really was up to her, that it was her business and that I respected that.'

'And that was how you felt?'

Keith nodded. 'Yes, it was. I wanted her to talk about it, but when she wants and needs to. There is no point in my trying to push someone into talking about things they are not ready to talk about. Once you do that, you take something away from them, you take away their autonomy, and that takes something from their own process. They know that they cannot now go with their own flow, as it were.'

'As if you would, what, leave them experiencing distrust of their own process?' Lorraine was being speculative in her response.

'Is it distrust? Maybe not conscious distrust, but it says something to the client. It sets an agenda that might not be in tune with their inner process, and I know that saying it like that can make it sound woolly, but I don't believe that it is. In fact, for me it is the bedrock of what I do. I empathise with my clients, with what they say, what they communicate, and with the process taking place within them. I want to say "the process that they are", because essentially we are in a state of process, all the time, and in a way it is that which we are seeking to empathise with in our clients.'

'Tuning into their process and allowing that to direct the session?'

'Very much so. It's subtle, or can be, and hard to quantify which is probably why it's not always really appreciated. We talk about relationship and connection, and we usually refer to it as being with the person. And that can in a way make it as though they are something fixed at the other end of the connection, but there is no fixity, well, in some people there is, but it's about connecting with the other person's process, their way of being, the dynamic intra-personal content.'

'Interesting phrase, "dynamic intra-personal content". It does sum it up.' Lorraine paused.' Do you want to stay with that or focus back on Katie?'

Keith's thoughts were already back with Katie. 'She has some very powerful intra-personal dynamics. That sounds so scientific, but the reality is she's fragmented. She's speaking through a very childlike voice at times, and this happened in the session I'm talking about. She talked about wanting to be taken away to somewhere nice. It was really powerful. And Katie herself as an adult also responded to herself as a child. It's been confusing to Katie and it has disturbed her sense of who she is, and I know she is struggling to get her head around some of this - whether she is who she is normally, or the part or parts of herself that emerge. But it was hearing Katie respond to herself that was so powerful, and that really does make it feel like three people in the room. It's one thing when a part of a client emerges, you relate to that part and it can feel strongly still one-to-one, but on this occasion Katie responded to herself, and she said that she was left feeling more whole, more calm, she had a more peaceful expression on her face.'

'What did she say?'

'"I'll take you away. I'll look after you", something like that.'

Lorraine felt her own eyes moisten a little, 'such a tender and human experience. Powerful too.'

'It was a kind of heart, no, world stopping moment. Katie said afterwards that she wasn't sure whether she had said the words or not, she had heard them but wasn't sure if they were just a thought, but I heard them and I am sure that the part of Katie that had emerged also heard them. That part faded. I guess in some way reassured. Some kind of connection must have taken place, maybe something integrated, I don't know, can it happen that quickly?'

'I don't know, and I don't think we understand these processes well enough. Someone hears a voice, speaks to themselves, a dissociated state emerges, and it is all to easy to pathologise it, label it up as a mental illness, give the person medication to contain or manage it and not fully engage with the person enough to understand them.'

'Back to seeing them as process persons?'

'Something like that. People are in process and sometimes their processes can be challenging, can be disturbing both to them and the people trying to help them, but that doesn't mean we shouldn't strive to understand and accept what is present. And there are still going to be times when people will need medication to contain them, but we just need to watch that we are not impacting on a process which, if supported, might actually be healing to the person. And we know that people do need to be helped so that they are not a danger to themselves or others, but we just have to be so careful that social control does not override genuine treatment, and the truth is that often what is called treatment is actually risk management with an underlying agenda of social control.' Lorraine paused. 'Sorry, strong feelings on the topic.'

'I know, I have them as well.'

'But I need to stay with you, not sound off. I think I need to process my own stuff somewhere else.'

'Well, Lorraine, don't process it out of existence. You know my thoughts and concerns about therapy as a way of restoring people to maintain their place within the social norm, and what does that mean when the social norm may itself be damaging, unhealthy, even fundamentally flawed and dysfunctional?'

Lorraine smiled, 'I know, anyway, OK, so let's get back to Katie.'

'Well, that was it really. Then the next week, well, another intense session. Katie talked of being depressed at times and how it was a kind of heavy, zombie like experience. She talked of wanting to be free, to be different. This was a really strong yearning. And she'd also talked about how awful it was, not just that, everything, her life, and I responded saying something along the lines of my wanting to hear, understand and respond to how awful it was. There then followed an intense silence. And then this scream. It just, how can I describe it, just cut its way out of her, it was so penetrating.'

'Mhmm'

'Then she spoke again as a child, talking about being lonely, only having her doll and teddy to comfort her. Talked of them being her friends. They were really important to her but Mister P got taken away from her when she went into care. She was able to keep her doll, called Dolly.'

Mister P?'

'Name of her teddy bear.'

'And he was taken away from her', Lorraine could feel herself frowning and a sense of how awful and inhuman that was.

'Someone probably thought she'd rather have a new one or something. I don't know, sometimes people just don't think, do they, and it clearly affected Katie.'

'Reason enough to scream.'

'She said she'd screamed at the time, one of many reasons for her to scream.' Keith was aware as he spoke of his own awareness of how much Katie had been through in her life. 'She also talked about being taken away from home, from her mum. She can remember it still. More screaming, and not just her.'

'No, I can only imagine. Can't have been easy for you to hear.'

'Not when you have a real sense of the person that was affected, and is still affected. It's easy to blame, I hope people do their best in these situations, they can't be easy. But, well, it was probably for the best, they must have felt Katie was at risk, but damage had already been done.' Keith felt keenly what he was saying. So much damage did get done to young children. Some were resilient, or had others around them who could provide the support and normality, usually in the form of consistency and caring that helped them find their own internal resilience, but there were many who did not have that and who, as a result, found it hard to cope with life.

'As so often happens.'

'And I know we can help people to turn things around, but I see so many young people these days who, I don't know, they are really struggling to cope in many different ways. Maybe it's always been like that, every generation has its difficulties, but today in the West, and no doubt elsewhere, it's so intense, and the need to conform to fashion, to looking right, all of that, it's a real pressure. And then there are the gangs, the culture that we see in the cities, kids literally not being able to move around outside of a few streets because they'd be in someone else's territory.' He shook his head, he'd seen a TV programme about it recently, and how community workers were having to bus young people from one area to another just to get them safely to youth clubs and other activities.

Lorraine had seen the programme as well. 'It was on TV the other night.'

'You saw it too?'

Lorraine nodded.

'What are we creating out there? It's madness and we don't seem able to stop it. Why don't we care enough about young people? We've created a crazy world in so many ways, our values are upside down, everything is just over the top.'

Lorraine put her own feelings aside. 'So intense. So, as you say, over the top.'

Keith took a deep breath but he wasn't going to go off on one over it. He knew he had strong feelings but he needed to use the time to focus on his clients. If he felt the need to go on more in supervision he knew he needed to take it to therapy, or to some other place to unload. He continued. 'Anyway, Katie started to talk more about the cutting, how it helps to relieve her stress, but she said she was careful. Said she sometimes cut on feeling down, that it gave her a focus and got her out of it, sort of cut through the fog, I guess.'

'Mhmm, can mean different things for different people.'

'Well, that's how it was, but then by the next session things had got out of control. But I want to mention something else before I get on to that, something that happened in the same session I've been talking about.'

'OK.' Lorraine acknowledged to herself what Keith had said waited to hear what more he had to say.'

'The child state emerged again, and she was picking at her fingers, really intensely and quite distressingly somehow. I hadn't seen her doing that since the first session or two. It was about her being so alone. I responded in the third person using her name, I really wasn't sure how much contact there was and felt I needed to speak like this. It just feels like I am speaking to a small child when it happens. And I suppose I am, it just feels right and yet I am sure to someone looking on it might seem quite incongruous. But it isn't.'

'You mean making observations, like, "Katie is picking at her fingers", that kind of thing?'

Keith nodded.

'I think that's what's needed sometimes in these situations. You are speaking to a child and very likely a highly traumatised one. You don't know how connected the part is either so in a sense using their name does anchor their identity in the dialogue. You say she was alone?'

'Talking about being alone, and what then emerged was a sense of self-blame, of blaming herself for her mum's problems. That happened after, when she was back in her adult state. She talked about missing her mother. She has such a range of feelings towards her, I guess the whole spectrum and she moves between them, but that was where she was then.'

Lorraine had a sense of the movement. 'So, again, a lot of fluidity?'

'I think it's like layers, and maybe that's linked to different ages and the way she internalised the experiences at that time.' Keith could see human emotions a bit like the layers that an archaeologist digs down into, unearthing periods in history. He felt like therapy could at times be like that from a psychological or emotional perspective.

'Different layers of experience with connected feelings and ways of making sense of things.' Lorraine sought to clarify for her own understanding what Keith was alluding to.

'And trauma.'

'Yes, of course', Lorraine responded.

'And then there was the last session, and, well, where do I start?' Keith shook his head, there was just so much that he could say.

'A lot going on?'

'A lot had already happened. She'd really gone and cut herself deeply. She talked about how scary it was because she knew she *had* to cut deep, *had* to hurt herself. That was different. It was more intense, and she did cut deep, said she needed to really see the blood. But it was the *having* to do it that shook her. And not being in control.'

'Not being in control?'

'She struggles with that, but now she was having difficulty controlling something that was directly causing her harm, and she knew it, but she couldn't stop. And she recovered memories of sexual abuse. She can see a man's face and she recognised him when it came back to her, but she doesn't know his name. So now she has to contend with that memory, and the *knowing* that it happened.'

Lorraine felt herself wince as she heard Keith speak. 'So she's cutting to hurt herself and that's linked up with the sexual abuse?'

'I don't know, the memories emerged when she was cutting. But she was already needing to cut deep. I think it's also about the blame she carries for her mother's death, feeling that she was "bad news". Within her is a very negative self-concept. It's not always there, but it's in there, part of the mix that makes up who she is and her sense of self.'

'And that was driving her to cut?'

Keith nodded. 'Probably, yeah.' He felt quite drained as he spoke. 'There is so much for her to come to terms with. Emotionally she is taking a battering at the moment.' And physically too, he thought to himself.

'So are you.' Lorraine needed to keep in contact with how Keith was dealing with the intensity of Katie's sessions.

'Yes, but I don't have to live with it twenty-four-seven, you know? It's not part of me and who I am.' Keith preferred to think of Katie and the scale of her difficulties rather than himself.

'Maybe not, and I appreciate what you are saying, but we also need to be aware of how you *are* affected, and be sure you are taking care of yourself too, as well as ensuring you are able to be congruently present in the sessions with her.' Lorraine felt insistent. Yes, she appreciated what Keith was saying, but as his supervisor she needed to ensure he was taking responsibility for his own well-being and ability to be transparently and authentically present and available for his clients.

Keith felt a flash of reaction. Yes, he knew Lorraine was right, but he also felt a deep need to keep hold of what he was saying. 'But it's not the same.'

'No, it's not, you don't have to live with what Katie has to live with twenty-four-seven, but you do need to be open to what you are experiencing and why.' Lorraine paused. 'I'm sensing a reaction from you to what I have said.'

'She's only a kid, Lorraine.'

Lorraine felt her internal sensitivity turn up a notch. She was unsure what Keith meant. Katie was a young woman. 'Only a kid?' She asked the question that was so very present for her.

Keith felt suddenly uncertain. She wasn't only a kid, but that's what he had said. And in a way she was as well, though not physically. 'Well, no, I mean....'

Lorraine was very aware of what they had been discussing previously and the way that aspects of Katie were coming to the fore from her past. She was being present in the session as a child as well as an adult. She felt a need to work with Keith in ensuring he was clear and was aware of where his reactions were coming from. 'She's there as a young woman, and there is a child as well, but she *is* a young woman.'

Keith felt himself taking a deep breath and was aware of a certain anxiety within himself. He voiced it, he knew this was the best thing to do so it could be explored. 'I'm feeling anxious.'

'Mhmm, can you say a little more?'

'A kind of confused anxiety, like losing your bearings, not sure about things. An uncertainty. Slight churning in my stomach, only slight, but a blurring in my head.'

'And these feelings are linked to what I just said, and you just said.'

Keith nodded, he was thinking about how he was feeling. 'Hmm.' He needed a moment or two to collect his thoughts. This wasn't straightforward.

Lorraine respected the silence. She could see the frown on Keith's face and so knew he was thinking about something. She wasn't going to disturb that process. She sensed, though, that something significant had happened and she was glad for that, and was determined to stay with it. She didn't believe in leaving things half resolved in supervision. If there was an issue it had to be addressed, and there was something about the way Keith had said what he had said that had stood out for her. It didn't match up, it needed to be understood, and not just with the intellect.

'It's the child, isn't it?' Keith had begun to speak. 'She's only a kid, and she is at times, and so much so as well.'

'Mhmm, the child is very present to you in the sessions.'

'Incredibly so, more sharply present in some ways than Katie is, I mean, you know, when she's being her adult self.'

'So there is something about her child-state, if that's the right way to put it, that is more real, more present, sharper to you, than Katie the young woman.' Lorraine made her response a statement rather than a question. She wanted to convey empathy and not simply force a "yes" or "no" response as a question might have done. She wanted to hold

Keith on this observation and let him move with it to where he needed to go.

'Hmm.' Keith was still thinking. Katie the child was very real, incredibly so, and his sense of communicating directly with that part of Katie did stand out, there was no doubt about that. 'When I speak to the child I know I'm on kind of full alert.'

'Like you are keyed up, it's more intense?'

'Definitely. It's just, yeah, it's like I'm much more tuned in.' He paused, 'and I guess that says something, not just about how I am when the child is present, but what may be lacking when she isn't.'

'Because it's less sharp with Katie the adult?'

'Sort of, and yet it feels intense with her too. But it's different.' He paused again, there as a lot to consider. 'Hmm. OK, so let's take this slowly. I'm feeling connected with Katie in her adult state, and I do, but there is something about the child-side when that emerges that is more intensely present and that makes me more intense as well, and so I'm left carrying that part of her more than the adult Katie.' A thought struck him. 'So am I at risk of relating to adult Katie in a way that is to some degree coloured by my experience of her as a child? In other words, could it get in the way? Could I be find myself relating to her when she is adult mode as if she is in the child state?' His questions were as much to himself as to Lorrraine.

'That sounds highly likely. But you'll be the best judge of that.'

'I was going to come on to something else that is part of this that happened in the last session. I think it's worth touching this now because it was powerful, once again.'

Lorraine nodded and waited for Keith to continue. Clearly there was something else that had happened and maybe that would help further to shed light on the process.

'The child, the young Katie was speaking again in the session, and this time was saying about how she wanted her mummy and she asked me if I'd be her friend. It was a really direct question, you know?'

'Mhmm.' Lorraine said nothing further and waited for Keith to continue once more.

'So I replied directly to her and said that I would be her friend.'

'And part of me wants to ask how that felt, and I also want to ask what happened next.'

'It felt very touching, very human, and, yes, very paternal as well. I really felt as though I was saying to a four year old girl that I would be her friend, no doubt about it. I wasn't playing word games, you know? I meant it.'

'I'm sure you did. And you would have needed to have been utterly authentic, she'd have probably known if you weren't.' Lorraine could imagine that a child who had had maybe no friends, who was so lonely, would really need to hear the authenticity in Keith's voice, particularly as she had been let down by adults already. She could see that Katie wasn't going to be in a place to trust that easily, except of course if her desperation for a friend overrode all of the distrust. 'And you weren't saying that in any way to Katie the young woman?'

'No. I meant it and I know that I *was* speaking to a child, absolutely. And that's what's so, I don't know, amazing in all of this. I mean, yes, I know intellectually that Katie is there as an adult, but in those moments of dialogue I actually know something else and that overrides it. And it isn't that I have to really think about the fact that I am relating to a child, it's spontaneous, utterly spontaneous. And I suppose that's why it is so powerful.'

'It's a genuinely lived experience, yes?'

'Exactly. And so, yes, I suppose it is no wonder that I end up carrying that sense of Katie the child so strongly. It is very present for me. But does it in some way override or affect my ability to be with Katie on an adult-to-adult level? I don't think so, but I am certainly open to the possibility that that might happen. I can see that now. I think maybe I needed to be able to see Katie the child more in context, I had perhaps lost sight of that. I was maybe feeling more intense, perhaps more connected, when Katie the child was present.' Keith stopped and thought about what he had just said. He needed time to process this. 'I need to take a moment to think about this.' He could see that, yes, Katie the child was more present for him and so, yes, it probably wasn't surprising that he referred to her as just a kid. The truth was that Katie the young woman was in fact far from being a kid, in fact given the life she had had in many ways she was no doubt extremely street wise and finding her own way to cope and survive in the adult world. And yet he also knew that for some people emotions could get left behind if not properly nourished by healthy human connection and relationship commensurate to the age of the person and their development. Physically a person might be an adult, but emotionally they could still be a child. He put that thought aside. Lorraine was responding.

'So, something about Katie the child affected you more deeply.'

'I think it's depth, or intensity, I'm not sure. Yet I also feel for the adult Katie too.' Keith paused. 'You know, I'm seeing two aspects of her but I'm not sure how helpful it is to keep them apart. I think that's where my problem is, I have to start seeing her as a single person, and that's what's happened, that's what I've lost.' Keith felt a sort of release as he spoke, a sense of "yes, that's how it is".

'You sound suddenly more, I don't know what the word is, clearer somehow.' Lorraine could hear from the way Keith was speaking that there was a kind of surety in his voice.

'It's the splitting. No, she's Katie and yes there is a damaged child-like part of herself, and maybe that part is dissociated, maybe it's to be explained in some other way, but it is her, part of who she is, and you know what happened after what I was just talking about?'

'Saying you'd be Katie's friend?'

'Yes, adult Katie also responded and said "so would I", and that was absolutely electric.' He could feel his eyes moistening and his own throat suddenly feel constricted.

'That is powerful. And that clearly affected you and still does.'

'It does.' He paused. 'Something about that sense of the two of them – I know I'm differentiating again, but that sense of…, I don't know, what was present in that moment. And then Katie talked about it and came to a point of acknowledging that as a child and as an adult she wanted her mum, that in effect they both wanted their mum. That was another powerful moment. And it sort of brought them together as well. And you know, that's what matters, that's what really is what this is somehow all about, them being brought together; Katie bringing herself together, becoming fully open to who she is and what has shaped her. The difficulty is that it brings with it memories that had been hidden from her normal awareness, the sexual abuse. That's there now in her awareness. It was known already in some way within her structure of self, no doubt, but now it's in awareness, and everything changes again. It's the *knowing* it happened, that's what she referred to, the knowing.'

Lorraine could appreciate that. She had herself been sexually abused as a child and she knew the experience of recovering a memory, and how shattering it could be. 'Yes, everything does change when you know something like that about yourself, and with that knowing usually comes all the feelings associated with what happened along with all the feeling you then have in reaction to what you now know. It's a double effect, if you like, you get hit twice. And, yes, it really does change you. And it changes everyone differently. You have to be with that person on their individual journey as they pick up the pieces, and it really is their individual journey.'

Keith was touched by the way Lorraine was speaking. She was very clear and yet reflective. It felt very immediate, having a genuine note of authenticity. He was struck with a strong sense that the authenticity came from reality. 'You know, don't you, from your own experience?'

Lorraine nodded, 'yes, I know'. She smiled. She had worked on it many years ago and still issues came up in relation to her experiences that she took to therapy. She knew that for her one of the significant features of the effect on her was the knowing that it did happen. It wasn't something remote that happened to other people. She knew how it was a human reaction to think that things wouldn't happen to you, or couldn't have happened to you. But when you know something terrible did happen to you, then you somehow know things in a much deeper way. And it wasn't just about depth, it was the fact that the knowing had no doubt within it. Like the person who experiences trauma in war directly at the hands of another human being, or the victim of torture, there is then a profound knowing of what a human being is capable of inflicting on another person. And that knowing changes you. It's not the same as reading about it in the papers, or hearing about it on TV. Even films don't capture it because however realistic it is, you know they are actors. It was the *knowing for real* that changed you, she knew that. She didn't feel a need to say anything further to Keith. This was his time, not for her to fill with her experiences. He'd picked up on her authenticity and she'd acknowledged he was right, and it was right to move on and back to exploring what was happening for Katie and how it was affecting Keith.

Keith felt himself going silent in response to what Lorraine had said. He didn't have any urge to want to know more. Her simple, confirming response was enough, along with the expression on her face. But where it did take him was into himself as a man, as being of the gender that is usually the perpetrator. And yet he also knew that his issues around that were not to in any way be compared to the experience of the target of sexual abuse. His mind went back to something Katie had said. 'She wants to cut him out of herself.'

Lorraine nodded, she could appreciate that. 'Yes, cut him out, get rid of him I should imagine, and every last remnant of memory associated with him.'

'But she can't and she knows she can't, and with her risky alcohol use there's going to be a temptation to drink more to get him out of her awareness again. And that is going to be such a temptation for her.' Keith was experiencing his own sense of the enormity of this. It was such a basic human reaction to want to ease or dull pain and if you had something that you knew could achieve that then it wasn't surprising that people turned to it. To say that he could appreciate that Katie was going through a particularly tough time was always going to be an understatement.

'It is, it will be. And she is going to need someone to be consistently present and available for her, who is not going to judge her, whatever she does, but seek to understand and to convey warmth, someone who can stand with her as she faces up to all of this.'

Keith nodded. He knew that should Katie continue to attend therapy that it was likely to be a long process. And, yes, it made him feel anxious, but it also made him feel very alive in the sense that he knew he had some really challenging work to do and that made him feel good. 'Yeah. It's not going to be easy, I can see that there could be so many difficulties and I'm sure to be bringing Katie back here very regularly.'

'That's OK. It's important. I don't know how she will cope, we must hope that it won't be in ways that are too damaging. But she is going to want to get away from herself, and we know she drinks, she cuts, she may make other choices.'

'And I think her sex life is another area of escape for her too. She hasn't spoken much about it but she has talked of being sexually active since early teens and that there have been occasions when she has been in situations where she hasn't been in control and has had sex when she didn't really want to. So, you know, the courts might not always see it that way, but to me that's rape.' Keith's view was that it was still too easy for men to get away with forcing themselves on women, despite attempts to make the law more effective.

Lorraine nodded but she wasn't going to get into a discussion on this. She kept the focus on Katie. 'So, Katie has a range of ways of trying to make herself feel different, and she now has an added reason to want to do that. Quite how it will change her we cannot yet know.' Lorraine wondered how Keith, as a man, would be in working with Katie given the issues that had now emerged. She knew that they had touched briefly on this in the last supervision session. She found herself wondering how she would have experienced Keith if he had been her counsellor when she had been working on her own issues. Her train of thought was interrupted by Keith responding to what she had just said.

'No, we don't, we really don't. I wish she had more support, though, more structure in her life. Without some kind of structure people tend to have more reactive lifestyles and if the thing you are reacting to is your own emotional and psychological processes, and they are difficult if not problematic, then the person is going to be struggling. It just feels like more structure would be helpful.'

'For her, or for you?'

'I'd feel easier knowing she had others involved. She sees the GP. There's a group she has attended to help her get into work, or training, that kind of thing. There are a number around these days, they're very good, but I'm not sure whether she's still attending that. I'm not sure what else she has. Is it my need to know she has more support? Maybe, but I also know that there are services out there that would help her, either to help with the sexual abuse in her past, the self-harming, just getting her life on track, there is a lot available these days for young people that really are young-people friendly. But given her past, I can imagine she's had a belly full of services who have maybe promised one thing but she's experienced something else. She's very independent.'

'And that's a good thing, there's resilience in that, but she also needs to trust others and that can only happen if they prove themselves to be trustworthy.'

'She needs to feel cared about, cared for. She needs to experience that fundamental of all human feelings – love. She needs to feel genuinely and unconditionally loved.' Keith paused. Yes, he thought to himself, that was it but how few people could or did experience this, really experience it. He continued. 'So often it is conditional, the 'I'll only love you if you are like this, or do that', rather than that much rarer but powerful quality of human love that has no conditions. For Keith, love was a word with so many meanings and could so easily be misunderstood. Yet he saw what he thought as "therapeutic love" as a key component in human growth. And he knew that it was a quality or tone of love that had to be genuine. It wasn't a 'falling in love with' kind of love and yet there was something about loving your clients in the sense of really caring about them as people, as individuals, as fellow human beings struggling to cope with whatever was making their lives difficult. It could pull on your heart and you had to be aware of this. It could be challenging. You had to be a human being with your client, and you also had personal and professional boundaries to maintain. You had to preserve the integrity of the therapeutic process, which was itself essentially about relationship. Could you really differentiate between human relationship and therapeutic relationship? Good human relationship was surely therapeutic to some degree. Yet you had to know your boundaries. He knew it could be exploited, that there were people who would use one person's vulnerability to satisfy their own desires or needs. And he knew this could be subtle as well.

'A lot of love. Comes back to that, doesn't it?' Lorraine knew herself how important this was. So often people's experiences in life seemed to close down their hearts and to Lorraine that was one of the tragedies of life. It stopped people caring in the way that they otherwise might. It was a lot to do with caring. People had cared about her as she had come through her difficulties. Knowing that people cared, really knowing, made you feel more valued, more able to feel something positive about yourself. 'And a lot of it is about caring and feeling cared for.'

Keith took a deep breath, 'yes, knowing that someone cares. So easy to think that no-one cares when you are only used to no-one caring, or no-one showing emotion, or when they do they only show anger, or they are inconsistent so you are never quite sure. Our intense world is too fast. You need time to care. People rushing from one thing to another. Everything hyped up. You know, I'm back to thinking about teenage gangs. There's a sense in which the gang members care for each other, they are like family for these kids. There are some fundamental human needs being met, but it's all got distorted, each unit looking after itself and attacking anyone who gets into their territory. Oh, I don't know. Katie's made no mention of being caught up in anything like that. But then, well, round here it's not such an issue. We're not in an inner city – and I know that's a generalisation, these kind of problems probably can exist anywhere.'

Lorraine wanted to acknowledge what Keith had said but also keep the focus on his work with Katie. 'I think we all have a lot to learn and, yes, love and caring, and genuine caring not the pseudo caring that we see too much of, makes a difference.' Lorraine was thinking of how too many people are in so-called caring jobs but whether they really cared about the people they worked with was another matter. 'And Katie needs to feel valued and cared about, and maybe that's what she is experiencing through the support she is getting, but the challenge for her is how she reacts to that. People can reject it because it doesn't feel right, it challenges their sense of being unloved and unlovable, as we know.'

'I know, and that's where it comes back to steadiness and consistency, doesn't it?'

'It does. It has to.'

'There's something else that happened in the last session. Katie went into a long silence and she seemed to be staring into space, but she said she was experiencing her life like it was a kind of film, going back through events over the years. It was very vivid. It seemed quite unusual to me, but it sounded as though it was like a whole stream of memories just started running, like a tape, I guess. One event after another, and I just wonder if that was also very significant in terms of her own integration.'

'It sounds important, like a flow of connection running back over her life.'

'Linking up experiences, like she was watching them but through her own eyes as they happened.'

'So that really does sound like it's a kind of memory stream. Fascinating.' Lorraine was intrigued by what Keith was saying. 'So what was happening for you?'

'I was maintaining the silence, keeping my own focus. It was clear something was happening for Katie in that she seemed to be locked into looking at something. It was strange and yet it felt trustworthy in the sense that the session had been a powerful one and she had been making inner connections, and, well, I'm almost at a point of not being surprised any more.' Keith was very aware that his sessions with Katie were certainly full of the unexpected, and he was too experienced to start to think that there were not going to be more surprises. He was aware that Katie could go into her self in silence, it just happened that in that particular episode a vivid experience had occurred for her. He remembered how he, himself, had had an experience in therapy. It hadn't been a re-running of past experiences but more of a kind of symbolic vision. He had been in the therapy room with his therapist and had suddenly started seeing light to the left of the therapist. And yet it wasn't really there, it was clearly in his head, but it had a special feel to it. It had certainly been an important experience in his own journey, representing an opening up with a sudden emergence of coloured light and energy like a fountain. But that had been his experience, and he had no doubt that people could have all kinds of inner experiences once they began to touch into deeper aspects of their own natures, and indeed when reaching into what some would consider to be the spiritual aspect of themselves as well.

'I get a sense of the moment-to-moment nature of the sessions with Katie. It really is a journey, isn't it? You have no idea where the sessions are heading?' Lorraine had been struck by the sense of one thing leading to another.

'No, I don't. They unfold and I can trust that. In a way it's special and I see myself as trying to not get in the way. I don't need to direct, not that I would, it's not my approach. Things happen. It's like within Katie's structure of self there is fluidity and movement. I have a sense of emergence. I can't say where it will lead, I don't know. I don't know how Katie will become.'

'And that's crucial, isn't it?'

'It is for me and for the way I work. I don't want to set myself up as the expert who knows how a client should be or ought to become. My focus is on staying with my client in the here-and-now of their experiencing I think there is a beauty and a kind of simplicity in this. That may sound a bit odd.' Keith paused, wondering how Lorraine was going to react.

'A beauty and a simplicity in the sense of going with the flow, you mean?'

'That's very much part of it. It seems to me that this is central. It is about my being able to be present in Katie's awareness, offering a set of human relational qualities which she can experience whilst she also connects with and experiences her own process. And as I say that the words just sound too complicated. It's simpler than I can put into words, but not simple in the sense of easy or simplistic. Rather it's disciplined and focused, but there is an ease when it happens.'

'When the process, the connections, happen?' Lorraine was trying to get her own clarity on what Keith was saying.

'Yes, and I need to stay there and be present, open, offering that warm acceptance, offering caring.' Keith nodded to himself. 'I'm back to caring again.'

'Conveying a sense of caring to your client.'

'Caring that's genuine because it is present within me. I do care about my clients, they matter.' Keith could feel his own sense of commitment to his clients and his therapeutic work as he spoke. These were important areas for him.

'I really hear that, you care about them, how they are, what happens to them.'

'They matter, and often, I don't know, I get a sense that in many respects society behaves in ways that almost suggests people don't matter. We allow rubbish food to be produced and sold, we cram people on trains, we have hospitals with bugs that no-one seems able to really tackle, people get virtually abandoned in old age, young people get left to their own devices and then get criticised when they get into trouble. I don't know, I just have this sense that somehow people don't matter anymore. The companies with the automatic phone systems that keep you hanging on and you end up lost in the maze. We are losing something precious.' Keith shook his head. 'But I'm off at a tangent again. When you consider someone like Katie, I mean, OK, the system has tried to support her, for better, for worse. But now here she is, starting adult life and in a mess. Does society care, really care? If she was doing drugs as well, or robbing then there'd probably be very little sympathy from a lot of people. We've got to get over all of that, see people as people.'

'That's really important to you, and in your work.' Lorraine had noted the passion in Keith's voice as he had been speaking.

'It is with young people. We shouldn't keep knocking them. Yes, there is a madness out there, we touched on the gangs, and yet they also give young people something as well. The need to bond is there, the need to express aggressive tendencies is there, the energy of youth. Why can't we work with it and create constructive outlets for it to flow into?' It frustrated Keith, he just saw wasted energies, potential talents left to rot almost. It may seem over-dramatic, but that's how he felt about it all. 'Anyway, never mind all of that. Katie needs at least to be offered more support, and she may or may not agree to it. And I can accept that, but when people find accepting help difficult because of the effects of damaging life-experience, it is so challenging. I don't think we talk enough about trust, and I think somewhere someone should be writing about the nature and importance of *therapeutic trust* in order to make this more explicit. For some people that seems to me to be *the* most important factor, particularly to begin with. Clients can't always feel or experience your authenticity, empathy and unconditional positive regard until they feel trust towards you. And I know they are bound together, but trust is also based on other things – consistency, for one, doing what you say you'll do. And, yes, it does link to congruence and authenticity, and I think that's often really important for the young people I work with. They don't want bullshit from adults. You've got to level with them.'

Lorraine had listened carefully to all that Keith had been saying. 'I'm struck by what you say about authenticity, and I think you are right, but I also thought what you said about therapeutic trust thought-provoking and I am left wondering where trust is now with Katie towards you. And I realise that it can only be speculation.'

Keith felt he needed to say more about what trust meant to him. 'I think trust is a strange thing, it's not always something you are aware of in a kind of conscious sense. Yes, it can be something on the surface, but it can be deeper too, a sort of inner knowing that the person you are with can be trusted although you might not consciously think about or dwell on it. However, it affects how you relate to that person and how you are when you are in their presence. Where there isn't this trust the person is likely to have defences up, and quite right so.' Keith could see how even without realising it people could put barriers up to other people.

'So I guess it is about giving off certain signals that then tell the person you can be trusted?'

Another thought had struck Keith. 'Of course, people can be damaged by life-experiences such that they actually don't want someone they can trust, or they want someone they can trust to be untrustworthy, if you see what I mean.'

Lorraine did understand what Keith was getting at. 'It gets complicated, doesn't it?'

'Some people may never have been exposed to trusting or trustworthy experiences in relation to other people. Or they might be so conditioned into being treated badly by untrustworthy significant others that they believe themselves to be deserving of this. They internalise it in such a way that they then seek the same experience. It satisfies something that they believe about themselves.'

'You think Katie's in that place?' Lorraine wanted to bring the theme directly into the relationship with Katie, anchor it rather than let it remain a theoretical discussion point.

'I don't think she finds trust easy, but I'm not sure she has got into a place where she wants untrustworthy people. I guess, and it is a guess, that at some level she may want to trust someone but she defends herself against risking this by clinging to her independence. These are just my thoughts, I'm not saying that's how it is. I don't actually know.'

'OK, so at least that means that she may want trust but needs to cultivate the capacity to respond to trust and to, as it were, trust any feelings of trust that might emerge within her.'

'And that's not going to be easy. And that's why I think my being consistent in how I am is so important, and why I need to be utterly authentic and genuine in what I say.' Keith felt a surge of energy as he spoke. It felt as though he was affirming something that, whilst he already knew it, was good to experience himself saying it. 'I feel in a positive place at the moment. That's not to in some way ignore the challenges to come, but I feel nourished from this conversation, like I am in touch with me and ready to be the therapist that Katie needs, and so much of that is about being a caring presence.' He paused. 'I nearly said "concerned and caring" and I'm wondering why "concerned" doesn't feel right.'

'You sense a need to communicate caring rather than concern?'

'I just wonder how it will be received. When I said that time about Katie looking after herself, maybe that came more from concern and she reacted against that, although I have said that since without the same reaction. So maybe something has moved on, I don't know. It's the independence thing again, I think.' Keith paused again, collecting his thoughts. 'Anyway, I've spent a lot of time talking about Katie today. I need to move on to other clients. Is that OK.'

Lorraine nodded. 'I think the themes of caring and trust are important, and being able to be authentically and consistently present. Yes, maybe there is a place for offering her ideas for support but only when this emerges out of that sense of connection, you know?'

Keith nodded. 'Yes, I know. Go with Katie's flow and if the urge to say something arises and it really feels like it is emerging in some way out of the therapeutic dynamic, I'll say something.' Another pause as another thought came to him. 'Maybe Katie's reaction to my suggesting she take care, I can't remember the exact words, maybe what followed has made me over-sensitive in some ways. If I'm genuinely concerned then why shouldn't I communicate it? That's about being authentic. I don't want to tell her to do something, or not do something, but I do want to be able to express my concern as a human being, as a person. And I also need to watch my sensitivity towards Katie the child. I need to remember to see her as a whole person, not let the child side of her cause me to risk losing sensitivity to the adult. I've got a lot to take away from this, and I'm already aware of looking forward to seeing Katie next week. I hope that it's been a better week for her, and if it hasn't been then I hope I can offer her therapeutic support to help her. Thanks Lorraine, I value what we have explored and shared today.'

It felt to Lorraine that Keith had done most of the work. She responded in ways that she hoped were helpful, but he had done most of his own processing. She wanted him to own that. 'You've done a lot of the processing today, Keith, and I think that's a reflection of how keenly you feel towards your work with Katie, and not just with her, with young people generally. It means a lot to you.'

'Yeah, thanks for that, but you need to have been the way you have been to allow me to explore things as I have. It helps.'

'Sure.'

The conversation moved on to other clients and other issues.

Chapter 11

As Keith sat waiting for Katie to arrive the following week, he was thinking back over his last supervision session. In particular, the question of how Katie saw him was present in his thoughts. Was her perception enabling for her, in a therapeutic sense, or did it cause an obstruction or some kind of block to her process? She had sensitive issues that might be difficult for her to discuss with him, and yet he also knew from his own experience that his being a man wasn't always a problem in relation to this. However he also knew that in some cases it could be. He knew that whilst for Katie there was likely to be a deep internalised knowing that men can (and for her did and do) abuse you, she also knew that she couldn't necessarily trust women either. Trust. Surely that was a key word. He closed his eyes and spent a couple of minutes clearing his mind of all the thoughts that could so easily take over. He needed to be clear and present for his work with Katie.

He took half a dozen slow deep breaths which he found this particularly helpful. It slowed him down, centred him. He nodded to himself and slowly got up, feeling quite measured in his movements, and headed out to the waiting area. He saw Katie sitting there, she had earphones on and was clearly listening to something, with a magazine on her lap. He walked over to where she was sitting and called her name. She looked up and smiled, closed the magazine and got up, switching off the music and taking out the earphones.

'Hi.' Katie felt good to be there. She'd had a strange week but nothing too dramatic, and she was glad for that. But it hadn't been easy. The memories from her past remained really difficult, and she had cut herself once, but only once, at a time when she had just felt a build up of everything and needed some kind of release. It had helped though she had also found it not to be quite as satisfying as in the past. She was more troubled by it. Something had changed in the way she felt about what she did. She was more uneasy with herself, it wasn't easy to describe, she just knew there was a difference.

She had drank a few times during the week, it had helped by taking the edge off things. The medication was still helping but she'd felt she needed something more. And yet even that she wasn't so comfortable with either. Everything seemed strangely empty. She didn't like it. She followed Keith to the counselling room. It was all very familiar to her now. It had seemed so odd the first time, not that she could remember it that clearly. She knew she had been quite different then. She had started something and knew she had to see it through. She wanted everything sorted quickly, but already she had been to more sessions than she imagined she'd probably come to. She liked things sorted. She felt more in control when things were like that.

Katie sat herself down and looked over at Keith who was also settling himself in the chair. What was he really like? The thought lingered in her mind. He looked not exactly old, but he must be in his late 40s at least. She didn't know much about him other than he did seem to be calm and steady, and she appreciated that, at least she did for her counselling sessions. Someone like that would be too boring in 'real' life. She wasn't feeling any sexual attraction towards him, it wasn't anything like that, and yet he had a certain kind of appeal. She couldn't really explain it. She heard him speaking and it brought her out of her thoughts. She felt herself flush slightly and looked down.

'So, how are things and how do you want to use the time we have today?' Keith as usual wanted to keep the focus open and he waited for how Katie would respond.

'Funny old week.' Katie looked up again, glanced briefly at Keith and looked to his left, focussing on the bottom corner of the Monet print that was behind him. The print was new, but it didn't hold her attention. She took a moment to decide how she wanted describe her week. 'Just find things aren't, I don't know, things don't seem the same, somehow.'

'Things feel different in some way this week.' Keith was naturally curious as to what Katie meant by this and he felt sure his curiosity was captured by his tone of voice. It was, and it encouraged Katie to say more.

'I feel uneasy, can't sort of settle. I don't know, it's like I feel…, I don't know, it's hard to explain.'

'Hard to explain this sense of uneasiness.' Keith kept his empathic response short and focused.

'I mean, yeah, a lot's happened, you know? Things I know about myself now. Makes me sort of want to forget things but then, well, you can't, can you?' Katie was thinking of her regained memories of being sexually abused but it wasn't just that. The experience in that last session of re-running her life had stayed with her. Something about her past was more vivid now. It was as if it was more 'in the present', so to speak. It wasn't easy to describe, though.

'Things you'd like to forget but you can't, they're with you now.' Keith was thinking in general terms rather than specifically with you now in this moment. He realised after he had spoken that what he had said could be taken as meaning that.

Katie instinctively took a deep breath. Yes, they were with her now. 'It's like, yeah, I'm sort of….', she paused, pursing her lips, wondering how to describe it. 'It's like I feel somehow like there's more of me. That sounds weird.' She stopped speaking again, it was weird, she knew she was still in a way adjusting to it all.

'OK, so something about feeling like there's more of you, and it's an experience that feels kind of weird.'

Katie nodded, she felt OK about hearing Keith saying back to her what she had said. It was how it was, but she felt a need to explain it more. 'It's like I know things about myself, well, some things I already knew but they're more real somehow, not that they weren't real, but, yeah, they're there. I somehow know them, sort of know them more as me. At least, I think that's what I mean.' Katie was aware as she was speaking that the words didn't quite convey what she was experiencing. It was as though she was using words but they were strangely detached from what she was using them to describe.

'OK, and it sounds really important to get hold of this. So what I am hearing is that the things that you already knew about yourself are now more real in the sense that you know them as being you in a much more immediate kind of way? Like you own them in a different way. Or have I missed it?' Keith was being tentative, he genuinely wanted to be sure that he understood what Katie was experiencing. What was her inner world like? Could he move around within what she told him in a sensitive way that would not disturb the psychological and emotional landscape and yet would enable him to experience clearly what existed, and then communicate that back to Katie? He felt this was an important exploration, as if Katie was sifting through her self-awareness to, in some sense, maybe re-organise something of her self-concept.

Katie listened to Keith and, yes, it sort of felt right. 'It's like, yeah, I've always thought I knew me but I didn't know, not really. Now I am beginning to know who I am, or at least more what's me.'

'Clearer about who you are, you mean?'

Katie nodded. 'It's not comfortable and yet it is as well; that's what's confusing.'

'The fact that it isn't comfortable and yet it is somehow comfortable as well? It's like a contradiction but it isn't?'

'It doesn't make sense but that's how it is.'

'Mhmm, can't make sense of it but it's what you know you are experiencing, it's a kind of knowing that is both comfortable and uncomfortable.' Keith hoped he had summed up what Katie had been saying. He very much appreciated her ability to have the self-awareness to explore herself in the way that she was. He knew that not all clients had this capacity, indeed he hadn't been sure Katie would be able to given the experience of the first couple of sessions and the long periods of silence.

'I suppose it's best to know, but, well, sometimes it isn't.' Katie wasn't really thinking about what she was saying, the words just came out in response to what Keith had said. She was thinking about what she now knew about herself and how she had been sexually abused. And it wasn't something she really wanted to dwell on. It made her feel not right, somehow. Knowing it had happened to her in one sense was like an 'and another thing' and yet it wasn't as well. It was deeper, more horrible, more infecting of her sense of who she was. She could feel herself recoiling from it as she thought about it. She had looked down as she had finished what she had said. She hadn't told many people and didn't want to. Keith knew, of course, so did the nurse at the hospital whom she hadn't seen since, her GP knew and so did Bernie, her friend. But that was all, and she wanted to keep it that way.

'No, sometimes it feels best left not known.'

Katie sighed in response to what Keith had said. It did sum up how it was, and it left her feeling saddened by it all. It wasn't a tearful sadness, more a kind of having to resign herself to the fact of what had happened. It left her not wanting to say anything else, but she didn't want to just sit and think about it either. Yet it remained very present in her awareness, the knowing, the image of his face, she knew the memory was there, inside her, with her now. She hated it, hated him, hated having to know what she knew. It replaced the sadness. She looked up and caught Keith's eye. 'Men!'

Keith guessed that Katie was probably dwelling on the sexual abuse and responded. 'There are some bastards out there.' He was also aware as he spoke that he was in part distancing himself from the perpetrators of sexual abuse. Yes, he was a man, but it was certainly not something he had done or wanted to do.

The anger was still with Katie as she looked down again. She could feel her jaw tightening as she picked at her left thumb with her right thumb nail. She wanted to dig her nail into her flesh, but the moment she began to press she felt a kind of voice inside her saying, 'going to hurt yourself?' She pressed a little more and then relaxed, feeling her jaw relax as well. Did she want to hurt herself? Surely she deserved better? She spoke quietly to herself, 'Fuck it, I'm a survivor.' They were words spoken only for her to hear. Keith had not heard exactly what Katie had said. He didn't respond but waited to see if Katie had something more to say, more to communicate for him to hear.

Katie wasn't in the mood for saying much more. It felt to her as though there wasn't any point. Shit had happened to her, big shit, and she wanted away from it all. She wanted to just get rid of it all. It wasn't, though, about cutting it out, she wasn't thinking in that way. It was about forgetting. It was about losing it all somehow. It wasn't something she could wash away, she wasn't thinking like that. It was more wanting to sick it up, really sick it all up from really deep. Feel it as it burned out of her, smell its stink. Something burning and rotting was inside her, deep inside her. It was beyond cutting out, it needed sicking up, spewing out, to get rid of it. She needed to feel it coming out of her. She'd make herself sick, that would help, she knew it would get it out of her system…, and she knew that it wouldn't as well. She took a deep breath and sighed again.

'Leaves you with a lot to sigh about, Katie.'

'I just want to get rid of it all. I really want to sick it all up. I can feel it inside me, hot, stinking, horrible. It's like I feel like I want to get clean but on the inside, like, yeah, like if someone could just blast me with a water jet on the inside, wash it all always, yeah, cool water. Flush it all away.' Even as she spoke she knew it was more than that, it needed more.

'Flush all the hot stinking horribleness away.' Keith responded to what Katie wanted to flush away.

'I'd…, yeah, just let it go. I'd feel better, I know I would. It's like all this stuff got put on me, in me, messed me up and I don't want it any more.' The anger that had subsided was rising once more.

'Mhmm, no more, don't want it any more' The tone of Keith's matter-of-fact response was affirming of how Katie was experiencing herself.

'Fucking shits, every one of them.' She closed her eyes and looked down, taking a deep breath as she did so. The seething anger was taking over. Katie was clenching both of her fists, her knuckles while with the tension. She could feel her nails digging into the palms of her hands. It felt good, very good. She could feel her jaw tight, her teeth clenched. She wished she could smash the people that had hurt her. They deserved it, each and every one of them. She didn't want to have to feel like this. The emotions continued to burn inside her, she felt hot, she realised she was shaking, the result of the tension in her body. The thought that was also with her was, "how dare they?", "how dare they have treated her like that?" Scenes from her past came to mind but she was not a passive observer as she had been the previous week. No, she was anything but passive. She felt the anger burning inside her, she hated each and every one of them who had hurt her. She lifted up her head, her eyes still closed, her head now slightly tilted back. She could feel the tension in her back as she did so, opening her eyes to stare at the ceiling. She gave voice to her feelings. 'Ahhhhggg'. She took in another deep breath, she wanted to let it out, she had to let it out. 'I learned to fight back, you know, but there was a time when I couldn't.' She hadn't planned to say that, the words just formed in her mind and came out.

She lowered her head once more to look over at Keith. She appreciated the seriousness on his face.

'No, I know, when you could fight back you did, but there were the times when you couldn't.' Keith could feel the tension within himself, he had tightened up as he had witnessed the anger rising within Katie.

Katie was back thinking of her early childhood again. 'It's not fair. It shouldn't have happened to me. I didn't deserve it. And yet, you know, yeah, it's messed my head up, I know that but, well, maybe it's made me able to look after myself, you know? I don't take shit from anyone, never have really since I broke that stupid kid's nose. Yeah, everyone had a go at me, but I knew he deserved it.'

'Something about that incident, yeah, and everything else making you more able to look after yourself.' Keith could appreciate exactly what Katie meant. It had given her a satisfying experience, it had enabled her to channel the anger and the hurt in such a way that it had brought her a sense maybe of her own personal power. He decided to comment on that, 'maybe gave you a sense of your own personal power?'

Katie smiled. 'I don't want to take anyone's bullshit, if that's what you mean.'

Keith smiled back, 'something like that'. Yes, he thought, he used words that were a bit too therapeutic. Katie brought them into the real world of language. He knew Katie had touched into this area in a previous session, but that never meant that insights might not be revisited at other times. He was aware that perceptions could change. The re-ordering of a person's structure of self and the shifts in self-concept that occur could take time, and often aspects of the individual's nature or experience needed to be revisited and seen from a fresh angle. It was very much a learning process which some people would think more of as growth or development. As far as he was concerned it was about helping people to get a truly genuine understanding of themselves and the events and experiences that had contributed to them being who they had become. Sometimes this then involved fresh understanding and insight towards those events and towards themselves. It could be subtle, it could be dramatic, it was his job to be a companion with his clients as they engaged in that process. And the goal? Well, it wasn't his to impose on a client. It would be as for their own actualising tendency to define in some mysterious way. He knew there was a deep mystery in this and there were times when he wondered whether there was some kind of link between this inner drive and something more spiritual.

Katie knew she didn't take grief from people, but she also knew that she wasn't always in the mood to stand up for herself. She could be verbal but there were times when her mood was low, when she just kept quiet, said nothing. She had the capacity to be both and that also confused her. She responded to what Keith had said. 'I don't always, though, I can be quite quiet as well, depends what mood I'm in.'

'Sometimes you can stand up for yourself and at other times you go quiet, that what you mean?'

'Sometimes, I don't know, I just know I don't want to say anything, I'd rather just, I'm not sure, I get sort of strange, anxious. I…, hmmm.' Katie looked down. Her thoughts had gone back to her past and she could suddenly see it all so clearly. Yes, how could she not have seen it before? But she hadn't and now it was as clear as day.

Keith felt the sudden silence keenly. It was sharp. He knew something significant had happened and he had a sense what it was about. But he wasn't going to pre-empt Katie in any way, rather let her find her own words to express her insight. It was an important part of her own process of clarifying and owning what she was discovering about herself.

Katie looked up. 'It's me how I used to be, how I learned to be. It's like, yeah, I knew it but didn't really know it, but now, yeah, it's clear, you know?' She sought acknowledgement from Keith of what she was saying.

'Like you can see something suddenly more clearly, it's real, sharper?'

'There's me like I was, shrinking back, keeping quiet, not saying much. That's how I was, how I became, but then I know I learned to be different as well. It's like, yeah, I knew that, but now it's different. I can't explain it.'

'Mhmm, it's the quality or depth or intensity of that knowing, right?'

Katie nodded. 'It's like I kind of feel…, hmm, this may sound a bit weird…'.

'Things that are new to us can often feel weird, that's OK. Go for it.' Keith hoped to encourage Katie to continue with her process as she was describing it.

'Well, it's like I feel sort of more me.'

'More you?'

'More, yeah, more...', Katie thought about it, 'more complete, somehow.'

'OK, so it's like having this insight, this knowing about yourself that makes you feel more complete.' Keith wanted to add something about bringing two parts of herself together, but that was his recognition and he didn't want to get ahead of Katie on this. He wanted her to make sense of it, understand it in her own way, using her own words, not his.

Katie nodded again. 'It feels a relief.'

Keith was glad he hadn't said anymore, that was not a word he would have used and he would probably have shifted Katie's focus into his own perception and away from her own flow of experiencing.

'A feeling of relief?'

Katie smiled, 'it is, and it's clear and yet, I mean, I still don't understand.'

'Mhmm, a sense of feeling more complete and of relief because of this, and it also feels hard to understand.'

There was a pause as a fresh insight became present for Katie. 'I don't have to be how I was, I don't have to react in ways that I learned as a child, do I?'

'Not if you want to react differently now.'

'I wasn't expecting any of this. It's sudden. It's..., yeah, shit.'

'Good shit?' Keith couldn't resist his response, the way Katie was speaking and the look on her face, whilst there was some puzzlement there was clearly a freshness as well. It did feel good from where he was sitting. He knew only too well that insight could come out of the blue in therapy, and at any time. That was the wonder of being human and of the therapeutic experience. You could feel moved in ways all of a sudden. Things could shift, and for him he always came back to the image of the jigsaw, as you look at all the pieces lying there in confusion and then you suddenly see one that might just fit in the place you are trying to fill, and the sense of delight when it fits perfectly. And how often that could suddenly lead to a number of pieces suddenly fitting into place; he was sure therapeutic process was like that.

Katie nodded. 'It feels good. I feel freed up, somehow. I don't have to be anything other than how I want to be. That sounds crazy. I know that, but I didn't, not really, not like I feel now.'

'Mhmm, you don't have to be anything other than who *you* want to be.' Keith spoke slowly and reflectively, holding the focus on what Katie had said through his empathic response.

Katie sat in silence for a minute, letting the words sink in and at the same time just being with how she was. Eventually she broke the silence, verbalising where her train of thought had taken her. 'I don't understand what has happened though.'

'That sounds like it is really important for you to understand what happened.'

'Is it like I'm different?'

'Can you say a little more about that?' Keith wanted to understand and to offer Katie an opportunity to understand what she was experiencing. He knew how putting your thoughts and feelings into your words could be clarifying.

'Like something's changed.'

'Mhmm, change can happen, and sometimes quite suddenly. Though it is usually as a result of a lot that has already gone on before.'

'Like, yeah, you reach a point where, yeah, everything's different.'

'And that's how it feels now, as though everything's different.'

'And I don't really know why. I mean, yeah, OK, lots of stuff has happened, you know?' Katie was thinking about the therapy and the trips to hospital, and really the last three months in general.

'Mhmm, you have had a hectic life.' Keith thought Katie was talking generally about her whole life, not just the recent past.

'Yeah, but recently, coming here, seeing you, all of this. Is it always like this?'

'It's different for everyone. It's a process. I believe people get insight when the time is right. You can't force it or push it. And for whatever reason, today you have seen something about yourself in a fresh, new and more real way, and it has made a deep impression even though it is hard to understand or put into words.' Keith felt it was right to sum things up a little as well as offering his view on the therapeutic process.

'But it feels more than something in my head.'

'Mhmm, like it's bigger, a different kind of knowing?'

Katie nodded quite intensely in response. 'And I feel sort of, yeah, more alive as well, somehow. Like I feel I've suddenly got more energy.'

'Mhmm, like a block has been removed.' Keith's response was very much his own perception of what Katie was trying to describe. It did sound to him as if a block had been removed and something was now flowing more freely within her.

'I know what you mean but it's not quite like that. It's more like…', Katie paused trying to capture in words what she was feeling. 'It's more like something has been lifted off of me, like, something that was holding me down has let go, but that's not quite right either. I don't know, and in a way it doesn't matter. I just know I feel different and I feel more how I want to be. And that's what's important.'

'Mhmm, OK, so let's not get too caught up in trying to find the right words, maybe they don't matter, what really matters is acknowledging that you feel different and it feels like how you want to be, yeah?' Keith felt his own energy lift as he spoke. There was a lightness in what he was experiencing.

Katie took a deep breath. She needed to stretch her back which was feeling a little stiff and she was aware that whilst she felt energised her eyes felt tired and gritty. She hadn't been sleeping brilliantly the last few days, but now she felt as though she probably would sleep better. She just knew she felt more relaxed. She hoped it would last although she wasn't totally sure about this. But she didn't want to dwell on that. She wanted to stay like this forever. It all seemed very sudden and yet it really did feel so real. 'I just feel how I want to be.'

'And feeling how you want to be is a good feeling.' Keith was pleased for Katie and yet he also knew that these kinds of experiences whilst often indicating some kind of a breakthrough, did not always last. Old patterns could fight back, seek to reassert themselves, almost at times as though they had a life of their own. Some thought that they did, that they had their own kind of energy and identity within the person's structure of self, and that they needed to survive as well. Perhaps Katie had made a change in herself that would be permanent, yet he also knew that change like this could be just a first step. Wars were not always won with the first battle. But what he had to remember was that Katie had been battling all of her life, not just since coming to therapy. Therapy had sharpened it up and now she was fighting with herself, with the patterns and attitudes and behaviours that she had established through her years of difficulty, and in an increasingly conscious way. She had done what she had needed to do to survive. It had worked for her, though he knew it wasn't always the case for everyone. Alcohol and self-harm had played their role in enabling Katie to cope. Yet he also knew that some people did take it too far, and with other drugs as well along with an even more risky lifestyle, with permanent damage or even death a possible outcome.

Katie was sitting for a moment just absorbing how she felt. She hoped it would last. There was no way that she wanted to start talking about things that might make her feel upset, that might in some way take her away from what she was experiencing. Yet she didn't want to just sit saying nothing either.

'I don't want to lose it.' She paused.

'It's important not to lose it, really important.'

'How can I stay like this?' The thought was strongly present within Katie's awareness. 'I mean, yeah, my life's been, you know, pretty shitty at times. How can I feel different about everything?'

The question hung in the air. It was a powerful and extremely pertinent one. How many times had Keith heard that question, or variations of it, over the years. A person gets a sense of how they can be, and they desperately want it to remain with them. Anything but lose that precious sense of feeling more whole, more complete. 'That's the question, "how can I make this last?".'

'I have to. I can see there have been all kinds of stuff in my life and, yeah, a lot of it I wish didn't happen. I'd like it all to have been different. But where do you start?'

'Where would you like to start?'

'With mum and me. If she'd been different, you know, maybe everything that has happened, well, it wouldn't have happened, would it?'

'Probably not.'

'So everything I've experienced in my life is based on how she was with me. If she'd been different I wouldn't have been taken away, yeah?'

'Mhmm.' Keith simply acknowledged that he was hearing what Katie had said.

'And then, well, who knows?'

'That's the unanswerable questions, the "who knows?".'

'Strange, but I don't hate her, not at this moment. I mean, maybe there is still hate somewhere but at the moment I feel very sad for her, and for me, for what I didn't have, what we never had.' Katie could feel herself going quiet and she felt hot. So much that never happened that might have been so different, might have meant she was a different person now, a different Katie anyway. But she had no concept of what that would feel like. It was hard to imagine how you would be and feel if you were a different person.

'Sad for what didn't happen for either of you.'

'I don't know how it could have been, but she would have had to have been very different as well, and I can't really imagine that. I find myself thinking of other people and sort of wanting her to be like them.' She thought of Mrs Albert. 'If mum had had time for me, I think that was all I needed, time, you know, and I don't remember that. I just have no memory of our being together in a way that was, I don't know, good somehow. I don't remember us playing together, anything like that. I just remember being on my own, being shouted at, sometimes being hit. I wish I had something else to remember from her.' Katie felt the emotions rising as she spoke.

The yearning in Katie's voice was deeply moving and Keith felt his own emotions rising in response. 'If only you could have some different memories.'

Katie had nothing else to say. It summed it up. If only…. She sat, looking down, wishing that everything had been different, wishing that someone could take away all that was in her head and replace it with something new. The good feelings she had had were fading. The contrast felt huge. She stared into space, totally absorbed in a sense of wanting those other memories and at the same time gradually slipping into a state of inner silence, a place that was blank. She shook her head slightly, the blankness was replaced with the thought once again of "if only…". But it hadn't been that way. She knew it. She regretted it. Katie knew she had lost something that she had never had. The sadness took over and she felt her eyes moistening and her throat drying. She closed her eyes and felt the tears trickling over her eye lids. She could not restrain the sobs once they began. Resting her forehead in her right hand, Katie supported herself with her elbow on the arm of the chair. With each sob her chest tightened. She felt weak, as if her whole body was tired. It wasn't a dramatically intense release of emotion, rather it had a strange reflective tone, more of a deep mourning for the things that never were, that never could be. The thought of the future faded as fast as it had appeared. It was the past that held her, the feelings associated with knowing that there was so much that she had been robbed of, so much that might have been so different. She just wanted someone to care for her, hold her, love her. She wanted to feel she could just melt into someone's arms and experience certainty, reassurance, a sense that someone wanted her, loved her, really loved her. If only…. The words kept coming back to her. She nodded to herself, and found herself taking a deep breath. The emotions were lessening, she wiped her eyes with the back of her hands and opened them, 'sorry about that'.

'It's OK, you have a lot of feelings and they have to go somewhere.'

The feelings were changing. Katie was aware of being a little less absorbed by them, as though something had caused her to step back from them, or them from her. 'It's hard, very hard.' Her voice had a tone of sadness and resignation.

'Hard to feel what you are feeling now.'

Katie nodded. She reached over to take a tissue and dabbed at her eyes and face. Her throat was still dry, she took a sip of water. She appreciated its coolness. She still felt hot. 'How do I cope with it all?'

'What do you think will help you cope?' Keith chose not to respond empathically but to invite Katie to explore what she thought would be helpful. It wasn't something he had time to think about, it just felt instinctively like the right response to make.

'I need a new life.' Katie looked up at Keith. She wanted him to tell her what she had to do to have that new life. She wanted someone to tell her, she was suddenly tired of having to always make her own decisions.

'What would that life look like, Katie?' Keith again invited further exploration, and again it had felt the right response. He knew he could have empathised and maybe as a result held Katie on her feelings of wanting that new life. But he felt connected to her and to the inner world she was exploring, and he trusted the promptings emerging within himself.

Katie took a deep breath. 'I don't know. Being somewhere nice, with good people. Yeah, having fun, you know, just feeling lighter.' She smiled as she finished speaking. She had an image of a beach somewhere, sunshine, having fun with people her own age. Yeah, having a few drinks, and not having all the stuff that goes around in her head, all the shit from her past.

'Having fun and feeling lighter, not weighed down.'

Katie's thoughts went back to her room. It wasn't good; chaos, really. She never had enough money, either, and usually felt shit as well because she'd drunk too much, or just because that was how she felt most of the time. 'How do I get out of where I am?'

'You mean in yourself?'

'I was thinking about where I live.'

'What would you need?'

'Money.'

'How can you get that?'

Katie tightened her lips. 'Get a job, I guess.' She wasn't sure whether it was what she wanted. She hadn't really tried that hard, and hadn't got much in the way of qualifications.

'What would interest you?'

'Don't know, really. Just some way to get some money.'

'Anything will do so long as it gives you money?' Keith knew he was probably being a little provocative, but he wanted to help Katie clarify what she saw herself doing. This seemed to him to be an important exploration, Katie's first focus in the counselling sessions on her future and what she wanted to make of it.

'Well, no, I mean, yes. I guess, well, something to do with fashion, you know? Hair stylist, maybe. Don't want to work in a shop, well, not one of those little places, you know? Proper shop, maybe, I don't know.'

'OK, so something to do with fashion, or something in a larger shop, that's something you could see yourself doing?'

'Yeah.'

Keith was thinking about the group that Katie had referred to in an earlier session. 'Are you still going to the group you mentioned before?'

'Sort of, I don't know, never really got into it I suppose.'

'Feel ready to give it another try?'

'Suppose I could. But it all takes so long, yeah? Why can't I just go and get a job now, start doing something, know what I mean?'

'Mhmm, it would be good to not have to wait, just get a job.'

'I need to be more patient, I suppose, yeah, I do need to get back into the employment group and, yeah, I can look around as well. Start to take it all a bit more seriously, I guess, be a bit more positive.'

'Serious and positive. Get involved, make a start looking around.'

'I need to. I can't just drift along like I am, can I, not really. I mean, it's not going to give me anything, is it?'

'I guess that depends on what you want. Is what you have now what you want?' Keith wanted to help Katie get her own clarity as to what she did or did not want.

'No.' Katie was very clear about that. 'Things need to change. I'm changing, or trying to, you know?' Katie was aware that the counselling and all that had happened in recent weeks had left her feeling different. She saw herself differently, and her life. Yes, it had been shit and still was, but she didn't want it to remain that way. Yes, she wanted someone to come and make it all better, but was that realistic? She could get shacked up with someone, maybe, but would that really be much better? She needed a life of her own. She liked her independence. She wanted to have fun, have some money, have her own life. She deserved it. 'I want a future, but it's like, yeah, I've got to sort out my head and I've got to sort out today, and tomorrow, you know?'

'Mhmm, sort out now before you can sort out the future, and sorting out your head is a part of that.'

'Big part.' Yes, she thought, it is a big part. 'If I could only keep feeling different, didn't get such stress and so depressed.'

'Feeling less stressed and depressed would help.'

'Doctor said she might give me some other pills if I got myself a little more settled in myself. I think she's afraid I might swallow them all.'

'Is that how you feel?'

'Not really, but on a bad day, I don't know. And when I cut really deep that time….', she shivered as she thought about it, 'I wasn't really me. I don't know. I need to feel normal and do normal things. And I need money for that. You can't do anything these days without money. I need a job.'

'Sound like you are pretty clear about that. Getting a job is the first step.'

'Doing what I need to do to get a job is the first step.' Having a job felt a bit distant from where she was at the moment. Katie could feel that it was a big step even though she also thought that was ridiculous and she ought to be able to go and get a job without a problem.

'Sure. What's going to help you make that first step?' Keith wanted to try and help Katie acknowledge what she needed to do. He felt it would be helpful to have some ideas anchored in some recognised steps.

'Use the group, start looking, get my act together, I guess. '

'Mhmm. That's a good start.'

It all felt like a lot and yet it felt as though it shouldn't be as well. Katie suddenly felt angry again, angry towards everyone and everything that had put her in the position she was in. Why did her life have to be such a struggle? It was easy to just get drunk, try and forget about it all, but it hadn't helped her, not really. She was where she was because of what had happened to her. But Katie knew she needed something else, something more from her life. Talking as she had done during the session had made her more aware that she did feel sad and angry about her past, and her present, but she knew she could feel different, she could put it behind her, she had to put it behind her.

'I need to get my act together and it's down to me, isn't it?'

'To a degree, but don't forget there are people out there to help you. Get involved. Get some support. Start with the group, yeah, see what else they can suggest.'

'Probably need to get some qualifications, don't I?'

'I'm sure it would help.'

'It's a lot.'

'Mhmm, big step, you're trying to break free of something that has held you back for so long.'

'Yeah, me, and all the shit in my head.'

'Mhmm.'

'This is good for me, isn't it, coming here, talking like this. I mean, to start with it was like, yeah, this is crazy. Don't know what to say, just sitting, you know? Nothing changing.' Katie was thinking back to the first time she'd come to see Keith and how awkward it had felt.

'Felt crazy, huh?'

Katie nodded. 'No disrespect.'

'None taken. Crazy world of counselling.'

'But it isn't, is it? I mean, shit, it's been like madness at times, I've never experienced anything like it and I still don't really understand a lot of it, but it's like, yeah, here I am, still having these crazy experiences but somehow I'm getting to feel different. It's not easy but it's like I've started something and don't want to finish, you know?'

'Mhmm, like it all seems madness and yet you know what you are experiencing and that tells you it's helping?'

'I think it is. I know it is, but it's like….' Katie paused. 'I felt really good earlier, but that's kind of gone, but it hasn't. It's like it's there, but not so close, somehow. I've got to do something about it all, haven't I?'

'Yes, and you have started by coming here and talking, but don't forget there is support and others who can help as well.' Keith didn't want Katie to feel she was having to do it all on her own. He knew society could be hard, particularly on young people. It gave them consumerist and often very self-centred values, encouraged them to take up all kinds of behaviours, many of which were addictive, in the pursuit of some kind of happy high that was always being marketed, and then blamed them when they struggled to find much purpose in their lives. Society needed to do more to help young people, but not just by setting up more support groups of various kinds, or even activity groups, but by people looking at society and questioning the underlying values that governed the way it functioned. Therapy could help the person on the inside, and encourage them to change in the outer world as well, but the reality was that society was in a mess in so many ways and it was not a nourishing climate for people trying to develop to their full emotional and psychological potential.

'Yeah, I know. I'll want to do it all my own way. I need to learn to listen. I'm realising that. You say sensible things. I don't always like it, though.'

Keith nodded, thinking that Katie had a lot of life still to lead and that, yes, she needed to find her own way, and she needed to be able to hear good advice when it was given as well. 'No, not always easy to hear what other people have to say, but it's something you're realising is important.' Keith glanced over at the clock and there were only a few minutes of the session left. 'We only have a few more minutes of this session left.'

'I don't think I have much more to say today. It's been helpful, it really has. I think I am making more sense of myself. It's not easy. I know I have missed out on so much and that the way I've been needs to change, but I also know that it's hard to change as well. But I have had a glimpse of how I can be, how I want to feel. I want to make things better for myself. I'll go back to the group and see what I can do about a job. I do need that, it would be good for me. But it's hard to see myself, you know, doing something. But I have to, don't I?'

'It's easy to slip into habits, and not working, or not feeling able to work or wanting to work can be like that. It's about getting into routines, and that can be difficult if you aren't used to them.' Keith felt it would be helpful to acknowledge the difficulty.

'I need to get my act together. And now I need to head off. Thanks, Keith. It's helping. I only hope it lasts.'

'There will probably be ups and downs still, but I sense that you have a clearer sense of what you want and a stronger desire to work towards it.' It felt important to acknowledges this and Katie was grateful to hear it.

'Yes, I'm sure it won't be easy, but I have to give it a go. So, I'll see you next week, yeah?'

'Yes, same time?'

Katie nodded and got up. 'Thanks. See you.'

'You too. Take care.' Katie headed out of the door and down the corridor leaving Keith to reflect once more on an intense session. He hadn't any answer to the question supervision had left him with, how Katie saw him, but that didn't matter for now. The session had been full and intense and he was pleased with how it had gone.

The room felt very quiet as Keith sat back in his chair pondering over the session that had just finished. So much going on for Katie, he thought to himself. He marvelled at the human being, at the depth of the unseen that we carry within us. Memories. The word stayed in his mind. How we carry with us the experiences from our past and the manner in which we have made sense of them. He knew that in many ways there wasn't as much understanding as there needed to be. We had theories, yes, lots of theories as to what happens, how and why experiences affected us. And yet the truth was we were still dealing with the unseen and there remained a mystery attached to it. Consciousness. Identity. Awareness. The brain. How did they all relate to each other? Is our consciousness and sense of self simply the product of electrical and chemical activity in our brains. Is that all we are? Or are we more? Did we have a soul? What did that mean? If we did, could it exist outside of the body, after death, for instance, as so many religions believed and some areas of scientific thought were exploring? These thoughts passed through his own mind, one leading to the next.

And why do human beings have such capacity to harm each other? For Keith that was quite a crucial thought. He heard stories of how young people, children, had been treated on a daily basis and he knew the horrors that happened, and far more frequently as far as he was concerned than society would want to admit to. And yet he also knew that there was such resilience as well within people, enabling them to survive, albeit in a damaged state. That damage could be physical, but it was certainly emotional, psychological, mental as well. And what about social and relational capacity, that could be damaged too. He was thinking about the group of people referred to as having personality or borderline personality disorder.

He anticipated many more sessions with Katie and he felt sure that they were likely to be as intense as the previous ones. He could see that there were some fundamental questions she had about herself and her past, and that there was likely to be further pain locked up within her. The way parts of herself had emerged into sessions, not dissociated to the point that she was unaware of what was happening, but certainly with a strong enough separate identity for them to take on a sense of being a distinctive 'part' of herself, meant that the impact of those early life experiences had been both traumatising and far-reaching. Knowing that she had had difficult experiences later in her childhood, he wondered whether these were likely to emerge more strongly as well, or were they more integrated into her usual awareness as 'normal' memories of events?

The one thing that he was sure about was that in his work with Katie, and other young people, he had an unwavering belief in the human spirit to adapt to circumstances and to try to make the best of situations. People wanted to survive. Yes, they may well do damage to themselves and others along the way, sometimes out of anger and frustration, sometimes the direct result of being brutalised, but in general human beings wanted to survive and to find ways of avoiding or containing pain. He felt Katie was heading in a constructive direction. That was what he would hope for her, perhaps all he could ever truly hope for his clients. And that constructive direction he believed was built on greater capacity for positive self-regard and authentic living, increased self-awareness and sensitivity to the needs of others.

*

As Katie lay on her bed a couple of days later she was aware the feelings of the counselling session had now faded. They seemed a distant memory and yet they also somehow remained important to her. She wanted to regain them but she was not sure how. She still had a sense of needing to do something more constructive with her life. She had noted down a few things to herself when she had got home:

Get a job
Only do things that make me feel good
It's my life – it's my future

She looked at what she had written, they all seemed such big steps to take. She'd got along to the group she'd planned to get back to and seen Bernie as well. She'd also been on the web and had found some support groups for people who self-harmed. She'd been pleased about that. It had felt like a big step. It was like she was accepting it was something she needed to deal with, really deal with. She had some contact numbers she'd written on a piece of paper, just in case. It had seemed like a good idea at the time.

Now, though, she wasn't so sure. She'd had a bit to drink that afternoon, and some guy she'd been with had given her a hard time, it had really pissed her off. She knew her mood had dipped. It was familiar in many ways but it also felt different, like she was more aware of how she was feeling. It was weird. Like she felt like she often did, but now she was feeling it more clearly. She couldn't make sense of it. What was the point in thinking about it. She felt like shit, that was all there was to it.

Time passed, her mood sank lower. The room was getting darker, she hadn't bothered putting the light on. She felt heavy. Her thoughts drifted over her life, so much shit. No-one caring, no one giving a toss about her. Only time she wasn't ignored was when she was picked on. And when she fought back she got grief. What was the point? What was the fucking point? It wasn't her fault, and yet it also felt as though it was. Familiar feelings were coming into her awareness. She was no good. She was the problem. She was the bad news. She hated how she was feeling, It still felt different, like she was experiencing stuff but also watching herself as well. It really felt so odd. She didn't like how she felt, and yet there was a feeling of utter powerlessness to do anything about it. Katie knew she had to have some relief from it all, it was getting too much. Darkness was closing in around her, and within her. She didn't want that. She didn't want to slide into that again. It felt more intense, like it was more threatening, more menacing. She had to stop it, had to, and she knew the only way she could do that. She pulled the cord above the bed and the light came on. She squinted, the light wasn't that bright but it was bright enough. She went over to the drawer. A voice in her head seemed to be saying quite clearly, "no, don't do it, it's not the answer, stay in control". Katie picked up the blade, her flannel and some tissues. "You don't need to do this, there are choices, you can make them." What choices, she thought to herself, what does anything matter. This is me, this is what I do. She walked back to the bed and sat down. The piece of paper with the phone numbers fell on the floor at her feet. Katie stared down at it, as if mesmerised in some strange way. She looked to her right, the blade sitting on the flannel. A familiar friend in so many ways, but a friend that she knew had started to hurt her, damage her, put her at risk. And yet it was still a friend. She looked back to the numbers and across to her left, to her phone. She felt herself taking a deep breath. She continued to sit looking at it. If she made a call, who would answer it? Would they be a friend? Would they? Who was her real friend? She looked back over to the blade again. "Can I trust you?", the thought went through Katie's head. "You cut me up, put me in hospital. I didn't need that." And yet it hadn't always been that way. It had helped her so many times in the past. But she'd never sat like this, hesitating.

Katie closed her eyes, she felt suddenly quite faint and nauseous. She simply didn't know what to do. 'I have to stay in control, I have to'. It wasn't a voice in her head, but her own thoughts. Her jaw tightened and her teeth were clenching together. She took a deep breath and opened her eyes, her heart was thumping like it would jump out of her chest. She looked up, then over to the blade, and back to the phone. She wanted relief, she needed some release. She didn't want to feel like this. A surge of emotion hit her and tears streamed from her eyes. She couldn't cope with this. It was too much. She had to get some relief, she had to. Katie reached out....

The voice on the end of the line sounded friendly, 'Hello, how can I help you?'. For the first time in her life Katie had chosen something other than cutting herself when she felt like this.

Some final thoughts

For Katie, there is much more ahead of her as she continues on a path towards reducing the damaging effects of her past on her present and her future. We live in a very stressful world, and for so many different reasons. Children and young people do not always receive the loving and supportive relationships they need. Parents and others in society have other priorities in their 'busy' lives. The causes of why young people, like Katie, have such a poor and impoverished start in life are many and complex. Or are they? It is easy to hide behind complexity as a way of encouraging feelings of powerlessness to do anything about it and to rely on the opinions of 'experts', who themselves often disagree with each other.

Actually it isn't complex. Children and young people go through the kinds of experiences that Katie went through because they are born into families and a wider society that simply does not *care* enough. Self-centredness and the selfishness that this breeds, can't be bothered, too busy, just want my own needs met, don't care won't care, are attitudes in society and indeed in families that have become all too present. They contribute to young people needing to find their own ways of handling their inner and outer worlds, as they seek to survive and get some fulfilling sense of self within a shattered emotional and psychological landscape that is the self-centred, quick fix, all-consuming and frequently addictive society that we see being held up to the world as an example to follow at the dawn of the 21st century.

For children and young people to have a better chance in life, they need a safe and secure family environment. They need parents who love them and who are prepared to put the child's physical, emotional, psychological and developmental needs first. This means that parents need to know how to be parents, and that is where we must start.

Then there are the schools and what is taught. Education for jobs is the basis for so much that takes place in schools, with the stress of endless testing and threat of being labelled a failure if you can't keep up. Whatever happened to education for life? Life is more than jobs. Life is about how we conduct ourselves in society. It concerns what society expects of us and what we expect of that society. Where do we see the importance of responsible citizenship being held aloft and valued?

There are many young girls (and boys) who are today 'alive and cutting'. Tomorrow some will be dead. It is not acceptable for this to continue and we must now, as a matter of urgency, ask serious questions of the values that underpin our societal norms and initiate national debates on the topic; and we need to ensure that young people contribute to and are heard in that debate. We need to take action to establish in people's hearts and minds an agreed set of values upon which we can shape organisations and, indeed, society.

I would suggest the following: a valuing of truth, a commitment to justice, a greater spirit of co-operation, a sense of personal responsibility and a clear vision and commitment to the common good. Such values must surely place the human needs of people, and that includes young people, first.

I could go on, but I won't. We can all look out at the world and wonder at the short-term, self-centred values that seem to drive so much that we see. I only hope that this book, by exploring something of the emotional landscape that can drive a young girl to self-harm, will serve to open people's minds and hearts to a fresh understanding and appreciation of the human tragedy that we are surrounded by. And I hope that the sense of our common humanity will be outraged and hurt, and that we will want to make a difference, a positive difference, to improving the experiences and life-opportunities of young people.

Richard Bryant-Jefferies
July 2008

Useful contacts for help and support

UK

Harmless

PO Box 9325, Nottingham NG8 9FB, United Kingdom
Tel: 0115 928 2468 (enquiries only)
www.harmless.org.uk
info@harmless.org.uk
A national organisation that provides information, support, training and consultancy to people who self harm, their friends, families and professionals.

British Association for Counselling and Psychotherapy

BACP House, 15 St John's Business Park, Lutterworth, Leicestershire LE17 4HB, United Kingdom
General Enquiries: 01455 883300
www.bacp.co.uk
bacp@bacp.co.uk

USA

American Counseling Association

5999 Stevenson Ave. Alexandria, VA 22304, USA
ACA Fax Number: (703) 823-0252
TDD: (703) 823-6862
ACA Toll-Free Numbers:
ACA: (800) 347-6647
FAX: (800) 473-2329
Website: http://www.counseling.org

Printed in the United Kingdom
by Lightning Source UK Ltd.
134798UK00002B/220-294/P